I0561747

My body seems to be backing away, but I'm not consciously moving my feet. Maybe the nearby fixtures are shifting from me, or the room has become much larger than it originally had been. I can't tell because the world seems to also be spinning and I can't control what's happening to my body or my mind. My stomach is weak and a scream is captured in the back of my throat, waiting to be forced free.

Praise for the Works of B. Hughes-Millman

"PURGATORY'S ANGEL is an awesome paranormal romance that fans of Sherrilyn Kenyon and J.R. Ward will really enjoy...No simple angels here."
- Examiner's Women in Horror Author, Danielle De Vor

"PURGATORY'S ANGEL is a must read! From the first chapter to the final chapter it keeps you wanting more. The battle between good and evil in its finest. B Hughes-Millman keeps you guessing to the end."
- Dana Thornock, Book Reviewer

"DARKEST FOREST is constructed properly and the characters developed in a most satisfying way. It turned out to be a compelling story line which I cannot wait to follow into her next novel and the series beyond."
- R. P. McCabe, Mystery Author

"B Hughes-Millman does it again in this installment of her Black Casket series. The execution of the emotional conflicts couldn't have been done better. I'll read this again and recommend it to everyone."
- Nichole Severn, Book Reviewer

"I love RESURRECTION'S ANGEL! The suspense, the plot twists, the characters - great story! - pass the hanky!"
– D. B. Sieders, Urban Fantasy Author

"With compelling characters, interesting subplots and plenty of paranormal action PURGATORY'S ANGEL is the kind of

book that keeps one up at night! Kudos to Ms. Hughes-Millman for some of the most well-written action scenes this reviewer has ever had the pleasure of reading!"
- Chantel Hardge, InD'Tale

"I loved RESURRECTION'S ANGEL. It kept me on the edge of my seat and my mind engrossed. I never knew what was happening next! All through the book I kept waiting for a dull part but it never happened. I read this one in less than a day!"
- MeLisa Holden Bruner, Book Reviewer

B. HUGHES-MILLMAN

A DARK ANGEL NOVEL

RESURRECTION'S
Angel

CITY OWL
PRESS

This book is a work of fiction. Names, characters places, and incidents either are products of the author's imagination or are used fictitiously. Any resemblance to actual events or locales or persons, living or dead, is entirely coincidental and not intended by the author.

RESURRECTION'S ANGEL
Dark Angel Novels: Book Two

CITY OWL PRESS
www.cityowlpress.com

All Rights reserved. Except as permitted under the U.S. Copyright Act of 1976, no part of this publication may be reproduced, distributed, or transmitted in any form or by any means, or stored in a database or retrieval system, without the prior consent and permission of the publisher.

Copyright ©2018 by B. Hughes-Millman

Cover Design by Mibl Art and Tina Moss. All stock photos licensed appropriately.

Edited by Heather McCorkle.

For information on subsidiary rights, please contact the publisher at info@cityowlpress.com.

Print Edition ISBN: 978-1-949090-12-3
Digital Edition ISBN: 978-1-949090-13-0

Printed in the United States of America

To every strong woman who has reached her deepest depths of pain and sorrow, then rose up to reinvent herself. May you continue to be the power in your own life that drives you to be your personal best.

PROLOGUE

Retrieving your soul from darkness comes at a price. Often times, fighting to reach the light means a piece of you is left in the grave. Sometimes, that lost segment could be the very fabric that once protected you from the world. You are left raw and naked.

The demons I once fought in my dreams were nothing more to me than defective souls. Without a past. Without a future. Until the night I killed Richard Stanton, I hadn't considered the ones left behind to grieve, those who loved the person in spite of their wickedness. Until the morning I woke with the stain of his death on my hands and in my head, I never cared what they may have contributed to the world. I only focused on what they removed from it.

Yes, Rick's obsession for me, to have me as his or to torture me until I begged for death, was reason enough to take his life. His sickness brought about his own demise. That Sarah had joined him long before I met her, was beyond unforgiveable. She was my only confidante and the one friend I trusted to dig an inch through the flesh to discover my soul. That I reveled in the kill, teased Rick's subconscious mind to destroy him in the most devastating way, is as morbid as I dare allow my mind to tread.

How far had I fallen to make them pay for their crimes? To this day, while I move about my life, I wrestle with the guilt I will forever carry, like the demon in the shadows who knows my tainted past.

After all that has happened and what I'd learned about Collin Leary, the one to whom I am now eternally wed, my heart is conflicted over what I feel for him. As much as I love and desire him, deep down, the realization of the life I'd endured due to a decision he had made for me—and, consequently, those I love who've died and the ones I've had to kill because of him—is far more than I can bear. He selected me before I was born, marked me as if I were property, then left me to fight the world with no one to help from the time I was seventeen. Had I known of his betrayal before I'd fallen in love with him, chances are great I'd have sought him out and killed him in his dreams. I've had no time to reconcile who he is to me, to what he's done.

Colorado is no longer a welcoming place for me. The painful history I have known can't be shaken from my core so easily. Everywhere I go I see Rick and Sarah, as if they're still watching me in the shadows, plotting my eternal demise. Worst of all, though, in my darkest hours I would always see Collin. Even now, in every restless moment that I ponder, I see his deep green eyes and breathe in his alluring scent. I try not to blame him, but I do.

Since the night I nearly allowed the demon to take my life, Collin hasn't trusted me to fight my own battles. Each evening, as I take a pause for the dream to materialize, I find no defective soul waiting to challenge me. He has taken my nightmares from me, turning me into a restless warrior in need of rehabilitation. And it is this that has rendered the realization within me: Colorado is too small for more than one dark angel. The passion I feel when near him isn't enough. I hope I can fully forgive him someday, but I know it won't occur any time soon. At least, not while my memories are still fresh and tarnished with his betrayal. I needed to run away. My heart nearly broke the day I decided to leave.

The Emerald Isles have been calling my name for quite some time. Especially since the day I learned this was the place of my birth. Unable to face Collin once the great battle was over, I left for my homeland, not telling anyone where I was going. Had he known, he would have tried to stop me, especially if he knew the result of our only intimate night together. I was gone before he caught scent of our child, growing inside of me.

Before leaving the only country I'd known for nearly my entire existence on earth, however, I made the journey to a place that once brought joy to me. The home my mother ripped from my life as we fled the murderers who kill in the night. I needed to make peace with the state of Washington. I had to smother the inner turmoil of my father's death, once and for all. My destination was Seattle. More directly, Whidbey Island.

CHAPTER 1

Resurrecting your soul from purgatory is a formidable undertaking for the weak of heart. And yet, I survived.

I remember kneeling in the pool of blood surrounding my mother's deathbed and whispering into the vacant air, *I will find you*. Now that I have succeeded in my quest, found and killed the one who murdered my family, I have no idea what to do with my hatred. I'm torn between my duty to protect the innocent and my distaste for killing the guilty.

Sea-Tac airport, this Monday morning, is surprisingly empty. The cold sterility of chrome stanchions and dark, gray barriers make me weak inside, remembering that rainy morning my father died.

The sun couldn't be seen that day as it peeked over the horizon. My cold hand clung to my mother's as she maneuvered the corridor. She counted the gates aloud as I did so in my head, searching for the one the ticket agent had written in red ink on our boarding passes. When we reached our destination, she stopped before approaching the attendant. Mother stood before me and took me by the shoulders, forcing a smile that would never calm me.

"This is a new beginning, Jaime," she had said, trying to convince herself more than me. I could feel it in the way her eyes combed the terminal as she spoke. I knew who she was searching for: Father's killer. Anyone who might also wish us dead. I can't remember another word that came from her as she spoke. My mind was caught on the words "new beginning." She promised. In my mind, I pretended as if it was possible to forget what I saw in her bedroom. I had never seen so much blood before that day. I wanted to live happily, carefree. Ignoring the monsters in my head, calling me to come out and play. Maybe their voices wouldn't follow me to our new home. Maybe they would be silenced once I was allowed to kill. I was naïve. They've never stopped haunting me.

Even today, as I reverse the path we took those years ago, the call of the demon is strong and fresh. The instinct to rest my head and let the dream take me to them is great with my recent reprieve from fighting. When will I have that new beginning she promised?

The terminal spills into a grand entry with a convex wall of windows, several stories high. The glare of early sun proves overwhelming to an anxious soul. But these feelings are easily concealed in this body I've learned to control. After decades of hate, anger and trepidation, I've done well to keep my emotions intact, hidden from the prying eyes of humanity. No one here notices the renewed dread welling up in me.

To once again breathe in the aroma of wet pine and sea air is a bittersweet reunion. With a burgeoning purse and only one piece of luggage in tow, I sign for my rental car and head toward the islands.

As I travel west toward the coast, I relax in my seat and take in the green vegetation mingled amongst tall buildings with a gleaming ocean in the distance. The entire time, I seem to be holding my breath, waiting for something to happen or maybe for someone to die. As I make my way toward the ferry docks, I see only shades of puce and emerald surrounding me, not crimson from forever-silent bodies littering the sidewalks or roadways of my mind. The clouds have cleared enough for rays of light to shine through while gulls squawk then swoop toward the water. My mind awaits the scent of death to reach my instinctual spirit, but the bustle of life encompassing me is nothing more than ordinary. I'm unsure if I can grow accustomed to ordinary. I've lived on the edge of a dark and twisted reality for far too long.

Once the ferry launches from the dock, I leave the confines of my vehicle and stand by the rail. Particles of sand and sewage churn in the water beside the vessel, filthier than I can remember, although, I didn't even see the water on my last trip across.

I didn't leave the car that early morning when I was still so young and innocent. The air was too cold and mother wouldn't allow me from her sight. I knew she wouldn't leave her seat. Her fingers held the wheel while her knuckles turned white. I didn't have to ask. She was frightened. At the time, I had no idea it had anything to do with me. As a girl, I could only guess it was from seeing the body of her husband in the bed beside her when she woke. Now, as I feel the tiny life growing inside me, I know her fear was for *my* life, not his nor hers. She was braver than I could have imagined possible. And I can't help but feel ashamed at the choices I've made since she has died. I'm not worthy of the lives lost to protect me. But my life isn't over yet. There is still hope the one inside me can take my place when I'm weary from the fight. Maybe I will die as my mother had, protecting my child from the evil I'd cast down into this hell on earth.

"You headin' for the distillery on Whidbey?" The voice coming from my left startles me.

"Um, no. I don't drink." At least, now that I'm pregnant I don't drink. I try to return my attention to the water, hoping the gentleman beside me will take the hint.

"Oh, sorry. You...don't seem like the typical island resident. A tourist, maybe?"

From the edge of my peripheral view, I see him eyeing my black leggings covered to above the knee in matching suede boots and topped by a hip-length leather jacket. Most would think I'm in mourning, or perhaps a ninja, being dressed fully in black. Both ideas are reason for someone to consider backing away. This *boy* isn't as talented at receiving clues as he is at admiring my body.

I peer down at his brushed blue jeans then allow my attention to trail up to his white t-shirt, pulled slightly taught over the muscles in his chest and arms. His physique almost reminds me of Collin. Although I know it isn't him, a part of me wishes it was. Aware that what is in my soul will show in my eyes, I take a deep breath and immediately turn from him.

"I have family in the area." My answer is curt and my tone flat with the desire to repel his unwanted attention.

"Oh? Well, I'm from Whidbey Island. Maybe I know them." He certainly is a persistent little shit.

Something suddenly turns me ill. The baby? My hormones? The handsome, but annoyingly curious man at my side? I'm unsure. The only thing I'm positive of, is that those at the rails on the level below were quick to scatter once my vomit started splattering the deck at their feet.

The next sound I hear from my left is a morose, "Oh, God."

When I finish retching my guts out, there is no one standing beside me or below me. Thank God this child has perfect timing. I wipe my mouth on the sleeve of my jacket and allow the wind in my face to soothe me.

The sky fills in with gray again as the ferry reaches the

shore. I set my GPS to Craw Road before shifting to drive. I remember, as a young girl, passing the sign when father and I went on our daily run. There was little in the way of industry, or even housing, when we still lived here. I'm surprised to see little has changed since then.

The main highway that traverses the island skirts a thick tree line. At times, the forest wall will make way for a lush meadow then swallow the horizon once again. I feel as if I'm finally home. When I reach Coles Road, I turn left into the trees and eventually right on Craw.

So many decades have passed since the last time I travelled this road. Still, it remains fairly consistent with the visuals my memory has stored. The small set of buildings to my immediate left are new and look more like a small farm than a distillery, as is printed on their sign. Clearly the one the young man on the ferry had referred to. Not far from the distillery is the final turn to my destination, a small, hidden road leading into a grove of trees. One might have the impression this path hasn't been traveled since the tires of my mother's vehicle sheared the gravel as she raced away. The drive is barely noticeable from the weeds that have overtaken the pale stones.

Just past an outcropping of pine and maple, the hard edges of a white structure come into view. My heart leaps with fear and anticipation. After all these decades, my eyes still fill with tears. Gripping the steering wheel until my fingers are numb, I'm afraid to move. This might have been a bad idea.

The door and windows are boarded up. Every pane of glass is broken. The front porch where I remember playing has fallen on the left side. Paint is chipping from nearly every inch. Dark shutters surrounding the windows have faded to gray. The windshield of my car is growing spotted with drops from the heavens, making it difficult to notice the finer details. Did they close up the house when they found Father's body? As secluded as this location seems, it could have been days, months. The thought turns my stomach sick again.

When I'm finished wiping retch from my mouth with a tissue I found in my purse, I rise to my feet and brush the wet soil from my knees.

"Are you all right?"

The voice from behind causes me to spin in attack pose. Before I can take a breath, however, the thick clouds above empty their heavy load of rain with a crack of lightning in the open meadow surrounding the house and a clap of thunder that shakes the ground.

"Let's go!" he shouts and grabs my hand, running in a full dash for the porch.

We're both gasping for air once we reach the landing. Through labored breaths, I recognize the man with water streaming down his face, leaning against the boarded door. He must have followed me from the ferry. What is his game?

"Tell me your family doesn't live here." He stares back at me with questioning eyes.

I turn from him, contemplating how much I dare tell anyone. "No one lives here. Can't you already see that?"

He takes the tips of my fingers in his hand and leans toward me. "Then why are you here?"

The touch of another man, gently cradling my fingers, makes me long for the comfort of Collin's arms. But that's not possible now. I pull my hand from him and tuck it in my coat pocket. Weakened emotions won't help.

The warped, rotting wood above us creaks from the weight of the downpour. Soon, the roof is shedding water between swollen boards and there is no place to escape the deluge. The soaked stranger searches the entry for a weak panel. Finding none that will budge, he moves to a window. Seeing a plank with loose nails, I join him in yanking on the slat and help him to work it free.

"Wow. You're pretty strong for the average girl," he says, staring at me in appreciation.

"I'm not a girl," I answer without turning my attention from the window. "And I'm not average."

Most of the glass is already broken through. I tap the remaining sharp edges from the frame with the heel of my hand then step inside, bracing myself with the slat above my head. Once under the cover of the familiar room, I'm stopped from moving forward by an invisible rope tied around my heart. The room is empty and musty. Webs hang from lighting fixtures, walls, and ceilings. The floor is covered in dust and shattered glass. The furniture we once draped ourselves over after an exhausting day is no longer here. The living room is bare. The rug we sat on while Father read stories by the light of a fire is also gone. Everything that once belonged to us seems to have been shattered into millions of particles of silt and scattered by the wind.

"I bet this was a nice home, once." An unusual take from someone who never lived in this broken-down building. I turn to him inquisitively. "Before the man was killed here, I guess," he finishes.

The blow of his words hit me hard in the gut. The wind is taken from my chest as I stare back at him. Being in my family home, the place where my father died, with some stranger who's heard our story, is more than my heart can bear. It takes every ounce of constraint to pull myself together and keep my stomach from convulsing in dry heaves. He reaches out to catch me as my body wavers, but I knock his hand away.

"What do you know? What have you heard?" I ask, staggering forward and catching the doorframe leading to the dining room.

"Are you all right?" he asks again and reaches for me once

more. His fingers hesitate then stroke the side of my cheek. "How did you hurt yourself?"

His fingertips lightly brush the scar left behind by Sarah's blade. "It's none of your concern. And quit asking me if I'm all right," I counter and turn from the room, headed toward the stairs for the bedrooms.

Each warped, oak board moans beneath me as my weight shifts from one step to the next. I skip the ones I remember from my childhood having creaked the most. My soaked hair drips down my back. Water falls at my feet as I creep forward, one by one, until I am finally standing in the entryway of their room.

"Did you know them?" he asks softly as he enters, startling me.

I didn't hear him approach, not one moan from the steps behind me.

"Nah, you're too young. Happened so long ago. You weren't born yet." He hesitates and scans the room with his eyes. "They say it was a man with his wife and daughter who lived here."

His eyes stop scanning the room and fix on a shelf above his head in the closet. At first, I don't see it. Then the object of his attention becomes clearer. The rounded corner of a paper is visible past the edge. He reaches up as my mind searches the past.

What did they keep there? Mother's hats? Off-season sweaters? As he pulls it into his hand, I see father, younger and alive, sliding the family picture album into its place. This stranger has one of those photos. My God, don't let it be of the family. He'll know. I don't look much different. At least, my appearance is close enough for him to make the connection.

I'm at his side in an instant and snatch the picture from his hand, shoving it in my pocket without looking at it. He stares back at me with curiosity clenching his brow.

"Stop this. I'm not in the mood for fairy tales. And you're rummaging through belongings of the prior owners," I snap at him.

He shakes his head, slowly. "The prior owners are dead."

A chill sweeps my spine.

"He was killed in his sleep by some psychotic killer...they said. And his family, wife and daughter, disappeared, never seen again. They searched the whole island, even the shore, for their bodies, but nothing." He moves farther into the room and kneels with his hand to the floor, brushing the dust. "I wonder if you can still see his blood in the wood—"

"Stop it!" I shout, then catch myself. I can't give my identity away. There's no telling who this person is or what he could become when he sleeps. "No more of your foolish bedtime stories. Nothing happened here. It's just an old house. That's all."

"Then why are you here?" he asks, studying my expression as if he can extrapolate from a flicker in my eyes, the curve of my brow, what this place means to me. I have to think quickly.

"My realtor was supposed to meet me. I'm looking for an investment property. But I can see now I'll have to level this structure and rebuild if I hope to gain any return. No one will buy a house in such disrepair and with silly rumors about murder," I answer, hoping my subconscious mind doesn't betray me. "I shouldn't have come out here with the stomach flu. Should've known they weren't a reliable agency, leaving me here in the cold, feeling like shit."

"I'm sorry, I thought maybe you... Can I buy you a cup of tea? Should make you feel better."

He looks so sincere, I nearly buy his helpful, boy-next-door act. But he's not a boy. And I'm not a naïve girl. My suspicious mind won't allow me to think this man is only an innocent soul, being friendly and making conversation with someone he thinks is very near his age. If he only knew that I was the girl who disappeared fifty-nine years ago today.

"Who are you? Why did you follow me here?" I finally ask.

I want to study his face, stare him deep in the eyes to find what he hides in his soul. But the past week has made me hesitant to search the fringes of anyone's intentions, afraid I might find the demon they are trying desperately to conceal. I'm not the person I once was. Instead, I turn from him, headed for the window.

So much time has passed. I remember the trees surrounding the yard far below when I would peer out my bedroom window at night. Now they've grown so tall, blocking my view of the neighboring land. The grass has been overtaken by weeds and wild shrub. As much as this was once my home, it now feels alien. Somehow, I expected to feel a connection to the house I grew up in and have missed for all these years. The child hidden deep within my soul had hope that I would find a lost treasure I'd left behind so many years ago. In my search I have only found more pain, destruction, and disappointment.

"I'm Daniel. I live down the road. When I saw you on the ferry, you looked like you needed a friend. That and, well, you *are* beautiful. Can't blame a man for noticing. I was behind you when you turned into the drive for this house." He hesitates a moment and I turn back to see him shaking his head. "I was worried. No one comes here anymore...except for children, intent on breaking what little glass remains on the fringes of the boarded windows. A favorite night-time story of this area is that the house is haunted by the dead. Silly, I know."

"Poetic. But what you failed to notice is that I'm not a ghost, nor a child. I'm nothing but a shadow. Shadows don't break windows and they don't need friends. No interesting story here. No pathetic damsel to save. And now you know. So, is it possible for you to leave? I prefer to be alone."

I walk past him on my way to the bedroom door and catch a hint of his scent, but immediately drive it from my mind. I don't want to know. I don't want to think that some night, soon, Daniel will have to die in his sleep. I don't want to know if he is really a demon with a dark purpose. I prefer to believe him an overzealous young man in pursuit of what he thinks is an available woman.

When I reach the hallway, I realize there were no floorboards groaning from his footsteps behind me and I turn on my heels. "I thought I told you to—" The room is empty. "Daniel?" There is no sound of human life echoing off the walls and the windowpanes. Only my words and the breath being forced from my lungs. I search behind the door, in the closet, rush through each room upstairs then down.

"Daniel? Where are you hiding?" My voice is more trepid than commanding.

I didn't see or hear him pass. My senses aren't so closed off that I wouldn't feel his energy. I rush to the living room window and visually search the yard. No one there. Not even a second vehicle in the drive. And I don't remember there ever being one. Had he come up on foot? I don't recall. I pull the photo out of my pocket and see the image of my father cradling me in his arms as a baby. Relief empties my lungs until I notice something familiar, drawing my attention. The man holding me, my father, looks exactly like Daniel. I spin in place, searching the room for him.

"Daddy? Is that you?" No sound echoes back. My voice is swallowed by the walls and I feel small in this house that once seemed so large.

With my body cold from the realization that maybe Daniel was never really there, I decide that returning to Whidbey

Island and the trauma of my departure was more than my weak spirit could take. I must be hallucinating. He couldn't have been my father. Best to return to the city and check into my hotel room. I'll need a good night's sleep. I have a long flight across the ocean in the morning.

CHAPTER 2

Most people think of Hell as a realm that swallows you, body and mind, into an eternity of physical agony and torment. They fear the fiery grasp of a recognizable Satan, the demon in red, forcing negligent spirits to toil in the furnace of the underworld.

I have felt the clutches of Lucifer at my throat and what I know is that Hell is, in fact, no such thing. Hell is not a place. Whether here on earth or in the after-life, hell is a state of mind that will rip your soul away as you claw the earth of sanity to avoid an eternal burial. In this condition of spiritual existence, resurrection is your only hope. Today, my energy is persistent with the strong intent to facilitate my resurrection.

My body and mind are still shaken by my visit to Whidbey Island. I hadn't expected company as I toured the house. My hope was to deal with the haunting memories of my life there then find a way to let them go. The presence of the young man named Daniel is beyond shaking. It's downright mind altering how much he resembled my father. Who the hell was he, and why was he so interested in me and my family's house? Was he really even there, or just in my mind?

The trip back to Seattle and my hotel room is shaping up to be uneventful. So far, no encounters on the ferry deck, no curious young men who disappear without a whisper of sound. I am left completely to myself. And it is liberating to feel free of prying eyes with wicked intent. The wind caresses my face and tosses my hair while cooling drops of rain fall over me. Taking in deep, refreshing breaths helps to calm me. I will not race away from Seattle this time. My mind isn't tortured with memories of a loved one's violent death. I'm taking it slowly, purposefully, as I make my way to an eventual destiny. Today, I control what happens in my life.

The hotel I choose is one of the most inexpensive I could find in Seattle. When I pull up to the drive, I can easily see why. The sign is barely recognizable from the road, having been tagged in red and black spray paint. Hm. Attractive. At least I'm close to the Space Needle. That sounds sarcastic even in my mind.

When I booked this room, I figured anyone tracing me to Washington would be thrown off my trail, expecting me to choose luxury over concealment. The guy on the corner looking for a fix? No problem. I am a dark angel after all. We'll see how Collin fares in his sleep this time. He's the one who decided to steal my demons. Tonight may be a busy evening for him. Sweet dreams, Collin.

After retrieving the key from the front desk, I head back to my rental to park nearer to my room and get my bag from the trunk.

When I enter, the room is musty and dank. A pattern of mold has taken life in the corners framing the window. The carpet is riddled with oval scars the color of night. The walls are stained with nicotine and the furniture reeks of stale cigarettes and whiskey. The décor is far from appetizing. If I hope to feed this hungry soul inside my womb, I'll need to find a restaurant a bit further from the hotel than I had hoped. Maybe there's a diner with authentic seafood and fewer drug dealers milling about.

I've spent far too much time seated on a plane, then a car, and not nearly enough out in the open air. This type of confinement just won't do. I need to stretch my legs and decide to set out in search of something this peanut-sized angel would allow to sit in my stomach for more than an hour. The pale gaunt woman at the front desk suggests a small Japanese restaurant five blocks away. Fresh sushi sounds palatable.

The sun is setting over the ocean, casting auburn rays into the azure sky. I'd forgotten how much I love Washington sunsets. Except for the sound of traffic and the aroma of exhaust, the evening is ending quite peacefully. There are far more cars on the roads than I remember, and the city has built up and out, encroaching on land that was once green and lush. Still, I feel a thread of connection that I can only explain as the last place I saw two people I love alive. But it is also the place I saw one of them die. The chill in the air causes me to pull the collar of my jacket forward then zip the front before shoving my hands in my pockets.

The brisk walk to the restaurant takes less time than I thought. I actually don't consider my surroundings until a strange man carrying a paper flower funnel with black lily-ish flowers stops me at the corner. His sagging jeans have the odor of a second-hand store and his accompanying black jacket once knew the inside of a dumpster. The stench of his last cigarette still hangs in the air like a cloud of desperation.

"Hey, baby, got a light?" he asks.

A quick glance reveals he has sandy brown hair and sunken eyes.

"I don't smoke," I tell him as I push the crosswalk button

on the light pole and wait.

I turn to get a clear picture of my environs: Boarded storefront across the street, pawn shop beside it, used clothing store behind me, an adjacent restaurant. *Shit!* That's the one. I'd just passed it. Had I noticed the *Discount Dim Sum* sign in the window, I'd have missed the guy standing behind me. Uh, yeah, I admit it. I was so desperate to eat sushi that I was willing to chance a hole-in-the-wall restaurant with a cheesy Chinese name. What was I thinking? I turn and head that direction, anyway, until the man grabs my arm and I patiently turn back to him.

"That's okay, baby. I don't really need a match. You're hot enough." *Ugh!* "Bet this smooth leather jacket feels nice against your skin. Those boots are some kind of sexy, too." He eyes me from head to toe and I roll my eyes. Then he pushes the flowers in front of my face. "Ever smelled Dark Angels?"

My heart stops for a second or two and I stare him down, wondering what he knows and why he wants me to smell his flowers. "Are you quite done? My interest is in sushi, not lame compliments." My words don't have the impact I had planned. They showed my discomfort more than my disdain. I turn away and pull my arm from his grasp. Before I can take another step in my intended direction, however, he reaches for me again and pulls me into his body.

"Now, hold on there, babe." He lifts his hand, filled with a black powder and blows it into my face.

"What...in the hell are you doing, asshole?" After brushing the powder from my face, I turn back to him with my eyes narrowed on his. "Do you enjoy breathing? Because you're coming dangerously close to losing your ability to do so."

Something he sees in the curve of my brows, or maybe the way I stare him down, makes his eyes turn taught and his forehead furrowed. Or maybe he smells death on me. I certainly notice the aroma of *dumbass* on him.

The dark pupils set in pale blue irises turn to a pinpoint as he tilts away from me. I've never had to use this skill on the awake, only the sleeping. And even then, there's no guarantee they'll realize they've picked the wrong woman to fuck with. Fortunately, this guy can see it, even smell it on me.

"S…sorry. I got the wrong girl," he whispers.

"No kidding," I answer and pull my arm, once again, from his grip. He backs away, nearly tumbling over the curb as he watches me in fear.

I turn the opposite direction toward my dim sum destiny. I hope to hell this food is good. I'd hate to think I walked all this way just to have a sour stomach and an annoying confrontation with the dipshit back there.

I walk in the door and let my eyes drift from the family sitting in a nearby booth to the painted red wall decorated in souvenir Chinese lanterns above each table. The lighting is dim and I worry the intent is to keep customers from noticing anything wrong with their food. In the rear of the restaurant near the kitchen, a small woman in her sixties sweeps a lock of hair from her face and waves her hand at me. "Sit anywhere."

I nod and find a booth not far from the door and slip in. The red vinyl seems to swallow me as I sink into the seat. Soon, the woman is at my table with a menu in hand. She doesn't pretend to be nice. No nonsense is her game. Just the way I like it.

"What's awful here?" I ask.

"Don't eat the tacos," she answers then sweeps the dark lock behind her ear again.

"Tacos?" My eyebrows raise in surprise.

"Yeah. Asshole thought it'd draw more customers. I told him we're not a buffet. Stick to what you know, I said. 'I know Americans like variety,' he said. Asshole put 'em on the menu anyway. Taste like shit."

"Fair enough," I tell her and scan the menu. "Scratch the tacos, how's the sushi?"

"Now you're talkin'," she answers. "He'll make it good. Just got salmon this afternoon. You get the Philadelphia roll. It's delicious." She winks at me and scratches "Phil" on her pad. "You want some saki with that. Ours is best in town."

"Um, no. No saki, thank you. I can't drink." I inadvertently place my hand on my tummy and she looks down. I can tell by the way she studies my movements she's smart as a cat-'o-nine-tails.

"Ohhh...I see. I'll bring coconut and ginger juice. You'll like it." She snatches the menu from my hands then glides off toward the kitchen again.

Within a matter of minutes, she returns with the drink, a delectable plate of sushi and a pair of chopsticks. I fumble with the damned things for a while before getting the hang of them and snatching up each morsel once they're doused in wasabi and soy sauce then topped with a slice of ginger root. The drink she suggested also seems to settle my stomach even before one slice of Philly roll touches my lips.

Turns out, the food is not so bad. A Chinese-Japanese, and surprisingly Mexican restaurant with discount dim sum, tacos, and sushi that doesn't kill me or turn my stomach inside out. I'm satisfied with the overall outcome of this venture. And the people are nice. The tables could be cleaner, but what do you expect from a hole-in-the-wall joint like this? They're busier than any of the others on this street. A bonus for me.

I finish and pay for my meal, but not before tipping the woman well. She smiles when she sees the $10 I left her under the Kikkoman. I start my journey back to the hotel to make a fair attempt at a good night's sleep.

The well-lit streets of Seattle remind me of my dreams,

walking toward danger without fear. At least, without the fear I knew in my early years. In those days, I didn't hold my head high as I do now. The idea that I could die young in a similar manner to my father or grandmother once I started hunting was a challenge my mind had difficulty overcoming.

My first kill was a fifteen-year-old gang member. I was eleven. Small and trembling. He towered over me by feet more than inches. The scent of death coated his soul. Mine hadn't yet been stained. But the kill was easy, simple. I allowed him only one slash of the knife before taking it from him then using it. His eyes rolled back in his head as he cursed me. I turned away before his body hit the ground. Couldn't bear to see it. I've done the same ever since. When I awoke, the stench of his death covered me and I've carried it ever since. Every demon I kill covers my soul with their demise. A weight I will never lift from my spirit. Although I know these killers have to be stopped, I still hate that I'm the one responsible for their ending.

As I finally fit the card key into the lock of my room, I let my shoulders fall and my body relax just a bit. I'm relieved my short excursion elicited no more than a minor altercation. My devil-may-care attitude may bring about more situations where I might meet up with someone in my waking hours who is less than pure of thought. Someone I may end up having to kill, after all. Have I learned nothing? How many sets of eyes were on me as I traversed the darker streets of Seattle? I can't tell as easily when I'm awake. Although I will protect myself and my child to the death if need be, I hope the necessity doesn't present itself, and that I'm not the one who entices the deadly encounter. No, I will do all I can not to kill anymore. Breaking a few bones to render the perpetrator a huddled mass of sobbing regret is an ending I can live with, however.

More hours pass by as I search the channels of the relic they call a TV in this room. Nothing worth capturing my attention except reruns of an old zombie hunter series. I've had bloodier battles. They should try harder.

After shaking the bed for bugs, or any other unknowns one might encounter in a hotel room of this stature, I crawl under the covers and let the pillow swallow my weary head.

Seems as though mere seconds pass before I feel myself walking the darkened path of my mind. The clothing on my body is a white men's dress shirt, much like Collin's the first night we went out. Couldn't be possible that I'm actually dreaming the full, nocturnal slumber of a dark angel, could it? This is unusual to me now. For the past month, I close my eyes then open them hours later without an intervening thought or memory. But this has substance, formation. I feel the lure, hear the heavy breathing of the monster in my mind and my forward progression into the dream falters, just as it had the first night I was drawn to one of them. Do they feel my fear? Do they realize my hesitation isn't for my life, but for my child's?

As I stand on the fringes of the shadows, I wait and watch as the dream forms before my eyes. Hello darkness, my greatest foe, where have you been? Soon, the mist of nothingness begins to swirl and a great wind gusts against my rigid form, tearing at my hair. A whisper pulls my attention to the right and I see the mattress on which my father had once lain, his lost life still staining the sheets and floor. Why did my dream bring me here? Does this demon have anything to do with my father?

Suddenly, I detect a familiar scent. "Go to the bed Jaime," a voice whispers from behind, startling me.

I instinctually reach back and grasp the sleeve of a heavy jacket. With a heave, I pull the demon over my shoulder and to the ground at my feet. The face I recognize well. The one from my previous waking confrontation, while on my way to eat. The stench of him permeates my senses.

"Who are you? Who the *fuck are* you and what are you doing in my dream?" I shout at him with my foot to his throat, still clutching his wrist.

He only looks up at me and laughs. As my temperature rises and my face begins to burn, the pressure of my instep on his airway increases, making him choke. I don't want him dead. I want answers. So I lift my weight a bit, allowing him the ability to speak.

"Answer me." The words roll from my tongue in a deep growl, but he isn't fazed, even chuckles a bit. "That's brave, laughing at the one who's about to end your life."

His blue eyes twinkle up at me as he smiles and takes a deep shuddering breath, then coughs until blood splatters my ankle. "I'm already dying," he answers, then laughs again. "You're only making it a faster transition."

"Or I could make it slow and painful for you."

I hold his wrist tight in my grip while turning until the bone snaps then crackles under the pressure. His screams of agony penetrate my soul and I hold back my revulsion. Then I lean closer to him.

"Talk."

Once he catches his breath, he turns to me and shakes his head. "You have no clue. They still know you and they *will* get to you. No one has forgotten you, Jaime Connor."

The sound of my name on his lips turns me cold. I reach down and lift him to his feet by the throat. "Who? Who're you with?"

He shakes his head then hacks and spews droplets of bright red phlegm onto my white sleeve. If this wasn't a dream, I'd be pissed. Moving swiftly to the wall beside the bed, I slam him against the barrier and peer into his eyes, trying to read his soul.

"You won't find the answer in there," he chokes out. "I'm more afraid of *them* than I am of *you*."

"We'll see," I tell him then slam his head into the solid wall his mind has created for this evening's escapade. He crumbles to the floor, his mind conjuring a disjointed nightmare, half in this scenario and half in another alternate state of unreal. Could be hours before he collects his marbles and his mind returns to play.

With the demon momentarily controlled, I turn to the bed and see the unrecognizable body soaked in deep burgundy. The torso barely appears human. The only recognizable feature is the face. The long, dark hair surrounding it is knotted and wet. I wipe the matted strands from her face to see deep green eyes fixed on a distant image, her mouth open and twisted into a scream—all are mine. Am I seeing my terrible fate?

My body seems to be backing away, but I'm not consciously moving my feet. Maybe the nearby fixtures are shifting from me, or the room has become much larger than it originally had been. I can't tell because the world seems to also be spinning and I can't control what's happening to my body or my mind. My stomach is weak and a scream is captured in the back of my throat, waiting to be forced free.

The demon knows more than I will ever be able to extract from him. If he knows my identity but isn't afraid of me, that means there's someone out there who truly scares the shit out of him. Someone who can kill me. Kill my baby. Will I be able to survive long enough to give birth to this child?

The fear I'd swallowed deep in my throat rushes upward in a torrent before I can tamp it back down. "Collin!"

I hear his name scream through the ether, but I don't

remember parting my lips. Are my thoughts an audible cry in this dream? Seconds pass, or maybe they're minutes, I can't tell. What I do know is the sound of Collin's voice frantically calling my name before powerful hands grasp my shoulders from behind. I spin to attack, but my arm is caught in mid-blow, so I swing with the next. Soon, both wrists are trapped and my screams are suffocated by a strong chest and Collin's tender voice.

"Jaime, shh…I'm here. I'm so sorry I was late. I'm so sorry you had to fight, babe."

His voice is soothing and I only want to stay there. "Hold me. Tell me you love me."

"Oh, sweetheart, I love you. I love you more than the ground beneath our feet. Every breath that whispers past my lips is yours."

My eyes raise to his in question. *What the hell?* He sounds like a girl. What have I done to him?

He must see my confusion because he strokes the side of my cheek and lays a gentle kiss on my forehead. "There isn't a moment throughout history that I haven't wanted to drink you into my soul and hold you there for all eternity."

I must be staring back at him dumbfounded. My jaw is dropped open and I feel my eyebrows pinch together. "What the hell has happened to you?" I nearly whisper, trying unsuccessfully to pull free from his embrace.

"What're you talking about, buttercup?" he replies.

"Who the *fuck* are you? Who are you, and where's Collin?"

"Jaime, calm down." His voice has suddenly changed, a little tauter than before. Slightly rounder and throaty. I step backward, but he reaches for my wrists again. "Don't go, Jaime. Don't leave me again." The eyes. I look into his eyes and they're not *his*. The color is similar, but paler, flatter. This isn't Collin.

As I pull free from him, I fall to the ground and scramble to my knees. By the time I rise to my feet, he's gone. The only person in the room with me is the unconscious demon and the dead Jaime doppelganger. And I begin to wonder if *she's* even real. I step carefully to the bed and reach for her hair. Before I can sense the coarse strands between my fingers, the corpse disappears. She wasn't really there. She wasn't me. It was only a nocturnal illusion. The bedding and the wooden frame are no longer my parents'. The room has become mine and the bed ours, the one I shared with Collin. What is the purpose of all of this? What are these demons trying to tell me?

The sound of someone approaching causes me to spin in their direction. When he appears in the shadows surrounding my dream, I hold my breath. The intruder has dark, wavy locks and deep green eyes. Collin?

I step back and he hesitates.

"Jaime?"

I want to move forward into his arms but stop myself. What if this isn't him, either? What if it's someone bent on turning me mad? He reaches forward.

"Don't touch me."

I glare back at him, cautious, studying his face, his eyes, the mannerisms I've come to appreciate and sometimes hate so much.

"Jaime—"

"What took you so long?"

"I was caught in battle with a demon. I'm sorry, I meant to… When I heard your screams, I killed him and—" he must recognize the sharp stab in my heart, maybe my pain reflects in my eyes, making him hesitate. "I rushed right to you." He takes a step forward and I take one back. "Jaime, please—" I see confusion in his eyes then hurt.

"There's someone else in this dream." My voice is still

untrusting, as if testing the waters. "He looks just like you." I stop short, still unsure if this is really him.

"There's no one else, Jaime. Search the shadows."

My eyes scan our surroundings, feeling for a pulse, a hint of a soul waiting for their moment to enter the heart of the dream. The darkness is hollow, empty.

"Just us," he tells me. "Well, and him," he says, pointing to the demon on the ground. "Did you do that?"

I feel the half-smile pull at the corners of my mouth then turn serious again, unwilling to let go of my emotions.

His lips curve upward to a boyish grin. "Let me come to you, Jaime. I promise I won't hurt you. I promise to stay benign," he says, and I'm reminded of the night at his gallery. The memory of how much I wanted him to hold me without the pain of broken ribs making me weak, comes flooding back. At my door, he said he would kiss me in a way he has kissed no other woman if he stepped inside. My body ached for him now just as it did then. He really is Collin. The realization ignites a fire in my thighs racing up to the curvature at their summit and attracting my full attention.

I lick my lips and he steps forward again, with his fingers outstretched. "Let me come to you, Jaime," he repeats.

Oh, *God*, his powerful energy teases every part of my body.

"Collin," I whisper, longing for him, reaching my hand forward to meet his.

Collin grasps my fingers and pulls me into his arms, meeting me halfway. "God I've missed you," he murmurs into my hair, clinging to me and kissing my temple.

My lips brush his throat and I breathe in the scent that is uniquely his. He's dressed in the white shirt he wore the night of our only true date. At this point, it's difficult to tell if I imagined him into it in my mind, or if it was him. My body reacts to his scent, the feel of him so close to me and I melt into him as if our skin is fused and we form a perfect puzzle. I long for his fingertips to tickle my flesh. I ache for him to discover my body as he did the first time we made love.

The passion also rises within Collin. The evidence presses against my abdomen, stirring my mind and my longing for him. I don't know if my desire is elevated due to my inability to hunt or the hormones raging through my body because of the baby, but I don't care. Either way, I want him so badly. More so than when we first met. I never knew I could react this way to anyone.

"Take me, Collin," I whisper, breathless.

He shakes his head in confusion. "No, not here, Jaime. Come back to me."

"Please. Please, I want you, now, in this dream. Don't make me beg."

He shakes his head at me, his eyebrows bent in sorrow. His denial makes the urgency take control of my senses. I want him, need him. And by the pounding of the blood through his chest, I know he wants me just as badly. Instead, Collin steps back and rubs his face with both hands then peers down at me. He's torn between his desire and his fear that I'll hurt him again. I can see it in the dark shadows of his eyes.

I step toward him and reach up to his forehead. "I can't promise I'll come back to you," I say, sweeping a lock of hair from his eyes. "At least, not yet. I need time. I need to process everything that's happened. If I don't, I'm afraid of what I'll do to you...and what it will do to me. What I *can* promise is that I will carry you in my heart. I will *always* love you, Collin."

Taking his hand, I place it on my shirt over my breast then trail it lower, over my ribs, through the dip of my waist then the curve of my hips until his fingers find the heat between my thighs, beneath the hem of the shirt. A groan escapes his lips as he forces his eyes closed and tilts his head as if trying to reason with his uncooperative conscience. He sighs then returns his gaze to me, his irises nearly glowing in the dim light. His glare pierces me with the color of gleaming emeralds surrounding a hint of peridot rimming his pupils. My breath is stolen by their intensity.

Collin gathers me into his arms, holding me close to his chest, and carries me to the waiting bed. He lays me gently on the covers, bleached white like pure down.

Then Collin glances sideways to the foul-smelling demon on the floor.

"What about him?"

Dismissively waving my hand, I shrug my shoulders and shake my head. "Oh, him. Uh, slight head jostle sent him to another dream. Should be at least another hour before he finds his way back," I answer, embarrassed at the idea I'm dying to make love mere feet from the inert image of someone sent to kill me in their sleep. What in the *hell* am I doing? *Fuck it.* I want him so badly, I don't care.

Collin waves his hands and candles fill the room. He is awash in the flickering light while his fingers gently lift my chin and my eyes follow to peer into his. He stares down at me, passion burning in his green irises. His shirt is nearly completely opened. Then he releases the last button and climbs up on the bed, straddling me. His patient fingers work to unfasten the shirt I'm wearing. The anxiety of his contained desire shows in his narrowed eyes and his teeth biting into his lower lip.

Before long, he lays open the two halves of cloth, exposing my breasts as my fingers glide across his chest and over his taut shoulders. My body aches for him while his finger traces a line from my chin to my cleavage then trails further downward and into my panties. I eagerly raise my hips to meet him as he slips them into the sensitive crease. I feel his eyes on me as I close mine and revel in the ecstasy he draws out in me.

The talent Collin displays while gently stroking and working his way deeper through the folded flesh draws out the animal in me. The cries of passion that escape my throat are all I can hear echoing through the darkness of my mind. I clutch the sheets at my sides until I feel his moist lips covering my nipple. Soon my fingers are laced through his hair and pulling his mouth into my tender flesh.

He slides my panties downward, past my knees to my ankles, then kisses the sensitive flesh of my inner thigh. My legs tremble with desire. He's taking far too long and the muscles in my body grow taut again as a wave of ecstasy rushes over me. The first orgasm takes me before he even begins. With my body flushing from the intensity of passion, he positions himself at my opening. The muscles in my groin and thighs contract in anticipation. My mind forgets that we're only in a dream and that I was there to kill someone, not find passion with a talented lover. *To hell with that.*

The surge of adrenaline through my body sends my mind into a frenzy, wanting him, needing him. My fingers dig into his flesh as he glides inside and becomes one with me. The gasp that escapes my lips releases the days of anxiety I've known since I decided to leave. The hours of dread I've felt since arriving in Seattle flee from me with his next thrust.

His teeth grind together as he throws his head back in an attempt to temper his hunger. But I crave the animal inside him and pull him back to gaze into my soul. The moment our eyes meet, his pupils dilate and the beast awakens.

With a force I haven't known from him before, he drives deep and hard inside of me. My legs curl around him and I only know this moment, this feeling of unfettered ecstasy. My body tightens as another orgasmic wave rolls through me, forcing an impassioned scream up my throat. Collin's eyes close as he attempts to stave off the rise in his blood, the surging in his groin. When his hips move rhythmically with the beat of my heart once again, I feel another rise arching my body and numbing my mind.

Again, I cry out into the night and Collin pulls back, moving to massage the spot only he can reach inside my abdomen, forcing another ecstatic wave to flood over me. His subtle motions, then dramatic thrusts, cause one rush after another to pour through me. I pull his mouth to mine, hungrily taking his tongue and sucking.

When my nails dig into the flesh of his arms in a frenzied moment, a groan escapes his lips and fills my mouth. Soon, his body grows rigid and he throws his head back. A deeper cry echoes through my mind as he plunges one last time to the core of my abdomen. Both of us cling to each other, afraid to let go, as our bodies ride the tempest from within. Soon he collapses on top of me and my body sinks into the sheets.

After what seems like an eternity, our bodies lie still, tangled and unmoving but for the pounding of our hearts and heaving of our chests. I've been swallowed into a blissful stupor, feeling the tickle of his breath on my throat. My mind grows clear as I wait for my strength to return. Collin's lips nip at my shoulder while I comb my fingers through his hair.

"*God*, I love you, Jaime," he whispers gently.

My heart falters. I love him, too. I know I should tell him, return his sentiment. But I can't. Just moments, maybe even an hour has passed since I told him I would always love him. Why can't I tell him now?

Collin lifts his head to peer into my eyes, questioning. His eyes close with the realization that I can't utter the words. *Damn it!* Why can't I just say them? Why do I still hold back emotions I want so clearly to express? My damned pride. Before I can force an apology past my lips, he turns from me and I can feel his heart breaking just as mine had so many years ago when I faced the brutal realization I was left on this earth alone. And I can't forget that it was his fault. His selfish deed that killed them.

His gaze trails over the edge of the bed to the demon on the floor. Dread takes over my thoughts as I read what his eyes don't attempt to hide.

"You know he has to die, Jaime."

I shake my head defiantly, knowing the truth I refuse to face.

"If I don't kill him, this dream will never end. What do we do then?"

"Stay here. Why can't we just stay here? Never leave this bed, this dream." My request is childish. I know there's no other way, but I can't face the truth.

Collin knows my torment. It shows in the creases around his eyes and in his forehead. He rises from the bed and I catch his hand.

"Collin, no."

He turns back to me and leans over, kissing my lips so soft. "Come back to me, Jaime," he whispers into my mouth.

"I can't. Not yet."

He takes a deep, sullen breath. "Turn away," he tells me, lifting my hand to place over my eyes. "Don't look."

I turn my face from him and tears roll over the bridge of my nose and to the white sheets beneath me. I take a deep breath and call out to him, "Collin, I love—" But my voice doesn't flow into the shadows of the dream. Instead, it echoes back to me from the painted walls of a small room. I'm in the cheap hotel, waking to a loud pounding at the door.

"Miss! Are you okay?" comes a muffled cry from the

hallway beyond.

Shit.

I gather my thoughts to discover the source of the commotion. Did they hear my orgasmic screams in my dream? Oh my God. Have I woken the entire floor? Pulling the comforter from the bed, I wrap it around my naked torso, stumbling from the covers and across the floor. With the safety bar latched above my head, I open the door enough for them to see my eyes.

"Are you all right, miss? There were screams coming from your —" He stops mid-sentence; his eyes fix on the scar on my cheek. Then his gaze turns to the door to avoid my stare. "There were complaints that someone was, well, maybe being hurt. I came to check." He forces his eyes back to mine, then past me and I step aside to show him I'm alone.

"I'm so sorry. I had a horrible nightmare and…I…it was so real. I…I'm completely humiliated now." I feign embarrassment and flick on the light to allow him to see I'm unharmed.

The light illuminates the healed, but still noticeable wounds in my shoulder that Rick gave me, and a multitude of marks across my arms from the others. I gather the flowered comforter around my feet and pull it tight under my arms. He ponders for a moment, his eyes darting from me and the stained comforter barely covering my nudity, to the door, then just past me as far as the narrow crack will allow. "Well…as long as you're all right. You have a good night, you hear?"

"Thank you, I will." I fake a smile and close the door, then take a deep, shuddering breath.

Shit.

CHAPTER 3

In the bleakest hours of desperation, when the world and all that is holy seems to have forgotten you exist, you might peer down to find the icy claws of desolation tearing at the very last shred of your resolve. When the final ragged thread of your humanity is broken, and you lose all that is left of the person you once knew, the one you thought you were and would always be, that is when you have found yourself devoured deep into the belly of perdition.

The emptiness I feel as I pack my lone bag and close the door to my hotel room is akin to a dank pit in my cavernous soul. And I wonder if I am running from or to the gut of perdition. Collin isn't solely to blame. He is merely the vessel for those intent on drawing me into their torturous web. Unwittingly, he led them right to me. Although I have vanquished those who seemed the greatest threat, I still feel the frigid clutches of Lucifer, pulling at my ankles to meet an eternal burial. I am resolute. My only hope of escaping the spiritual death I'm destined to know is to put distance between me and the Americas. Somehow, I must evade the fear that chases my soul and the dread that I might someday soon be forced to kill again in my dreams.

Before settling into my final destination, I want to discover the world, learn about other civilizations and hopefully leave behind the cynicism that has poisoned my soul for these many years. My heading is Thailand. I plan to explore the country and hope to meet people who are as tired of death as I. Those who see the woman I am, not my scars.

As I walk the airport, a familiar anxiety burns inside of me as I remember, once again, my mother's hand clutching mine. I need to take it slow. *Don't rush out of here or you'll regret it, Jaime.* The words echo on a continuous loop in my head. I have time. Plenty, as a matter of fact. No need to hurry to the terminal only to replay the scene in my mind once again. I've already shelved that book, and it doesn't serve me to pore over it again.

Up ahead in the concourse is a Starbucks. I can see their signature green mermaid sign and pleasantly accessorized displays from two magazine shops away. The aroma of fresh-ground coffee wafts through the concourse as I breathe in and hold the scent inside me, as if I could taste it through osmosis. I could use a cup of something warm and bitter right about now. But coffee isn't best for me in my delicate condition. A scone, however, and some nice hot chocolate are. A compromise is in order. Maybe I'll even have them add a dash of orange syrup to my drink. Mmm. The idea settles well in my stomach. It's about time *something* did.

"Welcome to Starbucks. What can I get ya?" A young man with a freckled nose greets me. His blue eyes sparkle far too much for someone like me whose soul has grown accustomed to darkness.

"I'll take a venti hot chocolate with orange syrup. You do still have orange syrup, don't you?"

"Yes, ma'am, we do."

Ugh! He called me *ma'am*. Why does that grate on my nerves? Maybe I'm finally feeling my age and hating the way it sounds on me. "Fine. I'll take that," I tell him, realizing my voice is too flat and bitchy, so I raise it a pitch or two. "And I'll have one of those cranberry-orange scones with it." I flash a fake grin any warm-blooded soul could see through.

"One venti orange hot chocolate coming up. May I have your name?"

His eyes seem to drill into me as I stand there dumb-faced. Then I feel my brows pinch in the center in a *what-the-hell-did-you-say* kind of expression. Why does he need my name?

He points a black sharpie at the side of the cup. "So we know who to call when your drink is done."

Shit. Has it really been that long since I've been in one of these joints? "Sorry." I think for a moment. Then, "Angel," I tell him like it's my secret stripper name and he smiles back at me.

He lowers the marker to the side of the cup with a subtle grin on his face. A teen-ish girl with brown hair pulled back in a tail reaches into the case and slips one of the scones onto a plate. Then her dark, innocent eyes turn up to mine. "You want this heated?"

Oh, baby girl, doesn't it show? I take my pastries like I prefer my demons. "No." *Cold*.

"Good enough," she answers and hands me the plate. "Next!"

Her voice startles me. I had no idea there was another waiting behind me. How could there be someone I never noticed; someone whose scent I didn't even catch a hint of, nor sense a change in my peripheral energy? I turn to note the tall man directly behind me with brown curls and hazel eyes.

"Yes. I'll have a venti iced latte. Oh, and one of those scones. Also, *cold*."

The emphasis he puts on the word is like he's read my mind. A chill sweeps through me. I can't feel his energy at all, as if he isn't really there. All of a sudden, my mind goes numb as I try to read his soul. There's nothing that speaks to me. His spirit hasn't one intimation of history to sense. Suddenly, I notice his eyes have met mine. A current shoots through me like a power surge as a voice behind me shouts, "Angel!"

The brown-haired man points his finger to the barista. "I think your coffee's ready."

"Huh? Uh, oh. Yes." *Oh, God*, was I staring?

I turn like a woman who's been mentally chastised, although I'm not sure why, and take my cup, still feeling his eyes on my back, my hair, then my ass. *Damn it! Why are men always prone to looking at my ass?* I take a deep breath and blow it out before turning away from the barista, who's already on to the next customer's drink. If I only had the power of invisibility. One of the many things that suck about being a dark angel.

Once past the counter, a quick glance around the room reveals a small table in the back corner. Ah, yes. A secluded area. I can sit out of the way with my back to the wall. There's no one sitting nearby, just the way I like it. I can hide and sulk while enjoying my treat, the only part of my venture into this shop that's made the journey worthwhile.

Although the edges of the scone crumble when my teeth sink into it, the flakey texture and tart cranberries are delightful and compliment the silky chocolate that I carefully sip. After another bite and a second gulp, I allow the muscles in my shoulders to relax while scanning the room. Old habits die hard, as they say.

There's a woman in a suit with a briefcase on the floor at her side and a phone to her ear. She seems focused and direct, neglecting the muffin on the plate in front of her. Periodically, she brings the cup to her lips, but barely takes a sip before speaking again. The man beyond her is relaxed in jeans and a t-shirt. His laptop is open as he leans back, enjoying a video that intermittently evokes a chuckle. A girl stands at the counter with her phone in hand, furiously typing a message to someone while impatiently awaiting her order.

My phone is tucked away in my purse. I have no desire to use it. There's no one I'd want to call or to whom I'd send a message. Am I the only person in this place without some sort of device stealing my time? Am I the only one in this world independent of an internet or cellular signal?

The man with brown hair is heading my direction. *No.* With a smile on his face. Damn. And here I thought I was being slick. He sets his iced latte and scone on the table beside mine as I pretend not to notice him. Training my eyes on the room, I take a tentative sip of my chocolate, attempting to ignore the adjacent personal space invader. As I stare ahead at the many people before me, electronically pacified by their various devices, my full attention is on the one nearby who is studying me as I pretend to study *him.*

"Cute cup," he says, and I turn to him, confused. "The…uh, angel wings. The barista drew wings on your cup." He points to my hot chocolate.

I turn the cup to see an abstract set of wings over the name Angel. "Oh, I hadn't noticed." I turn the cup back to its original position then take a sip and return to the distant patrons.

"Nice day to fly," he says, forcing me to cringe.

"Seriously?" I answer in a flat tone, still searching the room. "That's the best you could do to springboard a conversation?"

From the corner of my eye, I see him shrug. His face and neck turn redder than his tie. "I'm not good at this."

"Apparently." I almost feel sorry for him before reminding myself that most demons are terrible at picking up women.

Although he doesn't seem like a demon, I can't waste my time meeting people who will inevitably want to know more about me. I don't have the luxury of idle chat. I don't have an innocent backstory to make any conversation interesting. So, my choice is to lie and hope I don't forget, or tell the truth, and my truth isn't the sort that someone like him would understand. On the other hand, if he doesn't want to learn more about me, that only means he probably already knows who I am and doesn't need any further introduction. I learned my lesson with Sarah. That she only talked about herself should've told me she was a demon sent to eliminate me. Or a narcissist. Turned out she was both, and for that I had no choice but to kill her. Either way, this man is someone I don't need or want in my life.

"My name is Marcus," he says, jutting his hand toward me as if we were about to do business together. I glance down at his fingers, noting his well-manicured nails, then back up to his eyes, gently sparkling in his boyish face. Noting my reluctance, he takes a deep breath and tries again. "Yours is?"

"Disinterested." I turn my attention back to the room.

"I...I'm sorry. I just thought—"

"Please don't think, Marcus. Look, I don't mean to be a bitch, but I'm not here to find a boyfriend or any other kind of *friend*. I just want to be left—"

"Rebecca? I *knew* that was you!" A stunted woman with short brown hair resembling a football helmet, approaches the table. Good lord. "God! How long has it been?" she asks, with eyes like small, black beads blinking as she speaks. She slips between me and Marcus.

I sigh and look up at her. "You've got the wrong person." This is not my day.

The obvious appearance of annoyance on my face prompts her to wink at me. "You must not remember me. Amy Schneider. We took a Psych 452 class together a few years back, *remember*?" she says and winks again, then again and…again, until I finally get her game and wish she would stop winking. It's annoying the hell out of me and I'm not sure why, except that this has been an unusual day, and she reminds me a lot of Sarah. And what normal person sees a woman speaking with a man at a Starbucks and says to herself, *"Gee, I think I'll pretend I know her so I can separate her from this guy?"* This is such a Sarah move. "Abnormal Psychology of the Criminal Mind," she continues, still winking at me. "You were the best analyst I'd ever seen. How are you? Still working for the Seattle crime lab?"

"Amy…yeah…uh, no. I…don't work for the crime lab any longer. I'm the…lead detective in the…special…crimes…unit." I guess I learned something from watching numerous commercials for the various police dramas that populate the average TV channels. Or else I'm semi-plausible when pulling information out of my, well, let's just say it's a dark place that never sees the sun.

"Wow! A promotion? That's awesome!" She feigns impressed too well and squints her eyes at me like she's trying to be cute. Shirley Temple cute. I should recommend her for an Emmy. Or maybe not. Her act is maddening.

I know she is just trying to be helpful. So why do I hate her so much? Is it hormones, or intuition? Yes, I'm in a pissy mood, and that probably explains my unforgivable attitude toward the barista and Marcus. But my feelings toward this woman are undeniably targeted. I know there's something in her past. Or maybe her future. There's only one way to find out what that is.

"I have a table right over here. Come sit with me. I'm dying to hear all about your promotion." She waves her hand then grabs my drink and plate and leads me from my corner seat.

I stay planted for a moment, watching her ass sashaying to an open table, wondering what the hell just happened. Then I turn to Marcus. With an apologetic look on my face, I nod toward him and rise to my feet. He doesn't say a word as he watches me leave with my drink and scone, following the woman who I've realized, sadly, reminds me of someone I recently killed. Even worse, her pathetic display is my best opportunity to escape.

When I reach Amy's table, I plant myself behind the empty chair and lean forward, looking her directly in the eyes. Between the squints and winks I see more than she ever thought she could reveal. She's a demon and she knows who I am.

"I saw him follow you and thought you might need some interference." She grins back at me and my skin prickles. "Sit. Let's talk—"

"Thanks. But no. Have a nice day, Amy," I tell her and her smile slips away. I draw the last bite of scone to my lips and toss it in then turn from her.

More than two sets of eyes watch me as I stroll from the shop and into the wave of bodies rushing to their gates. The cup of hot chocolate is clutched in my grasp as my other hand clings to the strap of my purse.

Part of me is sad, knowing that Amy may be one of the next demons to die in her sleep. The other side of me shudders at the idea of what she may do to another in their dream before her life ends. One thing is for sure, she knows me and has plans to meet me in nocturnal battle. Unless she's more bad ass than she appears, she's destined to succumb to the dark angel of her dreams one of these nights. As for Marcus, there's no telling on what side of the black/white line he will fall. Maybe he hasn't made up his mind quite yet. I'm still perplexed that I didn't feel a thing from him, neither hatred nor love, only emptiness. If someone searched my soul as I did his, would they find the same? Nothing? Or would there be only darkness for them to discover? At this point, I'm not sure what composes my soul. That disturbs me more than I want to admit. Maybe that's why Marcus rubbed me the wrong way so badly.

When I reach my destination, I check in then sink into a chair near the outer rim of the ticket gate. In the event someone annoying sits next to me, I won't be trapped between them and another body. If I'm unable to turn away to avoid conversation, at least I can excuse myself to the restroom. I've never been a conversationalist. Social situations aren't exactly my thing, especially ones in cramped situations. I'd rather sink my teeth into Styrofoam than chat about the weather with a stranger. After decades of hiding from the world to avoid bringing attention to myself, I've become such a recluse. Is there no hope for me?

With more than an hour before takeoff, I note the area is fairly empty. The way I like it. A few scattered travelers are dispersed throughout, preoccupied with their electronics and I realize something I missed in the coffee shop. No one bothers anyone whose staring at their device. Maybe the Starbucks customers knew something I didn't but should have.

With my purse tucked snuggly at my side, I notice a woman with her husband and a young girl shuffle into the seating area. The child is, maybe, three years old. Dark curls fall to her shoulders. Her bright yellow sundress contrasts with her hair and bronze eyes. The eyes. They glint with the light of heaven as she studies those around her. Her busy gaze hesitates on me for longer than a minute. *Yes, little angel. You do still recognize me.*

The earthbound cherub smiles as if she can read my mind, nearly aware of my dark past, understanding I'm only a danger to those who will harm her. Soon, she will forget all she knows about the preexistence and who I once was and what I've become. She won't recognize me from anyone. I'll be another frightening, strange face in the crowd. Today, however, I'm a friend.

As I watch her rush to the window, her small fingers curled around one of her father's, and tugging him along behind her, I think of the child inside of me. Will mine look like her, be as anxious and as gregarious? Will her curiosity overwhelm me until I'm rendered helpless by her charm and left being dragged behind her like a sluggish pull toy?

I rub my abdomen, feeling the energy of the growing life, the spirit so powerful that both masculine and feminine energy radiate through my tissue and skin all at once. The life force of this child pulses out such an unusual energy. Around most pregnant women I can feel the boy or the girl she's carrying, even in the early stages. As much as I try, I can't tell which gender mine will be. Was it the same when my mother carried me?

The girl at the window turns to see if her mother is still nearby. Her dark eyes sparkle with the mischievous glint of a three-year-old when her mother waves back at her. She turns her face up to her father then back to the planes on the tarmac. I notice his brown eyes and dark hair are the color of hers when he smiles down at his daughter. I can't help but wonder if this baby will have the same mischievous glint in his green eyes and hair as dark as Collin's.

Remembering the last time I saw those green irises and deep waves, my mind is taken back to the passion we knew only hours ago. His eyes digesting me while his fingers excited my skin wherever he touched. His warm mouth drawing my flesh inside to be tasted by his moist tongue. I can almost feel him all over me as I slide deeper into my seat. A groan inadvertently escapes my throat.

Just as I silence the rising tide within me, a man in a business suit with a black briefcase and bright red tie sits in the seat beside me and turns my direction. Before he can utter one lame conversation starter, I swipe inside my purse, pull out my cell phone and turn my back to him. I decide to discover some apps in the Google Play store. There are so many to choose from, I couldn't help but download several. Much to my surprise, this phone works much like piranhas on a corpse. The world around me ceases to exist within seconds, dissolving the meaty distractions around me, while I lose myself in the many offerings I've never even considered before. I may become a download junkie before this trip is over.

Eventually, the room fills in with people. Coughing, sniffling, bored-beyond-compare-people who all have their own story. Their own destiny. Each of them has lost someone—to death, to divorce, to an unconquerable world that steals their time and their soul. Some losses go barely noticed by their keeper, while others etch painful memories into their hearts that can never be rubbed anew. A quick glance over my device to the faces around the room shows so many conceal a brewing storm deep inside. Seems the world is shifting darker in a desperate, senseless way.

The suit beside me hasn't tried striking up a conversation. I have my phone to thank for that. He anxiously rises to his feet as the doorway is pulled agape for passengers to begin boarding. I'm ensconced in my chair, willing to wait. I'm in no rush. With my phone at eye level, I play an addictive game where I fling rotund birds at poorly constructed objects to facilitate the death of devious pigs. Didn't even read the rules.

Just started playing and, look, I'm killing it. Literally. Seriously, I'm really fairly good at this game. And I thought killing demons in my sleep was a dark proclivity.

As the area is nearly clear of bodies I notice a boy watching me from over my left shoulder. I turn and glance back at him and his face puckers.

"What?" I could've removed the impatience from my dark tone but chose not to.

"My sister plays better than you." His eyes turn up in an annoyed roll.

"Your much older and much more intelligent sister, I would suppose," I answer with my eyes slack, showing his diss fell flat on me.

"She's three. Look, you have to use the bombs or you won't kill all the pigs, but wait to use them when there's a close grouping or you'll waste them."

I stare at him dumbfounded for a moment then sharpen my glare. "I knew that. I was just testing my mad skills without the bombs today."

He curls his lip then slackens his eyes in a mocking expression. I return his gesture. This kid I'm carrying inside of me had better never give me that look. A sinking feeling tells me I'll have to learn patience on my path to momhood. And I'm not known for patience.

As his mother grabs his upper arm and drags him toward the line to board, I search the instructions on the game to learn how and when to use the bombs. I actually suck at this.

The ticket counter makes one last call for boarders and I decide to rise and meander onto the plane. I don't relish the idea of being stuffed in a flying tin can for hours. Someone is bound to fall asleep. Chances are one of them will be me. Although the demon's call has grown more distant with time, the lure is still there. I may be lucky not to have anyone with ill intent on my flight. Ninety-nine percent of all transatlantic flights complete without a hiccup. There's no reason at all for me to consider this trip to be anything but average. But, then again, my life has never been anything resembling typical. And the number of humans with a demon lurking within is frighteningly high.

As I board the plane and the door closes in behind me, the finality of the latch locking into place sends a twinge through my spine. Down the aisle, merely six rows back, is the woman from Starbucks who called herself Amy. As our eyes meet, I notice she isn't winking or squinting anymore. Instead, she allows me to see into the deep darkness of her tarlike orbs.

This time, her ink-stain pupils reveal more than I could have extracted over a coffee cup. Is it a mistake? Are her defenses lowered in the surroundings of this aircraft? Or is she intentionally showing the blackness of her heart? Regardless, I'm able to move past the façade and take advantage of the moment.

Her lips curve down into a scowl. I nod then feel mine curve upward. There's something about being trapped on the plane with *her* that makes this seem... So. Damned. Planned. And I struggle with the demon inside of me that yearns to snap her neck. Now there's no way I'll be able to go to sleep. The need to hunt her down would be too strong.

My seat is in the second row. Window. No one sits beside me. I'm alone. Thank God. Not a soul to bother me on this long flight across the ocean. I can watch the clouds roll by without being showered with questions of my origin or my destination. I'm not sure I could keep my sarcasm in check once my patience wore thin.

What do I do for fun? I hunt and kill people like you in my sleep.

Sure, it would be an asshole answer, definitely a stunner and, no doubt, a conversation stopper. Maybe it would even shut them up for the rest of the flight. Luckily, I won't discover the consequences my smart-mouth answers might bring.

As I reach up to draw a pillow and blanket down, from the corner of my eye I catch the flight attendant pulling the drapes between first-class seating and coach. The glower of Amy's button eyes may be hidden from view, but I still feel them glaring through the wall of fabric.

The "Fasten Seatbelt" sign flashes and the pilot comes over the intercom as I slip into my seat. A flight attendant offers me some bottled water that I accept, then motions for me to fasten my lap belt. While the plane taxies, my mind returns to Amy and what she revealed to me. I wonder, once again, why she would let me past her walls to see what she carries in her black soul.

Although she hasn't yet killed, at least that I can tell, she fucked with a friend, destroyed her—mind and soul—over a man. Incredulous. She entered her dreams, night after night, and tortured her until the young woman was rendered to a heap of sobbing ruin. The boyfriend defended Amy, thinking his girl had lost her mind. And once the friend was gone—locked away *for her own safety*—Amy played the victim, stealing his heart and mind. Manipulative. Little. Bitch.

Is this the only thing Amy has done? Is there much more I didn't see that she was still able to keep from me as I stared into the small, round pits, drilling into her soul? I may never know.

Turning to the window, I pull the blanket up around my neck as the plane jolts forward and my stomach heaves with it. The ground beneath me grows smaller and slips further from me. I feel one weight being lifted from my shoulders as another begins to settle there. The closer to the heavens we climb, the more my soul lurches inside this form, panicked I may be struck down from the sky.

I desperately grapple the inside of the seatback pocket to find an air-sickness bag. The bag fills with liquid chocolate and scone. Merely the thought of it makes my body convulse in a series of dry retches. Thank God the curtain was drawn and Beady-Eyes didn't get the thrill of watching me retch upon takeoff of this transatlantic flight.

CHAPTER 4

M y heart thumps harder in my chest as I feel myself drifting farther from the Americas, nearly a world away from Collin. A solid mass seems to have settled in my chest as I wonder about him and worry that I may never see him again. It's my own fault, really. I'm the one who chose to run like a child. But am I really? Am I a child? Or just being too hard on myself? I'm sure Rick Stanton would have something to say about that. *Asshole*. Why do his words still haunt my mind, as if they have any foundation in reality? Why can't I get him out of my head?

The greater the distance between us, the more my thoughts pull toward Collin, wanting him near me, holding me, telling me it will be all right. All these years with no one to comfort me when I was in my darkest days have had chilling ramifications. Emptiness still scours my soul, turning me cold and abrasive. Maybe Collin was the only person, the one dark angel who could ignite the flames to melt my frozen, black heart. Only him. So why the hell am I here, on this plane? Shouldn't I be back there in his arms? How will I work through this feeling, this sense that I've removed the dagger he placed in my back and plunged it into his heart instead?

Damn! I'm so fucking confused. But I can't weaken now. I have to stay strong and follow through. This is the path I'm meant to tread. I have to find the piece of me that isn't a killer. That is, somehow, human. If I don't, there's a chance one of the rogues who hunts me will find the only way to turn me and make me one of them. I have to fight the darkness that's ripped at my soul all these years. If not for me, for this baby. This little angel can't endure the type of life I've known. I won't let him.

Running from myself may be the only way I know to fix it. To fix me. The dark cavern I'd stumbled into was devouring me. My self-loathing would consume everyone I loved as well. There's no place for love in the depths of despair. In a spider's nest of fury and revenge. I have to lose those ways. And I can't do it while I'm anywhere near Collin Leary. Maybe someday all that will change.

Right now, I feel too close to the evil that lingers in the shadows of my dreams. As much as I hate it, despise the thought of killing another person, I'm equally drawn to the excitement of the kill, like a woman to her lover. And I wonder if all dark angels feel this way. Or am I the only one? Have I known far too many hardships, seen far too much death, to feel the light of heaven ever again? Is there hope that I will know a moment without hatred in my soul? Until the day I no longer sense a small thrill up my spine at the thought of my next conquest, I'll dread the impending pull of sick and twisted thoughts while anticipating my next battle.

Only Collin seems capable of tearing me from the darkness. Since my mother died, he has been the only true light in my cursed life. Why did he have to *fuck* it up by being so damned selfish?

Shit! One minute I want him to hold me and never let me

go and the next I want him to writhe in pain for what he's done. I'm too torn. And I'm too weary from all the fighting. So damned confused. I need distance. A *lot* of distance. I'm unpredictable under such pressure. This is something I have to acknowledge and accept.

The plane lurches violently and a warning light above me illuminates with a resounding chime.

"We're experiencing some turbulence so I've turned on the fasten seatbelt sign."

The plane lunges and drops an inch or two. I'm all out of air-sickness bags.

"Please remain seated while we climb above the pocket and into smoother air."

As bile rises up my throat I reach inside the seatback pocket in front of me and find only magazines and a diagram of the plane. *Damn!* I'm going to vomit all over first class if I don't find something soon.

I stand and grasp the seatback in front and behind me, feeling unsteady and hungover. The nearest flight attendant staggers down the aisle toward me, fighting to keep her balance while checking passengers' laps to ensure their belts are engaged. Then she looks up to see me stumble forward into the aisle ahead of her.

"The captain has illuminated—" she begins and I clasp my hand over my mouth and force back a dry heave. "Oh, God, have a seat. I'll grab a bag."

She directs me back into my spot and reaches into one of the seatbacks from the rows in front of me. She returns with three hefty, foil-lined bags.

"This should get you through until the captain turns off the sign. Shouldn't be long." A look of compassion spreads across her face.

I nod before burying my face into the mouth of the bag,

spilling whatever could be left in my gut. How can a baby mess up my body so much? The two of us are going to have a little talk about this when he gets here.

After what seems like hours, but probably was closer to fifteen minutes, the beacon above my head is no longer illuminated and the captain notifies us we're free to move about the cabin. I rise to my feet again with the full bags in hand. The same attendant dashes toward me and takes my parcels then helps me down the aisle to the restrooms to wash. As I lock the door and turn to the mirror, I'm astonished at my reflection. I hadn't noticed how gaunt I'd become. Had I lost that much weight over the past few weeks? My pallor is ashen and my eyes sunken. I need fresh fruits and vegetables, lean meats and fish. I haven't eaten nearly as well as I should. And here I am on a plane for fifteen-plus hours, at the mercy of whatever they've wrangled up for us. I had no idea morning sickness could be this miserable.

The cool water from the faucet feels refreshing. This could be the remedy for when I feel a wave of nausea coming on. Maybe I could coax a wet washcloth from one of the attendants.

When I finish washing my face and cleaning my tongue and teeth with a paper towel, I unlock the door and step out, surprised to see Beady-Eyes waiting. Her eyes study me. Her mouth is screwed into a frown. The smell of death permeates her soul just as heavily as it does mine. Why didn't I notice it before? Wasn't just the girlfriend she made go insane. She's entered the dreams of others, manipulated them until they took their lives. I can smell it, see it in her glare. My skin prickles as I push past her and into the attendant's station.

"Could I get a wet washcloth?" I ask, watching from the corner of my eyes as Amy enters the lavatory and locks the door.

"Sure," one of the male attendants answers. "You all right? You were pretty green when you passed."

I smile and nod at him. "Bad fish."

He smiles back. Empathy shows in his eyes. "How about some crackers?" He holds out his hands and nestled in his palm is an individual package of saltines. A sigh escapes my lips. This is what I need. This will help tremendously. He presses several packets into my hands then smiles back at me.

"Thank you," I practically whisper, too overwhelmed to do much more than clutch the crackers to my chest and wander back to my seat.

I'd barely clicked my belt into place when the woman attendant who helped me before was at my side, handing me pillows. "I've tucked more bags in the seatback pocket in front of you. If you need more, let me know. Would you like some water?"

She tilts a bottle toward me, dripping with condensation as if it had just been removed from a cooler. My eyes are on the drop of water falling from the plastic container to the seat beside me, but my soul searches my past. Old feelings tear at my desire for a peaceful flight.

Whenever I've accepted kindness from a human in my past, it always turned out they were bent on turning me or killing me. The experience at Starbucks did nothing to alter this perception. My mind defaults to worn patterns and I turn my eyes to hers as a number of options flash through my brain.

If I were dreaming, I'd grab her wrist and break it as the bottle of water slips to the floor. Or I'd jam the heel of my hand into her face, cracking her head backward and breaking her nose, distracting her attention while I leap on top of her to snap her neck. Or maybe I would take the water and jam it, cap-first, into her abdomen and up under her ribs to stop her heart. All gruesome options I might have used in a recent past. But this woman isn't a threat to me. Her pupils are soft and clear of any demon intent. What the hell is wrong with me? Does Collin have these same impulses?

I clear my throat while the woman patiently awaits my reply. "Yes, please," I answer, taking the bottle from her and attempting a weak smile.

"Let me know if you need anything. We can get you more fresh cloths as you need them. Don't hesitate to let us know." She smiles at me, but the look on her face is like that of a mother, not a killer. I nod and smile again, pulling the blanket up to my chin.

How long have I been such an asshole? My paranoia of everyone around me has to stop. I know there's no solace in the clouds outside my window, but I search for it anyway.

The earth is so far away now. There's nothing but ocean for as far as I can see. I can't shake the cold grip of anxiety reminding me I'm trapped in this tin bullet shooting through the air. The feeling is so isolating. I don't ever remember feeling this empty and alone in a crowd of strangers.

CHAPTER 5

A fifteen-hour flight across the ocean, in itself, is a draining adventure. Flying to a continent and a country where I've never been before, by myself, and doing so while newly pregnant and the little embryo is wreaking havoc with my hormones–and, by extension, my stomach–is flat out insane.

I must have fallen asleep because my eyes open and the world around me is different. The seats of the plane in front of me are still here, but they're all empty. The aisles are dim, but the seating area is cloaked in shadow. The darkest I've known since I started hunting in my sleep. Does the fact that I'm dreaming on this flight mean I'm meant to have a fight? Right here? With everyone on the plane watching me? My heart speeds up as I rise from my cushion.

What am I going to do when I reach them? The muscles in my calves tighten, my sign that I'm hesitating too long and need to move forward. I have to resist. The last thing I need is to be jailed for killing someone on a plane in my sleep. I know I can't hold out for long. The monster's pull is unusually strong. Why can't I delay this battle? I've done it before. There must be something I can do to hold off the kill.

As much as I try, my will won't allow me to wait any longer. The urgency to begin has consumed me, and I take a step forward then turn into the aisle.

The plane jolts and I fall into an empty seat. The ping of the panel above my head alerts me to the glowing sign in the dark.

"The captain has turned on the fasten seatbelt sign so we need everyone to return to their seats." The voice echoes in my head as if it didn't come from an intercom.

This scenario won't end well. I can't obey the commands of someone who isn't dreaming with me. The captain's glowing seatbelt icon has no power over the outcome of this night. The crew has no idea someone's about to die on this plane. They have no clue that I have no choice but to find them and kill them first.

As I rise to my feet again, the ground beneath me lurches and I grab the seatback to steady myself.

"Ma'am, you need to take your seat." Her voice is barely more than a whisper from the shadows, but she is nowhere in sight.

I right myself and continue on, nearing the curtain separating first class from coach. I can't help but believe I'm being drawn to Amy. Her eyes told me she knows who I am. She's more than a demon. She must be a rogue, sent to take my life before we land in Bangkok.

A gentle tug on my arm alarms me. I grab hold of someone. My grip is tight, like a vise, and I hear a woman gasp, then cry out in pain. *Damn!* She's not my target. I pray she isn't one of the flight attendants who tried to return me to my seat. I immediately let go, but it's too late. I can tell she's been hurt. *Damn it.* How will I face her once I'm awake? There's no way to tell her why I injured her, let alone killed another passenger. I need to finish this before I hurt another one, or an innocent is taken before I reach my destination.

"Miss, miss, you need to sit down." The voice is the male attendant this time, but I rush forward to avoid his reach.

The curtain is pale, nearly translucent, and Amy glares at me from the other side. There are no others around her, no one who is sleeping is affected by our dream. They're somewhere else, on an island, in a canyon, maybe even their own bedroom, or wide awake, wondering what the hell I'm doing out of my seat and fighting with the flight crew.

The curtain separates on its own as I step toward her, my eyes drilling into hers. She knows I'm there to stop her. No matter what, I can't wake until she's dead. The smell of death permeates her soul. She stinks of it, now that she sleeps. She covered it so well while awake. Somehow, I knew, even without the stench, which means I've gotten better at sensing rogue angels. A plus for me.

Amy unbuckles her lap belt and rises slowly to her feet. I tilt my head forward and direct my focus on her. Her eyes flinch and she gasps. Was it something she saw in me? Maybe she's only now realizing who exactly I am.

Her hand reaches over her shoulder to her upper back. Now's the time. The muscles in my hand tighten as I reach for her. But before I make contact with the flesh of her throat, I feel a strong hand grab mine and yank backward.

"You have to go to your seat. It's too dangerous."

The man's voice is familiar, but I can't see him in the shadows. He's not part of the dream, only an intruder from the waking world. I shake his hold on me just as Amy's hand comes forward. The weapon—she's pulled it from behind her but it isn't visible to me yet. I won't wait for her to use it. She won't get that chance.

The plane lurches again and I'm thrown against the bulkhead as Amy is thrown backward and tries to steady herself with the seatback cushion. She appears dazed, her eyes glossing over. A most unusual expression. I have to get my bearings quickly before she gains hers first.

"Liz!" The man's voice shrieks behind me. "Call the air marshal."

Out of instinct I turn to see if there's anyone rushing me but see no one. When I turn back to Amy, she's holding her hand in front of her, staring into her palm as if something's written there. To me, it seems empty except for a swath of bright red.

The plane lunges again and her body falls forward, into my arms, but I don't catch her. Instead, I allow her to slip down my body and to the floor, slowly crumpling to a heap, as they always do in a dream. Half of her face is buried in her curled arm and a dark pool surrounds her chest. Her body goes limp. She heaves her last sigh. Her pupils constrict then dilate as the soul leaves her corpse.

With her life expired, so is my dream. I'm awakened to the glaring cabin lights of the plane and a man with a dark cotton shirt and jeans rushing to the woman on the floor. A hole like what could be caused by a hunting knife, drains Amy's blood from her torso. I search the seats and find no weapon. Someone else entered her dream and killed her before I did. That's why she reached for her back. The knife was already there. *She* was the intended victim.

Stunned passengers come to realize what just happened. There are gasps and whimpers of fear or sympathy spreading throughout the cabin. Some try to whisper, but their voices still reach my ears. "Did she do it?"

Oh, God, do they think I killed her? The plane drops and I lose my footing again. The pool of blood spreads across the floor and a tendril of crimson rolls toward me.

The air marshal turns, his angry eyes flashing at me. "Go back to your seat!"

My mind spins as I scan the faces of those leaning in to catch a glimpse of the dead woman. One of them is a killer. We're too far from Collin's reach, here in the clouds, for it to be him.

This. This entire situation right here, is the reason I avoid people. Nearly everyone I've known has ended up dying in their sleep.

CHAPTER 6

O nce the air marshal moves Amy's body with help from the flight crew, he comes to first class and closes the curtains behind him. The attendant I'd hurt in the dream ices her wrist in the front kitchen area of the plane, periodically leaning past the bulkhead to see if I'm still here. The crew whispers to the other first-class passengers and they leave their seats for the other side of the barrier between us and coach.

Once it is only the marshal, the attendant, and me, the marshal sits beside me and heaves a sigh. "Long flight from Seattle to Bangkok. Manifest reads you're traveling on to Nepal, Greece, then your final destination, Ireland."

I turn to the window. Small lights on the wing flash in the dark, at times temporarily obscured by a wisp of a cloud. "This'll go much faster if you get to the point."

"Okay," he answers and I turn back to him. "This trip isn't going well for you right now. What's your reason for this flight? You've never flown before. Suddenly, you're traveling halfway across the world. Oh, and a woman just happens to have dropped dead in your arms, twelve hours into your maiden voyage across the ocean. What's your purpose for this trip, business or pleasure?"

"You have a unique way of asking for my personal itinerary." My sarcasm doesn't seem to endear me to him. I clear my throat then turn to the window again. "I'm taking a sabbatical," I finally answer.

"From what?"

"From life," I tell him and gaze back into his brown eyes.

Eyes droopy from lack of sleep stare at me from a face grizzled with stubble. His red hair is short, but not overly. His expression isn't accusing, but changes with his next question.

"Like the woman back there?" he says, his words cutting through me.

"So that's what they call murder these days," I answer in a flat tone.

"Only when they're a smart ass. You know her?"

"Not really."

"A passenger saw the two of you in Starbucks together." His expression turns hard.

"I suppose she wanted coffee. But I selected hot chocolate. We both happened to order at about the same time. That isn't a crime, is it?"

"Do you have anything against coffee?"

"Not usually."

I wait for him to answer, but his eyes continue to study me so I turn from him and search for a good answer on the back of the seat ahead of me.

"Sometimes," I begin, then hesitate, "coffee isn't recommended." When I turn back to him, I realize I'd said too much. He knows.

"Is that what the two of you fought about? You have an affair with her boyfriend? Or did she have an affair with yours?" He looks down to my abdomen.

"Are you that obtuse?" Dumbass thinks I'm ignorant enough to stab someone over a man? *Jesus!* "*Look*, I was there, minding my own business. Some guy was trying to pick me up and she came over to intervene."

"And that made you mad?"

"No. That made me move. I wanted to talk to either of them about as much as I care to talk with you right now. And the entire situation ruined an opportunity to relax without anyone disturbing me." I shake my head in frustration.

"So why'd you kill her? Cold hot chocolate?"

"Now you're just being an ass."

"I am, but I still want to know why."

"I didn't kill her."

"There were three hundred and sixty-five witnesses to a murder behind those curtains. We already have you for assault and battery on a flight attendant."

"That wasn't my fault. I was asleep. I was dreaming. What do *you* do when someone grabs you in your sleep?"

"The last time someone grabbed me in my sleep, I rolled over and made love to her."

"Ugh! Seriously? You had to go there?"

He cracks a half smile, then turns serious again. "So, let's pretend I believe you were sleeping. Sleepwalking? What were you doing at her seat when she was killed?"

"You tell me. I was sleepwalking."

"That's not a good enough answer. You were the last one to confront her."

I have to come up with an answer that convinces him. But what? Of course, I'll have to lie. "You call that a confrontation? All I remember is standing on a boat with the waves rocking me back and forth. The next thing I know, there's a bleeding woman falling against me."

"You didn't see what happened to her?"

"No. As I said, I was dreaming."

"And you just happened to be standing in front of someone just as she died, a woman who intervened in a conversation with an unknown man, annoying you and ruining your hot chocolate."

"My hot chocolate wasn't ruined. Neither was the scone I had with it. I just didn't want company. It wasn't as big as you're making it."

"Then why did the crew see the two of you glaring at each other early in the flight?" He watches my eyes again. I suppose to see if I'm lying.

"Maybe it was because I wasn't feeling well and the last face I wanted to see after puking my guts out was hers again. I may not have wanted to be friends with her, maybe even thought she was annoying, but I don't typically kill people over perceived personality flaws. Is this something you often see on planes? Coincidental homicide?"

"You'd be surprised what I see on planes." His expression is stern but turns soft again.

"If I'd killed her, wouldn't her blood be all over my hands."

Realizing what I'd just said, I look down for the first time since I woke, trembling as I search my palms and the backs of my hands. They're clean, but there's a streak of red down the front of my jacket. From her hand, I suppose. I reach into the pocket in front of me and pull out one of the washcloths, now dry from time and evaporation. He grabs my hand and pulls the cloth from me. "Don't. Your clothing is evidence of a murder scene. In fact, I'm gonna need your jacket."

Evidence. Of course. My God. This is the first time I've been implicated in the death of a demon I met in my sleep, and I didn't even kill her. She was a bad person, but not my target—theirs. And I can't even tell him the truth. I remove my jacket and hand it to him then lean back in my seat. My focus falls on the headrest in front of me.

"You don't seem fazed that mere minutes ago you watched a woman die. Is this a common occurrence?"

I steel my spine to continue answering his insipid questions. "If you're asking if I've ever woken to find a dead woman at my feet, I'd have to say no. This is a new one for me." At least I'm telling the truth. This entire scenario has never happened to me before.

"Why aren't you crying like most people? Why aren't you afraid?"

Shaking my head, I turn from him. "I don't know. Shock, maybe. I'm not sure how I'm supposed to react or what you're expecting of me. What I do know is that I want to get this blood off me. Is that okay with you?" I throw the washcloth in frustration at the seat in front of me and let out a cry of frustration. "Damn it!"

"I'll let you go to the restroom and clean up once we're through here," he says and waits for me to compose myself. "I have three more questions."

My hands settle into my lap, fidgeting like a school girl waiting outside the principal's office as I try to force them still. A deep breath then slow release does little to control the whirlwind of emotions inside of me. "All right."

"What do you do for a living?" he asks, his eyes steady as they stare back at me.

"I'm in finance," I answer without hesitation.

"Where'd you learn to break someone's wrist so easily? I find it hard to fathom you became so strong counting money."

"I take karate lessons. I'm a fifth-degree black belt."

He nods and purses his lips, then rises from his seat. "Thank you, Ms. Connor."

I narrow my eyes at him and tilt my head. "That's Ms.

Leary. And you said you had three questions. That was only two."

His expression turns stern as he leans toward me and asks, "What color was the boat?"

"What boat?" I ask, unsure what the hell he's talking about.

"The one in your dream." He watches my expression carefully. Did a double back to try and trick me into revealing myself. If my eyes twitch to the side, it means I'm making it up–the entire dream–and that one neurological reflex could sink me.

I search my memory for father's boat, the one he docked at Whidbey Island. "Sea green with red trim. Ocean Angel lettered in black script on the hull," I answer, noting his eyes as they soften.

"You have a great memory," he says, and smiles. What in the hell is he talking about? "Your dream. I always forget mine. Maybe 'cause there was nothing worth remembering."

"I'm a lucid dreamer," I answer. "Now can I go to the restroom?"

"Yes. By all means." He steps aside for me to pass but grabs my arm before I'm out of his reach and I turn back to face him. "Just because I haven't turned this plane around doesn't mean you're free once we land in Thailand. If we were closer, I'd have had you in cuffs and answering more questions on U.S. soil. You're not finished explaining what happened. Not by a long shot."

Our eyes stay locked for what seems like minutes. "That's what I was doing? Answering questions? I thought we were playing pre-school games. My bad." I flash him one more disaffected glare like a teenaged daughter to her over-protective parent.

"You're not very likable," he tells me and releases my arm.

"I suck at faking it." My expression remains emotionless.

The corner of his lips pull upward into a grin. He's finally come to recognize we're not so different.

I turn back down the aisle and make my way to the bathroom, keeping my eyes on the door and ignoring the woman in the kitchen. What was a short distance only hours ago has suddenly become the length of five football fields, maybe longer, as I trudge forward on unsteady legs. Finally, I reach my destination and jar the door open with an awkward yank on the handle. Once locked inside, I collapse against the wall and slip down to sit on the edge of the toilet.

What have I done? I've never been connected to anyone who's been killed in my dreams. I should've looked beyond her, watched the shadows. *Damn it!* I was so focused on her, sure she was the one, that I didn't entertain other options. The same damned thing I did with Sarah. *Shit!* This could get messy real quick. I don't know of any angel who's been caught in this situation before. Certainly not my parents. My grandmother, either. I've been sloppy. In fact, my entire life I've been nothing but a daydreamer, stumbling from one defective soul to the next, using anger and brute strength to kill my demons. Not brilliance, that's for sure. Have I learned nothing over the years?

My legs are weak when I shift my full weight onto them again. My reflection in the mirror is so pale. This moment is no different than each day I rose from my bed after having killed someone. Maybe I didn't kill her, but I didn't save her, either.

This is the first time I've seen ugliness in the soul of the victim, too. Who am I that I'm also sent to save the deficient from imminent death? All this time, I've thought my victims were clean. Now, I can't help but wonder if I've also saved the life of people who have tormented others to their death. How will this affect my future when faced with a choice of saving the one being tracked by another? Will I hesitate, wondering how clean the soul of the victim truly is? It's not mine to judge, but will I do it anyway?

Splashing water on my face doesn't help to clear my mind. I can't scour away the image of Amy holding her hand out to me, coated in red. When she fell against me, against my jacket. My jacket. Her blood still stains the leather.

God, I can still see it, feel it, soaked through the layers and into me. As hard as I try, I'll never clean her DNA from the pores of the leather just like I'll never remove her death from my soul. Hers and all the others I've killed.

As hard as I try, I can't stop the tremor in my hands. Is this it? Is this the final plank to fall and destroy my sanity once and for all? I'm barely holding it together. How can I go out into that cabin? How can I continue to pretend I'm one of them? How can I still float the lie that I'm a normal person who has never killed? I can't stay in this bathroom forever. *Fuck!*

I have to go out there. Although the swathe of red is no longer visible, I'll have to do my best to forget what remains beneath the surface. For the duration of the flight, at least, I have to pretend her spirit doesn't call to me from the blackness of death, blaming me for her demise.

Taking a deep, shuddering breath, I wrap my fingers tight around the handle to unlock the door. The tremors are uncontrollable. When the door jerks open, the flight attendant startles. I take a step forward and freeze.

No one can blame her for being jittery. She'd nearly had her hand ripped off by a passenger she thought was harmless. Her eyes meet mine and my resolve is lost in her expression. A tear burns its way from the corner of my eye, then another. As they tickle my cheek on their path to my jawline, her face relaxes. What does she see as I peer back at her, feeling so ashamed? Does she recognize the aching in my soul? Maybe she remembers how weak I was when we first left the ground.

My body betrays me with a shudder, then another, and the muscles in my legs grow weary again. The weight on my soul is more than I can bear. My head is light. I sway forward, gulping air as if I'm drowning. I can't see for the tears flooding from my eyes, but I feel her hand grasp my bicep as my knees hit the floor. I peer up at her, straining to see her face through the fog distorting my sight.

"I'm sorry. I'm so sorry—" I can't help but beg her forgiveness until she cuts me off.

"No, it's not your fault."

"I didn't know. I was dreaming. I didn't know it was you… I, I didn't know. I never meant to—"

"Shh…shh," she whispers, as the sound of footsteps rush toward me. "She's okay. Help me get her to her seat," she tells someone on my right. "Listen to me. I'm fine. Just go to your seat and rest, okay?"

Taking a deep breath, I nod and rise with the help of the air marshal and the male flight attendant. I wipe my eyes and suck in another deep breath, then start toward my seat. As I pass each row, I realize the first-class passengers have returned and all of them were witness to my breakdown. On top of everything else, I had an audience. *Great.* For someone who rarely shows enough of herself in daylight to be recognized by anyone, I've become the star attraction on this flight into hell.

CHAPTER 7

Staying hidden in my seat by the window was the easiest part of the final leg of my flight across the ocean. Realizing my parents once took a similar trip with me as a small baby, I understand how anxious they must have been. Tracked by killers, they fled to America to hide me. Am I flying back into the storm they left behind to save me? Is the pain I knew in the west minuscule compared to what I could face in Thailand, or even Europe? I can't help but wonder what I'll find there as I search for peace.

The surrounding life–vegetation, motorized vehicles, and walking, breathing humans–becomes clearer as the plane taxies down the runway in Thailand. Part of me is filled with dread, wondering what will happen once I'm taken to the authorities. Another is filled with hope that I can leave behind my past. As the plane glides into the gate, the air marshal appears out of nowhere and sits beside me.

"We'll wait for the other passengers to depart before I put the handcuffs on you."

His words start my heart to pounding, but I do my best to hide it. Instead, I nod my acknowledgement.

Soon the last passenger lumbers past with his carry-on, shooting a sideways glance at me like the others. Thai police dart past him at the mouth of the plane and rush toward us as the cuffs lock in place on my wrists.

"The body's in the back," the marshal tells them and nods toward the tail of the plane. Then he turns to me. "Take the blanket with you." He loops it over my hands to cover my restraints.

"Thank you." Even this minor amount of compassion was unexpected.

"Let's go." He rises to his feet and helps me to mine then directs me from the plane with his hand between the scapulas of my back, pressing me forward.

The gate opens to brilliant colors of red and yellow, happily reflected in the carefully dispersed chrome stanchions with royal blue straps. A group of monks in orange habits shuffle through the terminal as other passengers search the surrounding signs for their destination or stride swiftly forward with purpose. The dread in my tight chest seems to be dissipating. Is it possible this is my destiny? As that thought enters my mind, a monk stops in front of me with his head bowed and his eyes closed. I stop and wait for him to continue on with the rest. Instead, he turns in my direction and raises his eyes to me.

"You find it...angel. What you search, you find." His voice is the brush of a bird's wings against my pain, striking my heart and healing wounds within. His small, dark eyes peer into my soul.

"How did you do that?" A tear rushes my cheek as I'm filled with sudden, unexpected joy.

A tug on my arm tells me the marshal isn't interested in what the man has to say.

"Beware one cast into this world. Dark one searches. He

will find you." His deep eyes are locked with mine and I can't turn away.

I should be stunned by the epiphany that Lucifer has his sights on me. I suppose that's a revelation I have always assumed. Instead, all that reaches my thoughts is the idea that this man knows what I battle in life. *How the hell does he know who I am?*

His hand rises from his side, palm up, and he holds it out to me as if he's holding the secret to my survival. "Your trials soon to end. You know beautiful life soon. Long time." Then his expression turns sad. "Until —"

The tug on my arm is insistent this time and I'm torn from the bald man in orange. His eyes follow me as I'm led away, down the terminal to an unknown destiny. Unknown, except to him. He sees what awaits me. Brilliant colors slip from my view, but I can only see him, craning my neck to see over my shoulder. He waits, stilled, in the middle of the walkway, his companions surrounding him while I'm led away.

The man at my arm pushes open a heavy metal door with his body and leads me inside a small, empty room with one desk and two gray, metal chairs in front of it.

"Have a seat," he directs me, "they'll be here soon."

I nod and sit, quietly studying the place. No windows. The walls are yellowed, probably once white. Paint chips in thick curls in places. The room far from exemplifies the happy coloring of the passenger areas. The desk is a 70s-style black metal with faux wood Formica top. The surface is covered in papers and an old desktop computer. It would be a miracle if that thing still works. The top of a weathered, wooden sofa table behind the desk is cloaked in yellow silk with an incense burner. Three individually framed photos of a woman and teenaged child dressed in white rest beside a three-inch statue of Siddhartha. The woman seems familiar, as if we've met before. But that's impossible. I've never been to Thailand.

"What was that, back there?" The marshal speaks up, slipping my jacket into a plastic evidence bag then sealing it. I must appear confused, because he goes on. "Those monks. They don't speak to anyone. But he spoke to you."

I ponder his words, careful not to reveal too much in my answer. I understood the monk's words, but doubt this man would ever appreciate, let alone believe them. "Are you a religious man, Mr. — ?"

"Nicol. Bill." He lays the evidence bag with my coat on an empty chair then drags an empty chair beside mine a couple feet away from me. He sits with his elbows between his knees, his hands clasped.

"Mr. Nicol. All right then. Well? Are you?"

"Not a bit." He looks me dead in the eyes and I know he's serious. "I believe it's all a bunch of bullshit. Just like the statues of Buddha they worship in this country, they're nothing but distractions."

"Then you would never understand."

"Try me, anyway." His stare doesn't leave me.

"Whether you believe it or not, Buddhists believe there is life before birth and after death," I tell him and meet his stare.

"Do you believe in it?"

"Yes. I do believe in it."

"You're telling me you believe all that silliness about gods and angels and demons?" His expression turns cynical and disbelieving.

"Yes, I do." I clear my throat, trying not to sound nervous.

His brows narrow and he cocks his head toward me. "What makes you so certain? You seem more no-nonsense than that."

"Personal experience." I go with truth to keep his trust in me.

"With what? Angels? Or demons?"

"Both." I answer matter-of-factly.

"And which are you? An angel or a demon?" He leans farther forward, studying my expression.

I take a deep breath, waiting for the right words to reach my thoughts. "You'd be surprised if you knew the truth."

"Try me."

"Let's just say, if you knew the truth about me, I wouldn't be in this room waiting for some guy to arrive and take my freedom."

"Are you threatening me?" he asks and leans back in his seat with a question in his eyes.

"Not at all. I'm just being straight with you." Searching past his irises, I find in his pupils the weakness he keeps hidden, a wife who died in childbirth. A pain shoots through my heart and I break eye contact. "You know, it's not uncommon for a personal loss to make someone stop believing."

His expression turns to incredulity. "How did you —?"

The door swings inward and a short woman dressed in a uniform seems to dash in on a wind. "I'm sorry to keep you waiting," she says in a thick accent but perfect English. "Is this the killer, Mr. Nicol?"

"We're not calling her the killer quite yet —"

"I'm not the killer, ma'am. I'm a witness. Sort of," I insert before Mr. Nicol has a chance to finish his response.

"And who are you?" she asks, impatient while she slips into her chair behind the desk.

I turn toward her to see she is the woman in the photos. "You have a beautiful son." I look into her eyes, making mine soft. "I'm Jaime Leary." I reach out my hand to shake hers.

The woman is speechless, turning pale as she studies me. Then her eyes drift down to the shackles on my wrists. "Have we been introduced before, Ms. Leary? You're familiar, like I've met you."

"This is my first trip out of the U.S." I recoil my hands and fidget with the tab on my zipper. Hopefully, her memory isn't for me trying to kill her in my sleep.

She narrows her eyes on me, still unconvinced. "I never forget a face. Even ones I've seen in my dreams. Maybe when I was in the Americas. Colorado, perhaps."

The realization hits me like a tidal wave. The curve of her dark eyes, crooked bend in her lips. She's aged since, but she's still the same woman under the creases of wisdom. "Oh, my God—" I whisper under my breath. It's been years since that night. The boy was only a baby. Turning back to the photo, I figure he must be at least twelve years old. "He's grown."

"Shit," Bill mutters under his breath. I shoot a quick sideways glance to see he realizes he may be on the losing side of this relationship.

"He's thirteen in that photo." Her stare is intense, like she's processing what she has just grasped. Her faith in a God may allow her to believe in angels. Hopefully, she will believe that night was more than a dream, also.

"Mr. Nicol, what happened on your plane?"

"This woman left her seat and approached another passenger." He answers as if he's already lost the argument.

"Approaching passengers is a crime, Mr. Nicol?" she interrupts and I feel his muscles tense without even touching his body.

"No, ma'am. A member of the flight crew tried to stop her and return her to her seat and her wrist was seriously injured by the suspect. The crew member is having x-rays as we speak." His eyes find mine with an accusing glare. Shame over the incident stabs at the cold space in my chest where my heart should be.

The commissioner shoots a quick glance my way, increasing my anxiety. "What about the other passenger, Mr. Nicol?" She taps her foot, her patience wearing thin.

"She died."

"How?"

"A hole in her back."

"And the weapon?"

"We never found one. Perpetrator hid it somewhere. We searched every passenger, including the suspect."

"And the plane? Did you search every seat, every overhead? Was there a trail of blood leading away from the victim's body?"

"Yes. We searched everywhere. And, no." He heaves a sigh. "There was no trail of blood."

"Why is Ms. Leary in my office with cuffs on her wrists?"

"She was the only one near the victim when she was fatally wounded. She's our only suspect."

"And there was a witness who saw her stab the victim?"

"No." His voice loses its force. "The victim...fell." He runs his fingers through his hair.

"Yes, Mr. Nicol?"

"She fell into the suspect's arms." He knows there's no chance he'll be able to make a solid connection between me and Amy's untimely death.

"Take these cuffs off her. *Now!*" She commands in her small, but still robust voice.

His gaze turns to me in surprise. Accusing, again. "Yes, Commissioner-General."

He pulls the key from his pocket and stands. I stand also and hold out my hands to him. Once the cuffs pop open, I recoil my hands and rub flesh where the metal indented my skin.

"You can leave my office, Mr. Nicol." Her voice is stern,

then softens. "Ms. Leary, please stay."

Bill looks over at me with mistrust in his eyes. He pulls my bagged jacket into his arms without taking his eyes from mine. In his expression is the indication he suspects some form of collaboration between me and the commissioner. The irregularity of this entire situation makes him suspect me even more than moments ago. Although I may be safe here in Thailand, my circumstances could change the minute I return to the states.

He shoots one last glare at the commissioner, which she ignores.

When the door closes, the woman who stands inches shorter than me, sweeps her hand toward the chair. "My apologies for the archaic furniture we have. Our office has little money for furnishing airport security facilities. Now, let me look at you." She steps into me and peers up at my eyes then studies my nose, mouth, hair, as I awkwardly search for a place to cast my gaze. "Don't be shy, dear girl. We're friends, aren't we?" she tells me in a confident and commanding voice. "At least, I hope we are." She turns from me and moves to her desk. "I have never forgotten you. My son wouldn't be here if it weren't for you."

"Your English is impeccable." I'm truly amazed at how well she speaks English.

"I spent many years in your country, working for NORAD. I had my son while I was there."

"He was, what, two months old that night?" The events of the battle return to me as if it had just finished. The demon had the babe lain across an ancient altar, a sword, strip of cloth, and large stone neatly placed on a nearby slab. Not too much unlike those used in a three-fold sacrifice. The moment he sensed my presence, he reached for the weapon most effective and swift.

"Yes. You have a good memory." She smiles back at me.

"For dreams, yes, I do, Madam Commissioner-General. But, how…how did you come to realize it wasn't just a nightmare?"

"Please call me Durudee. The sword that monster brought to slit my son's throat; as he brought it down to kill him, it sliced his shoulder before you caught it and used it to stop him. Ananda still carries the mark." She holds out the palm of her hand to me. "So do I, for also trying to stop the blade." A deep line interrupts the pattern of creases in her palm. I didn't see her catch the weapon's edge that night. Such a brave woman. My respect has grown.

"I see."

"Tell me, what happened on the plane, Ms. Leary?" Her smile is warm, but troubled. I know she has to file a report.

"I knew the woman was one who has killed others in her sleep."

"The victim?"

"Yes." I hesitate for a moment and she nods at me to go on. "I tried my best to stay awake, I truly did, but…" I consider how much to tell her and decide she doesn't need to know my weakness due to pregnancy. "A fifteen-hour flight…I just couldn't hold out. When I fell asleep, I was drawn to her seat. I had no choice. I had to go to her. Thought she was the one, that she was going to harm someone."

"But you didn't kill her."

"No, ma'am. Uh, Durudee."

"We can remain on first name basis. Anyone who saves my life and the life of my child has earned the right." She smiles briefly back at me then turns serious again. "But there remains the matter of the death on your flight. We still have a killer among the passengers."

"Yes."

"Did you see them?"

"No. I was focused on the victim. The killer took that opportunity to strike."

Her face turns pensive. "I suppose there's little we can do without a murder weapon and a suspect."

"It could be any of the passengers. Anyone asleep at the time would be a suspect."

"I might interview the flight crew myself. See if they noticed who was asleep at the time of the attack and search the backgrounds of the passengers they identify, if any." She picks up the phone on her desk and dials. "Please ensure that all crew on flight 2154 from Seattle are detained until I've had a chance to interview them. Yes. All who haven't already left on a connecting flight. Go, now!" She hangs up the phone and turns to me.

"Unfortunately, this could be a dead subject if the crew was too distracted by me, sleepwalking through the cabin."

"You may be right. You did injure one of them. But I'm sure she will heal from that. The victim, on the other hand—" She grows quiet and stares off into empty space then takes a quick breath before speaking. "I don't remember thanking you for what you did."

"Me? I'm not sure I—"

She holds out her hand and shows the scar from that night many years ago.

I shake my head in response. "There's no need to thank me. I was only fulfilling my purpose at the request of someone much greater than I."

"Exactly what *is* your purpose? Aside from your name, tell me, who are you?"

"I'm only the one who does as she's told."

"And that is?"

"I enter dreams to stop the death of an innocent. And

sometimes the not-so-innocent."

"That's an enormous task for any normal person. A burden such as this doesn't come without consequences."

"Consequences?" The way she says it makes my skin tighten and my body turn cold.

"Yes, like missing a demon who kills someone in front of hundreds of people without being detected. Something tells me the killer intended this to happen while you were standing in front of her. Someone who knew you and knew her past. Perhaps you were framed? Those are some pretty risky consequences."

Damn. I hadn't even considered the demon could be someone attempting to frame me for the murder.

"How often have you failed in the past? Other than last night, that is?"

Her words cut through me, although I understand her aim. "I've only missed the killer once before." Unable to face that tragedy, I push the moment from my mind.

"As a child," Durudee continues, "I had debilitating nightmares. All of my young life, my mother told me about powerful angels who save us from the demons of our dreams. She said they would protect me from harm. When I was a teenager my nightmares ended along with my belief in mother's stories. That is, until the night you showed up in my dream." She wipes her cheek as if whisking away a tear. "In the many years you've lived, you've saved uncountable lives, I can imagine."

My mind taunts me with the memory of Rick. "There are many more lives ended than saved in my..." I can't finish the thought. My heart aches with loss.

"Innocents?" Durudee asks.

I hesitate before the answer falls from my lips, as though regret had weight and substance. "No."

She scrutinizes me like an attorney. "You cling to the souls of the ones you killed to save another? As if saving an innocent life wasn't worth the loss of theirs?" Her words are measured and I turn to her, questioning her intent. "If you don't let them go, you will drown in the weight of them and the remorse you carry because of them. They chose their fate. As you said, you are merely the one who does as she is told. Is that not what I heard? Those deaths are not yours to keep. They are not in your trunk of belongings. They are owned by the one who forced you to kill them. The evil soul himself."

Her face is set, stern, and simultaneously, maternal. Her words are not unlike those Mother would have used after a treacherous night of fighting monsters. Maybe if every soul returned to be adjudicated in heaven, I would feel differently. There are souls who will never have the opportunity to defend their actions. I would have gladly sat on the jury for Rick, had he the opportunity for finding redemption. His fate, however, is final. I will never know if he could have been rehabilitated. No one will ever know.

"If you cannot move beyond your past, you will never find your future," Durudee insists. "Forgetting who you are and who you should be is a greater loss than the soul of one without conscience to respect the life of another. We all have a purpose on earth. When we accept that purpose, we assign new meaning to our efforts to fulfill it."

Her words fall like a seed in my mind, spreading through me and growing in strength. I don't own those souls. I'm not responsible for their actions. As much as I want to control everything around me, I have to learn to let go of those outside of my influence or reach. I have to forgive myself for taking their dark souls. Somehow, I must release what was, but no longer is, to the wind.

"Durudee, who are you? Your words—"

" — Are meant to save the soul of a friend who saved mine. Just an observation, but I felt you needed to hear this."

"Thank you," I whisper to this wise woman who seems more like an angel than an ordinary mortal.

"It is my sincere pleasure to point out what may be unseen." Her face is radiant, but the creases at the corners of her eyes soon smooth and her face grows serious.

"What? What's wrong?" I ask.

"Nothing. Just a fleeting thought that has no relevance to our conversation. I would like you to know, however…"

"Go on." My answer turns her eyes toward mine.

"As grateful as I am for your intervention, one thought still tortures my mind."

"Yes?"

"The others. Those who aren't sent an angel to help them continue on. I've often wondered, why me? Why my son? When there are so many who lose the battle, why save us?"

"I don't know. I don't know why. Why was I led to you? Why am I led to one and not another? I've never thought to ask myself this. I do as I'm commanded. I save people, then move on. The final outcome of my actions has never been revealed to me. All I know is the person lives another day."

The worry on her face softens and her smile grows once again. "Ananda. He is a doctor. Helps children at a clinic in the city. There's your outcome. A man who saves children, just as he was saved all those years ago."

"He's a doctor? He's that old? Wow. I had no idea so much time had passed since that night."

Her eyes glint as she studies me. "As a young boy, he listened intently while I shared the story of how he was saved to explain his scar. An angel in black rescued him from a monster of his nightmare. Now he's a big shot. Calls it a tall tale."

"Probably for the best. I'm better off remaining anonymous."

"I suppose you're right." She studies my face, my eyes, hair, again. "Hm. You haven't aged a day. Truly remarkable. I guess that's one of the perks of being a heavenly being." Then her eyes rest on the scar on my cheek. "But I see there are disadvantages, as well."

My hand instinctually reaches for the ridge of scarred flesh where Sarah cut me. "Yes."

Her eyes peer into mine, searching for words, or my soul. I'm not sure. Then she draws a deep breath and I hold mine. "Join me and Ananda for dinner. Please say you will."

"Oh, I'm, uh, not good company for anyone. And I really should be on my way."

"I get the feeling you aren't accustomed to making friends."

"It's complicated. I'm awkward in social situations," I answer, studying her expression.

"Nonsense. I insist. Here is a map of Thailand. On the back you will find Bangkok and any roads that may assist you should you rent a car for seeing the sights we have to offer. I suggest, however," she turns the map over to show the entire country and part of Laos, "that you not cross the border into Laos on your own. You may find some dangerous situations, although, I hear they have a beautiful flower plantation right here." She draws a red circle on the map to the northeastern corner, on the other side of the Mekong River into Laos. "I look forward to our dinner together. I promise not to tell my son who you are. But I would like him to meet you, even if he hasn't a clue why."

Peering down at the map, I consider her request. There could be so many reasons to move on and decline her offer to have dinner with them. I just can't think of one at the moment that is more compelling than my need to keep this woman as an ally.

After a deep swallow, I answer, "Okay."

That wasn't so bad. It's just a dinner, after all, isn't it? God, I hope there's nothing to be concerned about. My eyes search the room once again then fall on the picture of Durudee and young Ananda. So happy.

I'm awkward in social situations. What an understatement. Hell, I'm a social misfit, if I'm being honest. What's the worst that could happen while dining with someone I've saved from death as an infant and his mother who heads up security for the international airport of Thailand? A complete disaster, that's what. But it's only dinner. Right? I'll keep telling myself this until the evening is over.

***

The lobby of the Siam Hotel is intimidatingly extravagant. Large pots are garnished with fresh flowers of an exotic origin. There are fountains and extraordinary fixtures. The tiled entrance is polished until it gleams and I can't help but feel out of place. Durudee insists I stay here.

"Your reservations, all meals and incidentals have been paid. No credit card required."

"You're kidding, right?"

She cocks her head in confusion at my reply. This place is far too extravagant for anyone to be able to pay for my entire stay. A couple days? That has to be hundreds of dollars.

When I open the door to my 'suite,' however, I realize I was severely mistaken. The cost has to be more in the thousands. She doesn't owe me this. But I have no choice other than to accept. Perhaps the Siam Hotel owes Durudee more than the worth of a suite. She means no harm to me, but there may be something dark in her past, or maybe her present. Will this arrangement end in an expectation that I will fulfill another favor? Or will I find her in one of my dreams once again? This time, the demon I have no choice but to vanquish? This is the very reason I refuse to meet up with the victim. The circumstance of my stay here could devolve rather quickly.

The king-sized bed rests on an elevated platform, overlooking the formal sitting area lavishly decorated in creams and onyx. The floor is a dark, polished hardwood that matches my clothing. I snatch a fresh pear from a cream-colored ceramic pot on the cocktail table and take a bite while still touring the suite.

French doors open to a private courtyard, a small rectangular pool with waterfall fixtures on the wall above and a terrace with patio furniture. A spiral staircase leads me upward to another floor to find a private kitchen and dining area with an elegant entertaining room.

This may be exactly what I need, a stunning hotel suite that is like a penthouse apartment with so much more. I can wander outside and not be seen by the world. But why? What made Durudee put me here? Because she knows what I'm capable of in my sleep. Is it also that she would like my protection from her enemies? Keeping me close to save her once again? A woman in her position must have plenty of people who would want her dead. What will she do to ensure I'll never leave?

Okay, so the bathroom makes me want to forget about the potential that I may become a prisoner in this place. I mean, the square Jacuzzi tub. It's big enough for three, maybe four people. And I do need a bath. The white tiled walls above the tub feel cool, as does the black tile beneath my naked feet.

I can do this. I can relax in this suite, let the luxe of my surroundings envelope me. It's only two days. At least, that's what the concierge said.

Mmm, rich, scented oils beside thick, rolled towels. And they're all displayed so elegantly on this dark oak table. Every lavish fixture, each fine detail has been attended to sumptuously. As I turn the knobs, water flows from a spout shaped like a wide, flat mouth protruding from the wall. Soon, the tub is full, and the walls sweat the aroma of lavender and bergamot with my body bathed in warmth. My eyelids grow heavy with exhaustion. I struggle to keep them open. I want to enjoy this. Just ten. More. Minutes. Soon, my mind is surrounded by a hint of jasmine and an empty dark chasm.

CHAPTER 8

A long and cold hallway leads to a bedroom with pure white linen and black, tiled floors. On the nightstand is a plain lamp with a thin, black post and small, white shade. Black valances surround two tall, narrow, white chiffon curtains. There are no windows, only solid wall. What is this place? Hotel suite or someone's home?

The scent of jasmine surrounds me as I take a step forward then feel the tug of fabric at my knees. I'm in a red kimono with gold cord trim at the neck. Damn it. I've never owned a kimono in my life. Must be a dream. I reach up and unsnap the top closure at my throat as I'm drawn farther into the room.

A door to the left appears to be a bathroom. Steam snakes past the opening and I realize this is my destination. Crossing the threshold, I'm greeted with black marble counter tops and a full mirror from ceiling to floor beside the double vanity. Another opening leads to another hallway stretched into darkness. Flanking the corridor are closets of elegant men's clothing. Expensive suits made of silk and wool and crisp white dress shirts hang from black oak hangers. The man is large. Possibly 200 pounds or more from the size of these garments. The owner of these suits built this dream. Why would he want me to see his clothing?

"Don't keep me waiting," his voice calls from the dimness ahead.

The seemingly endless corridor opens to a spacious bathroom walled in mirrors with a great Jacuzzi in the center. In the Jacuzzi is a large, naked man, approximately 250 pounds, with hair the color of tar. His bronze eyes study me with appreciation.

"Atta girl. You kept me waiting too long. But now I see it was worth my time."

A clear box, nearly seven feet tall and five feet wide, boxes a woman in a corner beside the Jacuzzi. Her voice is muffled by the enclosure to soften her cries for help. Tears streak her cheeks. Her long black hair is tied in a knot at the back of her neck and her clothing is similar to the housekeeping staff at the Siam.

The surface of the transparent box is solid and thick, like bullet-proof glass. Her hands are red with blood that smears the glass in front of her. She must have been pounding so hard to get out that she spilt the skin and broke blood vessels. The poor thing is panicked and there's no way I can help her unless he dies. She appears hopeful when I approach the container. I want to console her...

"Don't," is all he says.

"Fuck off." I turn back to her in an attempt to discover a way to breach her containment.

"She'll be dead before you figure out how to release her." His eyes flash dark, then bronze again.

I've never seen that before. Who is this asshole?

"I'm the guy who summoned you here, that's who."

He's reading my mind. Bastard. How the hell does he do

that?

"I'm well-schooled in the intricacies of dream control. Every thought that passes each mind in my domain is mine to analyze. Now, pull up a chair. We have some matters to discuss."

A wooden chair appears on the other side of the tub and I turn back to him, my eyes narrowing in a glare. There are no weapons of use within my view. I study every inch of the room anyway, ignoring the nude man.

"No. The mirrors cannot be broken. No shards of glass to slit my throat. Sit, and we can talk about your situation."

"*My* situation? I'm not concerned with *my* situation. I'm here to improve *her* situation. Why's she here? What are your plans for her?" I rest on the edge of the seat and turn to him.

"Bait."

"Bait? For?"

"You."

A chill sweeps up my spine while I stare him down. As my mind attempts to penetrate his pupils, they sharpen to a pinpoint, hiding the evil lurking in his brain. I gather my thoughts again then ask, "What do you want with me?"

Roaring laughter fills the room, echoing off the smooth, mirrored glass. "You cut to the chase like a starving child, Ms.," he hesitates for a dramatic moment, "Leary." *Asshole.*

"Look, jackass, I'm not in the mood for games. Tell me. It appears you didn't bring me here to be your personal masseuse. What do you want?"

God, I want to stab him in the throat.

Laughter rolls from his throat again as he throws his head back. I watch his jugular vein wondering if there's a way to slice through the thick flesh of his neck before he can catch me and harm his victim.

"I had no idea you were such a bitch. Can't we have a nice

discussion? Can't we do a little—what is it you call it? Chit-chatting—without you looking for a way to kill me? Such wasted time, you know."

"That's debatable. You know, most people call someone, a friend, family member, when they want to talk. Tying up the help is a little extreme, don't you think? Why not be a nice psychopath and let her go?"

"Not yet." His face falls serious. "We have business to discuss. Then I can kill her, and you can go on your way."

The girl whimpers and I glance her direction, wishing I could tell her I can save her. Afraid I may lose two victims in one day.

"Why does *she* have to die?"

"You know damned well. I'm not ignorant. One of us has to die to get out of this. And I choose her."

"Now, you're just being a *prick*."

"I don't sacrifice for anyone." He lifts his soaked hand and sweeps it in a circle. "I've never had to sacrifice for anyone or anything. And I don't intend to start now."

I'd kill him if it weren't for the thought that there's something he has to say that I might want to hear, or at minimum, need to know.

"That's it. Your curiosity is piqued. Lean in and I'll tell you my wildest secrets."

"*Ugh*. No thanks." I try not to look into the tub to whatever may be floating freely there.

He throws his head back once again and laughs a full, throaty chortle.

"Look, jolly old elf, if you would stop cackling like you're torturing a Lilliputian, we can get on with this and I can get back to my bath."

Unfortunately, my insults only serve to humor him more. Then he wipes a tear from beneath his eye and drops his hand back in the water. "I should've hired you a long time ago."

"You brought me here to hire me? Sorry. I'm already otherwise engaged. And not as someone's court jester."

"As I can see." He nods to the string tied to my wedding finger. I stop fidgeting with it and lower my hand to my lap. "No, I didn't bring you here to hire you. That was a joke. I brought you here to warn you. If you get in the middle of my business, I won't wait to kill you and all you love."

"How original. A demon threatening me. I have no idea what to do." I keep my voice low, flat, and sarcastic.

"I don't think you understand the direness of the situation you're in. There will be more death around you that can't be explained if you aren't careful. The airplane incident was just the beginning. Stay out of my way, or I will use all in my arsenal to have you safely locked away." He smiles at me. "Or killed." His expression turns serious again. "Do we have an understanding?"

My jaw tenses. Did he have something to do with Amy's death? I don't remember seeing him on the plane. How the hell did he know about me and my destination, at least with enough advance warning to plan her murder and my indictment for it? Does he also know about my connection to the commissioner-general?

"Does this petty threat have anything to do with anyone in particular?" My thoughts inadvertently shift to Durudee.

"Very perceptive of you. And know this, your instincts will drive you to save the life of your compatriot. I'm giving you a piece of friendly advice. Don't allow it."

"Why should I take your *friendly advice*? I mean, I barely know you."

"I believe I've already mapped it out for you. You have no idea who she is and what you're dealing with."

"I, personally, could give two *shits*."

"You don't want to mess with me, Ms. Leary." His eyes crease as he stares me down.

"I'll keep that in mind," I tell him then stand and swiftly pull the chair from beneath me.

I swing it through the air in an attempt to crush his trachea. He catches it with one hand and launches from the water. I spin and rip the chair from his grasp then whip it around me to break it across his back. Pieces of wood shatter and splinter in slow motion, as if someone or something has interfered with time. I throw my leg between his to bring him down, but he disappears into the air. I watch the captured woman's eyes to see if she knows where he went. She watches me. Drops of sweat bead up on her forehead. Her red soaked hands press against the glass. Her eyes are wild with fear. Then she takes a quick breath as her focus jerks directly above my head the moment I see his reflection in the glass.

Before I can grab his hand, I'm lifted into the air. I reach for his hands to pull them from me, dig my fingers into his flesh until blood rushes from the wounds, but he doesn't let me go. With his thick fingers squeezing my shoulders so hard they could break, he throws me facedown into the tub. My head and body are plunged deep into the water, my lungs burning from the intruding liquid. I fight the hands holding me. Then suddenly, they release, and I breach the water, gasping and sputtering.

When I turn to the glass enclosure with the frightened maid, I find that both she and the loathsome man are gone. I'm in my hotel suite with water flooding the bathroom floor.

He killed her while I was floundering in the tub, releasing us all from the dream. It was his plan of escape all along. *Dammit*, I failed her. Who the hell is this guy and what is his story?

CHAPTER 9

The smell of curry and exotic spices infuse my senses as I enter the restaurant. The anticipated nausea is kept at bay for once. There's promise this cuisine is one I can enjoy during my pregnancy.

A tall, thin woman leads me through the restaurant. Durudee is already at the table when I arrive. Dark eyes that glimmered with hope when we spoke in her office are turned downward and strained with tortured thoughts. She didn't hear us approach.

"Madam Commissioner-General—" My escort interrupts her thoughts.

A barely noticeable startle unsettles her body before her eyes soften. "Thank you, Kaeo. Please let me know when my son arrives." Her attention turns to me. "Please, have a seat," she says and sweeps her hand toward the place setting to her left.

The décor of the restaurant is elegant, with white linen table coverings and chairs, surrounded with subtle black accents and simple but sophisticated lighting that brightens the room. With Durudee sporting a pale pink linen skirt and white cotton blouse, I feel out of place dressed all in black.

After awkwardly nudging my chair up to the table, I pull the folded napkin from beneath the silverware and open it in my lap. "The restaurant is...beautiful." And large, and wide open. And our table sits nearly in the middle. Being in the center of so many people brings an uneasy feeling. I don't like open space. At least, not in public.

She looks around the room as if seeing it for the first time. "It is lovely, isn't it? Mine and Ananda's favorite. We meet here, at minimum, once a week." I notice she hasn't looked me in the eyes yet. After a quiet moment, she turns to me. "How are your accommodations? Are they acceptable? Do you need a larger room?" A warm, comfortable smile spreads across her lips.

"No, no bigger room. Everything is far more than I expected and should accept." When I search her eyes, I ask myself, how do I tell her about my dream?

Her hand grips my forearm and I flinch. "It's the least I could do. And I will be offended if you don't accept."

I remove my hand from the table and place it in my lap then hold my breath and nod reluctantly. "The hotel is stunning."

"Did you get a chance to rest from your flight? You still have bags under your eyes."

"Yes. I did rest. And I want to tell you about that." Just as I was about to start in about my dream, a woman in her early twenties approaches the table.

"Can I get you some drink," she asks, setting a plate of egg rolls with translucent skin on the table and small appetizer plates in front of each of us.

"I'll have water," I answer. "With lemon, please."

"I'll have Cha Yen and please bring Nam Manao for my guest." Durudee smiles at me and pats my hand in my lap. "More refreshing than water, my friend. While here, you must try new things. And let's see a smile on that pretty face. You should learn to relax more often."

Realizing I'm holding my breath, I release it and nod my head. "Perhaps you're right."

"Now, what was it you wanted to tell me, Ms. Leary? You said you rested. Did you have any interesting dreams?" Her smile is strained, forced, like she knows something.

"Please, call me Jaime," I say, and she nods.

"Fair enough, Jaime," she answers and smiles. "Your dreams?"

I nod slightly then take a breath and release it to relax my shoulders, but they refuse to rest. "Do you have enemies who might want to harm you?" I ask, watching her expression closely.

Durudee releases a robust laugh that brings attention to our table. "My dear, any woman such as I would have enemies who want to harm her."

"I'm serious," I stress, nearly whispering. "Is there someone who would kill to get to you?"

The smile rushes from the woman's face and she begins to look every millisecond of her age. "There are many who would prefer me dead, Jaime. It comes with the territory. Now, tell me what you know."

"When I fell asleep in my room, I was drawn to someone who warned me to stay out of the way. He seemed concerned I would intervene when he attempts to take your life. What are you involved in, Durudee? Why does someone such as this want you dead?"

She seems to chew the words in her mouth before releasing them into the air. "What if I told you I came across something so frightening it would make even you quake with fear at it's potential?" Her eyes pin me in place. I stay silent, waiting for her to continue. "Have you heard of the flower called the Dark

Angel's Trumpet?"

Her words startle me. "I've heard of the Angel's Trumpet; a poisonous hallucinogenic that's caused many deaths in people attempting to harness it. Dark Angel's Trumpet is a new one on me." Then I remember the man on the corner in Seattle. He held a bundle of nearly black lilies that could pass for a dark version of Angel's Trumpet.

"It's a cross-breed. A hybrid," she adds. My silence while searching my memory must tell her I don't understand. She goes on. "They cross-pollinated Angel's Trumpet with black calla lilly. The dark flower has a potent pollen capable of rendering all who ingest it intellectually incapacitated while remaining a functioning being. The person seems rational while, in fact, incapable of rational or critical thought."

"Sounds like most politicians I know of."

"Yes, it most certainly does," Durudee answers with a slight chuckle. "But the ramifications are greater. This drug renders those under the influence of Dark Angel's Trumpet a slave to whoever controls them."

"So, are you telling me this flower is being used in place of date rape drugs?"

The memory of the scumbag on the corner the day before my flight made me cringe. Is that what he'd intended? Did he have plans for me? No. His intent was far viler. When I didn't fall for 'smell the pretty flowers,' he blew the powder in my face, probably made from pollen and the body of the flower. No wonder he was frightened when he realized it didn't work on me. Maybe the people who sent him were just as disappointed and an alternate plan was hatched. Amy, and now Durudee.

"This new drug has the potential to be used for date rape, yes. And worse." She can tell I don't fully understand what she's trying to convey. I wish she would let me peer into her eyes to see where she's going with this line of conversation, but she's guarded. "The person is under full control of the one closest to them. They will do whatever they say without question. Imagine the implications. Leader of a world bank forced to empty the accounts of every major corporation and transfer the money to a hidden account. Every trader on the floor of the Asian, or even the American stock market, instructed to sell every stock, all at once, crashing world markets. Their reach is infinite."

"The outcome could be devastating." I can't shake the vision in my mind, the black tubers clutched in paper by a hand that has known death. Then his appearance in my dream that evening. He warned me. No, he threatened me. He had to have known the naked man from my dream earlier today. One of his henchmen? Although, now, I'm not so sure I regret his death. But he was nothing. Just a pawn to them.

"The financial potential is the least of it. Imagine someone with the ability to control the actions of anyone, any politician." She hesitates and stares deep into my eyes. "A world leader and his or her entire security detail."

"Holy shit."

She nods her head.

The nuclear codes. That must be their end goal to achieve world domination. Lucifer's handiwork is all over this. His greedy fingers are itching to force the apocalypse. "How are you involved, Durudee?"

She frowns. "The drug cartel has been a scourge here in Thailand for years. Our previous leaders were corrupt, complicit in their dirty deals, but the people of Thailand are beyond fed up. Our new prime minister promised to end the drug trade within our country. He hired me to covertly oversee national security while I pose as a mild-mannered airport security chief. Jaime, I was exposed by the cartel. I have no idea how. Only the prime minister knows of my appointment. I can only guess he's been poisoned by someone close to him."

"Has he done anything that causes you to suspect he's helped this cartel?"

"Not that I know. I've checked to see if there have been changes to his security detail, passwords, safe combinations, codes; all are in place, everything as they should be."

"How long does the flower affect those who ingest it? Is this an indefinite mind-poisoning agent?"

"No, but it lasts hours, long enough to allow someone to cause serious harm to anyone, everyone being targeted. The world is unsafe as long as that flower exists. The cartel is willing to kill anyone to keep it secret and in their control." She hesitates, in deep contemplation, then turns to me. "Now it's your turn. What happened in your dream?"

I shake my head in disgust. "A naked man in a tub told me not to get involved, then killed a young woman."

Her eyebrows raise. "Naked man? Was he handsome?"

"Not in the least. Durudee, this isn't a time for jokes. They must've known I'd find out the rest from you. They already know of our relationship. I have an inkling they're behind the death on the flight last night. Must come as no surprise to you they want me to stay out of the way when they come for you. Obviously, they plan to enter your dream to avoid being implicated in your death."

Once the word escapes my lips, I notice Kaeo leaning over Durudee and whispering in her ear. I didn't even hear her approach and wonder how much she heard. How well can she be trusted?

As soon as the woman leaves, I lean over and whisper, "I'm so sorry."

She holds up her hand. "No need. I trust her to keep my

confidence. We have, let's say, a special relationship. And Ananda's finally here."

A tall, handsome young man with dark hair and eyes approaches our table. He leans over Durudee and kisses her on the cheek then turns to me. Wow, he's so striking, his features so angular, jaw so strong. The blood flushes to my cheeks, heating them up.

"Ananda, this is an old friend of mine. She lived in Colorado when we were there. This is Jaime Leary."

He places a strong hand on my shoulder then reaches out his right to mine. "It's a pleasure to meet you, Ms. Leary."

I clear my throat, peer down at the table, scan the room, then turn back to him. "Um, hello, Mr.," I answer, hesitating on my words. I don't know their surname. "Ananda." Could I be any more awkward than this?

His eyes smile at me before turning to his outstretched hand, waiting for me to take it. I grasp his palm and give a shake.

"You have quite a strong grip, Ms. Leary. You part of mother's security detail?"

Durudee bursts into laughter as I find myself doubting my choice in shaking his hand so firmly.

I knew it would happen. But I said yes to dinner with her anyway. There's every chance that when faced with a normal situation, I'll find some way to embarrass myself and screw it up. Do they see the humiliation, maybe even dread, in my eyes?

The two chat about everyday life while I sit and chastise myself for my awkwardness. I need to get over myself. This isn't about me. The dinner is about being a grateful guest of the woman to my right. Still, I can't help but study her son. For the first time in my life, I have an opportunity to meet one of the victims I've saved. This moment means more to me than

I can express or have ever anticipated.

He has very little accent when he speaks. Probably because of his early start in America. His voice is smooth, like melting chocolate in my mouth. His energy also feels so familiar. Like I'm home.

Ananda's dark eyes glint in the light when he glances my way. His smile is beautiful. That he is sitting directly across from me doesn't help.

Durudee smiles at me as if she can read my mind. Does she notice how enamored I am with her son?

"What do you do, Ms. Leary?" He flashes a warm smile and his white teeth attract my attention.

"Um, excuse me?" I manage to ask.

"For work."

"Oh, I'm…" I swallow, "in finance."

"What does that mean?" He laughs and leans forward.

Not helping. I feel my face flush again.

"I've managed banks, credit unions…I'm on sabbatical for a time."

"Is that what brought you to Thailand?" His stare is intense. I don't think I've seen anyone with a gaze that sees through my soul quite like his. That is, besides Collin. Why do so many of his qualities remind me of him?

"I'm just…travelling…around the world. Taking a little me time before hitting the grindstone. My work can be grueling at times."

"I can imagine." His gaze hesitates on me, his eyes gleaming. "What's on the menu today?"

My heart leaps in my chest before I realize he's speaking to his mother. Why is he affecting me this way?

"I think we should ask our guest, first, if she has any allergies. Jaime?" Durudee's voice snaps me back to reality.

"I…I think I'm good with most food. And I'm starving. I

wouldn't mind allowing you to order."

"Now, Mother, be careful not to order the hottest. She's probably not accustomed to our food." He turns to me and winks.

"Son, I can handle security for all of Bangkok airport. I think I can handle this, too." She flashes a knowing smile my direction.

Our secret. Even her son has no idea what she truly does for the government. I wonder how much of her work was kept from everyone around her when she worked for NORAD. Was it only a coincidence a sociopath was trying to kill her baby son back then?

"I was considering the tom yum goong, som tum and pad thai. Jaime, does that meet with your approval?" Both Ananda and Durudee await my answer.

Being a rookie at Thai food, I nod and smile. "Sounds…great."

Biding my time as our food is prepared, I barely hear the conversation between the two as my mind drifts back to my last night in Seattle. The man with the bundle of Dark Angel's Trumpets. I must ask Durudee more about the effect. Is the pollen potent enough alone, or do they require the entire flower for full effect? How many others feel no effect from the flower? Or am I the only one? After my experience with the guy in Seattle, and what Durudee told me about this flower, I can't help but wonder if they expected me to become one of their living zombies, following their nefarious orders. There's a great chance this storm has been brewing since I killed Rick and Sarah. More than likely far longer if they have an entire plantation and have already used it to control politicians for years from different countries, including America. Did Rick and Sarah know of this drug, these plans? In the end, they were angels loyal to Lucifer, after all.

Without looking up, I feel Ananda's eyes on me, studying me while I'm deep in contemplation. Durudee doesn't seem to notice, but I can feel her son analyzing my every movement even when not looking directly at him. His presence is so strong. Almost like he's a dark angel. But that can't be true. Could it?

"Do you..." he begins with a different inflection in his voice, then stops himself.

I gape back, realizing he's speaking to me.

"You look like..." He hesitates, as if unsure whether he should continue in this thread of conversation. After a moment, he tries again. "There's an image burned in my mind. I saw it every night when I..." His expression turns perplexed. "It's silly. Never mind."

Durudee and I glance at each other, prompting his active mind to search our intentions.

His hand falls to the table in front of him with determination. "I feel as if I know you. Every night as a young boy, a woman in black would enter my dreams, my nightmares, making me feel... Strange that you look exactly like her."

Durudee's eyes turn my way as she takes in a breath, but I make certain I'm the first to address him. "Our minds are funny like that. Generalized thoughts or images can alter when the slightest resemblance brings the greater embodiment to what we previously didn't clearly see. Apparently, I remind you of a dream that brought, what? Fear? Comfort? Neither?"

"Safety," he whispers, then falls silent, staring back at me.

I can't peer over to his mother without giving myself away. She told him about me over all those years. His mind conjured my image every night as a comfort to relieve him of his fear. He's made the link, at least, in his subconscious mind.

I take a swallow of my drink to appear nonchalant then

raise my eyes to his again. "The mind is a powerful protector. If you're prone to nightmares, I'm sure your subconscious invented someone to keep you safe."

"Oh, Ananda," Durudee breaks in. "You only remember the stories I told you as a child. The woman in the story, ironically, was also dressed in black with long, dark hair and green eyes. I used Jaime's likeness as a crutch." She turns to me and smiles as her fingers wrap around my wrist. "I'm not very creative. My stories were simply meant to put a fragile boy to sleep. That's all." Her voice had the calmness of a mother dove, cooing her younglings to sleep.

"Mother…" her son protests.

"Ananda. We're among friends. There's no need to hide your active childhood imagination." She returns her gaze to me with a glint in her eyes. "Apparently, he hasn't outgrown his belief in fantasy."

Ananda's eyes crease and his lips turn upward before he throws his head back. Laughter fills the restaurant, once again bringing unwanted attention to our table. "You're right. Of course, you're right. It's just a childhood dream. Funny, you're probably the closest I've come to meeting her while awake. I guess I've always wanted to meet the brave woman of my mother's fairytale." He turns to his mother, who appears to be holding her breath. "To my embarrassment, I carry the family's superstition gene."

He takes a sip of his water and swallows, then sets it down, purposefully, with his gaze locked on mine. "By the way, Mother, when did you say you met Jaime? After all, we did leave Colorado, what, nearly twenty years ago. Were you a small child, Ms. Leary, when you were friends with my mother?" His appearance darkens as he scrutinizes my expression. He knows. I didn't realize he was so young when they left the country. His accent is so refined. If I had known,

I'd have redirected the conversation.

"Ananda! You're being rude. Jaime has obviously carried her age well." She turns to me. "Please, forgive my son. Sometimes he's more suspicious than a gossipy neighbor."

"Mother, you know that isn't true. But I will offer my apology, Ms. Leary. I'm acting the fool this evening. Will you forgive me?"

His face is not as taut, but there is still tension in his jawline. Why am I not convinced he believes our feeble attempts to cover up the corpse of this conversation? Something in his eyes tells me he isn't buying it and is finding a way to unravel this bedtime story in his mind.

I glance from him to his mother then back again. "There's nothing to forgive. I'm perfectly comfortable with my age. I'm often mistaken for a teenager or twenty-year-old, more probably due to my size than my appearance. It's embarrassing, I have to say, to be carded at bars." *Damn it!* Why did I say that 'I'm embarrassed to be carded'? This is why I don't meet my victims. I'm a terrible liar and the truth is worse than fiction.

I force a smile and Durudee bursts into laughter. "I wish I had that problem, darling girl." She laughs again and Ananda smiles.

The server brings our plates and places three dishes on the table. One is a type of soup with shrimp. Next is a salad with green sauce and what looks like papaya. The third dish is a large bowl of long, thin noodles with large prawns. A silver bowl filled with white rice is set to my left. My mouth begins to water as I review the feast, deciding where to start.

I begin with the easier dish, the salad, and allow the other two an opportunity to serve their soup and noodles, carefully watching, hoping to not look foolish when it's my turn to fill my plate. I'm such a klutz, especially since I've been pregnant.

Not knowing their culture, I'm afraid I might not realize there's a unique system to serving the food. Once I've scooped enough of each onto my plate, I dig in. Ananda takes a mouthful of salad and chews. Then he swallows, and his gaze finds me once more.

"So, how old *are* you?"

"*Ananda!*" Durudee scolds, but I hold up my hand.

"It's okay, I brought this on myself. The fact of the matter is, Ananda, I'm seventy years old."

The table falls quiet as they both stare back at me with eyebrows raised and filled mouths agape. I hold my breath in response. Time seems to tick by without a stir. When I allow the corner of my mouth to curve into a sly grin, the silence is broken by Ananda's throaty laughter. Relief spreads across Durudee's face and I remember to breathe again as nearby dinner guests turn our direction.

Again, I'm silent, aware of being the spectacle of the evening. An uncomfortable circumstance for a creature who rarely pokes her nose farther from her hole than necessary. I can't help but wonder if those who have a beef with Durudee are somewhere nearby, watching our interaction. The thought makes me shift in my seat.

Peering from one table to another, I note those who glance our direction. A casual sweep from my right to my left reveals most tables swiftly returning to normal. Three tables, however, have at least one set of eyes frequently switching in our direction with greater than simple interest. Their dinner conversations seem less than casual. Out of place. I take the opportunity to commit their likenesses to memory. Four men and two women in all curiously examine us.

Swift movement from my peripheral left gives me a start and I tighten my muscles to keep my fists beneath the table. The server reaches over and removes an empty platter, as well as other spent dinner vessels, from our table. Durudee reaches for my wrist with a calm warning. Her reflexes are admirable. Nearly as developed as mine. Once again, I find myself wondering if there is more to her than I had already surmised.

Ananda also notices my flinch and trains his attention on me and his mother, analyzing our reactions. Although my muscles have fallen slack again, Ananda's attention hasn't. He seems to study me with an even greater interest. This may be the best time to make my departure.

"This meal was wonderful, Durudee. I wish there was more room in my stomach. I would have devoured much more."

"I will be sure to send the chef to your hotel room when you are ready to have more," she answers.

"Oh, no, that would not be necessary. As much as I enjoyed this meal, I would find it awkward to have someone in my room, cooking a meal."

She nods in understanding. "Of course. How insensitive of me."

"Please, allow me to pay," I tell her as I pull my card from my wallet.

"Unnecessary. The bill is already taken care of." She places her hand on mine and I feel her energy radiate through my skin and into the bones and flesh of my fingers.

Ananda wipes his mouth with the cloth napkin and rises from his seat. "Ms. Leary, please allow me to escort you to your hotel. It would be my honor, truly. I won't have to worry you might succumb to one of the death machines we call a taxi in this country."

Remembering the harrowing ride to the restaurant, I let out a slight chuckle. "Please, call me Jaime," I say.

"Yes, Jaime, you should let Ananda take you back. Not all taxi drivers in our city are as dangerous as my son would like to let on, but it would be a nice gesture and it can give you two a chance to chat without my prying eyes."

Suddenly, I'm worried at Durudee's intent. Is she trying to set me up with her son? She must realize that isn't a possibility. An angel and a mortal? It's not a conceivable match-up. Maybe I should have told her I'm married. And I don't want to be the one to hurt his feelings.

"Well, Ananda, I've grown quite fond of death machines. I mean, who would want to endure a boring ride to their hotel in Bangkok? I might be disappointed if I have to leave without a little heart-pounding taxi-riding action? Where's the adventure in that?"

He stops for a moment, thinks about my words with a pensive look on his face. "Well," he begins then turns to his mother for a brief moment. "I suppose if I must take you for what my mother calls a 'joy ride' in order to have the pleasure of your company for a while longer, you got it. Deadly speeds and dangerous turns it is. Ms. Leary, uh, I mean, Ms. Jaime, your chariot awaits." He bows with his arms swept to the side as if waiting for me to lead an entourage to the front door.

That's not what I had in mind. Something tells me he won't take no for an answer. Yet he has a charming way about him that makes it hard to say no. And I am their guest, after all. Refusal would be rude.

We reach the door and Ananda directs me around to the other side of a sporty, black Audi. Very unlike Collin's sensible hybrid. That thought causes a flush of guilt. But it shouldn't. I'm only accepting a ride from a friend. The door closes with a solid thud and he returns to the driver side and gets in, then turns to me.

"Are you ready?" he asks with a grin on his face.

"Ready for...?" I don't get a chance to finish my question as he shifts into gear and I'm thrown back in my seat. *Oh. Shit.*

CHAPTER 10

Ananda takes each corner like he's competing on a race course. I have to hold the dash with one hand and the armrest of the door with my other. Undoubtedly, my eyes are as wide as golf balls, watching the road, hoping we don't collide with another car, or worse, a solid building.

Ananda turns to me with a mischievous grin. "Is this heart-pounding enough for you?"

A snide comment comes to mind. However, he's already called my bluff once. Something tells me he wouldn't hesitate to take this drive to the next tormenting level. Aside from that, my food hasn't been digested in the least and Baby doesn't like this shifting back and forth as we cut right then left. My heart pounds blood through my veins as if I'm in a dream, preparing to encounter a demon. As much as I enjoy the stimulation, I have another life to consider, my child's. And his driving... For a pediatrician, he's a maniac.

"I thought you took the Hippocratic oath," I shout over the roar of the engine. "Isn't this style of driving in direct violation of that?" My nails dig deeper into the leather of his dashboard.

Ananda's laughter fills the vehicle as he releases his foot

from the accelerator. "Your sense of humor is appealing."

"On the other hand, my blood spilled on the pavement and splattered across this luxurious leather seat…not so much."

Ananda chuckles once again and I force a slight laugh in response. He's the son of a friend. At least, I hope she's a friend. For now, until there's evidence to the contrary, I'll assume she's an ally and coerce myself to lighten up.

Ananda is very unlike Collin. As much as my husband is subtle and sometimes brooding, this man isn't quite so serious. Yes, Ananda has his somber moments, but he seems generally happy. It makes me wonder if it's because of Collin's past? Our past and what we know that makes him like me, so downright dark?

"Although I barely saw the scenery zipping by at lightning speed, I'm pretty sure this isn't the way to my hotel. Seems we would've made it there within seconds after the initial propulsion." I give him a sideways glance, wondering why he hasn't slowed the vehicle and where we are going.

"You're very perceptive," he answers, showing two rows of perfect teeth with a big smile.

Why do I feel so good around him? Must be that familiarity I noticed at the restaurant. Has to be that I once saved his life. Or maybe my subconscious is reflecting the feeling of safety he has around me due to his childhood dreams.

"I thought you might want to see some of the city of Bangkok while here."

I flash a mischievous grin back at him, which surprises me. I had no idea I had any playfulness left in me. Typically, my mood is darker than my leather jacket. "I may have seen the entire city in two minutes. You are the worst. Tour guide. Ever."

His smile grows devious and I wonder what ideas he's

hatching behind that grin. That look makes me feel young and almost carefree, something I haven't felt in a long time. He has such a good, pure soul. Being near him is like a breath of fresh air.

The Audi negotiates city streets lit by bright signs on nearly every building. The writing is no longer Thai on advertisements. "Where are we?"

"Chinatown. If we hadn't just eaten, I'd suggest a great restaurant."

I chuckle before realizing I'm doing so. "No, no. I'm perfectly fine. Especially after my second death cab ride. This could be an ill-fated drive to my hotel. Worse than any Bangkok taxi, one might say. You may owe me many apologies by the time you drop me off."

"Oh, I'm wounded!" he says, grabbing his chest over his heart.

"And yet, I get the feeling you'll get through just fine."

"That's it," he announces. "Now I'm kidnapping you."

"Wait, what?"

I'm thrown back into my seat again as Ananda plunges the accelerator to the floor and the vehicle bolts forward.

"Hold on!" he shouts, ignoring my fingers already clutching whatever I can cling to.

"Whoa, this isn't cool! Where are we going?" I find the breath to ask while lights flash by and we peel through the city. "Your mother would never approve of this, you know."

"Yeah? Then this jaunt shall be kept secret," he answers with his eyes still on the road.

"How will you keep this secret? There's another person in the car besides you."

"Aahh, now, Ms. Jaime. Don't make me take extreme measures to silence you."

He grins devilishly, but I'm not playing anymore. My heart

is pounding in my ears, the blood being forced through my veins like a locomotive. My body wants to react as it usually does under this physical condition. Left uncontrolled, I may lunge for him out of habit. I may accidentally kill the man I saved as an infant.

We've left the city, now. I have no idea where we're heading. The urge to lash out pulls at my fingers and I force one hand deeper into the leather of my seat while the other still clamps the dash. This situation isn't safe. For him.

"Ananda! Stop the car right now!"

He throws a quick glance toward me. The grin slips from his face. Concern grows in his eyes. "Oh, shit." He pulls the car abruptly to the side of the road and flips on the interior dome light.

"Oh, God, I didn't mean to scare you," he says, pulling my clenched fingers from the dash.

I immediately recoil my hand. My fight or flight adrenaline rush is still pulsing through my veins. My entire body is throbbing with the desire to fatally wound. I might break a bone or five in his hand, his arm, the entire side of his body if I don't calm soon.

"Are you all right?" he asks, studying me carefully.

I take several deep breaths before answering. "Don't ever do that again," I tell him. "You have no idea what could have happened."

"I'm so sorry. I was only joking. Never intending to make you believe I was serious. You must believe I would never do anything to harm anyone."

After more deep breaths, my heart rate lowers to a normal level. I decide not to tell him the truth. Let him believe I was scared, not on the verge of killing him. "I believe you."

"I gave you quite a fright. Let me take you back." He pulls the steering wheel to turn the car around and I reach for his arm.

"Please, tell me. Where were you planning to go?"

"The river. The River Kwai."

"I've never been to the River Kwai. Can you see it at night?"

He shrugs his shoulders. "Not really. But it's a peaceful place no matter when you go. Day or night."

I ponder the idea for a moment. This might be something worth seeing. I need time to relax before sleep, and this may be enough to do just that. But I have to be sure... "Can I trust you to behave?"

He cocks his head at me and pinches his eyebrows. "I have no idea what you mean." The sly grin returns to his face.

"Do you promise to be safe?" I ask, remembering a conversation not too long ago. "You know, don't try and kill me. Because...I *am* dressed in black. And I *may* go full ninja and have to kill you first."

"Hmm, that is true. I suppose it would be in my best interest not to set you on alert. That is, if I want to stay alive."

"Good plan. Let's go." Poor guy has no idea.

I had no inkling how far the River Kwai was from Bangkok. Turns out the trip is far longer than I had anticipated, giving us far too much time for conversation. I'm not a girl who's accustomed to lengthy conversation with mortals. Thankfully, Ananda is good at filling in empty airspace.

"After we moved here, and I was old enough to drive, I came out to the river every chance I could. But then I started medical school and soon after I was too busy to take that much time. I haven't been here since I was nineteen. The water flows so peacefully. Everyone is respectful of the area due to the cemetery near the prison camp. It's sacred ground for us."

"Prison camp?"

"Yes, you know, the one that held American and European soldiers during World War Two."

"Oh, I do remember hearing of this place. Just never really thought about it. Isn't there a railroad bridge built by the prisoners?"

"The famous bridge. Yes. Called the Bridge on the River Kwai. A book and a movie were made with this name, also."

"That's right. I remember when that movie came out. Never saw it, though. I'd love to see the bridge, as long as you understand, this isn't a…date…" And at that moment I realize the mistake I just made.

Ananda laughs. "How could you remember when that movie came out? That was long before you were born—" His words trail off as if stolen by the night.

I shift in my seat, quiet, listening, as the night caresses the speeding vehicle. The dead silence tells me he's holding his breath. Why doesn't he say something? Anything. The emptiness between us makes the wind brushing past Ananda's Audi deafening. *Say something*, my mind screams at him. But there are no words to come. He's rolling his life, or maybe mine, over in his mind. Surely, he won't figure it out. How could he? Mortals always go for the logical explanation, not the real one, especially when it's so crazy. I can't wait for him to break this. I have to open the air again.

"The restaurant your mother selected was beautiful. Great ambi—"

"Don't."

I stop in mid-sentence and wait for him to finish.

"Don't," he begins again then takes a breath, "change the subject."

"I'm not sure I—"

"Yes. You know exactly. You and my mother are hiding something. I could smell it when I walked in the room." His expression is serious. Far more serious than I had seen yet, at least to this point in the evening.

"That could've been the Pu Pu Platter," I answer quickly, with the hope of flipping the conversation to something besides my background.

"Nice try, but that's Chinese." He almost cracks a grin, but his mind has a singular aim. "How old are you, Jaime?"

"Haven't you been told, it's impolite to ask a woman her —"

"Answer me." His tone is clear and final.

"My age is none of your business. I think you should take me back to my hotel now."

The tactic may be a dodge, one unlikely to have the desired result, but it may give me time to figure out how to explain this. When we arrive at the river in fifteen, maybe twenty minutes, however, he's going to want answers before returning me to my room.

"I don't like being lied to. You and Mother have a secret. I'm not taking you back to the hotel until you tell me what you're hiding."

"Then let me out here. I'll walk back." Crossing my arms and sliding back into my seat shows my dogged determination, as well.

"You won't make it back to the hotel. A woman alone on a road like this, after dark, doesn't stand a chance. Or, am I mistaken? If the woman is one such as you, Ms. Jaime Leary, does she have a chance?" He glances at me from the corner of his eye then returns his focus to the road.

"What're you saying?" I hesitate, waiting for the right words to come to me. *Shit*. Do I dare tell him? Would it hurt anything if I out myself, expose everything about me? Durudee already knows. He couldn't turn on me, knowing I saved his life. Could he? *Damn!* "Fine. When we arrive at the river, I'll answer your questions. Fair enough?"

"Yes," he answers, then releases the breath he's been holding. "That'll do. But I expect complete honesty. I can tell when people are lying."

Sigh. "Fair enough. Although, I don't know why you think I owe you anything. It's not like I've made any promises to you."

"No. You don't owe me a thing, except to be up front when speaking to me. That seems a universal sign of respect in any honest conversation, don't you think? I could turn this car around and drop your little ass off in front of your hotel. Is that what you want?"

I gasp at his expression. But he ignores me and continues.

"Yes, I said it. Your. Little. Ass. I could do that, all fine and well. But I think there's a history you know about me, about my past, and that gives me the right to assume you will be respectful and, at minimum, give me some sort of explanation. It would, after all, be the decent thing to do."

"I already said I would. You don't have to get rude."

The air is thick with unspoken words again. I barely hear him breathe. I barely breathe, myself. The tightness in my chest is a dull ache; one I want to vomit out of me but can't. Maybe telling him of his past will be cathartic, not only to him. Maybe I need this as well. I only hope he doesn't lose his marbles, or worse, think I'm full-blown nuts and have me committed. Oh, God, I hope he doesn't have the power to commit me. He is a doctor, after all.

When we finally pull off the road, it is just before the bridge, the famous one that got me into my current situation with the recollection of the movie. When he turns the key and the engine dies, we sit for several long moments. The air is too heavy, and I need to breathe. I force the door open and stumble out of the car like a clumsy girl on her first date. But this isn't a date, and nothing could ever happen between us. Nothing.

His door opens, as well, and I shut mine, glance toward him, then head down the hill.

"Hold on, you'll end up in the water if you aren't careful." He reaches the front of his vehicle and grabs tight to my upper arm, directing me toward the river. "Wow, you're awfully muscular for a—" He stops in mid-sentence.

"A what?" I answer. I've had quite enough of this and yank my arm from his grasp, then turn toward the water.

"You tell me," he shouts back

"You're not very—"

Suddenly, my right foot won't make its normal progression, somehow caught in a small divot, and my left foot isn't in any place to right my balance. My body hurtles violently forward and I find myself sliding over the wet grass down the hill. I roll to my side and curl in a ball to protect the tiny peanut growing inside of me while still careening in an unconstrained head-first skid, and the only thing to stop me is the water.

I barely hear Ananda mutter, "Shit!" then his footsteps chasing after me. When I'm close enough to make out the rush of flowing water, his body launches in front of me. My forward trajectory is halted, and my embarrassing impression of a human toboggan has been upended.

Both of us are breathless as we untangle ourselves from each other, then move back up the hill a safe distance from the flowing stream. I lower myself to the ground and perch into a comfortable position. I place my hand over my tummy to feel the tiny energy inside of me, thankfully protected by the layers of flesh between it and the world.

"What do you think I am?" I finally ask, once I've had a chance to recover.

"What?"

"All this talk about dreams. What, or maybe I should ask, *who* do you think I am? You're not superstitious. You have a mind that rejects foolish notions. Yet, you insist on entertaining some foolish notion."

"Is it foolish? I witnessed something as a very young child. I have the scar to prove it. I believed my mother for all those years when she spoke of a dream, the devil and an angel, maybe because I witnessed it. When I was old enough to understand what she was telling me, I took her words as honest. True." He shrugs. "Then I grew up and stopped believing in angels and devils. My culture teaches us they exist, but my scientific mind denies it. And yet, the vision I clung to in my childhood remained." Now he looks away, a sheepish expression on his face. It feels like he's worried I'll think he's crazy. "Her face, your face, was as clear as it was while we sat at the table. It appeared to me every night. How could I ever forget those eyes, those lips, strong while gently assuring me no one would harm me. I fell in love with that image."

A chill shoots through me as he waits, realizing what he's revealed. He fell in love with me long before tonight. Oh shit. This just got really awkward. Not for the first time during this trip, I wish I wore a ring.

He clears his throat, then continues. "I held her in my heart all those years. Then realized in my maturity she wasn't real. Imagine how I feel when you appear, the exact same woman, not having aged a day. At first, I didn't want to believe it."

How do I defuse this? How do I help him move on and live his life? Will the truth resolve his angst?

"Do you really believe I was someone in your dreams, helping you feel safe while you slept?"

"Yes. No. I don't know, dammit. I believe I saw

you...when I was too young to remember. And I believe your image stayed with me. But what I don't believe is that it was a dream. Dreams don't scar you."

"That's a lot of 'I believes' to take all this seriously, don't you think?"

"No. I don't think. Because you and my mother have done too much trying to hide something for it to be merely a coincidence. She put you up in her favorite hotel. Pulled strings, I'm sure, to see that you're in the nicest suite available. Offering to send a chef to your room. Mother owes you a favor, something she rarely allows going unpaid."

"You're being ridiculous."

"What do you know about this scar? How did I get it? Don't lie to me or I'll know." Ananda releases the top button of his shirt and pulls it to the side for me to see. A long-healed sliver of pale scarring streak from his chest to his shoulder. "I've had this as long as I can remember."

I soften my voice as much as possible and try again. I need him to say it. The answer must come from him. "How do you think it happened? How do you think I'm involved in this?"

"Like I said, I don't know. I want you to tell me. Tell me who you are."

"I can't. If you say it, I'll confirm it. But only if you say it first."

"You promise you'll answer me honestly?" he asks, and I nod my head. "Were you there?"

"Where?"

"In my dream. The night this happened. Were you there?"

I nod my head.

He hesitates and swallows deep.

I hold my breath.

"Okay then. Did you stop the man who did this to me?"

Again, I nod my head yes.

"Who are you?"

"Who am I, Ananda? What's your mind telling you?"

"My heart tells me you're an angel, but my mind tells me it's impossible."

"And you wonder why I can't tell you the truth. Most don't believe in what I truly am. You don't. And if I say the words aloud, you'll think me crazy. Why can't I tell you the truth? That. That is exactly why."

He takes my hand in his, studying it for a minute or more. His gaze shifts, following the sleeve of my jacket up to my shoulder then my face, my lips, then directly in the eyes. "Are you an angel?"

"Do you believe I am?" I know the potential leap from the unknown to this level takes great faith.

He studies me, searching for something, anything to tell him what to believe. His voice is barely audible when he finally answers. "Yes. But I don't understand how. Why are you here? Don't you age? Aren't angels supposed to stay invisible? Are you my guardian angel?"

"Whoa, slow down. There are too many questions to answer at once. I'll take them one at a time. First."

"First," he repeats then is lost in thought for a moment before continuing on. "Please answer for me, what kind of angel are you? What's your purpose?"

"I'm called a dark angel. We walk among people like, well, like we're normal, one of them. As normal as possible, I guess. I'm not very good at that part of it, though. At night, however, when we sleep, there's always a soul in need of saving. There are people, twisted souls, whose subconscious is so powerful it will kill them in their sleep. I stop a murder from happening, but someone must die before I can wake. The one evil enough to kill another is my target, every time."

His eyebrows press into a pucker. His mouth is agape. He

clings to my fingers as if it's his only grasp on reality.

"Next question," I practically whisper, afraid to break the spell of the moment.

He blinks his eyes, then stares blankly back at me. "You don't age?"

I smile, half chuckle. "No."

"You're really seventy, aren't you?"

"Yes."

"And my mother knew. She kept it from me."

"She knew, yes, but she didn't keep anything from you. She told you for many years. You chose not to believe after a time. What did you expect of her?"

"Has she known you all this time? Have you been around us? Watching over us?"

"No. That's not how it goes. I'm not a guardian angel. I fight the demon I'm led to. Each night it's a new victim, new demon."

"How did you meet up? Are you here in Bangkok for a reason? A reason that involves Mother?"

"One at a time. It's a long story. I'm not here because of you or your mother. I was honest when I told you I was merely traveling through. But she recognized me, at the airport, and asked me to join the two of you for dinner, meet you, and see who you've become. She's very proud of you."

The tightness falls away and a grin crosses his face. "She tells me all the time. I don't know what I would've done without her while growing up."

"You know, she helped me save you," I tell him.

His face lights up in the darkness. "She did? She never told me."

"The scar in the palm of her hand is also from that night. She caught the sword before I could. Your life was saved by your mother. I was only there long enough to kill the one who tried to take your life."

"My God. I never knew. She never told me."

"I'm not surprised. As long as you have her, you have your guardian angel. She loved you so much she was able to enter your dream and keep you safe. See? You've admired the wrong person all this time."

He turns toward the river, deep in thought. I pick up a small stone near my leg and toss it over the water. Tiny interruptions ripple the restless surface from shore to shore.

"How did you do that? I've never skipped a rock further than about ten feet. At least, not on this river."

"Angel," I tell him.

"Really? Do Angels know how to skip stones?"

I laugh out loud and shake my head. "No. Just messing with you. My father taught me how to skim stones on water, even when the surface was turbulent."

He returns my laughter, then stares into my eyes again with a smile on his face. "All those years, I prayed to God that you were real and that I would meet you someday. And here you are. To think, I considered myself a fool for holding on for so long."

"Another prayer answered. Not a fool after all." I force a smile that I nearly feel in my heart. Why am I so comfortable around him?

He seems to stare into my soul for far too long, then his hand rises to my cheek. His fingers follow the scar on my jawline then rise to my brow to brush the bangs back. I'm lost in the moment. I know I should stop him. I need to end this. Somehow, I'm mesmerized by his touch, the feel of the energy in his fingertips against my skin. He traces my brows to the summit of my nose then my lips. His light touch tickles them until I pull back, lick and bite the sensation away.

When I look down to my lap, I feel his hand at the nape of

my neck, pulling me forward until my lips meet his. His kiss is warm and soft but I can't do this. As much as I long for the touch of Collin, Ananda is no replacement. Even as I try to reason this out, my will grows thinner. Is this temptation I feel the lure of Lucifer? Is he the one toying with my emotions through Ananda?

I pull away from him, but he draws me back, staring deep into my eyes, and I'm weak. What is this hold he has over me? His lips part and they find me again, welcoming then longing as he grows hungry for me. I try to push back, but his arms are strong and my will to resist falters. I fall into him, allowing my body to melt against him while his mouth and tongue discover mine. I'm lost in a terrestrial heaven, Ananda's strong arm wrapped around me, clutching the opposite shoulder while the other hand holds a fist of my hair. Then the hand at my shoulder releases me.

A tug on my jacket distracts my attention from his lips. His fingers coax my zipper lower and I feel the cool air against my upper chest. One button, then another is loosened on my shirt and his hand slips inside. My blood rages through me and I fight the urge to reach for him, throw him to the ground and climb over him and draw out his sexual desire, just as Collin did with me.

I should stop this. It can't be. I'm married. I belong to Collin. But Ananda's lips feel so good on my cheek, my jaw, my throat, my chest. How could I deny myself? No! I can't do this.

"No. Stop, Ananda," I press my palms into his shoulders and push him back. "I can't. I'm married."

"You're what? Oh, my God. How can you be...? You're married?" The curve in his brows show betrayal. "Angels are allowed to marry? That's not possible."

"But they're allowed to kiss mortals? You're not making

sense."

"Maybe not. Maybe I don't want to make sense. Damn! Unbelievable! I find you and I can't have you. You married a mortal? Really?"

"No. I married another angel."

"Then... Why...? Why isn't he here, with you?"

"We have issues. It was an arranged marriage and, well, it's a long story."

"You seem to have a lot of long stories. Convenient when you don't want to explain something."

"Only convenient when the subject is too complicated for an hour or so chat on the shore of a river at night. Ananda, I'm just so confused right now. My arranged marriage is the reason I'm here, and the reason so many people have died. I'm just a perplexed angel trying to find myself, that's all."

"I don't understand."

"I don't expect you to. I barely understand it myself.

He sighs and grasps my shoulders with a gentle touch. After searching my expression, he pulls me into his arms and holds me, stroking my hair. He smells like the sage brush of Colorado and my heart aches. As much pain as I knew there, I still miss the peaceful moments and the man I left behind. I want to push him away, but I don't have the strength to do it.

After several minutes, he whispers into my hair, "I should take you to your hotel, but I don't want to move. Don't want to leave your arms. You feel like all the beautiful times of my childhood, all rolled into one moment."

The river babbles in the distance except for a snapping twig in the opposite direction that heightens my sense of alert. Ananda feels me stiffen and pulls back.

"What's wrong?"

"I heard something."

"That snap? This place is filled with odd sounds. They say

it's an echo of ghosts, of those who died making that bridge, or perished from abuse or starvation in the nearby camp. The night is filled with more unusual movement and empty clatter than any place I've known. I just call out to them, tell them to have a seat, and the noises go away. Maybe it calms me because I imagine them sitting beside me, enjoying the river with me. That's what I used to envision, at least."

"You're a beautiful man, Ananda."

He hugs me one more time then releases me and stands. His hand reaches down for me and I take it in mine to rise to my feet to avoid another embarrassing roll down the hill. As we stroll toward the car, I think of Collin and feel guilt. I've betrayed him. His poor choices don't give me free reign to do whatever I please. I may be a vengeful angel, but I'm not a cheater, no matter how good his touch may feel.

When we near the crest of the hill, I turn my eyes to the car and see movement in the shadows. Unaccustomed to letting coincidence slide, I search the darkness with keener senses. Nearly hidden in trees, someone waits for us. Three men dressed in black. Ananda sees them also and slows his pace.

"That's cozy. You lovebirds are cute," one of them pipes up in his native Thai language.

"Get off the car, low life. It's not for sale," Ananda answers in English.

They move forward, and I notice the black gloves pulled over their hands. The weather isn't cold here. Of the potential reasons for them to sport leather gloves in temperatures such as this, keeping their hands warm isn't one of them. Ananda pulls me behind his back.

"Don't, doctor. It's the girl we want," he continues, still in his language.

Part of me wonders if the man from my afternoon nap sent them. Do they plan to threaten me again? Assholes have no idea who I really am. Or do they? Perhaps they believe I'm more dangerous in my dreams than awake.

I push in front of Ananda and face the one doing the speaking. "What do you want from me?" I ask in Thai.

"No, Jaime, stay back. They're dangerous."

I sigh and frown at him. "Ananda."

"Yeah, okay, but—"

"No. No but. I'll handle this."

"You lovebirds quit fighting. We want the girl," the lead guy interrupts us.

I turn back to the three men and speak in Thai again. "I'm here. What do you want?"

He smiles and raises his hand, curling his index finger, beckoning me to come closer.

"Answer me."

"We have candy."

"I'm on a diet, asshole," I say in English, but they seem to understand anyway, and one to the left of the leader laughs. "Oh, so you're just screwing with me, using only Thai. Go jack off. I'm not interested."

"Listen, bitch, you come or doctor dies," the lead person answers in English.

"Jaime," Ananda says again, reaching for my hand and pulling me back, "get behind me."

"Ananda, understanding who I am, you should know better. Now, back up."

He stares back at me, puzzled, but does as he's told.

"Pussy!" one of the men shouts.

"Pussy?" I turn back to them and see the smirk on the one who had the nerve to utter it. The one word I hate more than Lucifer's name.

I march up the hill and past their front guy, knocking his hand away when he tries to reach for me. His wrist cracks like the snap of a twig. Screams of pain echo across the river. I grab the taller man behind him, who's nearly six inches greater than me and push him backward until he's up against a tree. The wind is knocked out of him and he gasps for air. His eyes grow large as he claws at my hands, unsuccessful in all attempts to free himself. The next man grabs hold of my arm and I let go with one hand and bring my fist back into his face. Blood sprays from his nose.

"Shit! Shit! Shit! Bitch broke my nose," he shouts.

"Pussy?" I repeat, and the man shakes his head frantically, still gasping.

Then a sharp stab in my side steals my attention. A long needle is jammed through the leather of my jacket.

"Bastard!" I slam the guy I'm holding against the tree and knock him unconscious.

Their leader backs away before I can elbow him. I reach back and pull the needle from my side and crush the syringe in my palm.

"What was that?" I ask. He only smiles and takes another step backward. "You *asshole*! What did you shoot into me?" I grab him by the jacket at his chest.

Keeping my eyes on the other with my peripheral vision, I pull the jacket tight around his throat until he nearly chokes. "Tell me!"

He grins and says in clear English, "Dark Angel." Then he gags as I pull the neck of his coat tighter to cut off his airway.

Rage boils within me. Do they really think they can get me to do their bidding by injecting me with their drug? "I'd kill you, but I want you to give your boss a message from me," I warn, forcing my words through gritted teeth. "It doesn't work. I'm immune, asshole."

I send his mind spinning with a fist to the side of his head, and he collapses at my feet. I turn to the last man. His eyes are wide with fear as he tries to run but won't take his eyes off me. His feet stumble over each other as he retreats, still holding his hand over his gushing nose as he rushes backwards up the hill. The other carefully backs away until I lunge forward. He stumbles backward then turns and runs full out.

Only now do I realize I haven't thought of Ananda since the moment I approached the four jackasses. I turn to see him farther down the hill, his eyes as wide as that of the two men I'd chased off. His mouth is agape.

"Are you all right?" I ask. He hesitantly nods. "Ready to head back then?" He nods again and doesn't move. I feel a wave of awkwardness flood over me and decide to speak slowly. "Do…you…want…me…to…drive?"

"Huh? No. Oh, shit. What just happened? Should I be afraid of you?"

"Honestly?" I ask, biting my lip. He nods again. "Only if you drive like an asshole again. Let's go."

CHAPTER 11

After traveling nearly fifty kilometers, Ananda still isn't speaking. Not sure if he's contemplating our kiss or the fight that followed. He seems to be searching the road ahead, yet it isn't pavement he sees. But I don't say a word. He has to be the one to break the silence.

Several more kilometers fly past and Ananda finally takes a breath. He holds it for so long I wonder if he's breathing.

"What was that? Back there. What happened?" he finally asks.

"I think, but I can't be sure, that you kissed me—"

"Not that," he says, interrupting my lame attempt to lighten the moment. "You barely flicked your wrist and broke that guy's nose. You practically lifted a two-hundred-pound man off the ground, nearly breaking the tree when you slammed him against it. Broke the wrist of the other guy with a slap of your hand. I mean, I've never seen—"

"Ananda. Angel."

He glances over to me with a questioning expression. Then it comes back to him. "You're a...that's right. I just never really...thought of it...in that way. I thought...I don't know what I thought. You're badass!" His face lifts into a smile. "No wonder you were able to save me from the guy in my dream. Wait. I kissed an angel. Not just a woman who looks angelic, but I. Kissed. An angel. A real, live, angel. I can't wait to talk to mother about this."

"Whoa, wait, Ananda. All right, your mother knows who I am, but I think you should slow down. Don't go rushing off and telling the country about me. Until recently, I've been relatively hidden from most of the world. I've stayed away from human contact as much as possible."

"I don't understand. Why shouldn't the world know about you?"

"You know as well as I. Imagine what tests the world leaders would want to perform on me if they knew. Scientists would want to dissect me. And the world militaries? What would they want from me? Bad people would want to destroy me. They already do. Why do you think those guys showed up back there? They were looking for me. They know I'm here."

He shakes his head in recognition.

"Corrupt governments? Undoubtedly, they'd want to control me or have me locked up. There's no way to win if I were exposed to the world."

"Who knows you're here? You said 'they.'"

"That's another story for another time. Let's just say there's an evil force on this earth that would like nothing better than to round up all dark angels and force us to join them or be killed."

"Dark angels. As in plural. There are more of you?"

I nod my head. "I'm married, remember."

"That's right." He goes silent for a moment. Pensive. Then turns to me, his lips drawn in a worried line. "If they know you're here, what will you do? It's just a matter of time before they come after you again."

"There's only one thing to do: leave. It's the only way to protect you and Durudee."

"But...who will protect us when you're gone? One might say we know too much. If they can enter our dreams—"

"Fight. Use everything within you, every ounce of energy. And remember that dreams have no rules. You can use that to your advantage if you can think to bring strength at your disposal."

"You're saying you won't be there if we need you again, aren't you?"

My heart falls in my gut. The best answer is the truth, no matter how much it may hurt. "I don't know, Ananda. My dreams aren't mine to control. I don't know who'll be there the minute I fall asleep. I can only hope that, if you and Durudee need me, I'll be there. But it's something I can't promise."

His eyebrows pinch together the way they do when he's trying to control the ache in his heart. He's done it more than once tonight. "Will you take my number and call me...text me if that's better, just keep in touch? I would like to know you're okay. Promise you'll do it?"

As much as I worry this is a bad idea, I agree. Would it hurt to stay connected? To someone, anyone, who isn't trying to kill me? At least, I hope he isn't trying to kill me. I trusted Sarah. Rick. *Shit.* No matter how much my suspicious mind wants me to mistrust him, I know I'll one day need an ally. I just pray I can count on him to have my back. This thought sticks in my mind the entire ride back to the hotel.

Ananda insists on walking me to the door of my suite. He gives me a tight hug, holding me for more than a minute, then releases me with a soft, "Good-bye." He doesn't turn back as he leaves.

Inside my room, the smell of jasmine fills the air and I wish the aroma could soothe me. Not tonight. I place the *Do Not Disturb* sign on the outside handle then close the door, double locking to keep out intruders.

As much as the hot tub looks inviting, I'm too exhausted from the evening and turn to my bed instead. The monsters seem insistent I come and join them. While braiding my hair down my back, I wonder if I'll see Fat Naked Guy. Tonight, I'll be prepared for him. And with my most comfortable and flexible black jammies on, I slip between the covers and fall into the darkness of my nightmare.

CHAPTER 12

Several long minutes pass as my mind wanders the dark corridors of the sleep world. The smell of jasmine greets me just as it had when I arrived at my hotel. Am I hunting inside Hotel Siam? There's no visual stimuli to verify my suspicions. Yet, as the thought enters my mind, a glowing orb appears in the distance, growing in intensity and becoming stronger with each step I take. I'm pulled in this direction, without doubt. Somewhere in the glimmer is the one, the soul whose light holds intent on dimming that of another.

As the fog of my mind separates and the glare crystalizes, I recognize my surroundings. Above me is a familiar street light at the mouth of the bridge on the River Kwai. My heart skips a beat, wondering at the significance. Does this mean what I think? My focus darts from metal supports to the pillars plunging into the river.

No one has stepped forward. At least not yet. Shadows cloak more than half the bridge. What lies beyond the light will be revealed soon enough as I step forward. Before my foot leaves the pavement, however, a hand takes my shoulder. I reach up in an instant, but my force is stayed when I hear the voice.

"Jaime?"

A shiver runs through me like a ghost. I turn to her with my eyes still scanning the surrounding areas of obscurity. "Durudee?" My voice betrays my lack of surety and her expression turns questioning, her head slowly shaking in an attempt to ward off my doubt.

"It's not me. I swear."

"What, Durudee? What do you mean it isn't you? Why are you in my dream? Are you here as the victim or—" I can't finish the thought.

"Jaime...it's all a mistake. I didn't mean to hurt anyone. I only wanted to save my son. You must understand how that is." Her lips are pale as she reaches for my arm and I instantly pull away.

I shake my head in reply. "No. I don't. What have you done?"

"Jaime," she pleads with me, but I know there is so much more that I'm unsure of. Is she involved with those who tried to drug me tonight?

"You sent them," I whisper, and she nods her head in shame. The air is knocked from me and I reach for a bridge support to steady my body. "Is Ananda involved in this, also? Did he bring me to the river to set up the confrontation with your three goons from dinner?" My heart tightens like a fist has plunged through the flesh, squeezing the life from me.

"They're not my goons, Jaime. And Ananda knows nothing of this. He's an innocent boy. He would never approve of what I have done, under any circumstance. You must believe me. I never meant for this to happen. They'll kill him. I know they will. They'll kill you, too, if you get in the way."

"Get in the way of what?"

"Tonight...I have to die. They will ensure it is so. If I don't, everything collapses. Their entire operation. Their networks, they're controlled by leaders, powerful corporate professionals, who are wrapped with the devil himself. Caught in Lucifer's grip, and Satan refuses to let go."

No wonder she knew who I was. She's working with the very demons and rogues of Lucifer. "There are many things the devil refuses to let go. I have never allowed that to deter me. Ever."

"You must believe me. Let it happen. Let me go."

"I can't do that, Durudee. I'm sent here to save you, no matter what you've done. This is my purpose tonight." The intent of her earlier question of how many I haven't saved, now becomes very clear.

The strike of footsteps echo from the emptiness behind me. They're coming for her. How many will there be? Sounds as if at least four. Will this be another life I won't be able to save?

"If their plan is to kill you no matter what, why wait 'till night? Why not in daylight?"

"To create sheer terror. To show anyone who will oppose them that their reach is beyond security walls and body guards."

Nocturnal kills as psychological warfare, not for any other purpose. This gang is merciless, doing Lucifer's bidding and intent on breaking me down until I join them. Tonight, they may find a worthy foe. Although, I must come to terms with the idea that, even if I succeed, she may still die.

"Why do they want you, Durudee?" The first of the goons leaves the shadows.

"Jaime. Just leave."

"I can't. What are they after other than political leverage?"

"I know their plan. The Dark Angel pollen, I used it to extract information from one of their guards."

Two more men in black suits join the one in front. I recognize them from the fight at this same river earlier in the evening. One who had his nose broken and the one whose wrist met a similar fate. Their pain controlled by narcotics, undoubtedly, they've returned for vengeance.

Another male and a female materialize from the shadows, headed our direction. The third male from the fight. But where's the naked woman-killer?

"What did you learn from him? The guard?"

"Well, they don't like you much."

"That's surprising." My sarcasm isn't lost on her.

"I hear you."

I turn back to her. Such a young and very American expression for someone her age.

"But the next revelation was their plan to mass-produce the plant to dump into the water supply of major cities around the world. They've already tested it in areas of the United States that are less noticeable — smaller towns, wide open areas — to see how easily they could infect a large area of the populace. People agreeing to some of the most ridiculous ideas their government officials proposed. They will need their own force to complete their final plan. I was sent back to Thailand by your government to follow the trail. It led me into filthy water I couldn't wash from my soul."

Her heart may still be pure, regardless of the mess she has found herself embroiled in. The undercover work she did in service of America has led her to this. How many others have fallen prey due to their work on behalf of a cold government agency that knowingly sacrifices people for their cause?

"Jaime, I volunteered for this mission," she breaks in, like she can read my thoughts.

"Where are the plantations?" I watch the group of five advancing our direction. Their stride is slow and casual like they're in no hurry. Maybe their repugnant boss is still trying to fall asleep and they're waiting for him. I feel another presence enter. Is that him?

"The fields lie just across the northeastern border, into Laos, just above the Mekong river. I gave you the map earlier," she whispers.

Oh, she is sly, this one. She slipped the map to me, hoping I would chase down the field and kill their mind control crop. "Tell me about the stability of the plant. Is it hardy or feeble?"

"It's a very stable and hardy plant. But it does have one nemesis."

"And that is?"

"Roundup."

"The weed killer?"

She nods.

Huh. "Is there anyone else besides you and me who knows this plantation exists?"

"I didn't dare tell any of my assistants. I have no idea who I can trust. Have no idea who might have been infected by the plant or turned traitor to save their life or the life of a family member. Everyone around me has or will betray me. That is, all except Ananda. Jaime, tell him I loved him more than any mother ever could love their child and that I'm sorry I brought him here to Thailand."

"I have no plans of doing that tonight, Durudee. My strategy is to get you out of this dream alive."

The group stops mid-way on the bridge, waiting. I step forward and wave Durudee to keep her behind me.

"They'll kill me anyway. It doesn't matter anymore. I betrayed my country. And yours. I betrayed you, the one who saved my son from these same people decades ago. I owed you my life and this is what I've done to you."

Her words turn in my mind and my stomach. What is she

saying? "You're talking nonsense."

"Listen to me. I knew about the murder on your flight before it happened. I was to bring charges and put you away. You would have died in prison, probably the first night. When I saw who it was, that it was you they wanted dead, I couldn't go through with it. I couldn't lock you up. I owed you my life and the life of my Ananda." She hesitates, lines of worry creasing her face as she watches me grapple with all she's said. "I'm sorry for what I've done. They have manipulated me like a puppet, using me to put away anyone who stands in their way by threatening Ananda."

"It all makes sense, now." I ponder her words then realize... "And the air marshal?"

"Yes. He was in on it, also."

I *knew* it! Bastard. Their reach goes all the way to the Americas. There's no telling how many in my government have been used by these assholes to accomplish their malicious purpose. So many of the appalling laws that have been passed lately now have a deeper meaning.

"Why aren't they moving?" I ask.

"I don't know. Maybe they're waiting for you to make the first move, step out of the way to let me go to them."

"Well, if that's what they're waiting for, we'll be here a long time. And I'm not that patient. Stay close to me, no matter what. Out of arm's reach, of course, but close enough that I can protect you."

"I beg of you, Jaime, let it be. Tell Ananda for me, then leave the country. They will let him be. If you will get out of Thailand. Go north. Kill their fields."

"I'm sorry, Durudee. I *cannot* leave you. I'm incapable of standing by while a life is taken. I can't."

"Then you must know, there is a soldier standing at my bedside. If I wake, still alive, he will behead me."

A sharp pain shoots through my core and my body turns cold. "Oh, my God. There truly is no way out for you." My eyes fill with tears as I realize the implication of what she's said.

"I would rather take the honorable death. Let me fight them and perish like a warrior. It's the way I would prefer to be remembered. A warrior." Her dark eyes stare back at mine, not a tear glints in them, only determination.

"Then we'll fight together. Like warriors. I would be honored to help take down as many of them as possible before the end."

"You mean, kill them all?" she asks, and I swallow back the word *kill* then slowly nod. "If that is what you must do. I understand fully. However, will you do one thing for me?"

"I'll try," I whisper, "what is it?"

"Will you give me the privilege of taking my life before they do?"

"What?" Another bolt of electricity shoots through me at her request. "No. I can't. I told you. Please don't ask me to do that," I softly plead.

"It's a matter of dignity. I would rather *you* kill me than one of them. There's honor in dying by an angel's sword, if your heart is pure. My quest to set this right purifies me to accept your fatal wound."

My thoughts trail to Ananda by the river, then the fight after. He'll know. He'll hate me. "What would Ananda think?" I choke out the words.

"That I died in my sleep, victim of a criminal because of the work I do. He will never suspect an angel ended my life. Tell him you tried to save me, because it's true." She smiles, but a tear escapes to her cheek, forsaking her strength. "Promise me."

If I do this, I will never be able to face him again. My

courage is broken like a fragile vessel. The air is sucked out of me as I stare into her eyes, gathering the strength to say the words I know I'll regret. "I promise."

Her warm hands reach up and caress both sides of my face as more tears mark a trail down each cheek. "You," she begins and takes a deep, shuddering breath, "are the second greatest gift God could have sent. Thank you." She sniffs and wipes the tears from her chin. Her face is set and prepared for her fate. "Now, let's get this over with."

I bow my head, my eyes closed. Then I turn my face to hers, my sullen resolve aching in my chest. "Are you ready?"

She nods her answer and we turn to those who await us. I dip my head downward with my eyes centered on the five. My hand instinctually slips to my abdomen and the tiny life inside. *Be strong my love.* I'll do all in my power to protect you.

God, forgive me for the lives I'm about to take. Although my request is to Him, it is myself that I'm truly asking for forgiveness.

We move forward, our gait steady and purposeful, skipping from one railroad tie to the next, swiftly closing the distance between us. With each fall of my weight on the dark planks, I force the dread of what I must do from my mind — not merely my promise to take Durudee's life, but the necessity to take that of those ahead of me.

At approximately six meters out, they synchronize, pulling swords from behind their backs and cutting the air in front of them before taking a battle pose, right feet on the tie ahead of them. The sword and forearm protect their faces and the left feet rest on the tie behind them, stabilizing their stance. I hesitate, search the shadows surrounding us.

I count to three, then dash forward, skipping ties as I bound for the front man. The muscles in his arm flinch and I bend backwards to avoid the slice of his blade. The metal skims my chest and abdomen. *Oh, shit!* That was too close. While the weapon takes a pendulum swing away from me, I reach for it with my left hand, twist it from its owner, and slice off his hand at the wrist. Tossing the hilt to my right hand, I turn and drive the blade up under his ribcage. He slumps forward, and I pull the weapon from him. His life force falls in a red puddle at my feet, leaking between the ties to the water below.

Without missing a beat, the two behind him continue forward with their swords slicing the air at the same time toward my throat. I lean backward, then bow to let the blades cross over me while mine continues a full circle above my head, slicing the abdomens of each of them and splitting them wide open. Before the weapon of the thug on my left hits the deck, I kneel on one leg and catch the hilt in my free hand. The freed sword on my right lands on the plank of my blade and I whip it backward to Durudee. With two swords in hand, I slice the air, then bring them to rest in front of me to make a protective X across my body. Awaiting the final two, my head bows while my eyes still watch them.

The third wave has already begun their advance, blades moving in unison as the woman among them spins past her companion, dancing over ties in a mesmerizing arabesque of motion. Making her way toward me, she avoids the bodies of her fallen comrades and swings her weapon toward my throat while spinning past me. I stop the forward progression with one sword as I also block a second whisking toward me from the opposite direction with the weapon in my opposing hand. Backing toward the female, I draw the male to follow, both slicing in syncopated timing. While keeping my eyes on both sides, I block and parry at varying intervals as my opponents move in for the kill.

With the distance closing between us, I have difficulty

making fluid movements that might surprise my adversaries. My swipes become tighter and faster in succession. Unable to move lithely, I miss a swipe and turn so that my shoulder takes the blow meant for my chest.

"Shit!"

"Jaime!" Durudee cries out.

"I'm fine," I call back in a strained voice, gritting my teeth and wincing each time I raise my arm to swing the blade. *Damn! Forget the pain. Remember what you were taught.*

Soon there won't be enough room for me to move and I could be seriously, even fatally, injured. But I have a promise to keep for Durudee and my child to save.

Shouting out into the emptiness of the dream world with a guttural cry, using my full might, I hit a support of the bridge with the pommel of the sword in my right hand, then spin to catch the blade of the male, but miss hers cutting the air toward my throat. From the corner of my eye I see another sword slice the air. Durudee's sword blocks the strike that would have connected with my throat. She slashes the woman's arm. Her screams are swallowed into the night. With her momentarily injured and distracted, I cry out again and hit another support with my pommel. I block a weak slice from her and parry a more forceful thrust from the opposite direction. One more agonized cry rolls up my throat. A third clank rings out as the hilt of my sword hits the upright and the prisoners' bridge whines.

My adversaries hesitate, glancing upward to the swaying bridge. The suspension above us yields to the pressure and a metal beam snaps. Taking advantage, I swing my swords and slice the throats of the two perplexed assailants. Blood drains into their clothing like deep red ink in the dark. Their faces contort in surprise then turn expressionless as they fall to my feet.

"Jaime!" Durudee's voice rises above the groan of the metal. "You did it! That was spectacular!" Then her expression turns sullen. "But you have one more." Her smile turns to sullen regret. She's talking about herself.

"No. Not yet. There's another,"

"But you promised."

"There's one more to kill before I can fulfill my promise to you." He won't get away from me this time.

Her eyes question me as she shakes her head in confusion. "I don't understand."

"If these five were the last in the dream besides us, we'd be awake now."

"You mean, you might not have killed me? You would have allowed me a dishonorable death, not the one you promised. How could you—"

"No. Durudee, I sensed another. He's waiting to see me take your life, so he can wake safe in his own bed. If I kill you, I wake immediately, and he gets away free. Your death will have no meaning. I must cut off the head of this snake tonight. He has to die before I wake."

"I don't care if he lives. Please, I beg of you, kill me now."

"I can't. Trust me. I'll give you the death you request and the honor you deserve. But you must be patient. The future of the world may revolve around this one person. If it's who I think it is, I've met up with him already and he has to die tonight." I remember the poor woman waiting for her fate, encased in a clear box as I struggled, ineffectively, to stop him.

Although she nods in understanding, I see her doubt.

From behind me I hear a slow clap of hands and the air of the bridge shifts like the wind. A sweet aroma fills my mind again as I turn toward him.

"The jasmine. It was you. At the hotel. Here." I stop and peruse the black slacks and white dress shirt. "At least you have pants. A definite improvement." He smiles back at me. "Still ugly, though."

He grins and offers an amused chuckle, then his expression turns sober. "You killed my favorite guards. I underestimated you." The smile grows on his face once again as I study his expression. "Just as you've underestimated me."

"Oh? Please share."

"Happily, you see, just as your friend's sleeping body has a guard standing over her with a sword, so does yours. I so enjoyed touching your lips as you slipped into REM, kissing you good-bye for the world." His glistening eyes narrow on me and I shudder. "Regardless of the outcome tonight. Both of you will die as you wake."

"Really? Why not just have them kill me now, before I ram this sword up your ass where it belongs?"

He throws his head back for a full, throaty roar of laughter. "You are a barrel of fun! Better than monkeys, I imagine. No. I want to be the one to play with you before you die." He steps forward with the confidence of a psychopath, circling his prey. "This could take mere minutes. Or, it could be drawn out far longer. Let's see how much time we can expend playing adult games, shall we?"

"Really, old man? You should be aware you are definitely too out of shape to play with me." I eye him from head to toe. "And certainly not my type. I prefer the mentally stable."

"I'm going to enjoy killing you," he answers with a smile.

"Well then, asshole, I see no other reason to hold back. I look forward to hearing your fat ass panting for air before I separate your head from your shoulders. In the meantime, let's see how painful I can make this for you…before we die. Because, you *will* suffer before I'm finished with you. I promise you that."

His laughter fills my head again. "You're certainly

entertaining for a bubble-headed bitch. If only the Dark Angel's Trumpet worked on you. You would make a great addition to my collection of powerful allies and sex toys." He begins to circle, but I turn to keep him in front of me.

"And you would make a great addition to my human skin stuffed sofa collection. Of course, we'd have to remove that unsightly growth on the top of your neck. That over-stretched pie hole flaps far too often for my taste. Now cut the bullshit and let's get on with this." I offer a sarcastic bow with my eyes still targeting his and the middle finger of my free hand extended toward him. "Shall we?"

I step forward. My feet stick in the coagulating blood on the bridge as I move from one crosstie to the next over lifeless bodies.

His lips curl into a devious grin. "If only we could've had more time together. I'm positive you'd have found a good reason to stay. After all, I find it unfathomable that you would let your husband die at the end of my sword. Yet, here you are and there he is and when I'm finished with you…" He shrugs. "Well, you can watch what I do to him from *Hell*. Or, maybe that's a proposition you wouldn't mind. Seems you may have replaced him, already." The shape of his face narrows and his flesh changes until he is tall and thin, his features handsome and familiar.

"Ananda!" Durudee shouts and moves forward.

"No! Durudee, it's not him. He's trying to fool us," I shout, holding my sword out to stop her from running to him.

"Jaime! I know my own son," she insists.

"It's not him, I tell you."

"Yes, Mother, come to me," the bastard calls to her, holding his arms out. "Let me kill you for Jaime. Let me slit your throat myself."

A gasp escapes Durudee's pale lips. "Ananda," she

whispers.

"It's not him," I whisper back to her. "His eyes, the voice. They're not the same."

"How about that kiss, Jaime?" He smirks back at me.

"Can you just…shut. The Fuck. Up. The sound of your girlish voice grates on my nerves." His laughter echoes in my head as I force the thought of his appearance out of my mind.

Now, only three meters from him, I take one more crosstie then lunge at him with both swords as Durudee gasps again, but he disappears before the blade can tear open his flesh.

"Asshole," I whisper into the air and turn toward Durudee, knowing he will materialize somewhere near her or behind me. One of us will see him first and alert the other.

Once again slamming the butt of my sword into the steel arch, I send the freed I-beam into a wave above me. When the end bows within my reach, I grab hold. Using the beam to hoist myself, I flip through the air and land on the deck, behind the spot where he had been standing, and slash my sword. The man appears as he dives from the tip of my blade. His appearance has returned to his original state. *Ah ha.* Just as I thought. He can't pull his dream-changing tricks when distracted. I need to keep him busy to keep his mind from changing the scene on me. Especially his form.

I rush forward with my weapons swinging in cross-circular patterns above my head and around my body. By the time I reach my tricky opponent, he's found two of the weapons his guards carried. The hilts drip with blood as he rushes to grab them. I can't hesitate and give him the advantage. Luckily, he's caught off guard by my aggressive attacks and is forced into defensive mode; ducking and dodging as I swipe again and again, driving him backward. Unable to see where he's going and protect himself, he stumbles over one body, then crawls backward over another. Seems surprisingly agile for his weight. On the other hand, this *is* a dream.

One of my blades sweeps toward him again, then the other without end as he rises to his feet while dodging my onslaught. I have him on the run. Unable to watch the ground beneath him, one of his feet slips in a puddle of blood and the second finds only an unstable surface on top of the female guard's outstretched arm. He turns to catch his fall and tumbles to the bridge. My advantage.

Casually walking to his side, I place my foot on his throat and hold my blade to his chest while he looks up at me in astonishment.

"So, I'm about to die, am I?" I ask, then release the pressure of my foot and crouch beside him. With one knee where my foot had been on his neck, I bring myself closer to his ear. "So are you," I whisper then smile.

The look in his eyes shifts and a smile spreads across his face. Shit! I just gave him time to focus and set a trap. The bridge shifts and grows wider, longer, and I leap backward. Gaping holes appear between the railroad ties. The swords slip from my grip as I reach for a support beam to keep from falling into the water. Durudee falls forward, catching one of the ties to keep from plunging into the water. My large adversary is gone. I know he's here, but with him hiding, I can't tell where. There's only one way to find out. The only swords left on the bridge are those clutched tight in the grip of the last two guards.

"Durudee, do you swim?" I call out to her.

"Yes."

"Are you a strong swimmer?" I ask.

She shouts back, "Yes."

I jump to the tie where the lifeless bodies dangle above the flowing river. "Jump. Meet me on the shore." I pull the swords into my hands.

"Jaime, that's crazy," she shouts back.

I smile back at her to tell her I have a plan. "I know."

Fear tightens her brows and lips when she lets go of the squared plank and falls. As soon as she hits, there's a second splash. My cue. I drop between the ties and hit the river. Swimming after Durudee to the shore, I search for another disturbance in the water. By the time I reach the beach, I've located him. The swords are still tight in my grip. Durudee is ten meters from me. I watch her face as I trudge through the shallow wash toward her.

The closer I come, the slower I get, studying her expression. He'll do it. He's too arrogant not to show himself when he's about to kill. I'm counting on it. She gasps for air and I feel a slight breeze. The expression on her face turns curious as she watches me watch her. Then her brows raise, and she sucks in a quick breath. Simultaneously, I slash both swords to my sides, then behind me, feeling them connect with a solid mass. An agonized groan meets my ears.

Behind me, my foe is on his knees with his hands holding his gut. Inky blood oozes between his fingers. Durudee meets me in front of him.

"Jaime, you have to do it now. Now's the time. Take my life."

I turn to her, knowing he has a near fatal wound, but could still live. "You both have to die at once."

"Can't you see he's dying? Do it before he dies and we wake."

"He's only wounded. I have to be sure," I tell her. With his hands covering his wound, there's no telling how deep the slice goes. Regardless, I hope he lingers long enough for me to think of an out, any way to not take Durudee's life. There must be another way. Delaying his agony is only another small motivation I can't deny.

His eyes turn to mine, his lips tight with pain. "Why don't you get it over with, Jaime?" he taunts me. "You know you desire more blood on your hands."

"Maybe I'm enjoying the way your face crinkles when you wince."

"Jaime!" Durudee shouts back at me.

"Okay, Durudee," I acquiesce. "How do you want me to do it?" I ask, stalling as long as I can.

"Through the heart. I want you to..." She swallows. "Pierce...my..."

My heart skips and I shake my head. The asshole chokes and his head has fallen to his chest. There's little time left. I may garner some amount of childish entertainment from watching him suffer, but I do owe Durudee my full attention, even if I would rather not do as I've promised. I understand why she wants me to be the one to take her life, rather than his assassin. To take that pleasure from those who planned her death is a sentiment I can get behind. And in her culture, it's more honorable to be killed by the one you betrayed than the one who betrayed you. Still, I'd prefer to find an alternative. Nevertheless, even if she lives the night, there will always be another minion of Satan, waiting for her to sleep.

The demon coughs and his body slumps further. Could be an act. Hard to tell. The voice inside me is shouting to deny her request. But, how can I? Honor is everything in Durudee's culture. And, she is a brave woman who has already suffered too much at the hands of Lucifer's agents. At the very least, she deserves to deny them the pleasure of killing her.

"Hold still," I instruct her, turning the hilt of the sword, shifting the positioning of my hand, and placing the point to the left and slightly below her sternum, between the ribs. The blade is parallel to the ground.

With the other sword at the dying man's throat, held in the

hand of my weak arm, I tighten my grip on both weapons. As I'm about to follow through, I notice a smirk forming across the demon's face. His shoulders straighten, and he pulls his hand from his abdomen. There's something in his eyes. Something he knows that I don't. My heart pounds in my chest. What did I miss?

"Jaime, now!" Durudee cries and I flinch.

My left arm pulls the sword back then forward in a pendulum swing as the monster glares back at me with a knowing twinkle in the corner of his pupil. With a swift motion, I drive the sword in my right hand deep into Durudee's chest, while pulling the other through the air toward the demon. Before my blade reaches his carotid artery and his blood can spill from the impending wound, his hand flies up and catches the blade making the sword disappear.

Hell. He was the one controlling the dream from the beginning, imagined the swords into the hands of his guards. Only *he* could remove what he's conjured.

The sword reappears in his right hand, pointed toward me. Before I can pull the blade from Durudee's chest to block him, he drives the tip of his blade into my abdomen and I scream out into the night. *My baby!*

I grasp the blade of his sword tight against my abdomen and kick him backward before he can pull the blade sideways to tear me open. His lips spread to a wider grin, then his laughter fills my head as Durudee sinks to her knees. My blood turns to ice as the tar pits of his pupils dilate and I realize I haven't sent him to his grave. He may be the one to send me to mine, however.

He rises to his feet, his glare piercing mine. In his eyes is a secret beyond this dream. Something I need revealed for my own survival and that of the people of this earth. I pull the sword from my abdomen and the one on my right drops to the dissipating ground beneath me as Durudee collapses.

Sucking in a deep breath, I immediately reach forward in my waking world with both hands to catch the assassin's blade swinging toward my throat. A sharp pain in my torso brings my hands to the hemorrhaging wound in my tummy, waiting for a sword to arc toward me and take my head in my weakness. To my surprise, there's no one here. He said someone would be here to kill me like Durudee. He lied.

I'm awake, in my hotel suite, my hands holding my life inside of me. There was no assassin sent to kill me as I wake. My room is empty. It was a lie. *Holy mother of God*. My hands shake uncontrollably as I realize what I've done. They hadn't sent anyone to murder Durudee, either. I killed her on a lie.

CHAPTER 13

The tear in my abdomen sends shocks through me like shards of glass. It is agony, nearly as torturous as the night I was impaled by a pole. But this ache isn't nearly as powerful as the thought that haunts my mind. The blade I ran through her chest, between her ribs, straight into her heart. The gasp of pain as blood throbbed from her wound, around my sword. Her glittering eyes, once full of life, dilating in death. When the sharp metal of his weapon ripped through me, I knew I'd lost two lives I once fought to save, Durudee's and my baby's. Will I ever forgive myself? My heart is heavier than I can bear. More than I've ever known before now.

Rising from the mattress is torment. But there is so much I must do before the sun rises too high in the sky. First, I must leave this hotel. Someone is bound to find a way to detain me and have me arrested. After I have a chance to clean up and dress my wound best I can, I pack my belongings ignoring the stabbing reminder of my last dream and check out of the hotel. A taxi whisks me away as I search my purse for the paper where Ananda scribbled his phone number.

"Watch every car," I warn the driver in Thai. "There's a big tip in the end if you aren't followed." Then I gasp and cringe from another searing spasm in my belly.

My brief conversation with Ananda is far worse than I anticipated. My heart is ripped from my chest—cold, hard, barely beating—when he refuses to believe I couldn't save her. After all he witnessed the night before, he won't concede that it was out of my control. Perhaps if I try harder to convince him. But I can't find it in me to pretend I did all I could. I know she would've lived had I denied her request, at least another day. If he had any idea what she was involved in, he would know her life has hung by a thread for some time. As much as he tries to hide his pain, raw emotions leak through in the crack of his voice while I deliver her final words to him. Without another sound from him, the line goes dead. I don't have a chance to offer an insincere apology. I'm numb with grief for Durudee, but more so for my baby. And I'm a monster.

Being cautious to protect my wound, I gather my backpack and purse, then ask the driver to pull over. I throw him twenty times the amount owed and head down the street. So far, there seems to be no tagalongs. No one following me. My first stop is a tourist shop to buy binoculars.

My stride is quick with my core protected from further injury. The half of a bloody sheet I wrapped tight around me is holding the muscles firm. Still, my arm across my midriff helps to steady me. The adrenaline coursing through my veins keeps me surprisingly vertical as I maneuver the morning crowd.

When my pace quickens, I notice a man behind me hasten his, also. A guard or an informant? I have to get out of the open. Spotting a clothing shop up ahead, I race through the throngs of people, past the door of the boutique and through the marketplace. My tag follows, but loses me in the sea of lives, allowing me to double back.

Inside the store, much of what is up front is traditional Thai clothing. Beautiful silk garments made in the traditional manner. This clothing is intended for tourists. Not someone who wants to hide.

Further inside are clothes influenced by western culture. Smaller fixtures display jeans, t-shirts, dresses, and skirts. Very little time passes while I flip through the rack to find something appropriate. After I pay, I pull on the jeans, a deep red shirt and pair of tennis shoes, leaving my black clothing behind in the fitting room. On the way out the door, I spot a hat and large purse. These will do nicely. I turn to the clerk holding a thousand baht. She smiles and nods, so I place the notes on the table where the items were displayed then dump the contents of my backpack into the purse, twist my hair into a knot and head for the door dressed in my new clothes and the hat covering my head.

With my hand tightening on the handle, a man dressed in black opens the door from the outside and holds it for me to pass by. Once outside, I turn back to see him question the store clerk who is by the table, slipping the money in her pocket and shaking her head. She tells him the person he describes is not there. Her eyes shoot a nervous glance to me as if she's urging me to go. She follows him when he moves through the store, insisting on searching anyway.

In the marketplace, several sets of eyes search the crowd. Men and women conspicuously dressed all in black. Those around the stores seem to be aware of who they are and how dangerous they can be. They do their best to avoid anyone dressed like them. The henchmen study every person who passes. Even with a change of clothes, there's no way I could pass through their gauntlet without a distraction. Chances are high of one of them stopping me. I study the shoppers. They amble through the market appearing casual, speaking with another person or striding confidently toward their destination, as if they don't even notice the menacing force around them. The searchers ignore groups of two or more.

That's it. I need a cover. And I just happen to see him heading my way. A twenty-something young man with dark hair, casual clothes like mine, and wearing a pair of wireframe glasses. He leads a bike at his side. Double bonus.

"I have a bike just like that one," I tell him in Thai.

He smiles, as if he wonders if I'm speaking to him.

"But I left it in Shanghai," I lie, trying to spark a conversation. But he keeps walking past me. "You have a nice face," I call to him and he stops and turns my way. "Can I walk with you?" I ask.

He peers around him, then back at me in surprise. The smile on his face grows wider and he nods his head. I speed up my pace to catch him, then hook my arm in his.

We pass guards on our left and our right. I pretend to have a focused conversation with my face turned fully to his. But my thoughts are on the ones who search for me. I speed up my stride, encouraging the boy to join me.

Within a matter of minutes, he tells me he's a farm boy who left his home to find a life in the city. I softly ask his name so the guards don't hear, and I ask how long he's lived in Bangkok, periodically turning back to the front of the store I just left. The guard is still searching.

"My name is Aat," he tells me proudly, figuring I'm aware that his name means *Daring*. "I moved to Bangkok when I was seventeen. I work here." He points to a stand of fruit in front of a small food store. I turn back to see the door of the clothing store fling wide and the guard rush out with black clothing in his hands.

"I'd love to see inside. And I need some fruit," I tell Aat

and squeeze his arm with my hand.

He smiles back at me. His eyes sparkle with hope. "Come."
He pulls the door open, waves at me, and I step past him.
Then he leads his bike inside and behind a counter. I stay near
the door and watch the commotion outside.

"Aat," I say and he stops and turns to me. "I also need a
bike," I tell him and nod toward his. He shakes his head
emphatically. Did I say it wrong? "No, no, no. I want to buy
your bike," I try again. Again, he shakes his head and speaks
too fast for me to understand his words. I raise my hands to
calm him, then reach into my bag to pull out two thousand
baht and show it to him. "Please. For your bike."

Again, he seems agitated and speaks far too fast for me to
understand. I put the money away then hold up my hands
again, trying to calm him, watching the door for anyone
heading our way. I may need to rush out the back door if he
continues to carry on like this.

"I'm sorry. I'm sorry," I try to concede. His speech slows
and I'm finally able to understand what he has to say.

"No, no. Not my bike. My friend. He sells bikes. Less cost,"
he protests. "You buy a new bike. This one doesn't work."

Oh. That's why he was upset. He didn't want to sell it
because it doesn't work. No wonder he was walking instead of
riding. He opens the door and directs my attention to a store
several meters ahead.

"You go there. He will give you a good deal."

Grasping his hand, I put some Thai notes in his palm and
close his fingers, staring into his eyes with appreciation.
"Thank you." He shakes his head, but I put my hand on his
cheek. "To buy a new bike. Please."

He hesitates, worry creasing his brow, then he grins back
and nods. I kiss him on the cheek then leave for the bike seller,
walking as if I belong on that street.

Purchasing the bike takes less time than I anticipate. I hand the clerk twelve hundred baht and accept the change before rolling my new ride to the exit. When I'm almost there, the door swings open and a guard steps in. His eyes search the room like a pro. My heart pounds in my chest and I turn back to shelves of bicycle helmets and kneel beside them as if I'm searching for one that will fit me. My insides are raw as if a metal instrument claws at my flesh. I hold my breath. Blood soaks my t-shirt, leaving spots on the bag each time it brushes my tummy. The young man who sold the bike kneels beside me.

"You need one?"

I smile back at him and nod. He selects one that would fit my head with the hat still on, then adjusts the straps for me.

"Two hundred baht," he tells me, still grinning.

I hand him three hundred and he tries to hand back the extra hundred, but I close it in his hand. He catches my eyes when they flicker to the guard at the counter. He nods, then stands and pulls me to my feet, keeping his body between me and the man speaking with his boss. Our gazes meet, speaking more than we dare say. He nods at the door and I turn away. He rushes ahead of me and pulls open the door, holding it for me to pass. I thank him as I pass. Once outside, I turn a sharp right. On my bike, I pedal slowly past the last guard on the street, keeping my eyes forward as he gives me the once over and turns his attention to the next person.

On the street, my speed picks up as I pedal past numerous impatient drivers until I'm nearly to the edge of the city. Once I'm far enough away from the market district, I ditch the bicycle and the helmet, then catch a taxi headed north.

The driver takes me to a car rental office where I drop a considerable amount of baht on the counter for their worst car and no questions. He shoves the money in his pocket, drops a set of keys on the counter and turns his back. The rusted heap I just bought may get me as far as Laos, but there's no assurance I'll reach my destination. Chances are, they'll report it stolen before the end of the day. Ditching it when it gives out will be the best result for the poor piece of worn out junk.

Once the starter finally turns over, I set out in search of a Thai equivalent of an Ace hardware store. Within an hour, I'm headed northeast to Laos with a trunk full of the Thai version of Round-Up and a map scribbled in red marker. Luckily, Durudee thought to write the coordinates so I could drive directly to the fields with my phone's GPS guiding the way.

CHAPTER 14

The three-day drive is torture. Blood still seeps from my wound at times, but the amount has decreased. Each unprepared twist sends fire, like molten glass, along the nerves in my abdomen. I force my eyes to remain open. My focus has to be the plantations. As soon as that's done, I can head to Ireland before I collapse. No planes this time. It's too risky. And no hospitals, either. There's no doubt they'd look for me there. No medical professionals could be trusted. This wound is too suspicious. I can't trust they wouldn't immediately call the police. I doubt I could even trust Ananda now. My baby has died. I'm sure of it. And with it, my heart. If this is my last act, to save the world from this flower, then I'd better do so before there is no strength left in me.

The sun dips below the horizon just as I reach my destination on the third day. I pull my car to the side of the road and reach for the binoculars in my bag to scan the horizon. The breath and my resolve are nearly ripped from me, seeing more than two hundred acres of plants, guarded by men in military uniforms with semi-automatic weapons. She didn't say there were so fucking many flowers. She didn't say there would be armed guards. I collapse to my knees, peering across at the vast fields. As I'm about to give up, a hiss fills the air, then sprays of water shoot from a sprinkler system across the field, feeding the plants. *Oh, shit.*

Scanning the horizon again, I search for the water that feeds the irrigation system. In the middle of the field I spot a containment pond. Calculating the number of cubic liters of water compared to the bags of poison in the trunk, I'm positive there's enough to bring down a plantation twice this size with this sort of irrigation. I'd prepared for a different scenario. *I'll be damned.* The plants will be doused with enough to kill them twice. But I still have the guards to get past. Military guards, nonetheless. When I focus my sight directly on them I notice something else. They aren't wearing any face masks. Nothing to protect them from the pollen? Is it because they're already under the control of the ones who planted these fields? Yes. I think I can do this.

Back in the car, I pack the binoculars into the glovebox and start the engine. Then I head toward the irrigation water containment pond. I pull my vehicle up to the water, then get out and march into the field and pick an armful of dark angels. While I'm still plucking stems, footsteps approach.

"Hands up!" he shouts, and I turn to see him with a gasmask on his face and a handgun trained on me.

Clutching the bundle of tubers in my arms, I tilt my head into them and take a deep whiff with my eyes still on him. The corner of his lips curve upward to a cynical smirk and he holsters his weapon, believing I'm controlled by the pollen. He took the bait. Smiling back, I step forward with *my* weapon clutched tight to my chest, biting back the pain in my abdomen.

"Hello," I greet him as he approaches.

He reaches for my arm and pulls me toward him, sending

shards of pain through my abdomen. When his face is close enough to mine, I pull off his gasmask and blow pollen into him. His eyes gloss over and the cynicism falls from his jawline.

"Are you my pet, now?" I ask, and he nods. "Show me. Bark softly for me." Without delay, the man lets out a solid *woof*. It works. *Thank you, God!* Now to get this finished.

"Now, my pet, I want you to call two of your boys and tell them to meet you at the containment pond, and pronto. Both of them. Got it?"

As I instructed, my soldier sets off to meet the two nearest guards, one at a time, and lure them to the field while I rest and try to control the pain. As soon as they are distracted by me, he removes their masks then I blow more pollen into their faces. I have three willing participants, thanks to the dark flower and its hypnotic effect on them.

Having these men here was more fortuitous than I originally thought. I overestimated my strength in light of my wound and level of exhaustion. I'll need them all to get this trunk emptied and the poison into the pond.

Warms the cockles when your bad guy does what he's told. "Good boy. You're being so obedient. While I wave pollen in the air, I want you to open the trunk of my car and start unloading all the sacks of fertilizer into the irrigation water for the fields. The flowers need the nourishment. Do you understand me?"

He nods his head again and turns toward the rear of my car.

"Wait!" I call to him and his progression stops. "You need the key."

The unaware little soldier returns and takes the key from me, then continues to his task. *Hmm.* Far easier than I thought.

While he opens the trunk and lifts sacks from the vehicle, I wave the pollen into the air, then wait as the rest of the gang arrives. The agent is fast-acting, quite a bit more than I'd thought. They're immediately set on task with that glazed look in their eyes. Not leaving anything to chance, I beat the lilies against my hand to knock free the last vestiges of powder and send it into the sky to fall on my helpful slaves.

Once every bag of weed killer in my possession is emptied into the pond, I sit back behind the steering wheel while the sprinklers continue to cover the field in glistening death to the Dark Angels. When I'm assured that every corner is bathed, I rise slowly from my car and turn to the captain of the group.

"Don't let the sprinklers turn off until this pond is empty, that's an order."

He snaps to attention and salutes. "Yes, ma'am!"

"That's a good little soldier."

I sure hope this works, or I spent a lot of wasted time. With the sun behind the distant fields, I get in the vehicle and head south, back into Thailand. The nagging thought twists through my mind as I drive: this was too easy. How were they not more prepared for something like this?

***

Long before the light breaks the horizon, the fatigued and abused vehicle breathes its last sigh. Its last gasp isn't nearly as far from the fields as I had hoped. At least we've breached the border. With my head weary from exhaustion and blood loss, I leave the car behind and head out on foot.

The sun is hot, too hot. Or it could be a fever. I only know that the drops of sweat trickling between my shoulder blades and down the backs of my knees help distract my mind from the burn in my abdomen. More than ten hours click by while I trudge too many miles to count, keeping to the side of the road. Won't be long before they realize what I've done, as their precious flowers wither to nothing. I don't kid myself that this was the only field under their control. At minimum, they have the capacity to plant more. Just not there. A small consolation for this weary mind. I can only hope my efforts derail their operation long enough for me to gain my strength. Whatever it is they had planned for this toxic lily, I can only hope there's not another plantation, or more seeds to start another.

The sun beats down throughout the day as my feet strike the road one after the other. The pain in my core is a dull ache that pounds through my body. I haven't time to replenish lost fluid. I'm barely able to keep going. Soon enough, the sun drifts past the horizon once again.

Few vehicles travel the roads I've chosen. Only two in the many hours that I've been here. My legs are weak, my eyesight failing, and I'm barely able to stay vertical, but the glint of headlights in the distance gives me hope and I wave my arms to catch his attention. The driver pulls to the side of the road and waits for me to climb into his rusty old farm truck. Barely able to pull myself up to the seat, my body sinks into the torn, filthy vinyl. He doesn't speak a word of English, so we converse in Thai. The better news is, he's going my direction. At least, far enough to get me a good distance from the Dark Angels and those who will be looking for me. Then I'll catch a ride with the next old car or truck heading further away.

The red of my t-shirt masks most of the blood making the fabric stiff at my midriff. At least I was able to put a good distance between me and Laos, regardless of how much damage it placed on my body and soul. Tears of frustration fill my eyes as I force my attention to the road. With my hands clutching the handle of my purse while I cling to the last vestiges of awareness, of my strength, and my consciousness. From the corner of my eye, I can't help but notice the farmer glancing toward the fresh circle of blood darkening my jeans. As much as I fight to stay awake and aware, darkness steals my will and I fall into a vacant, endless chasm.

CHAPTER 15

Startled by a foreign sound, my eyes snap open to a yellowed ceiling above me and a mattress on the floor beneath me. Hushed voices speak in Thai in the distance, wondering about me and from where I came. In a panic, I jolt up to defend myself, but the pain in my side and my weak limbs force me back down. A wet cloth falls from my forehead to my chest.

A fever. Infection. My wound.

The length of my braid is laid over my right shoulder and down my chest. To keep it out of the way, I suppose. The t-shirt and jeans have been removed. So has the partial bedsheet I wrapped around my abdomen. I'm only covered by a threadbare blanket.

My left arm feels nearly healed. On the other hand, my abdomen still aches, but the pain is far less.

My baby. Gone. Oh, my God. I was so focused on killing the flowers, I had no time to think of what their desire to preserve that flower killed in me. Another life lost.

I never had a chance to meet him. To hold him in my arms and tell him I love him. When I reach Ireland, there will be no bassinet beside my bed in the coming months. I could have taught him to fight. Like my father taught me. I could have made him a fierce warrior, like my family did for me.

Oh God. Why? Why did you trust that life to me? You had to know everything I touch I kill. Even the things I love. The ache in my chest is greater than the one in my abdomen. I can barely breathe, and tears burn my eyes. Another life lost. Another death on my hands. My own child. And Collin's. Will he ever find a way to forgive me? Collin could have stopped this from happening, had I stayed. How can I ever face him again? How can I face myself? What reason will I have to live, once I return to fighting in my dreams?

I roll to my side to rise to my knees, but the stabbing ache in my abdomen brings me down again. The farmer and his wife rush to my side, rolling me to my back.

"You stay here," she tells me in her language.

"I need to get up," I reply in my best attempt at speaking Thai. "There's a baby—" I begin, but she reaches for my hand and nods her head instead. "No, the baby died. Inside of me. My infection, it's the baby. It has to be removed or the infection will kill me."

She shakes her head and places the heel of her hand on my shoulder to hold me in place. "You rest, now. Your baby need rest," she answers and smiles.

She doesn't understand. "My baby died," I try again, sobbing and feeling ice spreading through my heart and into my soul. I'm so empty. So empty. "Right here." I point to the wound in my abdomen. "Right here," I repeat in English, this time. "The baby died inside of me. I need to have it removed," I tell her again in broken Thai.

She shakes her head again. "No. Your baby lives."

She takes my hand and places it beside the wound in the center of my abdomen. I don't believe her, but I keep my hand there with hope burning in my chest. There's nothing. She's wrong. Numbing bitterness robs me of my will and I grit my teeth in anger.

Then I feel it.

Only a flutter at first. Then the movement grows more prominent. When I look down at the wound, I realize it falls to the left of my bellybutton. He missed. Oh, my God. The baby was too small, and he missed. I must've been so wrapped with Durudee's demise, and what I thought was that of my child, that I didn't notice. Tears flood my eyes again and I can't control the sobs rising up my throat. Years of ache and hatred spill from me in tiny pools, streaming from my eyes to the hair at my temples. The woman pats my hand and replaces the washcloth on my forehead.

"You rest, now," she tells me, pulling the sheet to my throat. "Your baby lives."

My baby lives. My eyelids grow heavy with relieved exhaustion and I let sleep take me.

***

My eyes open again to find my environment hasn't changed. The bite in my belly is gone when I roll to my side and I'm able to rise to my knees. But my muscles are still very weak. My arms wobble as I try to keep my balance. Again, the farmer's wife returns to my side, lowering me to the mattress. She pats me on the shoulder to tell me to stay put as she leaves for her kitchen. Within moments, she returns with a steaming bowl, carved from wood. The spoon in her hand was cut and pounded from a piece of scrap metal. Rust pits the surface. Well, at least I'll get some much-needed iron to help with the lost red blood cells. And my body desperately needs the fluid. I take sips each time she brings the spoon to my mouth. My lips crack when I try to smile. Dehydration. It's a miracle I lived. Maybe, if I'm lucky, the one who did this to me believes me dead, also.

Seems as though I've been here in their tiny home for at least a week. If those who want me dead are still searching, it's only a matter of time before they find me. This may be the best place to hide, a simple farm house with little in the way of technology. And then I realize.

I swallow the soup in my mouth then turn from the next spoonful. "Does anyone know I'm here?" I ask her.

She shakes her head.

"Are you sure? No one?" I continue pressing her.

"No one. We afraid you bring death. We tell no one."

Oh. Good. And damn. They're a very superstitious culture. What must they believe about me? I came to them bleeding like a stuck pig. They can't have anything but fear for what my presence means here. I consider telling them I'm safe, that no harm will come to them, but think better of it. If word spreads of an injured woman found hitchhiking, the wrong person could be brought to their door. All of us may be killed. They need to fear my presence so much they wouldn't tell a soul.

"Fine. I won't hurt you." I point to my wound. "The devil, he did this. He will...he will kill all of us. Tell no one, or he will hear, and he will come. Do you understand?"

I spoke to her in her language. Of course, she understands. She nods and pats my hand like a mother to her child, then scoops another spoonful of soup. God, I hope she understands.

Within another day of downing as much soup and water as my shrunken stomach can handle, the strength returns to my muscles. I find the ability to walk and eventually journey outside. Turns out they live in the mountainous region of Mae Hong Son, near the border of Myanmar. The night the farmer found me, he travelled nearly two hundred kilometers to buy seed for the next planting season. He only travels that road twice a year. Our paths crossing at that exact moment was pure luck. Or somebody above looking out for me. A day later, an hour slower, and my corpse would have been found decomposing into the earth.

Chickens roam free outside the small building in which the couple lives. A goat bleats behind a rickety log pen, then kicks the dirt at its feet. Their crops are on a lower, flatter plot of land several kilometers away. The home is isolated and peaceful. But I can't stay long. My best avenue is to maintain my destination. Soon, I will need civilization. I'll need a midwife or someone to help me birth this baby. I place my hand over my tummy, feeling the growing fetus moving inside of me. I am so grateful he was small enough that the sword missed him.

In the evening, the husband returns, and a meal is laid out on a wooden table. A bowl of rice is set in front of the farmer, then me and the woman serves herself last. Another bowl with dark legumes, is also set in front of each of us. The same with a cooked vegetable I haven't had until now. Before I can reach for my food, the couple bow their heads in prayer, showing gratitude. Of all the years I've been on this earth, I've never once given thanks for what I had. And I had far more than this couple. The woman opens one eye and peers over at me until I close my eyes and bow my head. The prayer begins with a chant of five reflections.

Once they're finished, we eat. I shovel a heaping spoonful of rice into my mouth. The man and woman, however, separate a small morsel, lift it with their spoons and regard it, study it careful before placing it on their tongue with thoughtful motion. Each slight portion is chewed until every nutrient is extracted before another replaces it. I slow my eating and chew more slowly, thoughtfully, finding each bite more flavorful with patience and time. The woman smiles as my pace mimics theirs.

After the meal, they bow once again in thanks. The five reflections are repeated, and I feel my heart fill with gratitude for this couple. They may fear me, possibly despise me, but I am still grateful to them for not leaving me to die, and especially for showing me their grace, something difficult to find in this world at times. I decide not to ask their names. Having their identities in my mind could be treacherous for them if my thoughts are somehow robbed during a dream. After what happened in Bangkok, I can't take the chance.

The days that pass teach me patience I never knew before in my life. Each movement is deliberate. Every thought is on what I do, not my past, nor my future. My attention becomes more centered and focused. Within five short days, I am able to find deep inside of me the beginnings of the peace I have searched for. But I'm fully healed from my wounds and must move on. On this, the sixth night since I woke in their home, I tell them I must move on. A sense of sadness, mixed with relief, seems to cross their eyes.

We discuss my best route, through Myanmar, the northeastern edge of India, then into Nepal. Unfortunately, my travels will take me back through India and into Pakistan, Iran, and Turkey. Once I cross over into Europe, I will have the opportunity to breathe more easily. Until then, the farmer's wife gives me appropriate clothing and a hijab, instructs me on how to wear their clothing and how to speak. My dark hair keeps me from being seen as a total stranger. My green eyes complicate things a bit. "Speak Thai only," she warns.

The farmer and his wife load me and my belongings into their truck a few hours before dusk and drive me as far as they can. My drop off point is reached before midnight. They hug me and chant a prayer for my safety before releasing me into the night. I wave one last time before they pull the truck around and drive away.

The world awaits me. I put one foot forward, then the next, and begin my life anew.

CHAPTER 16

After traveling for months and experiencing the beauty of so many countries I've never seen before, I find I'm more at peace than I could have imagined. Some days, I eat with humble people, bow in prayer before their Gods, and meditate beside them in modest or elaborate temples. I learn to savor each moment as if it is all there is, say my prayers of gratitude, and feel thankful for all that I have in my life. My journey across the Far East and the Middle East is everything I never could have imagined in my past. The ache of Durudee's death still haunts me, however, regardless of how much I grow.

My months of travels finally lead me to my destiny. I arrive in the country I've loved in my heart my entire life. At the outset, I wander from one town to the next, touring castles and countryside I never knew existed. Sadly, I spent more time focusing on the past so that I never discovered the wonders of the world I was missing. Those places I'd seen in photographic form are greater in person than any picture could convey. As much as these sights will always be kept in my heart, reaching Dublin is the crowning jewel of my journey.

My arrival is greeted with a brief downpour, which the

locals say is commonplace. Afterward, rolling green hills glisten with dew outside this thriving but quaint city. This, the place I was born, is the siren song to my soul.

A sullen ocean rolls into the shoreline. The water foams and glints with afternoon sun. Strangers pass by, but none without offering some sort of greeting. It's peaceful here. This is where I'll find solace when I struggle with dreamless nights. Thankfully, no nightmares have crossed the threshold of my sleep since the death of Durudee. As much as I welcome this reprieve, I feel the bite of a chill that waits in the shadows. Someday my maternal protection will end, and I will hunt once more as they begin hunting me.

Discovering the city is my favorite part of this journey. Meandering from one friendly shop to the next lifts the heaviness I carry in my heart. Today, with umbrella in hand, I decide to follow the river, mingle with people, and breathe in the rich smells of Dublin before the rain rolls back in.

A river called Liffey flows west to east with quays buttressing the north and south banks. A gentle breeze caressing the river and the warming sun remind me of what I love most about Collin. Everything about this place reminds me of him: his breath on the back of my neck as we slept, the warmth of his touch whenever he caressed my body, and the green of his eyes when he stared deep into my soul. My heart aches with the desire for him to hold me again.

"Collin," I carelessly whisper into the wind and allow it to carry my pain and anger for his betrayal far from me. May the sting of his role in my suffering continue to fade.

When I turn away from the water, an older man with the deep green eyes of Collin's stares back at me. Just a coincidence, obviously, but I'm a bit unnerved all the same. When I turn in the opposite direction and spot a young woman striding my way, I notice her eyes are as emerald as the man's. She seems to peer into my soul, pleading with me as if she were him, my husband, begging me to return to him.

This is absolutely crazy. Surely, I'm only imagining it. One occurrence is unusual enough, but two? With irises his same remarkable color?

I turn back to meet her gaze before she reaches me, to find the color has muted to hazel. Relief falls over me and I take a deep breath before turning to the young boy clinging to her hand. His gaze meets mine and I realize that he, now, has Collin's intense jade stare. Soon, every face that meets mine has his shape, every wavy lock of hair is the shade of dark chocolate, and the eyes—the color rich as wet moss and staring through my soul.

Each of them gives the impression they are watching me as I fumble past, returning to my room at the small B&B in a panicked rush. The ache for him grows in my heart, forcing blood through my veins, pounding in my head. I'm overwhelmed, suffocated by his presence and missing him all at once. The effect is too much. My senses are on overload.

In a haste to flee the open quays and from the view of every person who regards me, I trip and tumble to the ground. Instinctually reaching out to break my fall, I grate my hand on the sidewalk.

"Are you all right my darling?" Collin's voice echoes through my mind, gentle and caring as the day after I killed Rick.

I turn and search for him. He must be here somewhere, to my left, behind me. But he isn't. It was merely my imagination. Am I going insane? On my right stands a blind man with a cup and a cane, shabby pants, and torn a shirt. All others casually pass by, ignoring me on their journey. Some drop coins in the man's container before meandering off.

"Ya didn't harm yerself too badly, did ya?" comes Collin's

voice again. This time from the man in worn clothing. "Ya may want to wash yer cut."

And the voice is no longer Collin's. The tone is cracked with age and a difficult life. He's blind. Wait. He's *blind*. How does he know I cut myself?

"The iron in ye blood. I may not see, but my gigantic *gaosán* is bloody grand."

I'm not exactly sure if he's insulting me, making a move on me, or simply making small talk. "Um, *gaosán*?"

"Aye, me beak." He points to his nose.

I breathe a sigh of relief. "Oh, I see. How…did you know what I was thinking? I…I should head to my room and look after this right up." I turn away from him but hesitate and turn back.

"Hurry up with ye," he says with a smile on his face. "Ye don't want infection setting in."

I think on his words. He speaks as if he knows me. My own angel. "Please, sir, tell me your name," I ask before moving on.

"Sir? Well, my lady, for someone so gracious, I will tell you my name. But you must come closer, so I can whisper in your ear 'cause it's a secret." His face is alight when I inch closer until his lips nearly touch me. "M'names Joseph," he says then kisses me on the cheek and laughs.

My lips pull into a smile, my palm holding the place where his mouth had just been, directly on top of the scar caused by Sarah's knife. This silly, naughty, old man. "Here," I tell him and press two hundred euros in the palm of his hand. "For you," I say and kiss him back on the side of his face. "Buy some new clothes, a warm mat to sleep on, anything your heart desires."

His grin grows wider as he rocks backward. "This old man hopes yer as pretty as ye sound. Thank ye for making me day, miss."

My face flushes hot with embarrassment while I hold his hand in mine, then pat it. "I'll see ye 'round."

"Ye bet ye will," he answers as I release his hand and wander away.

From the first moment I stepped out among the people of this country, I found them engaging. Even those who, unlike Joseph, have the blessing of sight accept me as I am without judgment of my appearance, knowing all too well the scars of holy incursion. Having so much in common, it won't take long to steep myself in their rich culture.

I'm no farther than a block from the river when the sky rumbles overhead and the clouds empty their heavy load. The sidewalk beneath me, basically everything within my view, glistens with rain. The umbrella stays in the bag at my side and I take my time finding my way home. A hot shower, then a nice fire will comfort me before bed.

Only two weeks have passed, and I've already made my decision. My backpack of belongings will find a home in the small studio flat I found for rent. I'll live above an electronics store, not far from the heart of the city. I plan to keep it simple, with only the bare necessities for now. A bed I can sleep in and sit on, as well as a stool to sit near the counter for meals. There's a fireplace for warmth and a narrow window for sun and air.

My nights are lonely, lying in bed and smelling the wet moorland grass on the wind. On these nights, I'm reminded of Collin. I hear his voice whispering to me as if he was by my side. I miss him more each time I hear him say my name. Tears fall heavy on my pillow as I think of him and the beautiful night we'd shared as one. I'm careful not to answer him whenever he calls, though, falling asleep with his name burning on my lips. After what happened that afternoon on the quay that I dared whisper his name on the wind, I'll have to be more careful.

The intensity of him calling to me fell like a blanket of snow on my longing for him, making my loneliness all the more unbearable. Whether the appearance of his likeness in every face I saw was only my imagination or an unnerving reality, I would rather not tempt fate. There's no doubt he would return to Ireland to be by my side if I asked. But I must do this alone. I've found peace. Now, I have to rediscover my strength, on my own, or I will always depend on him. I must find balance in my life first, before I can let him in.

With my last kill, I lost the fighter inside of me. My personality is no longer split. I no longer struggle with the longing to kill while hating myself for having done so in my past. My travels taught me to find my gentler side and smother the harsher portion of my soul, the wounded segment bent on revenge. The resultant metamorphosis exposes a tenderness in me I never knew existed. From the cocoon, something soft emerged, too weak to vanquish demons in the night. Unfortunately, if I don't find that balance between the hardened killer I once was and the pacifist I've become, I may end up being destroyed after all when I begin to hunt again.

I suspect the reason I haven't fought since I killed Durudee is my advancing pregnancy. The spirit protects me and my child in that way. To finally know sleep filled with amity is a welcomed change. Yet, as my pregnancy progresses, I become increasingly vulnerable.

The ones who hunt me will ultimately find me. I'm aware of them already catching my scent. I may not dream, but I feel them when I'm awake. Their energy grows stronger with each new night. Clearly, as I learned from Rick, the demons who hunt me for Lucifer want and need to turn me or they will have to kill me to stop any of my attempts to spoil their plans. Although I don't dare confront them in their sleep, I know they'll eventually come to me in mine. Soon, I'll have no choice but to fight again. This time it'll be a more personal battle—for the life of my child.

Most dark angels have husbands to protect them after childbirth. Because I've chosen to leave Collin behind, I'm the only one this baby has. A sense of regret fills my heart.

How do I feel so deeply for a man I barely know? As if I've loved him an entire life? His touch is familiar, like we met and have been connected since my birth. Like he's held me in his heart from my first breath. Is this the result of the sort of covenant he made to have me in marriage? A covenant he alone made without my consent. I'm beginning to forgive him for that because I do love him, and I know he loves me. But it is only a beginning.

Settling into my covers and watching flames lick and char the wood in the fireplace reminds me of the last time we touched. The gentle caress of his fingers setting my skin on fire, forcing me to pleasurable heights I hadn't known before. My body aches for him now, not only because of my elevated hormones. I want him more than I ever have. Tonight will be a challenge, with Collin in my thoughts and the new apartment on my schedule for tomorrow, I may never fall asleep. The rain taps relentless against the window of my room. No way I could go out to the ocean tonight. There's only one way I'll fall asleep.

With my fingers slipped just inside my panties, I breathe in the scent of Collin on the air and replicate his touch until I grow rigid with ecstasy. I stifle a moan in my pillow and bite down hard on the down-filled covers until my body falls slack once again and my mind is thick with sleep..

CHAPTER 17

My favorite moments are spent in the corner of a pub with a cup of tea in front of me, eavesdropping on a spirited debate over anything from politics to cobblestones. These Dubliners are wonderful orators.

From time to time a drunkard will make a play for me, raising the ire of other patrons. They treat me as if I'm one of their own, a favorite neighbor or younger sister. And when I rise from my seat to leave, one of them is most likely to notice my condition and offer their assistance to see me safely home. For now, I always accept, grateful for the company.

I train again, every day, as if I still hunt at night, mostly to keep my body limber and rebuild the muscle I lost while recovering in Thailand. The routine is structured to my changing condition, focusing on the most effective moves to protect my body. Someday I'll need the evolved skills necessary to fight raging monsters, to protect my child. I pray I'll have the strength and conviction when the time comes.

This evening, I head to my favorite pub in the Temple Bar District. I quietly sip tea in the corner while listening to various conversations around the room. I sit alone, playing with the braided ring on my finger, thinking of the morning Collin gave it to me and wondering if he still wears his. I try not to question if he'll still want me when I'm ready or if he'll forgot me as he had before? The thought of his rejection burns in my heart.

No more than an hour into the evening, one of the patrons waves his arm to me. "Come on, lass. Join us old coots in a pint o' Guinness and a chinwag."

I recognize the accent as Scottish, not uncommon around here.

At first, I shake my head, but they're insistent as several men pipe up to convince me. "We won't bite hard."

"Oh, so that's much better. But I must still decline," I graciously tell them.

"Aww... C'mon," they plead, practically in unison.

I search the faces of each of the men and reluctantly give in. "Oh...okay. On one condition." I smile at them with my eyes narrowed in a flirt. "You won't ask my opinion on politics. I can't compete."

Cheers rise to the ceiling as a chair is pulled to their table for me. They slap the seat to draw me over, but I hesitate at my table.

"I swear on me da's grave," answers an Irish gentleman.

"Yer da ain't *dead*," another man with a British accent answers and the table erupts in laughter.

A nearby woman turns to her friend and mumbles to her, barely loud enough to be heard, "Shite flies high when hit with a stick." Her friend nods and grins. They both break out in laughter as well.

Just as I shift in my seat, ready to stand, the tavern door swings open. In walks a man with dark, wavy hair and deep blue eyes.

"Jesse!" several voices call out. He turns to the crowd at the table and smiles, then directs his gait toward them. Before sitting, his eyes turn my direction and he hesitates, then smiles. The muscles in his strong jaw relax as his lips part to expose perfect, white teeth. I can't help but notice his dark shirt pulled taut across his shoulders before tapering at his waist. I take a swallow of my tea.

"Any chance this lovely lady will be joining us?" he asks with a hint of the Irish accent his comrades share.

I shake my head in disbelief that I'm actually considering joining them. "How could I decline such a generous offer?" I answer hesitantly then rise from my seat to a round of cheers and back-slapping amongst the men.

As I prepare to move to the next table, a distant voice whispers on the wind. I barely make out the words. "Dark angel."

The accent is inflected with a thick Irish brogue, nearly reminiscent of ancient times. The hairs on my arms stand on end and my heart skips a beat. My eyes search the corners of the pub. Have they found me already? I still have five more weeks.

"Are ya comin', lassie?" Jesse asks with a hand stretched toward me, his deep eyes piercing my soul. The scent of juniper fills my senses. Is that him? I had no idea juniper grew in Ireland.

I stare back at him for a moment, then feel my body jolt involuntarily. What the hell was that? Thinking quickly, I reach for my belly. "Gas."

Once again, the table erupts as two more women join in, giggling and pulling their chairs closer. The only available place to sit is to the right of the one they call Jesse. I take a deep breath, then slip into the vacant seat. The Scottish gentleman slides a Guinness in front of me and I smile, shaking my head.

"It'll grow that baby strong," he protests.

Jesse laughs with a subtle gasp of air and slides the beer back to its owner. "It's not my place to interfere, but you don't have to drink this if you don't want to." A bit of his accent is lost in the hushed conversation, and I wonder if he's merely a transplant to Ireland.

An older woman in the group, wearing a dark blue suit and white cotton shirt, slaps the Scottish man on the hand and moves the beer further from in front of me. The conversation progresses from there while I pay little attention. They want to know my age. I tell them the truth and they all laugh, of course. Most of the conversation is lost as my mind catches on Jesse's knee, brushing against mine when he turns to order a pint.

All eyes turn to me as one after the other plies me with questions, wanting my opinions of their country while giving me their impressions of mine. They seem to understand the political system of the U.S. far better than many Americans. I merely smile, often asking them to repeat a question. My thoughts linger on the overpowering energy of the man beside me. I've never felt such a strong presence. The baby in me jolts and I reach for my abdomen.

After enough time has passed, and my cup of tea is drained, I politely excuse myself and stand to leave.

"Please, let me walk you home," Jesse asks.

I smile and shake my head to decline the offer. Then his eyes soften, and I can't help but stare back into them. "I…" Then I sigh and search for a way to reject his generous offer. "You're very kind, but I assure you, I'll be fine."

"I have no doubt you'll fare well, me lady. Yet, the night can be filled with any number of treacheries that could befall a woman in such a delicate state as yours." He takes my hand as his lips curve to a grin. Electricity shoots straight to my core as

I gently tug it away. Who is this man? Am I feeling an attraction or repulsion? I'm not sure I can tell anymore.

"Jaysus H. Christ, Jesse. Yer offerin' ta take 'er home, not ta prom, ya fool," one of his friends calls out, his jibe followed by more laughs.

A woman's voice swells over the din. "Go on, missus. Jesse's the safest among this lot o' brutes."

He waits patiently as I roll the situation over in my mind. Then I turn my eyes to his and manage a grateful smile. "Thank you for your offer. I would appreciate your company."

"Atta girl," one man calls out and the women roll their eyes.

"You'll be fine, lass. He's a complete gentleman," a woman named Kate tells me.

"Unfortunately," mumbled her friend, and they burst into laughter.

"Okay, that's enough," Jesse interrupts. "I will be off escorting this young lady to her abode. I will catch up with ye muckers on the morrow."

He offers his arm and I take it with guarded hesitance. Once we are out the door and a block from the pub, I turn to him.

"Muckers, you called those at the table that. Isn't that rather harsh?"

"What? You don't call the people you like a friend?"

"Oh. A mucker is a...it just sounds so close to—" I stop in mid-sentence and he lets out a deep, guttural laugh.

"No...No. I would *never* call anyone I like *that* word." He laughs again.

The blood rushes to my face, turning it hot. So embarrassing. How could I think that's what he meant? I'm an idiot.

"Oh, forgive me. I have no idea what's gotten into me."

He shrugs and releases a last chuckle. "You're not from here. Surely we should give you a pass for mistaking a word or two." His Irish accent is almost lost, nearly American.

"Jesse." I try the word aloud as if saying it to myself. "Not your typical Irish name."

"My parents were Jewish. It comes from my father's side."

"Oh? Your parents aren't from here, then?"

"No. They came from Russia. Many years ago." His gaze is at some point far ahead of us.

"You didn't grow up in Ireland?" I ask, breaking into his thoughts and he turns his attention on me.

"Yes. Been here my entire life. Grew up with these people." His answer seems cryptic, like there's more to learn.

"But your accent. It fades to…well, American, from time to time."

He stops walking and glares back at me. "Does it?"

I watch his expression, study the curious bend in his brow while he studies me.

Then, he throws his head back and laughs. "Oh, that! I studied at Stanford University for two years, then returned with a terrible bout of homesickness.

"That must've been awful, being so far from home."

"Don't you feel the same? You're clearly a great distance from your home, and…" He turns his attention to the bulge at my waistline. "Perhaps someone you care deeply for." Although the words are in the form of a sentence, I sense the question in his mind.

"Yes. Well…there are people we miss who're unable to be part of our lives for a time, aren't there?"

"Yes, of course." He continues walking without speaking.

The Ha'penny footbridge crossing the River Liffey isn't far from the pub. I cross this bridge nearly every day. In the evening, my way is lit by streetlamps and lighted fixtures that

I find comforting. I can see much better on the waterfront than the rest of my trek to Parnell Street where I live.

As this stranger escorts me home, the whispers in the shadows at the pub are present at the forefront of my thoughts. They haven't stopped calling me. The further we go, the clearer it becomes.

"Dark angel—"

Many voices speak the words at once. The ancient brogue chills my skin. If these are rogue angels, they've been strong enough to last the millennium, and probably more powerful than any I've fought before.

Hesitating at the rise of the bridge, I wonder what waits for me when I reach the crest. The night sky is covered in heavy clouds. No moon this evening. Reflections from the streetlights play on the gentle waves of the river. A soft breeze smells of the distant moors. I close my eyes and take a deep breath. When I open them, I prepare to move forward again. Jesse has moved on without realizing I'm no longer at his side.

"Ya all right, Jaime?" The voice from behind startles me.

Turning, I notice the kind face of one of the patrons who I'd been laughing with at the pub. I believe his name is Curtis.

"Yes. I'm fine, thank you." Allowing a comforting smile to show I'm all right, I turn back and see Jesse waiting for me on the other side of the bridge.

"All right then, off ye go." He smiles and watches as I move hesitantly forward, wondering what else may be waiting on the other side of the bridge.

My gait is slow at first, increasing as I progress to meet up with my companion. When I reach him, his gaze seems to study me. "You all right?"

I nod and step past him, leading the way should anything go awry. Whatever calls to me in the dark could be harmless, but I'm not betting on it.

Once past the River Liffey, I follow the quay with Jesse doing his best to keep up with me. I lead him to O'Connell Street, then turn on Parnell to my apartment a half mile away. Passing quiet buildings and dark alleyways, I notice the whispering growing louder, as if they're impatient for me to stop and listen. My pace doesn't falter even as a light drizzle fills the air. I'm relieved. The mist will cover the traces of my spirit's scent until I reach my apartment. They shouldn't be able to track me back there.

As I arrive at the dwelling, I stop at the foot of the steps leading to my door.

"Well, this is it. Thanks so much for walking me."

Jesse seems befuddled, but I figure he'll get past that in no time. "I, uh, I could walk you to your door."

"No need. I'm well prepared to walk those steps without help. I've practiced for days now."

He releases an embarrassed chuckle. "Of course."

When he turns, I reach for his arm. "Jesse…really, thank you. Your kindness was beyond gallant." I lean in and rise to my toes to give him a kiss on the chin.

He reaches for his chin and smiles. "No, thank you." He nods, and nearly bows, then turns to leave.

I watch him go until he turns back to me and draws a line from me to the top of the stairs with his finger. Worry slips from my shoulders as I allow a smile to pull at my lips. I nod and turn. My feet don't hesitate to ascend the stairs. I lock the door immediately once inside, tarrying by the threshold for only a moment before heading to start a fire. I notice the bundle of lavender I'd purchased in advance of this moment.

In the small fireplace in the corner, dried paper and bark become my kindling. I place a split log in the center and another on top. Once the wood is engulfed in flames, I separate three dried branches of lavender and lay them in the center to smolder. I'll spend most of the evening tending the fire, ensuring my scent is well hidden.

As I sit on my bed, watching flames caress the wood, I wonder where he is tonight. Soon Collin's voice whispers into my thoughts and I close my eyes, letting my head fall on the pillow.

"Jaime—"

A tear traces my cheek as I open my eyes to see firelight dancing on the ceiling.

This evening I whisper back. "Collin...I miss you."

CHAPTER 18

The streets of Dublin are typically quiet late at night. Whispers of cars pass by, always in a rush to get home. At times, you'll hear laughter ring through the streets as couples and mates leave closing taverns. Infrequently, drunken tussles will temporarily interrupt the peace. Then all is blanketed in silence once again.

Night is when the baby is most active, stretching and kicking, sometimes hiccupping for a minute or longer. With my hands on my tummy, I speak to him and wait for him to stretch or kick. As much as I call this baby a *him*, I can only hope God hears my words and makes it so. If I'm taken from this earth as my mother had been—while he's still in his teens—I want a child with both mine and Collin's strength. One that won't have the societal constraints most women endure. I hope he'll withstand all this world and Lucifer will throw at him without flinching. Is it too much to ask that he has Michael's power?

Tonight, he lies unnervingly still. Not even a hiccup. Did the whispers frighten him? I rub my belly and stare out into the street.

From my window, I only see the fronts of other buildings, standing statuesque and commanding in the night. Soft light from dim streetlamps highlight features mostly overlooked in the day. I can't say I prefer day over night. Both bring pleasures I'm grateful to explore. My time in Colorado was spent dwelling more on my past than discovering new adventures and enjoying the wonders around me. Here, I visit new and glorious places, majestic castles, ruins of ancient lore and history, the sweeping moors, whenever I like. And in the night, I sleep now, without an interruption by demons haunting my sleep, so I don't dread the dark as I once did. Something I never knew in Colorado. Back then, I hated both day and night.

The sky finally opens and releases heavy drops of rain that pour from the clouds, tapping on the roof and dripping from the frame over my window. My mind feels detached from my body as I rise from my bed and pull a cloak over my shoulders. The door creeks as I slowly open then swiftly close it behind me. Floating down the staircase to the street level, I'm anxious to feel the rain on my skin. Something about the storm draws me. The elements — sun, wind, water, earth — tend to liberate me. My mind and body crave them.

My feet are bare as I make my way down the wet pavement, past closed storefronts and dark flats. Soon I find myself in the middle of O'Connell Bridge, staring at the river, mesmerized by its appearance. Large drops of rain make the water quiver. Reflected streetlights tear into pieces of gold and silver confetti on the surface.

These are the treasures I never noticed before. My life, so cluttered with darkness, had little time or patience for beauty. I'm grateful to have discovered this place. Comparing what I was in Colorado and who I've become here, I find a glaring contrast. My desire to play with demons has dissipated into the night.

There's no traffic on O'Connell Bridge as I walk the center line. Very unusual for a structure such as this — wider than it is long — to be so deserted. But I don't care. I'm glad to have the city to myself.

As I reach the crest of the bridge, a voice in the distance captures my attention. Unsure who or what it is, I continue on. Initially, I don't find it odd the lights on one end of O'Connell Street have gone dark. But then, the next set of lights turn black. The sky is still the color of pitch. A cleansing rain persists. More lights along O'Connell fade as familiar voices grow nearer.

"Dark angel — "

Burgh Quay lays ahead of me, the short segment of road intersecting O'Connell, running parallel to the River Liffey. Always brilliantly illuminated, Burgh Quay, too, is turning to shadows. Darkness is descending upon me as the whispers increase. The wind seems to blow through me and my flesh turns to ice.

"Dark angel — "

Blackness has reached the bridge as I watch, paralyzed as if I've left my physical form behind. The lights of Eden Quay on the other side of the river are also retreating. I'm surrounded by darkness. Why can't I run?

"Dark angel... Dark angel..."

Taunting voices encircle the bridge as blackness engulfs me. Their force taps against my shoulder and nudges my body one direction, then the other. Tentacles slide across my hand, burning me with searing heat. What *is* this? Fingers pull at my hair as I find my body once again. I immediately turn and run.

The streets are cloaked in shadows as I rush from the bridge, my heart pounding. Familiar landmarks fade as I search for the correct street to turn onto. The night is thick as tar and I can't read the signs, can't find my way with my mind in a panic. Every avenue, each alleyway, looks the same as any other. Am I going in circles?

The whispers follow, and I scrape my heel and cut the pads of my feet as I run from them. As I turn another corner, I realize I'm no closer to home than when I stood on O'Connell Bridge. I have no choice but retreat, my face whipped and slapped by the cloud of devils I must breach. My heart still races as I rush toward them while searching the darkness for an exit. My clothing is being torn by invisible hands.

Turning onto another side street, then deviating once again, I find myself in a dead-end alleyway. With my back to the wall, I watch the cloud descend upon me. Unseen hands hit, kick, cut and bite while I hold my belly to keep my child safe. They tear at my hands and the clothing around my bulging abdomen, trying to reach the flesh beneath. I swing my fist but hit nothing more than air. This thing seems to have no substance. I'm paralyzed in fear, and completely unprepared to defend myself so soon. Why are they here so early? Mother said dark angels are protected from demons while expecting. At least through the last months of the pregnancy. My long hair is torn as my screams echo past the buildings.

Crouching near the ground, I bend over to protect my baby. After twisting the longer strands of hair into a knot, I cover my head and ears with my arms. The sound of them calling me is nearly turning me insane, until a stray wind rushes the scent of moorlands to me. I can't help but call his name, wondering if he can see what's happening.

"Collin!" I scream. The force of my voice is more powerful than I ever remember.

His name echoes with the shrieks of demons, slapping me as they flutter away at the sound. My body shudders as my strength withers and I sob into my full belly, holding each side with my fingers. I'm afraid to look, unsure what I'll see. After a time of only silence around me, I lift my head to dying embers in my fireplace. I'd fallen asleep, allowing the fire to die. It was all a dream. *Oh, my God.*

My entire body aches as I lower my feet to the floor to revive the cinders before they return. The soles of my feet sting when they meet the wood. As I try to stand, my legs buckle under my weight and I slip to the floor. Rolling my feet to the sides, I notice thin cuts oozing fresh blood. My labored breathing doesn't slow as the realization takes hold. Peaceful dreams are a luxury of the past. They have found me. My nights will be occupied with a fight to survive.

CHAPTER 19

By the time the sun rises on this new day, I've been asleep no more than five hours. My restless night makes it more difficult to want to move. My body aches from the blows I'd received in my dream. Walking is painful on the healing cuts of my feet. Minor bruising colors my legs, trunk, and arms, but no place that will show in public. There is that burn. I'll have to remember to cover my hand. I'm grateful we're in the cooler season. Not unusual to cover up my body.

The nightly ritual of going to the pub must end. My wanderings will be achieved by day. I'd planned to make the change once the baby comes, but I'm forced to alter my life earlier than anticipated. At night, I'll have to tend a fire in my room to keep the lavender burning to cover my scent. I can't risk being out after dark, either. If I keep my old routines, they'll surely track me. There are many changes to be made beginning today.

The smell of fresh bread wafts through the window and under the door of my room, redirecting my attention and bringing a new food craving. I want some of whatever that is, wherever it originates, more than I could ever express in words. So, I pull on leggings and a loose dress with long sleeves and head to the market. The streets are bustling with activity as I step out into the sunlight. I'm excited by the energy of Dublin. It rejuvenates me despite the rough night I had.

As I make my way down Parnell Street, I breathe in the fresh air and rare sunshine. There's a hint of salty sea in the breeze. The taste lingers on my tongue. I never could have imagined I'd be someplace such as this, living simply and enjoying life.

Colorado brought many wonderful memories, but they were always tainted by the cautious voice in the back of my mind: Don't enjoy yourself too much, for tonight your world will change. Sometimes, I wanted to silence that voice and lose myself in the moment. Unfortunately, I never could. Here, I don't have that nagging warning. At least, not until last night I didn't.

The light ahead of me turns red and I stop at the corner to wait. As I keep my eyes directed downward, I feel the fixed stare of another on me. I turn my gaze to the street and surrounding sidewalk. Just as I notice him, a man across the road staring back at me, the overpowering presence of another soul beside me prickles my skin. From the corner of my eye, I note the neatly pressed garda uniform.

"Top of the day to ye," he greets me.

The voice is familiar. But who?

As I turn my face up to him, Jesse nods down at me, although his eyes don't match the smile on his lips. What does he think? What's going on in his mind? I merely stare back at him, struck dumb. *Shit*. He's a police officer. An Irish-fucking-cop. I force a smile, trying not to seem nervous. Or guilty of anything. Why is it that police have this effect on me? Because I am guilty. Guilty of killing demons in their town, that is. *Dammit*! I have new scars from last night's battle that he's sure to notice.

"Where ye headed?" he asks with a tone that doesn't tell me if he's making small talk or sees through me.

"Oh, on my way to the bakery. That's all." I sound too guilty. But I didn't do anything. So why am I trembling?

"Is that so?" He visually interrogates me, one eyebrow cocked higher than the other, as if I'd committed a crime. This is a great change from his persona when we first met. "Well, be sure to tell the Mannings I send my regards." He cracks an unconvincing grin and I force my lips to curve into a half-smile once more. He steps off the curb and leaves me behind. I watch him leave, forgetting I was headed the same direction. Damn. I've never made friends before, let alone one who's an officer of the law.

My feet soon find their way forward and I barely make it across to the other side of the street before the light turns red again.

Within minutes, I find myself in front of the bakery, wondering how I even made it there with my mind in a fog. Pushing through the door takes me out of my funk, thankfully. The smell is so delightful. They have the best pastries in town and I can order eggs and sausage for breakfast. Erika's working behind the counter today. She's an adorable younger woman with nearly black hair in a short, alternative page-boy cut with a jovial personality to match. Her parents own the bakery and she fills in for them part of the week. I can't help but feel my spirits lift whenever she's here. I always enjoy our short conversations across the counter.

Today, though, her demeanor is rigid, as if something is bothering her. I ask if she feels all right and she doesn't immediately answer. Large tears fill her blue eyes. Did something happen to her father? His heart? The reason he cut back his hours at the shop? When I ask, she shakes her head and holds out the newspaper.

Dublin Resident Beaten to Death in His Sleep, the headline reads.

My stomach turns ill as I digest the news. This isn't possible. Something like this doesn't happen in Dublin. I skip down the page to see if there's a picture. When I reach the photograph, I can't believe what I see. The photo is that of the kind man who spoke with me at Ha'penny Bridge last night. Curtis. My hands tremble as I remember the demon in Thailand. His abilities were beyond any I've seen before. Could he be the one attacking in a cloud of blackness, exacting revenge for the destruction of his precious flowers? My stomach turns inside out as the paper slips from my hand to the floor and I run to the bathroom to vomit.

Once I'm back at the counter, I order scones and a fresh loaf of bread to go, in case I find my appetite. For now, the thought of food curdles in my stomach.

As Erika leaves for the kitchen, the clank of the door jars me and sends my flesh cold. The air shifts and the room fills with the vibration of a stained soul. I turn to the man, his eyes sending a jolt of energy through me. My God, he's the one I saw on the street corner, staring me down, just before Jesse walked up beside me. I'd forgotten all about him once I saw the garda uniform. The blood leaves my face in a rush and I feel cold all over. His gaze drifts across my cheek to the scar on my jaw before traveling down my arm to the fresh burn on my hand. I pull my sleeve to the first knuckle on my fingers.

"Morning, me lady." His gravelly voice saws at my patience. He nods and his eyes narrow, black fingers clinging to a stained slip of paper.

I nod and turn away. His glare stays trained on me. I feel him, same as minutes before on the street. His breathing is heavy, steady. He has something to say. I don't have time for him. I don't want to have time for him. Where is Erika? He draws a deep breath, preparing for his words to fall into the heavy air.

"I know what you need," he says, then waits.

The air is thicker than I've ever remembered it feeling. Jesus, Erika! What's taking you so damn long?

"Did ya hear me?" he says.

I turn on him in a split second with my teeth clenched tight and my jaw set. "I don't want what you have, so fuck off." The words grind between my teeth. I glare into his eyes and someone behind me clears their throat. *Shit*. It's Erika.

I clear my throat, as well, and slowly turn back to her. She hands me my order and I nod apologetically when Erika attempts an awkward smile. She slips a package of scrambled eggs and sausage into my bag for later. I turn and push past the man with grungy skin and dark hair. What just happened?

My mind is numb as I roam the streets, on my way to buy food for the week. If it wasn't necessary, I'd have gone home and pulled the covers over my head.

Wandering among the pedestrians, I note a hint of fear in their eyes. How could this happen to one of their own? I feel grief I can't explain. This isn't like me. This isn't the angel that kills, then wakes without a thought of those who'd already fallen prey to the demon. Is the baby making me weak or rendering me soft? Or am I crumbling from the weight of all I've seen and done? Has the darkness that once shielded me from emotions fallen from me in my journey to Dublin?

This time, the death isn't as personal as family. Yet, I feel as if it is. I can't get the picture out of my mind. He stood there near the footbridge with concern in his eyes. I remember his laugh while we joked at the pub. His wife died of cancer a year ago. He has three grown children. I don't have to ask—I know he suffered. And I wonder if he died because of me. There's no other explanation. I hold back the urge to sob into my hands.

Tending to my chores for the rest of the morning, I work my way back to the flat before sunset. My actions are mechanical, like I'm inhuman. A part of me wants to remember everything about the poor man. A fragment of me wants to forget this even happened. I want to be cold, wish I was hard again, the unsympathetic demon killer I once was. Something inside me wants to desire the taste of their blood again, get angry and exact my revenge in a thorough and calculated way. Another wants to stay the person I've become, someone who can wander among the people without wondering if they'll try to kill me in their sleep. Will I lose the gentle soul I'd found hidden among the ruins of my life just to make the rogue angels who did this suffer? Am I going mad?

At my apartment, the smell of bread isn't as strong as earlier in the morning, yet the aroma still beckons me. When I pull out the breakfast Erika gave me, a slip of paper falls to the floor. Black fingerprints stain the surface, identical to the one the man at the bakery held in his hand. How in the hell did he...? When I was turned to Erika. Asshole must have slipped it in my bag. But what else? I search everything, the bread, scrambled eggs and sausage, to see if anything had been touched, contaminated. All appears normal, except for one small detail, the stained paper that still lies on the floor. Tempting me. Why do I hesitate so much? Pick the damn thing up!

The paper appears to be smudged with grease, possibly from a vehicle. He might work on cars. Or he could be another messenger of Satan, telling me they know where I am. Maybe he's just an asshole. The paper is folded twice. The English is curt, but the intent is clear.

"Find what you need. Warehouse dock 31. Three to five a.m. Come alone. Snitches dealt with speedily."

My fingers close around the paper and crush it to a tight ball. I was right. Just another asshole. The fireplace will consume it with the lavender.

Most of the rest of the day is spent around the apartment, cleaning and preparing for this evening, taking short naps when I can. I need to be awake enough to tend the fire and keep the lavender burning, sleeping in small increments and planning for the moment I'll fight them again. For the rest of my time I sit on my bed and ponder. I contemplate the choices I've made and whether they were best for me and especially this child. Should I have left Bangkok, headed straight for Ireland, and left their fields of Dark Angels alone? The person I'm becoming couldn't have done that. Despite what she had done, Durudee was an innocent who had been manipulated by dark angels, maybe even by Lucifer himself. Her death deserved some type of revenge.

Even if this isn't the same rogue of Thailand, it won't take long before word will reach him. His best chance of having me and my baby is when I'm vulnerable, as I am now.

Being in Ireland has helped me to forget old wounds, to forgive those who gave them to me, including Collin. The joys I know here are unlike any I've experienced since my father's death. I've grown to love the people. They've welcomed me into their embrace. That's one more reason I'm saddened by today's news. If I don't turn away, the one who hunts me in the night will kill them one by one. They'll find me in the hearts of those I care about and make them suffer. Didn't the demon threaten as much in the bathroom of my dream in Thailand?

I'll have to be a killer again. I have no choice. As much as I wither from the thought, it's the only way possible to protect my child and save these people.

Today I don't feel much like training. Tomorrow, however, I will begin again, strengthening my muscles, reinventing my skills, renewing my balance and sharpening my mind. They won't take another Dubliner as long as I have control. I'll protect them to the death if necessary. They won't take my baby either. That I can promise.

As the sun slips beyond the horizon, I set my kindling to a blaze again and place two logs on the fire. Three lavender branches are laid over the burning wood and the room is filled with the scent of smoldering herbs. As I sit on my bed with my knees bent, I rub my tummy and watch out the window. I can't stop my body from shivering while the faint whisper of persistent darkness roams the city.

"Dark angel… Dark angel—"

CHAPTER 20

The stout tang of a dark Guinness infuses my senses and nips my tongue as I reach for my pillow. At the sound of laughter, my eyes snap open to peruse my surroundings. Tables of men and women chat up one another as the barkeep pours another round of the brew.

Not like me to drift off while sipping my tea at the pub.

Wait. *No. That's not right.* I don't remember walking here. My last memory is of me sitting on my bed, listening to the night. How did I end up here?

My pulse races as I remain still while surveying my surroundings. Jubilant voices hang in the air. I feel as if I'm not truly here. In my dreams, I may move around the room, throw punches into the air a considerable distance past where I first lay my head to rest, but I've never awoken to find myself beyond the confines of my house, not even as a child. This is why I'm so baffled by my surroundings. *Am I really here?*

The bar is soaked with beer that the tender spills over the edge to the floor with his wet rag. Nothing different about the walls, the arrangement of tables and chairs. Every accoutrement of an Irish pub seems to be intact. There's a knob on the front door, as well. All is normal. So, why does this seem so wrong?

I search my mind. *Is this a dream? Am I awake?* It's not possible for all these people to be demons. The scenario doesn't fit. For me to be hunting in this bustling pub is entirely impossible and improbable. While hunting, it is always just me, the demon, and maybe a victim or two of his. So, this can't be a dream, can it? *How did I get here?*

Did I get out of bed during sleep, slip in without them noticing? Or am I merely a shadow, watching in my dream? I'm still in the same pajamas. Have I started repeating my old hunting habits, only now I visit friends who are awake, rather than sleeping demons?

There are familiar faces at the table ahead of me, seated at the bar, in a booth across the room. There are also those watching from the shadows, waiting for me to show myself. What is that? I don't typically see eyes in the shadows of my waking life. Are they demon or friend?

Regardless of the answer, I'm not safe here. And my presence puts everyone else at risk. But how can I leave without bringing attention to myself? Even a glimpse of my shadow from the corner of their eye could be dangerous.

Easing out of the chair, I'm careful not to let my stomach bump the table. While slipping along the wall, I'm also careful to avoid shadows. There's no telling what might dwell there unseen.

As I pass a table, empty but for a drained beer bottle, one of the revelers calls out. "'Ey, watcha' doin' o'er there!" Had he seen me?

Panic robs my sensibilities. As I hastily turn to see who called out, my belly brushes against an empty pint, making it wobble. All eyes at the nearest table turn my direction, but I don't wait to see what happens next. Rushing out the door and down the street, I head to the river, never hesitating until I reach Ha'penny Bridge. I don't kid myself that the eyes in the shadows didn't also see me leave.

When I'm finally to the river, I stop and bend over to catch my breath. My hands grip the rail tight as I gasp for air.

"Who's there?" a voice echoes from an alley nearby.

Is it human or angel? They somehow heard my footsteps or heavy breathing. I search the shadows, hoping there's nothing evil watching me.

Soon the form of a person emerges from the alleyway. Joseph, the blind man. The same worn clothes still cling to his body as he feels his way past the building and into the open night air. He didn't use the cash I gave him for himself? What did he do with the money?

"Is someone there? Jaime?"

I can't answer, can't put his life in danger. So, I start across the bridge on light footing, careful not to make a sound. When I reach the crest, I stop for a moment, searching the streets for an encroaching black cloud. The lights on O'Connell are still lit. Similarly, the quays on both sides of the river remain awash in light. Maybe I escaped unseen.

Looking over the rail and into the water below, I feel comforted and release the breath I've been holding. Reflected lights ripple gently in the calm waves, washing my body in peace. The muscles in my jaw relax as I'm lost in the smell of the salty sea and the rolling water below me.

I love this river named Life. As the flickering reflections mesmerize me, I'm reminded of the story of another young, homeless Dublin man.

Several years ago, he and his two pets, a Jack Russell terrier and a rabbit, were on the O'Connell Bridge when another young man tossed the rabbit into the river. The homeless man dove into the water, risking his life to save the helpless animal.

The bridge is nearly three stories high. The jump alone could have killed him. A wrong splash could have broken his neck. To him, the life of that animal was worth more. He became a hero to this town. I remember thinking what a beautiful story it was. The metaphor it has become for my own life sobers me to the cool night air.

What I must do now to save these people means I'll need to take a similar dive into danger. My efforts won't make me a hero like the man with his rabbit, however. No one can know the threat they face. If they had any idea, the peril to them would be greater, like a panicked, drowning man pulling his rescuer under with him. If I die, they'll be more vulnerable just for me having been here, for having known me.

No. That can't happen. I know what I must do. In time, they'll forget me. Someday, I'll return to being that face in the crowd, the one no one notices. Alone once again. A frozen heart, fighting to beat in a cavernous chest. An existence akin to the grave.

At that thought, a distant whisper breaks into my thoughts. I watch with dread as patches of darkness move across the city, like clouds of restless, black fog. The skin on my arms tightens into goosebumps, my hands turn cold and pale. They're calling me once again.

A couple on the southern quay saunter toward me, preparing to cross the bridge. *Damn.* I've stayed too long. Now I'll have to reverse course. Heading in the opposite direction, I rush toward Liffey Street then take North Lotts, staying in the shadows and avoiding congested areas. O'Connell is too busy this time of night with workers rushing to their homes. Parnell will be the same. I could possibly take alleyways, if necessary, although I'm a bit nervous about doing so after last night. But I can't risk anyone being overcome by rogue angels or demons; whoever the hell is following me. My conscience can't endure another death. Not tonight.

As I progress toward my flat, the voices of those seeking me grow louder. They whisper around corners, into the alleyways, rippling across the water and past the quays. The bastards are getting closer.

I'm almost to Parnell and the whispers are nearly upon me. If I take Cumberland Row, past Avondale House, I'll be close, practically home. But as I near, a group of teens at the corner slow my progression. After Curtis was killed last evening, I won't take any chances drawing the demons past another Dubliner. If Curtis died because he spoke to me last night while the demons tracked me, I won't take any chances they will turn on anyone I pass in the night. Unless they leave, I can't go this way. The shadows are advancing rapidly. They'll be here soon. And my sides are cramping.

Rushing, panicked, I hold my belly as I move up Cumberland then turn left on Britain Place to backtrack for a block. From there, I can slip up to Parnell where I'll be near my building. In doing so, I put myself closer to those trying to find me. I pick up the pace, although it's not easy with the muscles in my sides twisting into a knot.

As I near Parnell once again, two drunk men saunter past, arms wrapped around each other as they happily stumble home. To avoid the two catching a hint of me, I duck into an unfamiliar alleyway to search for an alternate route home. As I wait in the shadows, out of breath and huddled near a brick wall, the dark cloud oozes past the corner and seeps toward me. My blood races like an adrenalin shot through my veins. Are they drawn to me by the sound of my pounding heart?

"Dark angel…"

The sound of them so close turns me frigid. My fingers grow a paler shade of white.

The black cloud slithers along the pavement, caressing the

sides of the building. With dread clutching my heart, I rise and rush forward. The cloud hesitates a fraction of a second before engulfing my body. Blackness descends on me, just as it had last night, throwing me backward against the building and taking my breath away as invisible hands begin slapping my face and tearing my skin and clothing.

"No!"

My voice echoes between the buildings as I struggle to fight them off, unable to see from which direction their limbs come. Am I drugged? I can't discern reality from fantasy.

Turning one direction, then another, away from the onslaught of a gyrating cloud, I defend myself as best I can, but inevitably fail. Is there nothing that'll stop them? How could a demon or even a rogue angel, conjure this sort of environment—in a dream or awake?

Seeing no other recourse, I dart through the demons again, miscalculating the direction and winding up in another dead end behind a set of tall buildings. My breathing is erratic, my body shudders uncontrollably. The only way out is a fire escape and I leap to pull the ladder to me. Before I can grasp the second rung, clawed hands pull my ankles downward and I return to the cold pavement with a jolt.

This time, I swing my fists into the whirling mass. My blows meet no resistance as I throw one arm then another. There's little to no substance to these monsters. How can this be? Is this how I die? Torn to pieces the same as my father? The thought drives me to near hysteria and I scream with each slice of my hand through the dark air. Fear suffocates my will and I can't breathe, gulping for air as I remember the pool of blood at my knees and father's frozen face, twisted with pain.

No. This must stop. I'm not thinking clearly. *Take a deep breath, Jaime. There's the baby to think of.*

I slow my breathing, then try again, striking out into the

dark mist, using the greatest force my arms can provide. After three more swings, I connect with an unseen limb reaching out for me and it swiftly recoils before another attacks from an alternate direction. There *is* something there. With determination, I turn and swipe with my fist, turn and swipe once again. As much as I fight, however, my efforts do little to harm them. Nothing I do forces them to flee. It merely lessens the number of blows. Taking a deep breath and gritting my teeth, I lash out once more with every ounce of strength in my body.

It doesn't take long before my arms grow weary while their fingers claw my pajamas, tearing them to shreds. Sharp nails penetrate the fabric, ripping the flesh on my belly, scoring and searing the freshly healed wound given me in Thailand. When I reach down to protect my abdomen they claw my arms. *They don't want me. They want my child.*

"No!" My cry echoes between the buildings.

All around me, the haunting voices shatter all attempts to strategize. All rational thought is ripped from my mind in the cacophony of voices. "Dark angel... Dark angel...," their voices whisper, overlapping as they call, driving me to the ink-stained edge of insanity.

I can't protect myself from these demons. They're too strong. What kind of demon is this? I've never met anything like this before. My hands tighten on my belly and my fingers dig into my flesh around the limbs of the infant inside. If I hand him over to them, their voices pounding through my brain will end. If I could only...

NO! What am I doing? The monsters are in my head, taking control of my subconscious mind. Damn them! I need a distraction to drive them out.

Backed against the wall, I turn away to protect my child, repeating the words to a lullaby my mother often sang to me.

Tears trickle down my face as I gulp for air and sing.

"Loo-li, loo-li, loo-li lai-lay. Lay down your head and I'll sing you a lullaby. Back to the years of loo-li lai-lay."

Taking a stuttering breath, I force myself to recall the words. Another verse. Remember another verse.

"And I'll sing you to sleep and I'll sing you tomorrow. Bless you with love for the road that you go," I squeak out, through clenched teeth. Claws of demons tear the clothing at my back as I cry out in pain then take another gulp of air and continue. "And may you need never to banish misfortune." My voice cracks and I search for the words of the next line. Another sharp pain is followed by blackness invading my mind with their voices climbing one over another. I gasp and begin again. "May you find kindness in all that you meet."

A deep, shuddering breath interrupts the lullaby and beyond the agony, I feel a stream of tears meet under my chin. With my eyes squeezed closed against the pain, I resolve myself to a cruel fate. Prepared to meet my father and mother, I barely hear my voice whisper the favored verse I always begged her to repeat.

"May there always be angels to watch over you." The frayed nerves in my flesh force me to wince and swallow the ache in my heart, before allowing the final words past my lips. "To guide you…each step of…the way…"

With the cloth ripped from my body, razor-sharp nails cut deeper into my flesh as they sear the wound. The smell of burned flesh sickens me. The taunting whispers enter my thoughts once again, but I'm too weary to fight it anymore. With my hands over my ears, I scream out in agony.

Their cuts dig deeper into me and I begin to falter, brought to my knees in torment. My body grows numb and my frail mind drifts to Collin. He'll be the last of us. The last dark angel left on earth. What horrific battles will he know before meeting his own dark fate?

Just as the thought crosses my mind, Collin's scent reaches me and I breathe him in, failing to ignore my agony while feeling his love surround me. The warmth of his touch rushes through me like the blood in my veins. There's hope.

Tears tickle my cheeks as they roll to my jaw. My throat is raw from screaming, when I finally whisper his name. "Collin, please. Help me."

The minute the words are uttered, I feel him near. The tearing fingers instantly cease and demons shriek as they rise to the sky. Soon, there's nothing left but the smell of Collin and the sound of my rapid heartbeat. His warmth fills me, as if his arms cradle me in the night. Warm blood trickles down my hips to my thighs.

Facing the corner with my eyes still closed, I whisper to him again. "Please stay."

His voice whispers through my head, "Soon."

My eyes burn with a stream of tears still washing down my face. I turn from the corner and I'm alone in my room once again. The fire has nearly died, so I wipe the tears from my cheeks, and take a step forward to stoke the embers. As if I've been ripped open with a fire iron, I cry out in pain. I must reach the fire before they return. I swallow a whimper as I bend to place another log. The shudders wracking my body force the branches of lavender in my hand to quiver. If I can stay awake through the night to keep adding lavender to the fire, my scent will be covered and should keep the demons at bay. I have to find a way.

I cringe when the blanket I wrap around my shoulders clings to the thick blood coagulating at my sides. I refuse to examine the cauterized cuts that seep a moment longer while hungry flames swallow an ashen log, engulfing the wood as the demons had me.

In my mind, I hear Collin whisper again. His voice wraps around me same as my blanket.

"Jaime." Only now, I'm not devastated by thoughts of his betrayal. I can only feel a love that patiently waits beyond the anger and my stubborn soul. I revel in the sound of his soft Irish accent and it quiets my tremors.

"Collin."

His scent surrounds me, and I feel his lips near mine.

"I love you," he whispers. His breath is warm against my mouth.

My eyes burn as I force back the tears. "I love you, too. And I miss you," I choke out. His spirit dissipates into air before I can finish the words. "Forgive me."

Soon, I'm alone. Although, I know Collin will be here in spirit when I need him, I'm aware that he can't help me fight until he arrives in person, at least, not really fight. He may chase them away for another day, but they never seem to be fully gone. Will he be able to answer my cries the next time I need him? There's no way I'll be able to protect myself. The thought causes my heart to skip a beat as the lavender is dissolved in the flames.

CHAPTER 21

A sharp stab of pain jolts me awake. The tears in my side send shocks up my nerves as the cells regenerate and heal. Each small movement still takes my breath away. The time is only 3:24 a.m. The fire is fading, so I rush to stoke it to life and lay more lavender to smolder. I wonder if this even helps. Is this demon even tracking my scent, or do they already know where I live?

Somehow, my world isn't any less complicated with the morning light soon to arrive. There are too many issues to consider now. I face a power I've never experienced before. I can't hurt them, can barely seem to touch them, while they not only harm, but kill. How do I fight something I can't grab hold of? My core shudders at the thought.

For the first time in my life, I realize I need more than my wit and physical strength to fight this. They seem to only attack at night, after I've fallen asleep. But I've also found myself in places other than my room. Am I somehow leading myself directly to them? Contemplating my best course of action, I set out. There's much to prepare before a new night closes in.

The air is thick as I step out of my apartment. Like a blanket of dread had fallen over the city. Sirens wail in the distance.

What is that?

With a shawl thrown over my shoulders to stay the night's chill, I follow the lights and the sound. There's a gathering of people on the quay, watching the medics cover a body on the cold ground. Every face around me looks grim. There is no one chatting about everyday matters. No smiles greet me as I pass between them. Something bad happened. My trepidation grows.

The feeling in my heart is familiar. I'm suddenly that same scared girl once again, killing demons and missing someone desperately, someone who could protect me from the evils of this world. No matter how hard I fight it, I feel helplessness turning like a blade inside of me, ripping me from all that's kind and clean. I'm propelled backward to a time when I knew nothing but darkness and self-hatred, a time when I wanted to crawl out of the cavern but didn't know how. Until I met Collin. His passion made me want to live again, slowly washing away the filth I felt clinging to my body and soul.

How can I be at this turning point yet again, the juncture where I lose myself to hatred to save those around me? And this baby, what does it mean for him? Can he survive my anger? Will my abhorrence turn him against all that is good?

My ears are tuned to the conversations around me. As I make my way through the crowd, I can't help but notice the expressions of those I pass. When they see my face in the light from the flood lamps, they do a double take, noticing the unusual scratches. *Damn!* I didn't think to cover them up.

Nearing the corner, I hear two gentlemen talking. "Gave every penny he was given to others in need. Poor blind cuss. It's bloody wrong."

As they see me, their voices trail off and the conversation ends. Concerned eyes trace my arm down to the hand with cuts and burn marks. Self-consciously pulling the sleeve to my fingers, I hurry by, feeling their eyes following me. The scream is caught in my throat as I realize who they're talking about. The dead body, the man on the cobblestones with a sheet pulled over his head, is Joseph. Jesus, why? Why did it have to be him? My gait falters and I reach for the rail that runs the length of the river to steady my body. A young woman with red curly hair and blue eyes reaches for me. I wave her away and rush past her. Eyes are on me, but I have to leave. Have to go before I fall on the cobblestones. My God, why him?

I stumble across the Ha'penny bridge to the other side of the river. My apartment is to the right, but I turn left. Instead of heading home, I veer toward the warehouses further away from my flat. Warehouse dock thirty-one. I hope they truly do have what I'm looking for.

The warehouse district is quiet at four in the morning. No one has arrived to load or unload trucks. Ships have anchored in the harbor, waiting for someone to liberate them of their bounty. Goods shipped from China or Europe, even the Americas, await their transfer to another buyer or distributor. Salt is heavy in the air the closer I am to the shore and my destination. I pass dock twenty-nine when I hear the shuffle of feet. Whoever it is, they're not very quiet. Someone knows of my presence. My senses turn up as I search my surroundings. My feet barely make a sound. Movement in the shadows to the right of me. Then the cool muzzle of a Glock sporting a homemade silencer presses against my temple.

"Don't move." His voice is deep, but smoother than the guy from the bakery.

Whoever it is, they don't know me, it's clear. If they did, they wouldn't be foolish enough to give me a moment to think. As I reach up, I slide my head backward, then turn away to let the bullet and the flash from the Glock's muzzle fly past me. I twist the gun from his grasp, then press it into his forehead.

"Where the fuck is he?" I shout at him while backing him to the wall.

"Who?" he asks, his pitch a bit higher.

"The asshole who lured me here, that's who," I shout back. "Is it you?"

An arm from the shadows cuts the air to my side. I reach behind me to grab his hand, then crush until the blade in his clutches falls to the ground. He drops to his knees beside me, gnashing his teeth in pain but trying to keep from screaming out.

Another person advances on me from the right. I jam my palm into the first man's throat to hold him against the wall, then turn the gun on those approaching.

"I wouldn't do that," I warn. "I'll kill you all before you can make one mark on me." Fortunately, they don't know that I wouldn't kill, just maim them.

The man whose throat is wrapped in my fingers gasps to breathe, pulling at my hand with both of his.

"Is this why you brought me here? What a damned waste of your time," I tell them, my eyes darting from one man to the next.

One of them steps forward. His face is familiar. The man from the airport in Seattle. The one at Starbucks. I'm dazed at the realization. Here, I almost thought he was clean. Had hope he wasn't this crooked.

"Mathew?" I ask, nearly as if we're old acquaintances with a history.

"Marcus," he answers, and his attention crawls down to my belly.

"My eyes are up here," I reply.

"Damn," he says and shakes his head. "I imagined you to be badass, angel, but I think I may have underestimated you," he replies with a smile.

"What the *fuck* do you want?" The words practically spit from my mouth.

He takes a slow breath then releases it. "Well, since you asked so nicely. First, I'd like you to let go of my guy." He nods toward the man in my grip.

The goon struggling beneath my hand stills as I contemplate my move. Better to free him. I can fight more efficiently without him in the way. Should I have a need to fight, that is. When I release his throat, I motion with his gun for him to join his buddies and turn my back to the wall.

"Why are you following me?" I ask, then turn back to Marcus.

"I asked myself the same question about you, when I saw you down by the quay in the Temple Bar district last month. Then I realized it was only kismet that we met at the same place."

"So, you sent your guy to contact me. To lead me here. Why? I'm not a party planner, I don't do balloon animals, if that's what you have in mind."

Marcus chuckles and wipes his chin. "Oh, a party planner you are not. Well, I normally wouldn't have bothered you at all and would have left you to your own devices, shall we say. But you appear to have some troubles sleeping at night. And there seems to be a black cloud following you everywhere you go. And I don't just mean the whispers on the night. You're bad luck, angel. But I might be able to help improve your lot."

"You've seen them?" I ask and he nods. "What do you know about it, the dark cloud?" I ask, dropping the hand with the gun to my side.

"Not sure. Never seen any shit like that b'fore. But you. You are a definite sleepwalker. Although, the first night I saw you out on O'Connell bridge, I thought you were a ghost. Could barely see an outline of you."

"What?" My head spins as I gather the loose ends of the past few days. I walk into town in my sleep. My body? My soul? Or both? How is this possible? I turn back to see Marcus studying my face.

"You haven't answered me. Why are you following me?" I ask again.

He releases a gust of breath. "Not following. I see everything that happens in this town at night. It's what people like me do." His eyes turn serious. "What about you? What are you doing walking around my town in the dark?"

"Apparently, attracting killers and thieves in my sleep." I turn my eyes to him, chasing my fear and steeling my soul.

Marcus laughs and slaps the man nearest him on the shoulder. "We're not thieves, my friend. We're entrepreneurs. Come, have a look."

The men surrounding us make an opening as he leads the way toward Dock thirty-one. I study each of them, wondering if any have souls so dark I'll meet up with them in one of my dreams. Once I'm hunting my typical sort of demon, that is.

"So, angel, what is your real name?" Marcus asks as he approaches the back of a semi-tractor trailer.

"Angel is good enough," I answer, keeping my eyes on the shadows to avoid any surprises.

"What you need," Marcus smiles and pulls on the latch of the door, "is a weapon." The door of the trailer shifts. The hinges whine as the opening widens. One of his men reaches inside and pulls a box to the ground. Once the lid is pried open, the glint of the long, black barrel of an assault rifle catches my eye and I shake my head. "I need a knife, or a sword, or both, and not a prop or souvenir. What I don't need is a Kalashnikov. If I'm even able to do any harm to that mass of whatever the hell that dark cloud may be, a gun won't be the tool to do it with. Sadly, the sort of knives I need, as you must be well aware, are illegal in Ireland. So, unless you have black cloud demon repellent, thanks, but no thanks. You don't have what a person like me is in search of, after all."

Marcus says nothing. His smile widens. One of his men jumps up into the truck and tosses a box down to Marcus. He sets it on the ground and motions to the man to his right. The sealing tape is sliced open the length of the box. He bends the flaps back and pulls out a smaller box, longer than it is wide, and hands it to Marcus.

"Is this what you're talking about?" Marcus says, taking the package from the man and opening it to pull out a knife. He holds it in the palm of his hand, lifting his arm an inch, then dropping it back to the start.

"I'll be damned. You just might have a fucking black cloud exterminator."

He grins back, still balancing the blade in his open palm. "Several, to be exact. Seems rather light, well-balanced. Not a toy. Or a souvenir. Here." He reaches his hand toward me. "You try." The blade is cradled in the palm of his hand with the tip facing him as he proffers the weapon.

I take the handle between my thumb and the first knuckle of my forefinger and weigh it carefully. He was right. Light, balanced, fits easily in my grip. Not bulky. Sure enough, it is possibly one of the finest I've seen. Not a display item. And very illegal. But murder is illegal, also. Then I heave a sigh and hand it back.

"What do you want from me? No one gives a contraband throwing knife to someone without a string attached."

Marcus removes the blade from my hand. "This is what I

do. I sell knives, swords, and guns. You have money. There's no give here. In my world, there's only buy. And I have what you need. The real question is, how many?"

He awaits my answer, but my mind is caught on only one word. "Swords?"

His smile returns. "Nihonto. Tamahagane steel, folded sixteen times."

"A katana."

Two men jump into the back of the truck to retrieve a box. The feeling is like Christmas, waiting for them to open the packaging and hand me the sword, hilt-first. I unsheathe the weapon and examine the blade.

"Beautiful," I whisper, breathless with excitement. The blade is sharp enough to shave the hairs on my arm. "One. I'll take one. And five of those throwing knives."

Marcus nods his head. "Excellent! That'll be two thousand euro."

"What? I don't carry that kind of money around with me. Who does that?"

"People in need of what I sell." Marcus takes the katana from my grasp and hands it to one of his guards.

I want that sword. I need that sword. And those knives. I have to find a way to get them. The katana is returned to the box as the impulse to snatch it from them rises in my veins.

"I tell you what…"

The men stop, and Marcus returns his attention to me.

"I'll get the money from my account as soon as the bank opens. It's only hours away. Then, can you deliver the product to me? Say, I meet you back here around eleven a.m.?"

Marcus shakes his head in disbelief. "Do I look like a legitimate wholesaler? No. I don't do exchanges in the light of day." He turns his back to me. "Come back when you have the money."

"I may be dead before tomorrow. I need this now. Can I write you a check?"

Marcus shakes his head and motions for his guy to jump out of the back of the truck. "Let's get outta here. The sun's nearly up and this angel is playing us."

"I'll pay you double. Four thousand dollars. Let me take them now. I'll meet you anywhere of your choosing. Put the money in an envelope…"

Marcus releases the doors before they're completely closed. He turns to me with his focus targeted on me, contemplating.

"If I die before I can buy those weapons, you've lost a client and a hell of a lot of cash, Marcus." I wait as he weighs my offer in his mind.

Then he nods and his smile returns.

"At the beach. Ten-thirty. No sooner. No later. Wrap the money in a plain towel and leave it at the top of the ridge near the north shore of the bay. Someone will be waiting."

He hands me the katana and I release the breath I'd been holding. "I'll be there with the money."

Marcus narrows his eyes at me. "I know you will."

I unsheathe the sword once again. This had better work.

I'm taking, shall we say, one last stab at it. Collin isn't here. If he's on a flight, he'll never be able to reach me when, not if, they come for me again. These demons have substance, even if they seem to be ghosts. If I have the right weapons, I may be able to kill them or, at least, chase them away once and for all. I still wish I knew how Collin is involved with these monsters, and why the sound of his name chases them away. Tonight, maybe I'll find the answer. Or maybe these demons will be dead.

The last of the blades is handed to me, still boxed, in a canvas shopping bag with handles.

"Go directly home using back streets. If you're caught with

these weapons, I don't know you and you don't know me, kapiche?"

"Don't worry. I wouldn't admit to knowing you if my life depended on it."

"What're you gonna do with that?" he asks, nodding to the katana. "Anyone notices it, you'll get turned in."

I roll my eyes at him and sigh. "Do I look like a rookie?" I ask and slide the sheathed sword down the side of my pant leg and pull the shawl over me to conceal the unusual bulge.

Marcus's eyes level on me. "Ten-thirty. Don't be late."

I glare back at him, saying nothing while adjusting the sword to feel less awkward when I walk. I hope no one notices me. I had better have a plan in place long before I go to sleep tonight.

The street is still in darkness as I make my way through back alleys. Soon, the main streets will bustle with people on their way to work, tourists drifting through shops, and I will be just returning home from my foray into the seedy side of Dublin, which brings another matter to mind. To learn that Jesse is a garda is an even more unsettling development. His loyalty will be to his badge, as it should be, not to a simple woman he met at a pub. That he knows me will bring him closer into my orbit, and possibly when I need him to be the farthest from me. How long before he forgets our friendly chat and grows suspicious of me for the murders of Curtis and Joseph, two men I knew who were brutally murdered within weeks of my arrival?

If I don't get this matter with the rogue angels or demons settled soon, I'll be forced to find a new home. I may have to return to the United States, even if those who want me dead are awaiting my arrival. If I wait to meet up with these demons in my dreams, they'll always have the advantage by deciding where we'll fight. Tonight, I pick the venue and I'll do it while I'm still awake. This fight will be on *my* terms. *I* control the place and, hopefully, the outcome this time, as well. If all goes as planned, two deaths will be avenged before the night is through.

CHAPTER 22

T here's much to prepare with no time for what is necessary. Most of my day is spent planning while tearing strips of black cloth to tie around my thighs. I recall the route I usually take to the Temple Bar District. My mind searches the roads and alleyways for the place a fight could be staged with little to no interference by an innocent bystander. If I can get these rogues alone again, I may have the advantage, whether it be in my dreams or in my waking moments.

By the time I finish, I'm exhausted and lie down for a quick rest. Just a small nap before nightfall. With lavender laid beside my pillow, I drift off peacefully before my battle.

When my mind stirs again, I awaken to find the sky has already turned black. *Damn! I'm late!* I quickly gather the knives and tie them to my thighs over a pair of black leggings, concealed by the knee-length, long-sleeved dress. A long, plaid shawl pulled over my shoulders covers those I've strapped to my back, including the low-hanging katana. Taking the main streets to the river, I cross to the Temple Bar District where they're sure to find me. They've led me there in my dreams and followed me from that direction while awake.

When I arrive at the pub the usual crowd is assembled, not as jovial as before. Mostly they keep in tight groups and talk in low tones. One of the women notices me from before and motions me over. Waving to her, I tilt my head to the lone table where I usually sit. Tonight, I stay as far in the shadows as possible, watching for the rogues who wait for me. If they're as brazen as they've been in the past, they'll search for me, calling throughout the town even if I'm still awake. Like how I heard them the first night as Jesse walked me home from the pub. As soon as I sense them, I'll leave, move toward Ha'penny and take the fight toward the warehouses across the river.

The barmaid brings my tea and I sip it conservatively, keeping alert to anything unusual. After sitting for a time, I feel a set of eyes following my movements. A quick scan of the room doesn't reveal them. There doesn't seem to be anyone else paying attention to me. Just my imagination? I can't afford to ignore my intuition. If someone is tracking me, I'll be prepared. I probe the shadows again. As I do, the door whines as it swings inward and Jesse walks in.

Bloody hell. Why him? My jaw tightens, and my teeth grind together. I shift the katana on my back and pull my dress low to ensure it covers the blades at my thighs. *Don't let him notice the sword behind my back*, I pray while adjusting the shawl to conceal it.

After the way he eyed me on the street, I can't afford to hope that tonight he's a friend I can trust. I've learned from Rick and Sarah. If I'm lucky, he won't notice me, and I can slip out while his back is to me.

I return to perusing the shadows, starting from my right, beneath scarred tables dripping with spilled beer. I scan the corner behind the bar and the stools to the left corner. There. There was movement, I think. Is it the one I'm looking for?

The one waiting for me to move so they can call out in a chilling voice. Is there really someone or something there? Harmless introvert? Malevolent demon? I keep my thoughts on them while I continue to scan the left of me to the door and back to the shadows behind me again. The darkened areas under the tables seem harmless as well. All is quiet except for the one corner. Whoever or whatever is there hasn't made any moves yet. I wait to see what happens.

Half an hour passes and my cup is near empty. The tea has grown cold and I begin to think they won't come for me tonight. From the corner of my eye I notice Jesse still standing at the bar, talking and laughing with a small group of men. When the barmaid hesitates at my table to see if I'd like another cup, Jesse turns and his eyes catch on me. I decline the tea and rise from my chair, move to the front of the table gather my shawl around me. A swath of the plaid fabric swipes an empty bottle on the next table and I catch the bottle before it hits the floor.

"Excellent reflexes, Jaime." I feel his hot breath on the nape of my neck and note the scent of palm oil and men's cologne. When I turn to him, his eyes seem to penetrate me, and I swallow. The feeling of his presence suffocates me as I place the bottle upright on the table. "How're ye doin' this fair evenin'?" he finishes, placing a hand on the table.

"Hello, officer…" I look at him as if I trying to remember his name.

"Jesse. Please, call me Jesse." He waves his hand to the seat as if he'd like me to join him.

"Yes, of course. How are you?" Instead of returning to my seat, I shift my feet backward toward the door.

"Ya can't leave yet. I just got 'ere."

I force a smile and nod. "Ah, but I've been here a while and I need my rest, the baby you know," I tell him, patting my very round tummy lightly.

"Yes, the baby."

Hanging on the end of his sentence is the light whisper I've grown to recognize over the past few days. Searching the shadows and corners, I feel more eyes following my movements.

"Dark angel..." The persistent whisper sends chills up my arms.

Studying Jesse's expression, I see he can't hear them. He seems to be unaffected and continues on. "I was hopin' to buy ye another o' what yer drinkin'."

Chuckling softly to sound relaxed, I say, "I would love to, sometime, when I'm not pregnant and can hold more than a cup before making it home to the privy."

He bursts into laughter. But I'm impatient to get out of here. A dark cloud forms in the shadows of the tavern, moving toward me like fog on the moors. Their whispers nearly drown the noise of the rest of the room.

"I have to go if I hope to make it home in time." I tap his arm with my hand and rush toward the door.

He looks confused, but I don't care. My aloofness ensures his safety as well as mine.

When I reach the exit, I pull on the handle, but it won't open. Yanking several times does nothing to jar the wood from its surrounding frame. Even with all my might, it doesn't budge a centimeter. I turn to the barkeep with concern, but he merely shakes his head and shrugs, heading toward me to help get it open. The feeling of Jesse's eyes studying me as I desperately yank the handle, drives me to fight even harder, but the door won't budge. Standing back from the exit, I watch as the men slam their fists then bodies against the frame, then yank again. The door is locked.

No one can leave, and no one can get in, not even Collin.

I'm not dreaming. I'm awake. I must be awake. So how do they have me trapped? And what will I do when the mist of demons reaches me? I'm growing convinced they're demons. I've never known rogues to make their fight public. And I've never fought in a room filled with bystanders. Nothing like this has never happened in the waking hours and the knowledge of how badly this could play out forces my heart to beat faster.

Fog, the color of night, is forming beneath the tables and growing thicker with each breath I take. Grabbing the thick arm of the barkeep, I ask, "Do you have a back door?"

He looks at me as if to say, *of course.* "In the back."

"Take these people and get out of here, now."

"Why the hell would I do—?"

Before the words can escape his lips, the whispers grow louder, more fervent. People start to look around. The room grows quiet except for the whispered voices calling me. *Fuck.*

"Dark angel… Dark angel…," turns the air cold.

Without thinking, I slam my fist against the frame of the door, crushing the wood with my untethered blow and sending splinters flying throughout the suddenly quiet room. All eyes are on me, including a now more cautious, and suspicious garda. *Shit.* I turn toward the barkeep and take a controlled breath.

"What's your name?" I ask him.

"Sean," he answers in a faltering voice.

"Sean, if you don't get them out of here this instant, there'll be more than two people killed this week in Dublin." I say it calmly, but he takes it as a threat.

Eyes narrowed, Jesse steps toward us. "What do you know 'bout those killings?"

Turning my attention to him, I speak through clenched teeth. "You see the black cloud forming in your bar?" I direct their attention to the darkness enveloping the free spaces between us and the wall, eliciting gasps around the room. "That isn't smoke. Look harder, smell the air, you know it isn't. It is something, someone, dark and malicious. They're intent on killing someone. That would be me. If you get everyone else out of here, no others have to die tonight. Do you understand me?"

He nods in stunned silence and turns to Sean.

"Pub's closed, everyone," Sean belts through the bar in a deep voice. "This way, folks!" He nervously shuffles patrons to his backroom, periodically turning back to the demon mist invading his bar. "Quickly! Quickly!"

Jesse grabs my arm. "What's goin' on?"

I turn to him with my jaw set. "I don't know enough and haven't the time to explain what I do know. If you want to live, get out. Now."

The center of the tavern is the best place to fight, but there are tables and chairs in the way. Immediately, I set to overturning and shoving them to the sides to create an open arena where I can move freely. Once the space is cleared, I back up to the bar as the pub's patrons scatter to the walls. Some follow the barkeep to the back door while others watch in awe at the black cloud materializing in front of me, taking pictures with their cell phones. Damnit! I wish I didn't have to do this here, but here goes nothing. I slip the shawl from my shoulders and reach for two of the knives strapped to my thighs.

"What in bloody hell—" Jesse starts toward me.

"I don't have time to explain, Jesse!" I tell him before he can say anything further.

Sean returns to the front with those who'd followed him. "Back door won't budge. What in the bloody hell!" He repeats, stopping in place, awestruck by the cloud that has tripled in size.

Without taking my eyes off the cloud, I shout to them. "Everyone stay out of the middle of the room until I say so."

"Jaime—" One of the gentlemen I'd sat with nights ago, steps toward me.

"I'm sorry, but I don't have time to chinwag right now," I answer in a clipped tone.

Jesse reaches for me, "Give me those knives before you hurt yourself."

Pulling my arm from his grasp, I forget to check my strength once again. In my haste, I bring my hand down and tear a half-moon chunk of wood from the bar with my fist. "Shit! I said not now, Jesse!" I shout, then move around the room.

"My God! There's a plugged lash in the middle the pub, trashin' the place!" I hear from a man in the crowd. "Savage!"

"I haven't a fecking idea what's happenin', but I'm uploadin' this hatchet to the internet," replies another.

"Craic show ya got tonight, Sean!"

I don't know if I should be relieved the crowd is mostly mesmerized, and not as frightened as I am. *Jesus*! The age of internet. This could get even more messy, though, when shit gets real.

My eyes stay on the black form, wondering what final shape it will take. "If you all will listen to what I tell you, we might make it home safe tonight. Move to the back of the bar and stay away from *anything* that's glass. Throw every bottle or pint, everything breakable, to the floor. Don't approach me and don't go near the dark cloud. Got it?"

Jesse moves toward me again. "Jaime—"

"Jesse!" I turn to him and he leans into my face.

"Get out of my way and let me handle this!" he snaps.

"You don't understand. I'm the only person in this room

who *can* handle it. And I'm still afraid." I stare back at him. "You don't know what you're dealing with here."

"But you do?" He has a really good point.

"No. But I have, uh, skills." I hope he finds a way to trust me and let me try.

"I can't let you do this. Back up." He throws his arms out to the side.

"Wait! You don't have a weapon."

"You don't even know what this is, Jaime," he answers. "How do you know if I need a weapon?"

"I don't know. There's some substance to them but not much. I can only hope that the knives I have will be useful. I suspect this thing is what killed Curtis and Joseph. They did this to me, attacking me in the night." I pull up my sleeve to show the deep scratch and burn marks. "So, it only makes sense to have something."

In the light, the formless figure appears more like the color of tar with an outline of several arms, as if the mass is more like a bundle of spirits. A grouping of souls in unison. Not rogue angels, not ghosts, either. *What the hell?* Is that why I couldn't hurt them? I was punching air. There's barely any physical form. Fortunately for me, the more I wait, the more there seems to be substance to them. Maybe not fully spirits. I can only hope that, if I can't reason with them, the blades will be enough to finish the job.

"Holy Jesus, Mary and Joseph. Jaime," Jesse whispers to me, "you can't fight that. Ye're pregnant for the love of God."

"This wouldn't be my worst experience since I've been pregnant, Jesse," I answer, and realize I may have said too much. When he peers back at me with his brows tightening his forehead, I shrug my shoulders. "Morning sickness. Pure, unadulterated hell." I turn back to the cloud before he can ask any further questions.

As they move toward me, I step forward, holding my arms crossed at my chest, with the blades facing away from me. When the darkness reaches me, Jesse reaches for me to pull me out of the way, but I shove him back against the bar and bring one arm back to slash the thick mass. As I do, a shriek fills the room and I swing out with the second arm before Jesse gains his footing. Thank God, they feel pain. Another cry echoes as patrons in the bar shout their excitement. They still believe this is a show, not reality. *Damn it.* I don't know if I can focus with a cheering section. My concentration could be easily broken if I take my mind off what I'm doing.

From the corner of my eye I see Jesse has recovered. He charges the black mass, but it immediately throws him back against the bar again. He attempts one more bout but is tossed back like a rag doll, just the same. The crowd doesn't cheer this time, realizing this may not be what they thought. Sean leaves the back of the bar to come to my side, but I shove him backward.

"Please, Sean, stay back."

The cloud circles me, then hesitates, the same as a sentient being plotting their strategy. The smoke seems to have even more substance and density than when we met up in my sleep. Within a breath of time, their darkness converges on me, arms reaching for me from all directions. They pull at my hair before I slice the dark atmosphere again and again, causing some of my brown locks to fall to the floor as their shrieks fill the air. Soon the mass hovers in one spot. I can only think they're assessing the situation.

"Dark angel..." they repeat like a canter in a hollow cathedral.

"Your vocabulary is rather limited, wouldn't you say? Why don't you speak to me?" I call back to the writhing darkness.

This time I don't wait for them. Dashing forward, I charge

into the middle of clawing arms, turning one direction, then the other, cutting the air and anything in my way. The howls are deafening as I slash and turn, jab and slit. The blades are working! Soon a form falls from the grouping of spirits to the tavern floor. When I turn to see the monster on the wooden floor, I realize the mistake as a boney claw reaches for me to exact revenge.

I'm knocked in several directions by the force of their blows, then thrown against the bar beside Sean. From the corner of my eye, I see male patrons growing angry while women gasp in horror. Sean grabs a full bottle from beside the register.

"No! You can't fight them! They've already killed!" Remembering the dead spirit on the floor, I turn from him to shout to someone nearby. "Try the doors again!"

While I'm preoccupied, Sean advances on the gyrating cloud. Before I can stop him, he swings the bottle, breaking it against a body in the mass and causing more shrieking. In the waking world, they can be hurt by blunt force. I'll be damned. The demon cloud turns on him, grabbing his clothing and pulling him into the swarming limbs and clawing hands.

"No!" I shout in a panic. As Jesse rushes forward, I grab his jacket, throwing him backward. "I'll get him! Don't move!"

With my head down, I dart into the swirling cloud, searching for a mortal. Nails claw at my face and tear at my clothing. The knives in my hands are knocked to the floor as another blow splits my chin. My face burns and I don't have the knives to protect me, but I have to find Sean. When my hands reach his sleeve, I pull him toward me, then shove him from the mist. I raise my arms to pull the katana from the sheath strapped low on my back and begin slashing again.

As the sword splits the air, high-pitched screams fill the room. Soon another body falls to the floor and I back out of the mass, still slicing at writhing bodies, until my back is against the bar once more. There are two bodies on the floor, both aged, gray forms that look almost human and already long dead. A new form of demon? Sean stands to my left, severely cut and bleeding, shaking his head in shock. He'll be fine.

Other spectators cling to the walls, watching the battle, careful to stay out of the way.

The mass of evil finally slows its movement until there's definition to the individual devils inside. As they take a human form they separate around the room. I wait, watching them all, knowing one of them is sure to be the leader. Their attacks were to too well planned to be a disorganized set of bodies without one of them orchestrating their movements. I'll speak with the one in charge. Seems they're just as eager to speak with me.

"Dark angel… Ye know ye can't survive."

Jesse moves toward me, "What do they mean? Why do they call you dark angel?"

I hold up my palm and shake my head. "I promise your questions will be answered. This isn't the time." I return my full attention to the demons before me.

"Why? Why don't you think I can survive? Who are you?" My voice is strong and commanding. I sense they don't appreciate insolence from a female and it pisses me off.

"Ye know who we are, dark angel. Use yer senses and ye'll see."

I breathe in the scent of those circling me to both sides, behind the bar, so I don't lose track of them. The smell of dirt fills my mind, ancient soil, scattered across the isle, across the centuries. I'm confused. The scent is infused with wet, moorland grass. Celtic symbols appear in my mind, an ancient language from before the recording of time, before Christ walked the earth. *Druids? Are you fucking kidding me?* My jaw tightens with the realization.

"What do you want with an archangel?" I watch as the clouded appearances grow clearer, their gray faces creased deep with time. Pale hair falls to sunken shoulders.

"We want ye and yer offspring dead."

My body shivers as I force my fear back down my throat. "Why?"

"This is our soil, the land of our ancestry. We protect our people from death brought on by yer kind."

I shake my head, my teeth still clenched. "How dare you say you're saving these people from me? You killed two of your own with your vicious attacks."

"They were loyal t' ye. It was written in their souls, poisonin' the pot."

"You have no idea what was written in their souls. They were harmless. Kind, loving people."

"And yer harmless yerself? Ye never hurt a soul? Tell 'em, dark angel. Tell 'em what yer kind does."

I look around the room at the frightened faces, still clutching their cell phones high enough to record. All turned toward me, begging the answer. "I protect."

"Is that what ye call it? Yer kind of murder is protection?" The voice hisses from the lifeless mouth of the druid leader before me.

"We don't murder. We protect from murderers. Dark angels hunt them at night."

"Killin' 'em in their sleep, is that not right, dark angel?"

"No. I mean, yes." There's a gasp from the crowd. The mortals standing around the room stare at me in shock. Curtis and Joseph were killed in the night. I have to think fast before the crowd believes I killed them in their sleep. These demons may be convincing enough. "We kill in our sleep, but only those who have also killed. We're sent here to protect the people of earth from dark forces like you, trying to harm them."

I can't tell if the druids understand. Their dead expressions don't shed any clarity. Then the leader speaks again.

"Who gave ya the power to be judge, jury, and executioner?"

I turn to the speaker for the druids. "God."

A rush of voices travel around the room.

"Yer God has given ye the ability to use yer power for evil. Not all dark angels kill only murderers."

"And I find *them* as well. There are dark angels who turn bad. I'm not one of them."

"What 'bout the child ye carry in yer womb, dark angel?"

His words catch me off guard, the same with those surrounding me. Five druid spirits move toward me, knocking the katana from my hands. One of them grabs my throat while the other tries to force my arms behind my back. I rip my arms from the cold clutches, reach for the two knives at my back then plunge them into the chests of two of them. I'm rushed from behind. The two weapons are knocked from my hands. Before I can reach the last knife at my back, the three others grab me and wrestle me to the floor, holding my arms and legs. As much as I kick and fight, I'm unable to tear free. Either they're much stronger than archangels or I'm much weaker from pregnancy. Seeing me overcome by the spirits, several people around the perimeter of the pub rush the ancient spirits to save me. Their advances are instantly abated with a sweep of an arm, each thrown back against the walls as if they were toys.

I can't let them hurt these kind people who have taken me in and accepted me. But I can't move. I smell the moorland grass and vaguely hear Collin's voice in my mind, calling to me. Is it a dream, a memory? Am I losing my mind?

"Collin," I whisper, knowing our next reunion will be in heaven.

Jaime, call for me to come to you, his voice whispers back, barely audible.

I shake the thought, knowing it must be my imagination. There's no possible way he could help me now. Unless he slipped into the tavern before the entrances were sealed, like in a dream, his body and spirit are locked out of the tavern.

Several hold me to the floor as their leader approaches and lowers himself over my body. I fight to free myself, but I must be weakened from fatigue, maybe even the baby is draining my energy. Or maybe I have to face that these druids are stronger than me.

The leader tears the cloth around my abdomen. I fight the arms pinning me even harder through my panic but they're far too strong. My heart pounds in my chest. How is it possible?

"We can't just stand 'ere!" Sean shouts. He lunges toward me.

Others in the pub join him, chairs and broken bottles in their hands as weapons, unaware of the strength of these druids that I can only suspect have been lured by Lucifer into killing dark angels. The concerted attacks of these heroes are immediately halted, and bodies are tossed backward with little effort the minute they advance.

"Stop! Leave them alone! They're one of you!" I shout to the druids to no avail.

Again, I hear Collin, this time shouting into my mind. *Jaime, call my name, now!*

When I open my mouth to call him, the leader's long nails slither over my burgeoning belly to just below the bulge. His nails, like razors, sink into my flesh to reach my baby. I hear the distant scream without realizing it's mine. My sides, nearly numb from shock, only feel the trickle of blood. The scent of iron fills my head. My strength fades as I fight their grasp. They're too strong. All seems hopeless in the face of my struggle to live. I turn to the shadows to see the one I noticed earlier, watching. Are those green eyes? It can't be.

Then I hear his voice shout my name. *Jaime!*

"Collin? Come to me! Help me!" I cry, and the druids are momentarily stayed.

"I'm here, Jaime," his voice calls back from the shadows, not my mind. Can't be.

My heart pounds in my chest at the sound of his voice. He's here. I can't believe he's here. Then I realize—he sat in the corner and watched? He didn't jump in to help? *What in holy hell?* Did he want to see me suffer? Or teach me a lesson? The thought weakens my resolve and I start to cry. I can't believe I need him to protect me after all.

"Please help me," I sob. "They want our baby."

"They won't touch our baby, Jaime. Do you trust me?"

I nod, not fully sure that I do. My breathing grows heavy with my sobs. "I can't see you."

"I'm here." His voice echoes around the room and I turn to search for him.

"Stay out o' this, Leary," the druid leader hisses.

I'm stunned. How do they know his name?

"Not a chance. She's my wife." He moves out of the shadows closer to where I'm pinned to the floor. My heart skips a beat at the sight of this man, this beautiful man, calling me his spouse. I want to melt into his arms.

The druids seem restless, shifting their weight and loosening their grip on me. For some reason, they seem to fear Collin.

"That means your child is only half druid descent. Unprotected by yer blood." Their mouthpiece answers, tightening his grip on my abdomen to try to rip my flesh free. I scream out in agony.

"Stop!" Collin shouts and the windows in the room rattle in their tracks as the druid releases me and rises to face Collin.

What? What in the hell is he talking about, "half *druid descent*?" Collin descended from druids? Does that make him protected under their covenants? At least protected against other druids?

"You're wrong." Collin's voice roars throughout the bar, causing the room to grow quiet.

His words are controlled, but his anger is palpable. His expression turns dark with fury. Even *I* feel a tremor ripple through my body at the rage in his eyes.

"My baby is pure druid descent. His mother is of the O'Connor clan."

My mind spins at his revelation. How could I not know this? And how could the druids not know it as well. Don't they know all the families descended from their covenant? Is it because my family left when I was so young, changing my scent *and* my name?

"Why do you think she could fight you so well? Only a druid could kill another. You know it as well as I."

"Yer dark angel wife is a danger to the survival o' this people."

"Be careful what you say about my wife," he answers with jaw set tight, "as I'm a dark angel too." His eyes narrow at them. "And I know she would protect these people with her life. If you want your spirits to survive, I'd suggest you leave her be and *never* return for my family again."

The room falls silent and the druid leader is motionless, his eyes practically penetrating Collin's form. Collin's lips pull tight as he glares back at the soul in front of him.

"If you *ever* threaten her life, or the life of my child again, she won't be the only angel sending druid spirits to Hell." He bends over and lifts my katana into his hands, pulling the blade slowly across his body to his right shoulder in a striking pose. "I'll kill you all before you lay another finger on her."

Not one soul stirs as Collin faces down the dark leader, preparing to finish what I'd started. Seconds pass as if they're minutes. I hold my breath, waiting for someone to speak or move. Then Collin lowers his head, his eyes directed toward the leader as if he's about to fight. The druids recognize the gesture as much as any dark angel. Their continued existence is threatened.

The hold on my arms and legs releases and the spirits slip over my body as they congregate in the center of the tavern. Their leader bows his head to Collin in concession. Their dark essence combines into a cloud once again, slipping along the floor, gathering their dead amongst them, until all signs of their presence in the tavern are lost in the shadows.

Once they dissipate, the pub erupts in excited conversation and cheers while Jesse and Sean rush to us. My name is called many times, but I only want to hear Collin.

My body is numb. I haven't the strength to make it to my feet on my own. The amount of blood spilled on the floor is more frightening than the tears in my flesh are life-threatening. Still, I feel weak and nearly lose consciousness when I push up to my elbows as he kneels at my side.

"Are you all right? My God, look at the blood." He strokes my face with his brows pinched as they do when he's worried about me.

"I'm fine. Just a little abrasion." I peer down at the shredded cloth exposing my abdomen and the torn, red-streaked flesh. The flow of blood is slowing. Looks worse than it truly is. "What in the hell took you so long?"

"Welcome back, Jaime Connor." The glimmer in those

beautiful eyes, and damn that smile, melting my heart. I'd forgotten how much I love the way he looks at me. I can't take my eyes from him while his hand brushes the hair from my forehead.

"What?" He asks as his eyes crease with his smile.

The trickle of a tear rolls onto my cheek. "I can't turn away."

Reaching for the droplet, he chuckles subtly and wipes it away. "Why?"

"I don't want you to leave."

"I'm not going." His face shows pride as his hand slips over my large tummy.

"Am I dreaming? Are you really here?"

He smiles and nods. "You're awake and I'm really here."

"You're not leaving me?" I want to believe him but find it difficult after he came to me in my thoughts those nights but didn't stay. Is he truly here?

He shakes his head, still smiling. "I won't leave you. You only have to tell me *stay*."

"Stay." His smile grows as the word leaves my lips. "Stay." Then I think about his words. "Why didn't you stay last night when I asked?"

"I was across the ocean, trying to get to you. But I'm here now."

"Don't ever let me leave you again."

Collin laughs and gathers me in his arms, lifting me to my feet. "I promise I'll never give you a reason to leave me again. You did pretty good with those druids, you know."

"Not *that* great. By the way, you never answered me. What took you so long? They nearly killed me *and* our baby."

Sighing, he stares at the floor for a moment before returning his focus to my eyes. Almost seems ashamed. "I wanted to help. But when you left...because of the contingency on our union...anytime you push me away, I can't come to you until asked." The pain on his face is obvious as he turns away.

"But wasn't that over when I accepted the covenant?"

"No." He answers immediately, nearly cutting me off. His eyes glisten down at me again. I hold my breath, staring into his soul and feeling the pulse of his heart. "The contingency will always be there. My fault. If I had done it correctly from the start, there would be no contingency and, well, I'd always be here, even when you're being stubborn."

I almost laugh at the insanity of it all. The entire matter of contingencies and covenants seems ludicrous. "Nothing can change it, not even me?"

He shakes his head. "Not even you."

Collin seems so different. He's changed since I last saw him. There's still that internal strength that radiates confidence. At the same time, there's a quiet humility when he looks at me. Has fatherhood made him lose his selfish tendencies.

A crowd of Dubliners surround us, now, chattering about what happened, some speaking with animated excitement, some straining to hear our conversation. "You know, we're gonna have to leave here, now. After all this...these people may run us out with pitchforks."

"What do ye mean ye have to leave?" Jesse stands beside me with his hands on his hips. "Yer muckers here very well won't let their own li'l angel fly the coop, now will they, miss? Oh, pardon me, I mean missus." He regards Collin respectfully. "Besides, yer not allowed to leave the city 'til we get this whole matter sorted out. And I'm afraid it'll take some time."

Collin puts his arms around my shoulders and pulls me close, whispering in my ear. "Whatever you choose. I'll follow you anywhere."

"I love it here, Collin, but I'm afraid of the consequences."

"We can discuss this later. For now, let's get you home where you can rest." He pulls me in for a tighter hug then steps back and puts his hand on my belly. "I'm not used to this being between us."

I scowl at him. "Get used to it. He'll be there for the next eighteen years. Or more."

"He?" Collin grins at me. "Or she?"

Oh, be still my heart. I grin now, too. "Or she."

Suddenly, I feel awkward that the tavern's patrons are witness to our most personal moments. I'm not a fan of all the attention, either, having never fought in front of an awake mortal before, let alone a crowd. I have no idea what to say.

"Yay! Jaime, yer our hero!" one person shouts.

Why would they say that? I didn't save anyone. I lower my head in shame. "No, I'm no hero. Two people died because of me."

"Yes, Jaime. Yer our hero. Ye saved us," another shouts and reaches through the bodies surrounding us to pat my shoulder.

But I didn't. I didn't save one soul. "I'm not a hero. I'm sent to protect you and I failed."

I can't tear the idea from my mind of what Curtis and Joseph endured in their last minutes on earth. Their kind hearts made them targets of evil intent. Then my mind drifts to Durudee and deeper shame fills my thoughts.

"I've had many battles in me pub, but I've never seen anything the likes o' this. Yer a wonder, Jaime. And my pub will always be known as the one where an angel fought the devil. And she was pregnant to boot."

With all that's happened, we can't stay in Dublin. These people have an image of me greater than I can carry. I'm part immortal and part human. My human-like mistakes will be amplified because I'm an archangel. Now that they know about me, the scrutiny will be unlike that of other mortals. We could never live a normal life. At least, as normal as life gets for a dark angel such as me.

Collin sees the look on my face and squeezes my hand, then leads me toward the door. As I take my first step forward, however, my head suddenly feels light. After taking another step, the sensation like a knife tearing through my abdomen brings me to my knees.

Collin is speaking to me, possibly shouting at me in a panic, but I can't hear him. All I know is the ringing in my ears and the excruciating pain throbbing through me won't let up. I feel sick and the room seems to have been turned off kilter. Jesse, Sean, and others around me are also shouting, but not a sound reaches my mind as their mouths contort with excitement.

People are rushing, scattering. When I reach for the floor to steady my quaking body, my hand slips forward in a thick, red puddle. I peer down to see the pool of blood at my knees, dripping from my palm and fingers. The bar and the strange faces surrounding me blur to unrecognizable. The pressure on my knees lifts and my body feels as if it's rising to the sky. I can't feel Collin's arms holding me, nor his fingers pressing into my flesh. Is he carrying me, or am I dying and my soul rushing to Hell? A flood of fresh air across my face tells me I'm outside the pub.

The street lights that typically glimmer along the Temple Bar District are mere pinpoints. Their brilliance flickers then dims, the same as all else around me. There's no sound, only a hum in my ears until I hear Collin's voice shout, "Jesse, can you go any faster? She's bleeding badly!"

My mouth moves to beg him not to take me to a hospital,

but I don't know if the words came out. I struggle to stay awake, remain lucid, but I'm suddenly very tired and lose the fight. Everything seems so far from me now, and I can't hear my own heartbeat. I can't feel Collin's hand in mine, but I know it's there. I know it's there. *Don't leave me, Collin.*

I want to squeeze my fingers around his, to let him know I'm all right. But I can't. My muscles won't move. I feel one more sharp pain, then nothing.

CHAPTER 23

Lights flash then dim, flash then dim, until another strobe captures my attention, sending my thoughts jumbled and shattered to shreds of unintelligible nothingness. There's no weight or substance to my body. Could be a dream. Or death. Is this how Hell feels?

What was once blurred and indiscernible has sharpened to a finer clarity. I'm floating down a cold corridor, my teeth chattering with incessant rhythm as fluorescent fixtures pass above me.

"Stay with us!" The woman is Irish. This can't be Hell, but it surely isn't Heaven either.

My body feels detached. I want to run, but I can't seem to move.

The pulsing in my heart is weak, nearly non-existent as I work at moving my extremities, forcing my fingers forward until they obey. Some sensation returns. Not all. *Beat, heart, beat.* Why won't it obey? More mobility returns to my limbs. So does the feeling. Something covers my nose and mouth. *What is this shit?* My heart skips a beat then charges like a bull in my chest, incited by my anxiety. When I reach up to pull the object from my face, rip it off, a hand grabs mine and tells me to leave it be. That Irish woman's voice. *Bloody hell.*

Who is she? Another demon, for fuck sake? Doesn't she realize *I can destroy her*? The fury she inspires pulses through my weak body, protecting me from danger. My heart may be beating slower, but the slowly surging adrenaline will soon change all of that.

The more coherent I become, the more a section on my forearm starts to sting and I reach for the area of irritation. Something foreign protrudes from my skin. Whatever the hell *that* is, it doesn't belong there. Once again, the Irish woman reaches for my hand and tells me not to touch. *What?*

This is *my* body. Who the hell *is she?* Who *is* this woman? My mind races as I consider my surroundings. A corridor, lights, someone I don't know. I don't remember walking here. My last memory is of the pub. Now I'm here. Am I dreaming? Or am I awake? I don't remember coming in the door. I must be dreaming, and this isn't a harmless woman. She's a demon. But there seems to be more of them around me. Where did all of them come from? Did they find me because of the battle in Sean's pub?

Another fluorescent light flashes above my head and I'm reminded of Collin's memory, the night he and his first wife fought off numerous demons until they were overwhelmed, and her throat was slit. Have they found me, too? Will they work in unison to kill me and my baby?

The fighter instinct in me takes over and I'm suddenly grabbing the hand that has mine and throwing the person over my body, across the corridor. Her squeal tells me she'll probably not try that again. Another tries to hold my arms down and I do the same with them. As I do, however, a searing pain shoots through my abdomen and I barely catch my breath. What are they doing to me? Is that naked asshole from Thailand here, cutting me open like the sneaky bastard he is?

A cry of agony doesn't release my torment, and I roll to my side. There has to be something sharp nearby that I can use to protect myself. Where's my katana?

I need to escape their hold and then kill one of them to escape the dream. My head is light again and I fear losing consciousness. I have to fight it. If I'm too weak, they'll have me. But wait! Is that Collin? In the distance, running toward me with someone at his side. They're here to help me. Relief flows through me at the sight of his face.

"Collin." I try to call to him, but my voice only comes as a whisper. There's another woman behind him. Who's that? A demon sent to stop him? I clear my throat and try again.

"Collin, look out…" I gasp as loud as possible.

"Jaime, no!"

What? What did he say? Did he say *no*? My body is struck weak again at his words.

He can't be a part of this. He couldn't have turned against me. Could he? Has he turned rogue? Pretending to be on my side, pure of intent until I trust him again?

Another stab shoots through me and a warm sensation floods my body. The woman with Collin has planted a syringe in the tube coming from my arm. She sent something into my body.

"No, Collin…" Lying on the pad beneath me, I reluctantly relax and lose control of my limbs. "Don't let them kill me…don't let them kill our ba…by."

***

Dark waves of cool then warmth flow through me as I try to force my eyes open. A hiss at my side heightens my senses and I pull open my eyelids a crease to an assault of brilliant light through my lashes. I blink the weight of sleep from my eyes and allow my pupils to constrict before opening them wider to the glare.

My body has no sensation; my fingers are numb. When I tighten my muscles to lift my arms, they won't move. I fight to raise them, but they're held down by a strong restraint. My eyes follow the sheets to my wrists, wrapped in cloth straps sewn to the bed. Even in my weakened state, with slight effort, I could tear them from the mattress. Tensing my muscles, demanding them to move and obey my command, the threads shred and the cloth rips free. The first to go are these tubes in my arms.

As I search my arm with a numb hand, I hear his voice call to me. "Jaime, no!" *Traitor.*

I shoot a glare that would have brought him to his knees if I had the gift of deadly vision. *How dare you? How could you?* My words catch in my throat so that they can only be heard by me.

He dodges my right hook and grabs my arms, holding them tight to keep me still. Betrayed once again. I try to cry out but can't. My voice is gone, and my throat is on fire. *Damn! What did you do to me?* My husband. My betrayer. *How could you do this? I thought you loved me.*

As my rage mounts, he leans over me and kisses my lips and cheek so gently, I almost believe he cares. My teeth still grind together with fury. I lean forward to snatch his lip in my teeth, but he moves before I can latch on.

"It's okay, Jaime. You're in a hospital." He smiles at me and for the first time since I left him in Colorado, I'm able to really look into those eyes. The ones I love too damn much.

A woman in nursing scrubs rushes in. "'Old her while I give her a sedative."

In a rage, I shake my head. Collin holds up his hand. "It's better if you let me calm her. She's only frightened because she doesn't know where she is."

"Are ye certain? 'Cause she looks feral to me." She waits near my bed, the syringe still in her grasp.

Collin smiles his comforting grin. "If you give her that, she'll wake the same every time. I promise you that. I can calm her. She won't hurt anyone else. I'll stay with her until she's settled and fully awake."

Did he say *anyone else*? I hurt someone? Not a demon, a person? I'm mortified at the idea. My whole purpose here on earth is coming undone, like a centrifuge separating matter. Instead of helping, I'm hurting. With my emotions taking over, my ability to save grows weaker. How much longer before I'm incapacitated and killed by my own failings?

Collin reaches for a tissue. "It's not your fault. You didn't know." He blots the drops under my eyes, then unties my left hand, giving it a soft brush with his lips. "If I woke up surrounded by people poking and prodding me, I'd have reacted the same."

The nurse checks the gadgets around me, her nametag reads *Nancy—Nurse Nancy. Beautiful.* An IV in my hand gives me clear fluid. Another in my other arm gives me blood.

Then I notice it. Something feels wrong.

Studying the room, I see pumps for the fluids and monitors to show my heartbeat and respirations. I can clearly see the peaks and valleys marking my life force. When I look toward the foot of my bed I can tell there's something missing. I can see the foot of the bed. No bulge in the way. When I reach for my belly, there's no mass of a child incubating, waiting to be born. Patting the area, I find my tummy is numb and empty of life. No baby. Just thick, empty skin. Panic rises up my throat as my eyes search the room. *Where's my child?*

Fury obliterates my commonsense, and again, my hands ball into a fist, preparing to take someone out of this world.

This time, it's Collin I'm wrestling with. What did he do with my child? I'll kill him before he takes another breath. The bastard leans his body over mine, pinning me to the mattress to protect his *ass*, knowing what I'll do to him once I work my hands free. Why didn't he leave when he took my baby?

"Stop, Jaime, it's all right." His voice, however, doesn't console me. *Asshole!*

From the corner of my eye, I see the nurse backing away from my bed, reaching for the syringe in her pocket. "Thought ye said ye could control her?"

If my hands were free, I'd break her jaw to shut her up. As I tense my muscles, ready to throw Collin off me, I see concern grow in his eyes. He knows what I'll do to him. He's lucky to have survived this long.

"Sweetheart, calm down," he tells me in a poor attempt at a soothing tone. Noticing my focus away from him, he turns to the nurse with the syringe in her hands. "You're not helping," he tells her through clenched teeth. Then he whispers in my ear, "Shh, it's okay. It's okay. Our baby's fine." He turns to the nurse. "Get her baby from the nursery. Go now."

The nurse hesitates for a moment and my eyes narrow on her, preparing to attack.

I sense Collin's fear growing as he addresses her again. "Do you want me to set her free? If you have any sense, you'll go."

The woman steps backward, puts the syringe in her pocket, then turns and leaves the room in a rush.

Holding my arms under his body, he reaches for my cheek and kisses me, whispering in my ear. "You're gonna start bleeding again with all this fighting. Our baby's fine. She's just fine."

His words stun me into submission. My arms fall limp. *She?* I clear my throat and try to speak, but the words still won't come out. Why can't I speak? I put my hand up and tap against my trachea and try to clear my throat again.

"It's only temporary. They had to intubate you, so they could put you to sleep." I scowl at him to show my disapproval. "Jaime, you were bleeding. You nearly died." I see the memory cloud his eyes until they glisten with unspent tears. "They had to take the baby early to save you. And to save her." He must notice the fear in my eyes again because he kisses my hand several times, shaking his head. "She's fine. She's a beautiful baby girl with her mother's eyes. And, hopefully, not her mother's fiery temperament."

A silent chuckle escapes my mouth. How dare he make me laugh when I'm in distress?

Little time passes before the nurse returns with a rolling bassinette. Inside is a small baby swaddled in a pink blanket. The woman apprehensively reaches over and pushes the button to raise the head of my bed just a bit. She recoils her hand when finished, as if I might gnaw it off should she come too close. She keeps it up, one of these times I just might.

"Can't raise ye more. Ye've lost too much blood and yer pressure is still low. Ye'd pass out." She tucks the pillow behind my shoulders and I give her a forced smile.

The nurse turns to leave us alone, but hesitates at the door, turning back to us again. "They said yer some kind o' angels, right? Black angels," She grasps the cross hanging around her neck and clutches it tight in her fist. Collin and I don't answer, wondering what's on her mind. "Does that mean yer baby." She seems uncomfortable with her own words and can't look us in the eyes. "Enjoy yer child. She's beautiful." She closes the door behind her and we're finally alone.

I shake my head at Collin and he smiles. "I know. It's all right. They don't know what to think of us."

He lifts our tiny girl from the bassinette, gently snuggling her before laying her in my arms. The scent is so similar to Collin's musky Irish dew. And she has a hint of Asian seaweed, also. Maybe from the packing in my wound at the farmer's house. Another scent overpowers the rest. The smell of a fresh-from-heaven soul, the reason the earthbound fall in love with their babies. I could take in her scent all day. Can't keep my lips from kissing her skin. I want to breathe her into me.

Looking her over–fingers, toes, tiny chin, sweet little nose–I wait for her eyes to open. When they finally do, I see they're not mine, but his. Someday, when they have their true color, I bet they'll be as deep a green. I can tell already.

"Oh, baby Taylor," I finally eke out in a coarse, barely inaudible whisper. My voice may be hoarse, but at least now I can make a sound.

Collin cocks his head to the side. "Baby Taylor?"

His accent has grown thicker in the short time of being among his countrymen. Mmm.

"I love that name," he says with his intoxicating gaze heating my soul. My heart is overflowing with love. For them both.

"Collin," I whisper, then hesitate.

"I know. Don't worry. I have that already worked out."

I'm not sure I understand what he means or that he really knows what concerns me. I don't know if he sees the improbability of us staying where mortals know what we are. There's danger to us, but more danger to them. The battle in the pub will become an historic event everyone will share. We won't be able to run from it. There's no way to quell the excitement that will certainly arise initially. The disappointment when they realize we don't meet their expectations is soon to follow. If we find a demon among them, we have no choice but to kill it. Some won't understand.

After that comes animosity. Our friends could turn on us. We'll have no peace.

What's worse—those who hunt me, no doubt, have their tentacles in every country of the world. They would soon learn of the dark angels here, including every one of their friends. Anyone we allow ourselves to care about would be in danger because of us.

"Don't worry. Trust me. I already have this worked out." He's reading my thoughts and sees I'm not comforted by his veiled promises.

"How?" I manage in a slightly louder voice.

"You'll see." He gives me that smile he reserves for times when he's being slick.

"Collin Leary—"

"Trust me." His eyes penetrate my soul.

In my current emotional state, I couldn't rule out the chance I will suffocate him in his sleep if he betrays me once more.

His eyes narrow at me. "I know that look."

I only smile back at him with a sardonic slant to my mouth. Better to keep him on his toes.

"I know *that* look, too," he says, then raises his eyebrows in a sultry way.

Good. We have an understanding.

"Jaime..." He breathes in deep and I see there's more on his mind. "I don't think I've told you..." Sighing deeply, he hesitates for a moment before going on. "I don't know how to say this to you, so I hope I don't confuse you. It may come out all jumbled. But I'm gonna say it anyway. In the States, when I saw you in my dream before we actually met—"

"Collin...don't."

"No. I have to. I need you to know. There's much you don't understand. When I saw you, I couldn't believe you'd shown up in my gallery like that."

"Collin, it's over. Please don't go through this again."

"Please, Jaime. You have to know. I've rehearsed this so many times over the past few months. Damn. I still can't find a way to say...what I want you to understand...I tried to find you. I searched. So long. It was like you disappeared. I thought maybe... Maybe they had... I thought I would know if you were killed, like your parents, but I wasn't sure. I finally gave up. Devastated. Then, a few years later, there you were. Like you had risen from the dead."

Shaking his head, he stares off in the distance, trying to hide the pain in his eyes. "After what happened to my wife, my...first wife, Elizabeth. When they killed her, I...it was too late. I'd already said the words. To protect you."

"Words? What words, Collin? What are you saying? What did you say to protect me? I don't understand."

He stares back at me with fear and confusion in his eyes. Then he shakes his head. "Nothing. Nothing. I was afraid. For you. And afraid *of* you. Part of me wondered if you knew what I'd done, setting up the advance ordinance that caused Elizabeth's death. That caused the death of your parents. And what I did to... I wondered, believed, that you wanted revenge. Deservedly so."

"Do you mean turn rogue? How could you begin to think something like that of me?"

"Because I...I knew what you'd been through. Other angels have changed under lesser circumstances. I..." He stops and shakes his head again. "That night, in that dream, I knew there was a demon, didn't know who it was. I prayed they weren't with you. I wanted to believe you couldn't do such a thing, turn rogue."

"If you truly knew me, you would have known it wasn't possible under any circumstance."

"I know that, now. I just…" He hesitates and heaves a deep sigh. "If I found out you had, I couldn't have found a reason to continue fighting. That night, you killed the demon, but you were also fighting *me*. Like you knew. Like you knew I…"

A moment passes without a word between us and I have to break the silence. "Collin? Like I knew what?"

He turns back to me. His eyes close in despair. "I didn't know what to think. The thought kept going through my mind, if they could turn *you*."

"But they didn't."

His eyes turn up to me, studying my face. "No. Couldn't. No matter how hard they tried. I respect you so much for having endured what you have and staying true to yourself and your family. I'm ashamed." He draws a deep breath. "My role in causing so much of your agony."

My heart drops a beat. He doesn't know, yet, that I didn't stay true to anyone. Not my vows, and definitely not my parents. I've acted shamefully. While hunting. I let demons touch me inappropriately, then used the blackness in my heart to make them suffer before they died. My parents never taught me that. Am I any better than a rogue angel? Am I any cleaner than the demons I kill in the night?

Taking a deep breath, he wipes a tear from his eye. "I don't know if I could ever love anyone more than I do you." He stares deep into my eyes, sending a shock through my body. Will he always have this power over me? "I've never had so much passion and desire for anyone. Oh, God, this sounds so sappy."

"Go on. I like where this conversation is going."

He laughs, then smiles back at me. "You're all I can think of during the day. At night, I fight as if I'm defending you. These struggles… They've made me stronger than I ever thought I could be. I think I'm nearly as strong as you now. At least, at fighting demons. You may need more help with handling druids, though," he says, and laughs.

Then he grows serious. "When I was there, in Colorado, without you for the past few months, I wanted to die. The emptiness I felt was devouring. I don't ever want to feel that way again." He pulls me into his arms with Taylor pressed between us. "I couldn't live if anything happened to you. Wouldn't want to."

I'm stunned into silence. What could I say to this revelation? He went on after Elizabeth's death, but couldn't without me. I could never tell him how close I came to dying only months ago. To tell him there's another who is smarter and stronger than me would only cause him more unnecessary fear. I've grown accustomed to fear, carried it like a cloak most of my life. How could I do that to him? How could I tell him that although I found peace in my travels across the Far and Middle East, I still have a deep fear trapped in my soul that this rogue in Thailand will find me? No, find *us*. He has no conscience. Would have no scruples against killing babies. Taylor will always be at risk as long as he lives. And searching for him to silence my fears would put us all in danger.

This latest battle has weakened me, physically and emotionally, once again. I couldn't face someone who could kill my child to get to me. I would rather die than let that happen. I would die inside without Collin and Taylor in my life.

As he snuggles his forehead against my cheek, I feel a tear tap my shoulder. I'm stunned into silence. I had no idea how deeply he felt for me. How do I tell him I feel the same about him when I'm not used to expressing love or even friendship to anyone? I closed off my heart to everyone after my mother died. To love another always meant heartache. History has shown me that everyone I care about will die a violent death.

My defense mechanisms wouldn't allow me to mourn my parents the way I wanted. That was when the wall grew around me. And yet, he was able to slip through a hidden passage I didn't know existed.

As much as I'm humbled by his words, the pain and anxiety I once felt has begun to consume me again. Tears roll down my cheeks, soaking Collin's hair before he pulls back to peer up at me. My heart might break again, remembering the past and dreading my future.

I sense him reading my thoughts and turn my eyes from him.

"You need to mourn. You deserve to cry. I mean, really cry, so you can let it go. It's the only way you'll be whole again, the only way you can be the person you were before heartache robbed you of happiness, stole your youth."

"I'll never be that person again," I answer, then swallow back the sorrow caught in my throat. "She died long ago when my parents were killed." I can't smile, even if I want to.

Collin frowns, understanding my pain. "I know. I'll be here for you. While you mourn and while you heal. I love who you were, who you are, and whoever you become, even if you turn into a tyrant." He smiles back at me in that way that melts my heart and makes me want to fight to resist his charm. *God*, why can't I let go?

Little Taylor's body jerks in my arms and I peer down at her. A moment later, she jerks again. Hiccupping. *Adorable baby*. My Baby. Our baby. I hold her closer, my tears anointing the dark curls on top of her head. This beautiful child is half Collin and half me. As far as I had gone into darkness, this little light found me anyway. I have difficulty believing she grew inside of me.

As much as I've known and nurtured self-hatred for what I have become and what I must do, I never could've imagined wanting to duplicate myself. Yet, looking into her face, I see me, in the beginning, before sin took over my life. Before hardness took hold of my heart. Will she, too, grow to kill demons with a strength unmatched by any man, except maybe one? I already assume she's an angel just like us.

She's a part of me, as if her body is another extension of mine. To hurt her would be no different than an attack on me, only more. I would defend her life more voraciously than I would my own.

Collin moves to sit in the chair beside me. His face beams with pride. I'm so glad to witness this moment. There's no doubt in my mind he'll do everything necessary to protect her, just as I would. He leans over and kisses me again.

"Collin?"

"Yeah?" he answers, his eyes still gleaming.

"How do you know so much about my family and my past? You know all these things about me and I realize I don't know *anything* about you *or* me. I thought I knew who I was, but now... Last night you said I have druid ancestry. Is it true?"

"Of course it is."

"Well?"

"Well, what?" He grins playfully back at me.

I sigh at him. "How do you know these things?"

"Jaime, I followed you, remember?" I can see there's something else he hasn't told me.

"Ah, no, Collin. That's not good enough. Tell me the truth."

He chuckles. "Sweetie, it's very simple. The truth is, well, we're related," he answers quickly, then nervously scratches the back of his head.

I'm cautious with what I say next. "You mean we're married, right? Not like we're siblings or first cousins or any sick thing like that."

Suddenly his expression becomes serious. "Yes, we're married...and...we're related in another way."

Now I'm concerned. "What?" Taking a deep breath, I let his words digest in my mind for a bit. "But. We're. *Married!*"

He looks at me as if he's surprised I shouted at him. "Shh, the baby."

Sigh. Answer me. I grit my teeth.

"Yes, we're married. We're also distant cousins. Emphasis on *distant*. Doesn't matter. We're so distant you'd have to dig deep into the archives, all the way back to the Nemedians to find it."

"I don't know who the Nemedians are."

"Don't worry. That's a really long time ago." I glare at him sideways without saying a word, so he takes a deep breath and smiles again. "Prehistoric, okay. Is that far enough?"

"Why didn't you tell me this before?" I spit out my words in rapid succession.

He smirks at me, forgetting I'm a woman whose body is raging with hormones and who can harm him very easily.

"Wasn't there enough against us when we finally decided to make it official? As I remember, you didn't especially like me when we joined."

"At least I didn't *hate* you."

"Yes, you did."

Wrinkling my nose, I shake my head stubbornly. "Nope, didn't hate. You're making it up."

"You said the words, 'I. Hate. You' right after you hit me." He stares into my eyes while I search my memory of that night.

"Okay. I did say I hated you, but it was a temporary hate. I got over it pretty quickly if you remember."

The sensual look in his eyes shows he remembers all too

well. "Yeah."

"Stop thinking like that. There's an innocent baby in the room."

"You started it." He gives me that look.

Sighing in frustration, I have to turn away. I already feel my pulse reacting to him and my breathing becoming shallow. He still has that effect on me.

"What's wrong, *Jaime*?"

Knowing I'm turning red, I still won't look at him. "Stop it." I lift little Taylor's fingers with one of mine.

Laughing playfully, he puts his arms around my shoulders and nuzzles my neck while looking down at our baby. I don't ever remember feeling this much love for anyone as I do for Taylor, and the dark angel sitting next to me. I know I would do whatever it takes to protect them.

"Collin?"

"Yeah?"

"I'm sorry. I should've never hit you. I'm really sorry."

He smiles and nuzzles me again. "I forgive you. Just don't ever do it again."

"Promise."

CHAPTER 24

The drip, drip, drip of liquid into liquid is reminiscent of an idea, maybe a thought, perhaps a dream of long ago. The muscles in my shoulders tighten with every drop. Anticipating the next as if each tiny splash has meaning. Every splatter is coated in red. Durudee's color of red. The shade she wore when she was found the following day. The puddle rolling from beneath her bed just as my father's, then my mother's, rolled from their death beds. Will Ananda realize that the wound couldn't possibly be made by a swift sword, but a purposefully placed and directed weapon? When it registers with him that I lied, will he also want my blood? Will it ever end?

I wake with a weight I thought I'd left behind. Didn't I try to kill this part of my personality? Will the part of me that knows self-loathing ever die?

The IV beside my bed leaks saline from the bag above my head to a reservoir. Drip, drip, like Durudee's bright red blood into the River Kwai. It nourishes my body with fluid to help my heart keep pumping.

Thu-thump. Thu-thump.

And it feeds my mind to continue to hate. Hate myself. For

stopping the heart of an innocent woman. For betraying the friendship of her son with a lie. Did they know this would be the result?

Were the monsters I met in Thailand watching me from the shadows of my dreams before I left Colorado? If so, they would know how fragile I was, how deeply I abhorred killing. Wouldn't it make sense that forcing me to take the life of an innocent woman would drive me over the edge of insanity? Did they watch as Collin made love to me in my sleep? Did they revel in my pleas to let the demon live and remain in the dream? Oh, how empty I feel.

Curling my arms into my chest, I notice something is missing. Taylor. Where's my daughter? I search the room. Her bassinette is gone.

Oh, my God!

My heart pulses and forces blood through my veins like a racing vehicle. I can't catch my breath. Did they take her when I fell asleep? Did someone with bad intent take her? Someone who would like nothing more than to torture me?

Collin's asleep in a nearby chair. His chest rises and falls with each breath. His hand jolts, fingers curl to a fist. I want to wake him but know I can't. He's asleep, so he's caught up in a fight. This would be the first I've seen him battle a demon since I left Colorado.

When his body jerks, I startle with him. His eyes pop open and his focus grows intent, but not on me. He isn't awake. Knowing what's happening, I watch him closely. Anger in the eyes of a hunter. I've seen it before. The rage I see in him now is foreign to me. His jaw tightens like he's grinding his teeth. He never gets this angry in a fight. What's happening? Then his arm swings out, his body twists and a guttural cry rises up his throat. Soon, his muscles relax, but his eyes turn to me with fury burning them a brighter green than I've ever seen. They are like the eyes of a deranged killer. After a moment, or two, he recognizes where he is. I anticipate a smile when he notices me. Instead, his face turns grave, then panicked as he rises from the chair and rushes from the room.

"Collin! Collin!"

A nurse dashes into the room. "What's happened? Are ye all right?"

"I'm fine, but my husband…" I don't know what to say, so I point to the door.

Lines of worry cross her face and she rushes after him. Wondering what to do, wanting to follow, I look up at the bags of blood and saline hanging over my head, still feeding into my arms. The thought crosses my mind to pull the needles. I've decided it best to stay, though. I'm no help if I climb out of bed and fall to the floor. Instead I'm left waiting and wondering where he is. Does this have to do with Taylor?

Clipped voices come from the hall, followed by the clap of running feet, Collin's voice shouting at others. An alarm sounds in the hallway. Nurses call orders and more feet clap on tile. My nails dig into the sheets, puncturing holes.

Time drags on as fluid drips into the reservoirs above my head, blood, saline, blood, saline, like a painful dirge, pounding in my mind. I pick at the covers, tearing frayed threads from the cuff of the blanket, glancing up at the IV tubing. When will this torment end? I don't know how much longer I can wait. Soon, this bed will be bare if I keep pulling threads.

After too many minutes of pacing in my mind, my nerves feel raw and any sudden noise in the hall makes me jump. I can't wait any longer and reach for the needle in my left arm just as the door swings open. My body and mind jolt at the sound and I turn to see Collin, his eyes red with tears. Our daughter is clutched close to his chest with his hand cradling her head. My breath catches in my chest as I wait for him to tell me.

Behind him, a young nurse rolls the bassinette into our room. She has an unusual expression when she turns to leave. Fear? Anger? My concern grows deeper. When Collin reaches my bed, he kisses little Taylor on the head before placing her gently in my arms. Then he kisses me on the forehead and forces a smile, but I'm not comforted. I try to smile back, but can't, understanding something's wrong. I'm curious to know what he saw in his dream, but not sure if I'm ready for it yet. He'll tell me soon enough, when I can take it, or he can find a way to tell me without stirring unnecessary fear. Or is it? Unnecessary?

After drawing a deep breath, he clears his throat and I can hear the fear in his voice. "Taylor stays in our room until we leave."

As I cradle our daughter, Collin lowers the steel rail on one side. With a sober look on his face, he sits beside me. His head comes to rest on my pillow with a hand gently placed on Taylor's back. I turn to kiss his forehead just as a tear trickles down his cheek. I couldn't be more frightened. Not knowing is killing me and my hands begin to tremble as I hold my daughter close, anxious to know what he saw in his dream.

"Jaime, there's something I have to tell you."

"What now?" I close my eyes and hold my breath, bracing myself for his newest revelation.

He hesitates, his eyes searching the room. Then he draws a breath and begins. "The reason I didn't leave the States right away isn't only because I couldn't come to you. Mostly, it was because I learned something shortly before you left." He takes a deep breath to prepare himself for what he's about to say next. I tremble inside, wondering what has him so shaken.

"There's another rogue who knows who you are."

"I know." My confession causes him to falter and he stares at me in question. "I felt him just before we woke from the dream. The dream where you…" His eyes dart toward me, then downward. "When Rick and Sarah died."

It's the same one. The rogue I met in Thailand. I feel it in my bones. I won't tell him about how he nearly killed Taylor. And me. It would wreck him even more.

When he releases his breath, I know it isn't due to relief. "I met up with him in a dream, Jaime. He's strong. Much stronger than me."

"Does he know where we are?"

Collin shakes his head slowly. "I don't know. I just don't know. He knows about our baby. I fought him, and it was like fighting you, maybe worse. He nearly killed me. I had to take out the demon to get away from him, to return to you. That happened the night before you called to me, asking me to stay." He hesitates for a moment and I can see the memory haunting his mind. "I didn't come to you before then for fear he'd follow. But when I saw what was happening to you, I had no choice. I knew the druids would kill you if I didn't intervene. And in my haste to reach you… Jaime, I think he's here. He threatened to kill Taylor if you didn't go to him."

My God. The ghosts of my past still plague me: Father torn apart in his bed, Mother bleeding from her mouth, a gash in her side, throwing clothes into suitcases. The thought forces a shudder through me. My stomach turns as memories flood my mind. I can't drive away the image of Mother's horrific death. The battles I've fought on my own since. The pain, the fear. The dread of knowing I would go to sleep and do it all over again. The battle with Sarah and Rick. I thought it was over until I went to Thailand. I can't relive that again. I can't feel that again. They'll use Taylor to get what they want from me. If I had only let them have me. My *damned* pride.

"Everyone would be better if I'd died years ago."

"Don't think that way, Jaime. It's not true."

"It will never stop. Do you understand that, Collin? They will always be there. They will always come for you and Taylor to get to me. How can I do this? How can I sleep every night, knowing they'll always be there and your lives will always be in danger?"

"Because you're greater than they are. That's why they want you so badly. Because they fear you. You were sent here at this time for a reason. Your strength and your ability to strategize is above any of them. They knew you'd endure more than any other angel, but they also knew you were capable of overcoming what was heaped on you."

I shake my head, unable to believe his words. "Not anymore."

"Yes, you are. They're morally deficient. They have no conviction for truth. They prey on the weak to try and build their numbers, hoping to create strength. But they'll never have it. They want you because you're the strongest, physically and intellectually. Right now, you're weakened because of your pregnancy and all you've been through, but your mind and body will change when you're healed."

He strokes the back of Taylor's head. "You can't miss out on her life. She needs you, and *I* need you. If they kill you, there'll be no one to protect her while she's growing up. I can't even protect her, not the way you can. And I can't promise I won't die myself of a broken heart."

"That's not fair." I try to control my tears, holding my child and feeling helpless. "You don't know what I was becoming before I met you. I was already nearly one of them. I just hadn't said the words yet. My life had come to the point where I wondered who the demon really was. Sometimes I thought it was me. I went through my life, doing what I'm meant to do, and would continue to do so until I died, growing weary, hating myself." A shudder racks my body. "You have no idea how badly I wanted one of them to finish me off. When I first met you, I desperately hoped you'd be the one. Then I realized you were here to save me instead."

Collin watches me patiently, holding my hand and brushing the hair from my eyes as I cry. "At first, I thought I was there to save you, too. When I saw how you killed Rick, then Sarah, I realized my calling isn't to save you from death, Jaime. I wish I could be the one. I want to be the man, that man, your protector. But you know I'm not strong enough. There's only one who is, and that's you. You're the one who has to save you. I'm only here to remind you of who you are and to give you a reason to live." His eyes search mine, but I turn away, unable to let him see what I carry in my soul.

"I want to feel that again, like I want to live. Even when I thought you would kill me, there was something there, something about you that brought meaning to my life, took my pain and made it bearable. When I came here, I thought I could make a fresh start, that I wouldn't have to go back to being lost again. But I was wrong. I would have no reason to live without you and Taylor. If anything happened to you, I wouldn't survive. The only way to protect you is to become the cold, hard killer again. Take lives without a thought."

"No. You don't have to be that, either. To survive or to save me and Taylor. You only have to be smarter and endure. Just this one. Just one more battle."

"You can't promise this is the last one, Collin. You know for a fact there are others out there, waiting for me to make a mistake."

"Jaime." He sighs and shakes his head. "You're right. I can't say for sure, but I can tell you that I hope. I hope this is the final one. I pray that this one will be the last rogue angel who hunts you. I pray that when the others see how you kill him, they'll realize it's a lost battle to go up against you. If so, then we can go back to fighting the brand of demons who aren't stalking angels in their sleep. But I can't promise anything. I can only tell you I'll be there for you. Every night. Until this rogue shows himself. And when he does, we'll fight him together. Our combined strength will pull you through."

"But, Collin, don't you see? Because of this, we'll never be able to sleep without taking Taylor with us, into our dreams. At least until she's old enough to fight on her own. And even when we take her with us, the danger to her is greater."

"She'll become stronger because of it, just like her mother." He stares, softly, back at me. I want to feel reassured, but I can't.

"Or she'll die."

"No. I don't accept that outcome. You made it through, and so will she. Her battles are no greater than yours were at her age. I know you. You'll defend her with every part of your soul. You have something they don't. Love."

As I stare at him for a stretch of time, I hear the sound of footsteps pass my room, the machines pumping fluid into my arms, and the monitors beeping softly. He's right. They don't have love. That's why they only smell death. They fight out of hatred, not with their heart. And they don't have a man like Collin at their side either. He'll defend Taylor to the end. Just like me.

"I promise, once this is done, we'll live a normal life. I told you I have a plan."

"And?"

He smiles at me and shakes his head. "It's a surprise."

"Aaah! Collin Leary!"

"Yes, Mrs. Leary?"

Mrs. Leary? He always knows how to make me smile, even

when my nerves are as frayed as the cover on my hospital bed. "What makes you think I'll take your name?"

"Because I know you already did." He grabs my shoulder and presses his lips into mine. Soon my heart is racing and my chest is tight from the breath I'm holding. Collin Leary can be very convincing.

CHAPTER 25

Within a day, my wounds are healed, and they release Taylor and me from the hospital. Collin and I agreed to find an apartment on a lower floor in another part of town. He took care of the arrangements before asking me, having no doubt in his mind he could get me to concur. When he pulls up to take us home in a new Mercedes, similar to the one he owned in the States, I shake my head. I'm not sure how we'll pay for the car. He'll have to be more frugal and find a good job that'll help pay the bills. Reading my thoughts, he only smiles, a reminder he has it handled.

We arrive home to find our apartment filled with baby furniture, clothes and toys for Taylor, and everything else I need to feed and care for her. I didn't think about getting any of these things before she came. *Surprise.* I was more concerned about the spirits following me than what my child would wear or what she would sleep in. What's wrong with me? Sometimes I think the only thing I can prepare myself for is a difficult kill. Being a parent is going to be a challenge.

The idea that Collin wasn't the one who bought the baby items is even more troubling. Somehow, the new landlord learned we weren't prepared for the baby and spread the word around town. Those who heard of our situation pitched in and bought all of this stuff.

Our first moments home are awkward as we sift through all the items they'd left for us. Collin is just as shocked as I, especially that someone entered our apartment to put all these baby gifts in here while we were gone.

The gesture was so, well, nice. And unusual for me. Typically, nearly everyone I know is trying to kill me in my sleep. Not showering me with gifts. That nagging feeling in the back of my mind is hard to silence. Old habits die hard, they say.

When Collin opens the refrigerator, he finds it filled with food, cartons of milk, bread, butter, full meals in foil containers. Very thoughtful, still disconcerting for us. I can see how they were being helpful, but after what I've been through and the knowledge that someone repeatedly invaded my home in Colorado, I can't ignore the chill running through me. Another reason we couldn't possibly stay. I will have to work on convincing Collin of this.

For the rest of the day, we put all the clothes away, keeping cards with names of those who gave them in a box. There are so many pink dresses, baby sheets, rattles, and stuffed animals, it looks like a Pepto-Bismol factory exploded in our apartment.

When nearly everything is appropriately placed, I sit on the bed, trying to convince myself all will be fine and the gifts were a thoughtful idea. That is, until Collin walks in. He holds a red box in his hands.

"I found this on the kitchen table." He hands me the card and I open it carefully. The note reads, *To the Little Angel*. No signature.

The look on Collin's face is more concerning than the unsigned note. I hold my breath as he lifts the lid and shows me the contents of the box. All of the clothing is black. A dress, hat, socks and shoes, all the same color. No one gives a newborn black.

Collin immediately calls the landlord as I slip into a soft chair near the fireplace, suppressing a shiver as I hold Taylor close. First, he thanks him for his thoughtfulness then asks who delivered the gifts. We're relieved to find out he had collected them in his business across town. When there was no more room in his office, he and his maintenance man delivered them later. He doesn't remember what had been dropped off, only that there were so many boxes he had to use a delivery truck to bring them. More than once, he shares with Collin how the town is excited to have a guardian angel in their midst.

My concerns aren't relieved. We still don't know if the one who bought the black clothing was in our home. I have a suspicion they already know where we live. After more contemplation, Collin calls the landlord again and tells him we lost our door key, asking if he would change the locks. The promise to replace them in the morning doesn't console me. We need a deadbolt. Maybe two. Until then, we're vulnerable to attack in our sleep. Anyone able to enter our home while we sleep—as it turned out Rick and Sarah, the rogue angels back in the states, often had—could cause harm to us while we fight, just as they had with me in Colorado. Even worse, someone could take Taylor. The many potentials are too much to allow them space in my mind. We'll have to sleep in shifts.

This entire experience is a heavy weight to carry. At another time in my life, I thought I was invincible. I thought I would never make the mistakes of those who came before me. Now, with my daughter to protect, I fear my skills may not be enough. If I turn to glance in one direction, I may miss a danger coming from another. I'd missed so much when I lived in the States. In those days, I took my eyes off the shadows. Once Sarah and Rick entered my life, even prior to being introduced, I relinquished control to them without realizing it.

This new rogue is stronger than any I've known. He has a greater ability to strategize, as well. Could I be undone by someone better prepared? I've always studied my physical surroundings, not considering what hides from my view. Could I lose my life to my own inability to study the shadows?

Collin finds me brooding in the living room and kneels beside me, knowing what I'm thinking. Thankfully, he can only read what I allow. My most guarded secrets are still mine, for now. His scent interrupts my thoughts. His eyes, so filled with love for me, bring my desire for him to the surface. He studies me, reading me like an art show pamphlet. Sometimes, I hate that he can get this far inside my head. But I'd opened my mind up to him in Colorado, revealing the pathway he now treads to my thoughts too frequently. Too easily.

"Collin," I whisper, unsure of how to tell him.

He kisses my forehead and whispers back. His breath tickles my face. "Yes, my love?"

I shake the dread rising up inside of me. The memory is too painful. "When I was in Thailand…" I hesitate.

"I know," he says and kisses me again.

"You know? Know what?" I ask as my mind flashes to the kiss on the River Kwai with Ananda, black lilies, and finally, being wounded with a sword.

"Everything." He kisses me again.

"The flowers," I begin.

"I know," he answers.

"The sword?" I ask.

"That too." He replies, putting his hand over my abdomen.

"But, how?" He couldn't know all.

"You let your guard down in the hospital. And I saw." His eyes are soft and loving.

"Then you know about…" I start, then hesitate.

"Him, too," he answers with no anger in his eyes.

"Can you ever…" He stops my words with a kiss on my lips.

"You forgave me, didn't you? I love you. Of course, I forgive you." His eyes gleam into mine.

I don't deserve him. But I do love him with every ounce of blood that rushes through my veins.

His finger lightly traces my arm from shoulder to hand. Sorrow creases his brows as he weaves his fingers through mine, then pulls them to his lips, leaving a trace of his Irish scent on my flesh. How could I grow to love someone as much as I do him in such a short time?

As he draws his mouth closer to my neck, I close my eyes in anticipation. His touch seems to melt away my concerns, every drop of pain I've known. His lips on my skin make me tingle beneath his breath. Before I'm aware, he lifts me and Taylor into his arms and carries us to the bedroom, then lowers my feet gently to the floor. After placing our daughter in her bassinette, he turns to me.

That look. The heat consuming my body. My eyes flutter closed as the smell of Collin fills the air. His pheromones entice me. So long. It has been far too long since I've known his hungry gaze on me, tasting my passion and teasing my resolve. His finger traces the line of hair at my forehead to my jawline, making me tremble and falter in my weakness. I want him to take me, ravage me with his touch, feeling every parcel of flesh within his grasp.

When I turn my attention to his face, that strong jaw, olive skin, and those deep, green…wait. There's something different. Something missing. His eyes don't match his smile.

Not anymore.

The image of my father creeps into my subconscious mind. He swiped a lock of hair from my forehead after one of our runs. His lips were curved in pride, but his eyes spoke a different language. Confused, I remember stepping back. The contradiction. He knew. My father knew it was his last day on earth, our last race to the front steps of our house.

Is this why I'm stepping back from Collin, now? Why is my heart thundering in my chest? He isn't hiding anything more from me. Can't be. Or is he? What does he know?

His brows pierce in a pained curve as he reaches for me and I take another step backward.

"Jaime?"

Am I being silly? Why am I afraid? What am I protecting? My heart, or my pride? The distance between our bodies is less than a meter, yet my fear stretches like a chasm from my soul to his. My body shivers with the heat of a raging fire, a meter from where we stand.

The pain in my chest is too great. I turn away. Collin closes the distance between us. I feel him mere centimeters from me. The ache in my chest betrays me. *Damn it!* My love and desire for him is greater than my fear.

Collin's hand draws me into his arms. He lifts my chin until my eyes reach his and I'm lost in them, once again. The shadow behind his pupils is gone. Clearly, I only imagined it. He won't hurt me. I won't lose myself. We're joined for an eternity. The protective impulses in my mind reject the notion. I see my father's death bed. Everyone I've ever loved has been lost, killed. I'll lose him the same if I allow myself to love too deeply. I squeeze my eyes tight to block out the memory.

"Jaime—"

"I...can't—"

"Don't. No matter what happens, I'll always be here with

you."

"You can't promise—"

"Shh… I love you. Now is all that matters."

"Collin—"

My protest is captured in his mouth as his lips cover mine and his tongue gently tastes my breath. The moan that escapes me releases months of repressed fear. My armor lifts, exposing my frail heart. My soul is bared and rendered weak. As my knees buckle, Collin lifts me in his arms and lays me like a feather on the covers of our bed.

His eyes steal my attention as he brushes my cheek with the tips of his fingers.

"I love you, Jaime." His words fill my mind and I can only think of them, on a constant loop in my mind, *I love you, Jaime. I love you, Jaime.*

His lips find their way to mine and I'm lost, falling into the depths of darkness where his passion takes me.

Leaving the mattress, he unbuttons then peels the shirt from his shoulders and lets his pants drop to the floor. Then he reaches for the buttons of my blouse. Languidly, enticingly, he slips me from my clothing and we're soon lying naked in each other's arms. His finger traces my leg to my abdomen and he bends down to kiss the scar where I was cut open to take Taylor. His feather touch rises over my breasts, to my shoulders, my face. His warm lips meet mine again and I melt into him, wanting him, but knowing we must wait. Hours rush by like seconds as we touch and kiss—our fingers exploring each other until we're too tired to lift our hands. Our bodies lie together, intertwined in one another. The way it should be. For the first time, I feel every bit the wife of Collin Leary. Not only giving up myself to the man but possessing him as my own. No interference by another. No judgment by anyone. No fear. Without notice, we drift off to a deep sleep with Taylor in her bassinette beside the bed.

***

When my eyes open again, I find myself in a lighted hallway. Am I sleeping? Am I dreaming? The plain walls and glossy, over-waxed floors are unfamiliar. The tiles beneath me are translucent blue-green, like a body of clear water, glistening with each step I take. Although, in my mind, I sense Collin nearby, I feel completely alone. I'm taking this journey on my own, without him.

The thought hits me like a charging locomotive. I'm panic-stricken. Where's Taylor? The thought is a tempest, tearing my thoughts in all directions. My heart flutters and I can't catch my breath. If I don't control the fear consuming me, I'll be lost and so will this battle. I know that, this time, I fight for me *and* my child.

The soft wail of a crying baby piques my attention. The timbre is soft at first, but grows louder as I continue on. *Taylor?* I turn in circles. There are no exits, no intersecting hallways. Only long, white walls stretch to each side of me. No seams mar the panels, not even where they join to the floor.

I start forward, increasing my pace until I'm rushing down what seems like an endless corridor. The crying grows more frantic and my heart races harder. If they hurt her, I swear the hours of torture I'll release on them will be my sweet revenge. The moment the thought crosses my mind, I feel I'm not alone. Skidding to a stop, I search the corridor behind me, then ahead. Someone else is here, reading my thoughts the instant they enter my mind. I search my senses.

Is it Collin? No. Another soul waits for me to discover them. God. Not the one I met in Thailand. Please, don't let it be him.

"Taylor?" I call out, unsure why I expect her to answer me.

Her crying continues and I grab the hair at my temples as tears flood my eyes. *Please don't hurt her.* "I'm coming, baby. Momma's coming," I choke from my ragged throat.

Only two choices present themselves to me, ahead or behind. I choose forward and continue searching for Taylor. Her cries echo through me, penetrating my flesh, making me shiver. Would they harm her before I can reach them? I can't allow fear to control me. I must push it out. How can I save her if I can't control my weakest thoughts?

That's the key. I must use my mind, not my might. How do I defeat this imaginary place and whoever built it? My strength isn't all I have. Then Taylor shrieks like she's been hurt.

No! "I'm coming, Taylor!" I shout through a narrowed throat, but her cries intensify, forcing the feral archangel in my soul to force out all fear.

An electrical current courses through me and the power within me coalesces, combining with the adrenaline in my blood. With a cry rolling up my throat, I rush forward, down the hallway at unusual speed. With no idea how far I've traveled or to where I'm running, I suddenly realize the end of the corridor is rapidly approaching. I slow my stride, but not soon enough. My shoulder and hip absorb the impact of the wall. Not even a dent mars the surface. A barrier contracts with impact.

My lungs burn from gasping to fill sufficiently to match my heartbeat. Bent over, I catch my breath for a moment, pondering this room, this dream. Once I recover, I turn the opposite direction. Nothing there. Nothing. Only a long passage. A blank wall lays at the other end. Taylor's cries don't cease. Her voice is strained as she grows weak. I can't reach her.

Frustration wells up in me and I scream until my throat

aches, hitting the walls, fighting against myself as though attacking a rogue angel. The repeated impact of my fists turns my knuckles wet with fresh, red blood. As much as my bones ache, I don't stop. I don't care. The realization has set in. I can't reach her. I can't save her.

The walls echo my howls without compassion. I'm losing. The awareness falls heavy on my shoulders, forcing me to the floor. "Taylor, baby. I don't know how to find you." My voice echoes down the hall, then returns to me. "I'm sorry. I'm so sorry, baby."

At the sound of my voice, I stop and listen. My voice echoes off the walls, but not hers. Her voice echoes through my body. I search the walls, then my gaze falls to the floor. My reflection is clear in the glaring shine of the tiles, but the image isn't mine. I'm wearing a white nightgown while the emulation is in black leather and holding a crying baby in her arms. Dropping my palms to the floor, I pound with bloody fists, screaming until the person turns. When I see the face, my voice is caught in my throat. The face staring back at me is mine. My limp body falls through the floor as if it has no substance.

I jolt forward and my eyes snap open. I'm lying in bed with Taylor in her bassinette beside me, crying heavy tears. A dream. Not the sort a dark angel endures. No fight? That never happens. My nightmares always include a demon, one I must kill before I can wake. This one didn't. Is this how humans dream? A mortal nightmare? How can that be?

I cradle Taylor in my arms, both of us sobbing together until Collin wakes and reaches for my shoulder. He kisses my cheek before leaving for the kitchen to make a bottle. By the time he returns, she's calmed and takes the formula eagerly.

After kissing me on the neck, he sits beside me on the edge of the bed. "No matter what, Jaime, you won't be alone. I promise, I'll be there for you."

When I peer into his eyes, I see his determination. He smiles at me in that knowing, sensual way that lets me know it will be okay. I lean back in his arms and snuggle up to him with Taylor suckling the formula from the bottle in my hand.

Chapter 26

The sun breaks the horizon and I refuse to move until a knock on our apartment door rouses Collin. Neither of us fought demons last night. The rogue didn't come for me in my dreams. The maintenance guy is here, though, to change the locks.

He's rather early. I decide to pull on a robe and sit in a chair in the living room with Taylor in my arms. Collin stands nearby, talking with him and inspecting his work. He refuses to leave me or Taylor alone with anyone anymore, no matter how benign they might seem.

Oddly, the maintenance guy seems overly interested in me as he talks with Collin, often turning to look over his shoulder in my direction. I assume he's curious about the person who fought the cloud of devils in Sean's tavern. From what we overheard at the hospital, the whole town is talking about the incident. At least, I want to believe that's his motivation. The feeling in the air is awkward, though, and my body reacts to his glare, shuddering as if I'm cold. Once again, I find myself paranoid at his scowling glances. My mind drifts to the box of black clothing someone left on our table.

What should have taken only minutes, turns into more than an hour of not having the right tools, going back to his truck to get the right tools, talking to Collin while watching me. After enough time passes I find my nerve and rise to take Taylor to her crib. Then I return with the red box in my hands.

"You helped bring all the baby gifts into our apartment, right?" I ask, holding the morbid gift at my side.

He stares back at me suspiciously and nods.

"Do you know who left this?" Holding out the box, I lift the lid to show the black clothing inside.

"I've never seen that before." His eye twitches, betraying his lie.

Unsatisfied, I close the box and show him the look of it and the card that was taped to the lid. "You haven't seen this? It wasn't with the other items you brought in?"

He shakes his head again. "Nope."

"O...kay." My intent is to let him know I don't believe him. Maybe he'll trip up under pressure.

Now I can't help but wonder how well our landlord knows his employee, and how well we know our landlord. Could either of them be behind this message from the one who still stalks me?

"How long have you lived here? In Dublin. How long have you lived in Ireland?" The question was blunt, but I felt it necessary to ask.

"All my life."

"And you've worked for this company how long?" My eyes narrow on him.

"Four years." His voice cracks under pressure.

Collin looks on, studying me. He knows why I'm asking. His curiosity is piqued, also, and he's more careful to notice everything the guy does, analyzing every glance in my direction from that moment on.

From the feel of his energy and the smell of his essence, I can tell the young man isn't a rogue, but I wonder if he has ill will toward us. He has the propensity to commit harm. I can sense it in his eyes. My body reacts to him as it does to any demon I meet in the day. My stomach is sick, muscles tense, and my whole body shivers. I guess I'll meet him again in a dream. The greater trouble will be explaining to the townsfolk who believe I'm an angel why he had to die.

From this point, the maintenance man finishes his work more efficiently and leaves with only a head nod to Collin's show of appreciation. I merely sit in the chair, observing him more intently than he does me. I want to make him uncomfortable. Want him to know I'm well aware of who he is. He'll make a mistake, show in my dream sooner than later, and I can rid this town of one more demon.

Once we're alone, I move to the sofa and Collin snuggles in beside me with his arms around my shoulders. "I've learned to trust your instincts. You're much more in tune than me," he whispers into the hair at the nape of my neck before leaving a kiss burning on my flesh.

I think on his words and remember my mistakes with Rick and Sarah. "Not when it comes to rogues."

"Yeah. Couldn't believe you almost fell for a rogue."

"Don't do it, Collin. Don't take that road. You were pretty cozy with Blondie until I came along. And I ended up having to kill her, too."

"Don't remind me." His voice trails off in deep contemplation. "Why do you think we can sense demons, but not rogues?"

"I was wondering the same." I listen for Taylor a moment, then relax in his arms. "Maybe, since rogues were once like us, we're too comfortable with them. Of course, they've killed. So have we. I think we've overlooked that so often we don't even notice they're angels, let alone fallen ones."

Collin falls silent in contemplation. Just as I'm about to drift off to sleep beside him, he gets up to put kindling in the fireplace and set it aflame. Two logs placed on top, then three branches of lavender. The fire instantly envelopes the dried sprigs and I recall the red box on the table. I rise from the sofa and retrieve the box with black clothing. Standing before the hot flames, burning strong and passionately over the logs, I toss the box in and watch it being devoured. The devil who sent it can receive its ashes through hell. Collin watches with me for a moment, then glides his fingers over my arms, gently telling me he approves.

After what seems like an hour, but is merely minutes, he leaves the room for the kitchen, fixes two cups of tea, and brings them to the living room. As I sip, the flames grow higher over the logs until it burns hot and fierce. My mind drifts off, thinking about the rogue who still hunts me.

I go over the night in Collin's gallery, not the dream, the actual night. While standing next to Mandy at the front of the building, I felt the same as I did while watching the maintenance worker change the lock on our door. After she left, my feelings didn't subside. Then the lights went out and the fear was greater. In the back room, I trembled as if I'd been locked in a freezer. Were there demon eyes on me as we made our way through the dark? Was this new tricky rogue also waiting in the shadows?

Collin turns on the stereo and starts soft Celtic music before returning to my side. We sit for a time, snuggled in each other's arms. I contemplate my past fights, mostly the one with Rick and Sarah. Reviewing what happened may help me know how to fight this one.

After having gone over everything in my mind, my preparations and the execution, I return to the present. My dream of last night is still caught in the forefront of my thoughts. Was there a hidden warning I missed? Or was it a reflection of my inner dread? I can't decide. Angels don't dream like normal mortals.

Since there were no other dreams last night, for me or Collin, it's like the calm before the storm. Even my prenatal reprieve from fighting didn't prepare me for this. Dreaming without a demon or a rogue angel trying to kill one of us is something we've never experienced, and I'm unsure what to think of it.

Is the new rogue playing with us, studying us? Studying me? Or maybe trying to find others to join him in destroying me? Is he preparing just as I am, knowing this battle won't be easy? I'm positive he watched the one at Rick Stanton's home, dissecting my every move and motivation. Unfortunately, he knows me better than I do him. He's seen me raw, at my worst and at my best.

I don't know how to prepare for a fight like this where even Collin is afraid of the killer's abilities. Why have I been left alone without the power to overcome these challenges? As Rick once asked, has my father in heaven deserted me? And if so, is it because of my past indiscretions? I'm a dark angel. I'm expected to be imperfect.

The feeling of Collin's lips on my temple calms me. The touch is not intimate or stirring, only comforting. He knows passion must wait until this is over. I have to use that instinct, not for pleasure, but for hunting a prey that also hunts me. He understands this as much as me.

The rest of the day is spent quietly in front of the fire, savoring tea and holding Taylor, talking with her as if I may not see her in the morning. If the fight happens tonight, I don't want to wonder if I'd said good-bye to her or shown her enough love before I die. Such a distraction could cause me to make a mistake.

The sky grows dark with night, yet we wait as long as possible before heading off to bed. This time, I don't leave Taylor alone in her crib. I collect her in my arms and slip into bed beside Collin. In the last minutes before succumbing to our dreams, he leans over me, cradling Taylor's face with his hand while kissing me as if it will be his last opportunity. Then he nuzzles his face into my neck and shoulder.

My body lays still, watching moonlit shadows of windswept trees dancing across the ceiling. Anxious outcomes occupy my thoughts until I can no longer separate them into reality versus fantasy. All become one as the weight of my destiny forces my eyes closed and I drift into darkness.

The hollow sound of footsteps echoes in my mind. My eyes snap open and immediately set to searching the room. Collin is gone, and I'm no longer wrapped in our covers. Instead, I'm walking the same corridor of the previous night's dream. The walls are still blank and the floor transparent with a bluish tint. This time, however, Taylor is nuzzled in my arms, pressed against my chest. Why here? What draws me to this place and for what purpose? Is this where the battle takes place?

Taylor sleeps soundly, unaware anything is amiss. I wear the same white gown I wore in last night's dream; spaghetti straps are the only fabric covering my shoulders. My arms are cold and I pull my daughter close to keep her from getting a chill. Thankfully, I thought to wrap her in a soft blanket before falling asleep.

I'm unsure what's expected of me at this point, so I move forward as I had in the previous dream. My feet are chilled by the cold floor. My body shivers, not only from the cool air. The smell of the room reminds me of Sean's pub, as if there are others surrounding me, watching as I move down the hallway.

Searching the walls, I feel them there, eyes watching, studying my actions, baring my soul without permission. Still, there is nothing but a plain, seamless barrier between them and me. Are the ones who watch those who will ensure my demise? These partitions are more daunting than the shadows of my dreams.

My guard is still up as I search for shadows that aren't there. The entire corridor is alight. Slim chance of a surprise attack from any shadows, a necktie around my throat or a board cracking my ribs, but that doesn't mean someone couldn't breach the walls. This is a dream, after all. Whoever constructed this pathway could change the rules at any moment.

When I reach the wall at the end of the corridor, I stop, turn back as I had last night and remember the image of me in the floor. My eyes turn downward to see if anyone is there.

Similar to the previous dream, an image of another is reflected in the floor below me. My reflection still wears a black leather jacket and pants. As I kneel to get a closer look at her face again, she turns and reaches her hand to the surface above her, my floor. When she does, I feel my arms pull downward. My grip on Taylor slips and I fight to hold her to me. The power is greater than mine, though, and before I can scream, she's ripped from my grasp. As her body reaches the floor she slips through, into the arms of the other woman.

"No!" I shout at her.

But the one who holds her is me, now in the white gown I had been wearing. When I search my body, I realize the black leather is now clinging to *my* arms and legs. What does this mean? Panic sets in my mind. Is someone trying to tell me my darkness will see me lose her, be the reason for her death? Or am I to think my desire to keep her safe puts her in more danger? My heart races as I pound on the floor, screaming for my baby. My other image holds her close to her chest, comforting Taylor as I claw at the transparent tiles above them.

Strong bands wrap around me and I prepare to fight back until I hear Collin's voice calling out to comfort me. I open my eyes to find his arms encircling me and his lips caressing my face.

"I don't understand!"

He pulls me closer and kisses me more. "I know, baby. I know. But you will. When you need to, you will."

As I lower my head to the pillow, Taylor safe in my arms again, I find it impossible to sleep. Instead, I search my mind for the answer, hoping I don't send my child to her death.

CHAPTER 27

After another night of demon-less dreams, no one attacking either of us, Collin and I have grown frustrated. We can't help but believe the rogue is intentionally not showing himself. Is he somehow creating these dreams to study me, learn what I fear most? I've changed since I moved to Ireland and he must sense that, learning as much as he can to find the best way to fight me, maybe turn me once and for all, or take me out of the game completely. As long as I'm alive and fighting demons, I'm a threat to him as much as he's a danger to me and my family.

We can't give him more opportunities to study me, though. The more he watches, the more he'll realize my weakness is Taylor. She'll be at greater risk. The best way to draw him out is to go out into the open. Show ourselves in the light of day and hopefully flush him out of the weeds. Or, is it more apropos to say, from behind the wall? If he knows we're searching for him, he'll want to finish this before I learn his true identity in the waking world. At least, that's our hope.

The waiting and a minimal amount of sleep is wearing me down. To worry each day that it will be my last is destructive to my fortitude. The fret that they'll find Taylor and take her before I can save her frays my determination. The dread of going to sleep each night, wondering if it will be the night I lose everything I love, is greater than my fear of death. For these reasons, my nerves are unraveling and I'm unsure how much more I can take before I lose control completely.

Collin prepares breakfast while I feed and dress Taylor in one of her new outfits. Afterward, we assemble the new stroller then head into town. The stroll is slow and purposeful, both of us smiling like we're only out for some fresh air with our new baby, not as if we're searching for the devil. When we finally reach Sean's place, we hesitate outside, searching each other's eyes and mentally preparing ourselves.

As we step into the dark room, the patrons don't recognize us at first. There are few people inside, being the middle of the day. Sean, however, notices us immediately.

"Jaime! M' friend! Come inside and let me see the wee one o' yers."

His bright face brings a smile to my lips. "Sean, how are you?"

He gives me a big hug and slaps my back like I'm a plow horse. Knowing my strength, he's not afraid he'll hurt me. I love that about him. "Well, Jaime, all is well, now lemee see the lil' angel," he says and leans over the stroller to peek inside.

His words, 'little angel,' cause me and Collin to lock eyes. Will we ever get over the urge to rip our child from anyone who refers to her so? Will we find comfort with that term now that a killer has also used those words?

Sean reaches inside Taylor's bedding and lifts her into his arms.

"Careful—" I reach for him, then stay my hands.

Before we can say another word, others in the bar crowd

around her to catch a glimpse of the dark angel baby. The overwhelming attention is what we hoped for, but I'm still ill at ease. I only agreed so we could draw out the rogue. The anxiety is greater than I'd imagined, tearing at my subconscious and devouring my resolve. I'm unsure how long I can allow them to touch her before erupting.

My attention stays focused on Taylor as she's cooed over and handled by strangers. Collin watches my reaction as if he's entertained by my anxiety. My breathing comes heavier and I feel his eyes laughing at me. My muscles tense with each new person who reaches for my daughter.

"Enough!" I shout to a stunned crowd and take her from them. The bar falls silent.

"She looks older than I expected," Sean finally pipes up. "Do angels develop faster than humans?" He turns to Collin.

"Where are her wings, Jaime?" another asks and laughter echoes through the pub as I cringe.

"Will she fight demons soon, just like her mother?" comes another query.

Their questions are harmless, but unnerving and I want to shout at them, tell them they're idiots. My defenses grow thicker while answering each of their questions.

Collin shoots me a disapproving glare and I return his sentiment. "Jaime's tired. She hasn't had much sleep since the baby, and I'm afraid she's growing cranky."

He pats me on the shoulder like I'm one of his buddies, one he's just insulted with a poor joke, or maybe I remind him of the trashy blond he toyed with up to the moment we first met. *Dammit!* A powerful bout of angst is turning me inside out and he's treating me like a plow horse. Or a child.

"Don't patronize me, Collin," I respond through gritted teeth. How dare he speak about me so disrespectfully in public?

Anxiety grows inside me like a virus, expanding and raging through my blood. I want to run from them, return to our apartment. Why can't I lock myself in until the rogue shows himself? I know this was the plan, but I can't stand here anymore. My breathing grows shallow. I have to leave. I'm not in control of my senses.

"I'm going home." It's best for all involved. I'm a person who uses my past to kill demons in my dreams. I fear that remembering my past, his past, in the midst of this perfect storm in my waking world won't end well.

I turn toward the door, but Collin catches my arm.

"Jaime—"

"Collin, let me go!" I snap back at him. My fight or flight instincts kick in. I can't breathe. I have to leave. *Now!*

"Jaime, no!" he answers, tightening his grip on my arm and pulling me to him, sending unabated adrenaline shooting through my veins.

Something snaps inside me. Rage unlike anything I've felt since my time at the hospital, curls around my self-control and rips every shred of reason from me. My jaw aches from gritting my teeth. She's going home with me, now, but Collin's grip won't allow me to leave his side.

Without thinking, I shove Collin with all of my might. Collin's jaw makes a loud crack against the door frame of the pub. The moment his body collapses against the brick, I realize what I've done. My spirit is deflated in the dank room. I just hurt my husband. How could I? He turns back to me with anger in his eyes, holding his chin.

What have I done? Is this what I've become, the changed person he promised to still love? The pub is silent. I search the faces surrounding me, their eyes creased in fear, mouths agape.

"Collin," I begin but the words choke in my throat, "I'm

so—" Tears fill my eyes and he glares at me as if I'd betrayed him. I have.

I've completely lost my mind. My eyes close to shut out the world. I shake my head. This isn't who I am or who I'll become. I have to fight this rage. The wait for the battle has to end. If I don't fight, I may be lost to insanity. Maybe that's their plan.

Awkwardly dragging the stroller to me, I lay Taylor inside and cover her in the plush blanket then head out to the street. Collin doesn't stop me this time. The eyes of those who witnessed my loss of control watch my every move. I feel bare in the middle of a city of strangers. How could I allow my emotions to get the best of me? Have I already returned to the person I was in Colorado? Maybe worse?

Why don't they have shrinks for archangels? Being thrown into deadly battles night after night here on earth, we surely need someone to listen to us and tell us why we're not so screwed up as we think. Any person who's seen too much battle, human or angel, would crack under these circumstances. I'm no different. And I hate that I could crumble so easily.

Rushing down the sidewalk, I haven't gone too far before Jesse's patrol car pulls along side of me.

He gets out and tries to stop me. "Jaime, I need to talk to you."

"Not now, Jesse. Not today," I warn him and continue on.

"Jaime. I need you to stop and talk to me right now." His voice is forceful and demanding.

I turn to him with my teeth clenched. Collin walks up behind me. "I said, not now, Jesse."

Collin steps in. "Jesse, she's upset over something that happened. Can we talk about this tomorrow?"

A crowd gathers around us, some whispering about what

happened in the pub. Jesse continues. "I'm afraid this can't wait. Jaime, I received a warrant from Thailand asking us to extradite you."

I'm confused at what he just told me. "I don't understand. For what?"

"There were some unexplained murders. Ye're their only suspect. They plan to press charges against ye."

I stand reeling from the shock of what Jesse just told me, frozen in place. Sean steps in front of me and puts his hand up to his friend. "Now, Jesse, ye know she's been here for months. And that's just daft. She saves people, not murders them. Ye can't do this to our own Jaime."

"Sean, these murders all happened before Jaime came to Ireland. One o' the victims is an airport security chief who tried to arrest her for a murder aboard her flight from the U.S. The others were the security chief's guards. All killed in their sleep by someone with excellent sword skills. Ye've seen her in action yerself. Ye heard the druid's warnin'. Besides, at minimum, she was carrying contraband weapons in yer tavern. The law is the law. I have no choice but take her into custody so ye might as well get out o' me way."

I peer over to see Sean's jaw hanging agape as he stares me down. He and the others from his pub don't seem to know what to think. It's entirely possible he believes I've done what Jesse says. I shake my head to tell him I'm innocent. His eyes tell me he isn't convinced. Then Collin steps forward.

"Jesse, you can't take her. Those people you talked of, they must've tried to kill her. There's no other explanation for this. She was only defending herself. She must've been attacked. Do you really believe she could kill those people? Surely she wasn't the only person in Thailand who knows how to swing a sword."

My heart breaks and I close my eyes. Durudee. Yes, Collin,

I could kill an innocent. I'm guilty. The thought eats away at the desire to defend my actions.

"Sorry, Collin. There's nothin' I can do. She has to go to back to Bangkok and tell 'em what happened, herself."

"Please, listen to me, Jesse, there's someone who followed me from the States. They're bent on killing Jaime. If they get their hands on her... They've threatened our daughter to get to Jaime. They want her and they'll kill her *and* Taylor if they have to."

"Do ye have proof of this?" Jesse asks.

Collin runs his hands through his hair. "It's not possible. But I can tell you it's true."

Jesse shakes his head. "I'm sorry, Collin. Me hands are tied."

In desperation, Collin grabs his arm. "Listen to me! Do you know anyone who's new to this city, just moved here in the past week from the States or Thailand?"

Jesse looks down at Collin's hand on his arm, then narrows his eyes. Collin releases his grip. "The only ones I know are you and Jaime. Look around ye, Collin. This city is filled with tourists. How will I know a visitor from a *rogue angel*, if such a thing exists?"

"Jesse. If you put her in jail, she'll be vulnerable with so many prisoners around her. She could be killed in her sleep."

"She'll be protected, Collin," Jesse answers, his patience growing thin.

"You can't protect her in her sleep, Jesse. They'll come to her in her dreams and they'll kill her with the help of all the other inmates there!"

"Collin, how do I know yer little story 'bout angels fighting demons in yer sleep isn't more than just a tall tale? Maybe the demon is staring us in the eyes at this minute. Now back away or I'll have no choice but to take ye in with yer wife."

Sean steps forward again. "Jesse, ye can't put her life in danger after what she did for us, can ye?"

"How many years have ye known me, Sean? Do ye think I do this lightly? Think about it for a pea-pickin' moment. What did she do for us, eh? Do ye even know? If they really are angels, she got Curtis killed a couple weeks ago because of the demons that followed her. Not just Curtis, but Joseph too. Two people died, or have ye forgotten? And they're not the only ones."

My ears are perked up now. What does he mean?

Collin asks my question for me. "What're you talking about?"

Jesse turns to him in an aggressive gesture. "Scotty, found in his bed this morning. A deep hole in his chest, just like the others she left behind in Thailand. Sean, it's possible she killed six people in one night before she ran away."

My heart stops. Scotty? Who was Scotty? I search my mind to recall the people I've met. Then I remember the man who told me his name was Seamus. They called him Scotty because he was from Scotland. This isn't happening.

A chill floods through me, like my blood has turned ice cold. How could he be dead and I not know about it? Why didn't one of us dream to stop his killer?

Jesse's anger shows in his eyes and his set jaw. "Sean, she may not be saving us. There's a possibility she's killing everyone who comes near her. She's better off in Bangkok. Let 'em deal with her there." Jesse pulls out a pair of handcuffs and my eyes tear up realizing what's happening. This isn't possible.

Collin reaches for his arm again to stop him, but I step forward and hold him back. "Collin, no. I'll go. We'll get this fixed. I don't know how, but I'll fix it, okay? There's no way they can convict me of killing them. They have no evidence I did what they're accusing me of."

The handcuffs encircle my wrists pulled tight behind my back. Jesse leads me to the car and helps me into the back seat before driving away. Despair fills my heart as I watch Collin holding Taylor, looking lost as the patrol car pulls away from the curb. The last time I touched him I hit him. I doubt I'll ever forgive myself.

Now is the best opportunity for the rogue to hunt me in my sleep. I'm still weak, have no way to defend myself and Collin may not be able to find me in his dreams to be there to help. I'm on my own and I'm more frightened than I've ever been.

CHAPTER 28

After Jesse books me, I'm led to a small cell, away from the general population. He called it solitary confinement. They consider me too dangerous to be left with other inmates.

The cell is small with gray cinderblock walls and a solid door with peeling green paint. There are no inmates in any of the other tightly contained cells of solitary. The only life here is mine. If anyone fights me in my sleep, no one will hear my screams. In the morning, this cellblock may be empty of life.

The rest of the day I spend pacing the cell, trying to figure out what I'm going to do. If I live long enough to be extradited to Bangkok for Durudee's murder, there'll be no way to explain how it happened. That alone is enough to cause worry. And that's only if I live that long. They have no physical evidence, but that doesn't mean they haven't planted some. I know the rogue angel had people in positions of authority there. I visited Durudee. She put me up in a hotel. Those things tie me to her. However, what I face when I sleep, the unknown outcome of this night, is even more intimidating.

When they bring my meal, I'm not hungry enough to eat. The tray still sits on the floor beside a worn cot. It is the only furniture in this room and what I'm expected to sleep on. I don't want to sit on the filthy, stained mattress, let alone sleep on it. In fact, I don't want to sleep at all. I'm caught up in total disbelief over my situation. I've never been suspected before. The anxiety alone might destroy me before I meet the rogue. This is the opportunity he needed to have me to himself. He planned this and I didn't see it coming. That display at the bar might have even been his doing to plant suspicion of my violence and abilities.

In time, I grow weary from all the pacing and lay, apprehensively, on the mattress to think. But I can't concentrate. There's no way to strategize. The plan to have Collin there, to have my back, and search for anything I might miss, was my best defense. Maybe Collin wouldn't want to be here for me anyway, even if he could, now that I hit him. I need serious training in anger management.

There's no way to make amends for what happened today at the pub. Before I die tonight, I won't be able to tell Collin that I lost control and I'm sorrier than I've ever been about anything. I won't have the chance to tell him that he and Taylor are my world. He opened up to me to say how much he loved me, but I never told him how I felt in return. The weight on my shoulders makes my chest ache and I close my eyes to force my mind to rest.

"Collin, I'm so sorry," my whispers echo in the cold room. My breath comes in frozen puffs of vapor.

"Jaime," he calls back to me and I sit up to listen. "Jaime," he whispers again.

"Collin!" I scream and run to the door to pound on it. "I'm here!"

"Jaime!" He's on the other side, turning the handle.

As soon as the door opens, I see his beautiful face and throw my arms around his neck. "I'm so sorry, Collin, I'm so sorry. I have to tell you how I feel before—"

"Shh, shh, I know, but we have to be quiet." This is unusual. He's acting strangely.

"What're you talking about?" Then I realize there are no guards with him. "What're you doing? What's going on?"

"Jaime, you're dreaming. Look at your clothes."

I'm not in the jeans I'd been wearing when I was locked up. Instead I'm in that same white gown I'd worn the past two nights in my dreams. My bare shoulders chill in the frigid air.

"How are you here?"

He shushes me again, searching each cell as he pulls me by the hand down the corridor. "I told you I wouldn't let you fight alone," he whispers.

We leave solitary confinement behind and move on to the corridors leading to the prison's commons area. There are no other souls here. The jail is completely empty. We're not in the Federal Corrections Facility after all. We're at Kilmainham Gaol, the old jail, now a museum. The realization hits me. We're missing something.

"Collin, where's Taylor?" As the words leave my lips I hear the sound of a baby crying. "Taylor!"

The panic must show in my eyes as Collin grasps my shoulders and shakes his head. "No. They won't hurt her."

The look in his eyes isn't comforting. He knows he can't promise something he has no control over. There's no guarantee they won't harm her.

In the open area, we turn in place, searching the empty levels of cells and dark shadows just beyond, listening for her voice. Then she cries again; down the hallway, straight ahead. We bolt forward in unison and Collin releases my hand as he rushes ahead of me.

At the end of the hallway is a closed door. Collin reaches it first and fights with the mechanism to open it. As I reach him,

I hear Taylor's cries on the other side.

"Hurry, Collin!" I shout, unable to control my panic.

The latch finally turns and the door inches open enough that I can slip through. Collin continues to push it open, but it slams back against him, closing and locking on its own. We've been separated.

I pound on the door. "Collin!"

His voice is muffled on the other side and I wonder if he can hear me calling to him. When I reach for the handle there is none. My body goes numb. I'm locked in and he's locked out. My situation is no better than before he showed up at my cell. I stroke the door with my fingertips, knowing he's on the other side, fighting to get in, knowing he won't succeed.

"Collin, I love you. I love you more than I could ever imagine loving anyone. Forgive me. But I have to leave you to find Taylor. When you wake," I take a deep shuddered breath to build the courage to finish, "tell her I love her. Don't let her forget me." I hesitate a moment longer, then turn the direction I last heard Taylor's cries.

Alone, I head to meet my destiny. A destiny I once welcomed, but now fear. I must steel myself for this. I'll need every ounce of strength I have left to survive. Then Taylor cries out again and my body falls weak. The sound echoes from a distance to my right. My heart pounds as I turn in the direction of her sobs.

Tears trace my cheeks as I cry. "I'm here, Taylor. Mummy's here."

I want to console her, wish there was someone to console me. I want Collin's warm hand holding mine, telling me it'll be all right, even if we both know it won't. My chest aches. Tears flood my eyes until I can't see. I take another shuddering breath then wipe them away. As I do, Taylor cries out again. They're hurting her to draw me to them.

"I'm coming, baby. Mummy's coming." I can barely choke the words from my narrowed throat.

My declarations to Taylor aren't as much for her as they are for *them*, to let the bastards know I'm coming for her. Taking another deep breath, I move forward again.

The room is long and oval-shaped. There's a tall set of metal stairs ahead of me, leading to the next floor. The doors to each of the cells are open on all levels. Briefly searching each room as I pass, I wait for someone to find me. I know they're here, and I'm positive they have my daughter.

When I reach the stairs, the smell of jasmine rushes my senses and my muscles fall weak, again. He's here. The one from Thailand.

The form of a man appears from one of the cells on my level, stopping just past the doorway. He is wearing a white t-shirt and jeans. No baby in his arms, though. His face seems familiar, but I'm not positive in the dim light and the distance between us. If he's the rogue from Thailand, he seems far slimmer than last I saw him. Or is this one of his victims?

Stopping at the railing, I look up the stairway to see where it leads.

"That's not the way out." The voice is nearly familiar, with an oddly different inflection from what I recognize. An Irish acquaintance with an American Midwest accent? "I know, I've confused you. Yer used to hearin' me talk like this."

"Jesse? What're you doing..." Then it hits me. Jesse's a rogue angel. But is he the one from Thailand? The guy in the tub. Did he make me see him as larger than he really is so I wouldn't recognize him while awake? Oh my God.

"I wondered how long it would take you to make the connection. You're pretty smart, Jaime Connor. But I expected you to be quicker than this." He smiles as he moves closer.

I'm discomforted by his calm appearance. My body shivers

and my feet ache from the frigid floor. Taylor cries out again. As I turn toward the sound of her voice, he reaches for my shoulders.

"She's fine, Jaime. She's being well taken care of."

My anger gathers the strength in my body and I turn back, throwing my fist at him full force. He stops the blow with his forearm and swings back at me. When his knuckles strike my cheek, I hear the bone snap before I'm thrown to the ground. The pain is nearly bearable. Blood drips from my mouth as I push up from the floor.

Collin was right. He *is* stronger. If I'd hit any other man that hard, they'd have been rolling on the floor with a fractured arm. Even an angel couldn't have taken a blow like that without feeling anything. With one swing, he cracked my cheekbone. I've more than met my match. I've met a superior fighter.

With frightening calm, Jesse watches me. When I rise to my feet and push away from him, he reaches out and grabs my arm, pulling me to his chest. Fighting against him, I yank my arm to get away, but his strength is greater than any I've known.

"You know, I like this gown on you, Jaime. So, feminine. Much more so than the clothes you usually wear." I glance over at him as if to say *get to the point*. "Oh, don't get me wrong. Black leather is stylish enough. I just think you look more angelic in white, don't you?"

I glare back at him. "Where's my daughter?" My body trembles and I can't make it stop.

"I told you not to worry. She's in good hands."

"Who has her?" I swing at him in panicked succession but miss each time.

With little effort, he slaps my face, sending shards of pain through my cheek where the bone was broken, then laughs at me. "Are we gonna do this all night, Jaime?" Gaining his composure, his expression turns serious. "I don't mind, but we could be doing something much more productive, don't you think?"

What does he mean by that? Does he want the same as Rick?

He rolls his eyes. "*No*. I don't want *that* either."

He's reading my thoughts. How can he get into my mind so easily?

"Yes, *scrumptious*, I find you enticing, but that's not what I'm up for at this juncture. We can discuss that later. In the meantime, you know what I'm after."

My soul.

"That's right, Jaime Connor. You hit the nail on the head. I have a hard-on for your *soul*. I've wanted it since I learned you were coming down to this planet, much like the rest of those who follow *you know who*." He chuckles and points to the floor like he just reminded me of a private joke. "Silly, I know, but I've been waiting for this moment for the past seventy years. You might say I'm very persistent, or patient. Being here, now, makes me tingly all over." He's being flippant, but I'm far from impressed at his antics. Something tells me his fortunes are tightly entwined with Lucifer's. I will never be enamored by someone connected to Satan himself.

I swallow back the lump in my throat, unintentionally showing my fear. "You know that won't happen."

"I didn't kid myself that it'd be easy. I've watched you for a long time. I know what you're capable of. My advantage is, I've seen you fight, know all of your signature moves, having studied you over the decades, most recently in Thailand and now here. I've been able to train myself to your habits, strengthen the weaknesses you might exploit with your superiority. Unlike other rogues or demons, I've been able to render myself invincible against you. Someone we both know intimately would give his right arm to see me succeed tonight. And I must admit, he practically did to give me an extra edge." He raises his eyebrow and smiles. His smirk sends a shiver through me.

Lucifer.

"Although I may be much stronger than you, now, I don't like to leave anything to chance. That's why I made sure I had an ace in my pocket." He nods and his eyes turn toward an open door down the hall from us. Someone stands at the entrance to a cell, holding a baby.

"Taylor!"

When I rush forward, he grabs hold of my shoulders again and pulls me back. I turn and swing my arms, hitting his face with closed fists, one after another. He takes my blows until the fifth swipe, blocking it with his arm again. This time, my leg sweeps the floor and knocks him to the ground. Then I move toward Taylor, but his hand catches my ankle before I'm out of reach. Yanking backward, he sends me to the ground with a jolt.

Rising to his feet, he stands above me as I push up to my hands and knees. "Not bad…" he says with a cynical smile and wipes blood from his lip. "Not good enough, though."

The smirk slips from his face and he kicks me in the ribs, sending me to the floor again, gasping for air. He crouches beside me and wipes the hair from my face as I struggle to breathe, my ribs on fire as if I'd been hit with a board.

"Oh, yeah, I failed to share this little tidbit with you. I've studied *your* weaknesses, also. I know what motivates you and I know how to take you down with your own strength."

I don't want to believe him. But there's overwhelming evidence he has the ability to finish me.

"Jaime, it doesn't have to be this hard. If you weren't so

stubborn, we could be through with this and you'd have baby Taylor in your arms right now." I glare at him for using her name. I hate the sound of it on his lips. "You can't avoid it. I have a feeling I'm gonna say her name several more times. Though, I'll leave it up to you how I use it in the sentence. Should I say, 'Baby Taylor needs to die now?'" His voice is shockingly cheerful as he speaks such evil.

"No!"

"Yes."

The way he says it, with such glee...

"You deranged bastard!" I swing at him and he catches my hand.

"You're right. I am deranged. But, so are you. Haven't you noticed? *I've* noticed. Hah, every rogue, even your husband knows the infamous Jaime Connor is damaged. We've watched you hunt. It's plainly obvious. Yet, I don't really blame you. You've seen so much, viewed the bodies of your dead parents. That alone is enough to make someone..." He snaps his fingers in my face, causing me to recoil. "Now, you revel in the kill, like you can't get enough. You play with them like they're mice. Capture and release, capture and release, until you've played them to death. You love the way it feels and hate the after affects, the filth you can't wash from your body, or your mind, no matter how hard you scrub. That's why I'm here, really. It's pitiful watching your talents being wasted. What I'm offering you is a way out."

"What you're offering is damnation." Every angel knows that joining Lucifer seals their fate. In death, their soul is sent to pure darkness, an eternity of inner and external emptiness. Worse than hell, you are lost to all that is kind and lose yourself in madness. I could never join him. Ever.

"Don't consider it damnation, Jaime. Consider it baby insurance. Because, precious little kitten, I'm dangling your daughter's life by a thread above your reach. And I'm giddy with curiosity to know if you'll keep jumping at the string like a circus animal. Or will you join me to save her?"

A growl rolls up my throat as I lunge for him again, this time my fingers reaching for his trachea, intent on ripping it out. He knocks my arms away with one hand and backhands me with the other. I flinch at the fire shooting through my cheek.

"We're getting off track now, Jaime. The brawling, this mud wrestling we're doing here, isn't getting us anywhere."

My breath comes in heaves, partly from fighting with him and partly from fear for Taylor. He wants to wear me down so I'll do whatever it takes to save her, even turn. I have to remember that. I can't give him what he wants. I can't lose my soul to the darkness.

"Jaime, don't think of it that way. Think of it as getting *rid* of the darkness. Imagine not ever having to kill again in your sleep." I turn back to him in surprise. "That's right. You'll never have to fight another demon in the night. You'll be free to live a normal life, like all your friends around Dublin."

As great as that may sound, I know there's much more to it than that. His kind stalks dark angels and anything holy that's left here on earth. They'll kill the innocent to get to them, as well. Something I could never bring myself to do. No matter how he colors it, there's no way to minimize what happens when we finally meet our end. The eternal darkness that surrounds the souls who've turned, it's more than I can imagine. I might as well be dead.

"There are worse things than eternal darkness, Jaime. Think of your healthy, happy family. Your child in your arms, husband at your side. Then think of your world if they should both die a horrendously painful death. Will your life be bright and sunny once again? I think not. Besides, princess, with me at the hem of your crinoline, you'll never die. You'll live forever, protecting your husband and child from killers in the night."

"I wouldn't waste my time on you. No matter what happens tonight, there'll be others, other dark angels, to send you to *Hell*."

"Hmm. If that were true, I still wouldn't be concerned. You're the strongest left in the fight, Jaime. If I can end you so easily, what makes you think any others would have a chance against me? Besides, there are no others to avenge you. The three of you are the last. You, Collin, and Taylor. And if you join me, your husband and baby won't have to turn. I could care less about them. They can continue running the hamster wheel, fighting demons, night after night, if you like. They'll still be the last, while you do your dark deeds at my side. And the best part is, your family will be protected. No rogue would even attempt to hurt the family of the queen of rogues, knowing you'd destroy them. Truly, this is the best and, might I say, *only* way you can defend your family. Don't you see how great we would be? You and me together, more invincible than Batman and Cat Woman."

"Are you a child, Jesse?"

He laughs at my comment, so easily amused.

"Oh, no, Jaime, or shall I call you Jerrica? I'm not laughing at your silly slight. I find it entertaining you still think of me as Jesse Hennessy. Truth be told, that's not my angel name. You should know damn well who I am."

I'm stunned for a moment. What did I miss? There's no possible way I knew him.

"Okay. I'll bite. Who the *fuck are* you?"

"Jerrica, remember, the baby."

Fucking pretentious asshole. "I don't care. I don't care who the hell you are. I want my child!"

"Now, now. In due time. I'm surprised you aren't the least bit interested who has your life in his hands at this moment. Aren't you even a tiny bit curious?"

"Fine. If it will shut you the hell up. Tell me."

"Now that's my girl. In the preexistence…you knew me as Michael."

My mind spins. The floor beneath me seems to have dropped. I reach for the railing to steady myself. It isn't possible. I would've smelled him. I would've known, would've sensed his presence on earth.

"It can't be. I would've known if you were…"

"But I am."

A gasp escapes my throat and I back away. How can it be? They turned Michael?

I grit my teeth until my jaw aches. "You mean to tell me, I've fought all these years while you've already turned? Bastard! I fought beside you!"

Asshole feigns surprise. "Oh, did you think I was that Michael. No, sugar plum, not *that* Michael. I'm the Michael who stood in the shadows of the archangel who fought at your side. Now how silly is that?" He throws his head back and laughs while my face burns with anger and humiliation. "Oh, my God, you should've seen you're face when I told you I was Michael. It was precious. Simply precious."

Fucker. While he's preoccupied with his horrendous joke, I lunge at him, knocking him backward. He swipes his fist and I duck, then turn to run after Taylor. Before I can go five steps, he catches me and throws me across the room. Before I can gather my senses, he's at my side, lifting me by my hair.

"You will never learn, Jerrica."

"Fuck off!" I spit at him. "You flatter yourself. I didn't know you in the preexistence. I wouldn't have wasted a millisecond of my time." I spit on him again.

He slaps my face, once again sending a shock of pain through my swollen cheek. As much as I try to abate a wince, I'm unsuccessful. Each tightened muscle, every flinch serves to strengthen the pain. But I refuse to let him see me physically weak, regardless of my failing emotional state.

"Calm down or I'll put you in time-out," he snarks back at me. Asshole.

I roll my eyes and turn to the person holding Taylor. No matter what happens, they'll die tonight. And if I have my way, so will Michael.

When I search the shadows, I see it isn't the maintenance man. I'd suspected he'd be here. Instead, I can tell it's a woman.

"No, it isn't him. I've only used him to help get that package into your apartment." He hesitates, takes a deep breath and releases it with a sigh. "So far, that is. I'm sure I'll find another use for him later."

Once again, I rush the woman holding my child, but Jesse stops me, holding my hair in one hand and turning me to face him with the other. My breathing grows labored as I fight to be freed. He tightens his fist and knocks me, releasing my body to fall to the ground and leaving my jaw aching from the blow, possibly fractured as well. I can feel my face swelling from the cracked cheekbone on one side and injured jaw on the other. But I won't let him see the fear in my eyes.

I push the pain from my mind to get me through the night. I can't be distracted by my physical weakness, even if this is a dream. Only time can heal what a demon causes in a nightmare of their own devices. If only I could heal my nocturnal wounds with a simple cognitive suggestion.

As I glare up at him, he reaches down and pulls me to my feet by my hair, then pulls my face to his. Impatience flares in his eyes. "I've had enough of this, Jaime Connor. Choose now.

Do you join me, or do I direct her to kill your daughter?"

I turn back to the woman holding Taylor, wondering if I knock him hard enough to the ground, would I make it to her before he catches me again.

"You won't make it, Jaime. Even if you do get past me, Taylor will be dead before you reach Nancy."

Nancy. *My nurse?* I turn to her and she forces a weak smile. I'll kill her.

"And I'll let you. As soon as we have an agreement."

Suddenly, I can't think, my mind won't allow me to mull over what's happening. There has to be a way to end this without them killing my child and me in the process. No matter how hard I search for a positive resolution, I see no path that leads to a satisfactory ending.

Tears tickle my cheeks as they roll to the corner of my mouth and down to my chin. Still, I am unwilling to face that I've been defeated. I can't turn. I can't become a rogue angel, even knowing the consequences if I don't. They'll kill her, then he'll kill me. By that time, I'll wish for death anyway. I wouldn't want to live without her.

"Okay." I try to sound controlled, but my voice betrays me, doesn't sound like my own. Tears force their way to the surface. "I'll give you your answer. I just want to see her." I begin sobbing, unwilling to believe I have to choose from two dire endings.

"What're you going to do, Jaime? I need your answer first. Verbal confirmation will be sufficient." His voice is strained. His patience is running low.

The minute the words leave my mouth I'm damned. I can't say them. I can't do that to Collin or Taylor. There's no way I could drag them into Hell with me.

My hands shake uncontrollably as I swipe a strand of hair from my eyes. "I have to hold her before I can decide." My words are forced out between shuddering breaths. "You know I can't run. You have me trapped. I just want to hold my daughter so I can decide."

"Make your choice, now!" he shouts in my face.

"I can't!" I scream back. "This is my daughter! You know I can't fight with a baby in my arms. So, what are you afraid of?"

His jaw loosens, but his fingers stay wrapped in my hair. Letting out a heavy sigh, he motions for Nancy to bring her to me. When she places Taylor in my arms, Jesse's fingers unravel from me and he allows me to hold my daughter, unfettered by his clutches.

Taylor's soft face turns peaceful again as I coo her to sleep. I hold her tiny hand in mine and sob even harder as I sink to my knees. She lays in my arms, so trusting, unaware her mother is considering letting her die a terrible death. But I can't do that. I'd rather snap her neck myself to save her the pain.

Jesse's foot taps the floor. "Don't start thinking foolishly, Jaime. I know you can't kill your own child. Now, if she were an adult, like Durudee, for example."

"Shut the hell up, you bastard!" I shout back.

He feigns a gasp. "In front of the child?"

I squeeze my eyes tight and force every thought from my mind. I can retreat to that hidden cavern in my mind where only Collin has been allowed to reside. The room in my soul where I used to go when life became too much for me to deal with head on.

As the echo of his voice fades, I hear Collin whispering to me.

Jaime, I'm still here. I'm here for you and Taylor.

"I'm waiting, Jaime." Jesse taps his foot again.

I look up to him. He didn't hear it. He can hear my

thoughts, but not Collin's.

Closing my eyes again, I listen for him, pretending to still sob.

Trust yourself. Remember what you did to Rick. You used his mind to kill him. You can do it again to save yourself and protect Taylor.

My eyes drift to the levels of prison cells above my head, the catwalks around the perimeter where those who once lived here stood. I imagine them standing there now, watching all that's happening to me, to Taylor, here in this prison, while remembering my dreams of the past two nights. Jesse wasn't there, watching me in my sleep. I'd have known if it was him, especially now. There was someone else, behind the walls watching. Not in the shadows. They were trying to help, not frighten me. Could it be my ancestors, trying to show me the way to win this insurmountable battle? Were they there in my dreams, knowing it'd be the only way they could communicate with me? Were some of those ancestors also the druids who now understand I'm one of them? Could it be they've been in my mind, like Collin, giving me the tools to survive?

I need to keep the connection broken so he can't read my thoughts. I remember a tune my mother sang when I was scared as a young child. Hopefully, he won't be able to read me past the innocence of a children's song. Taking a deep, shuddering breath, I begin to hum. At the same time, I remember the image of me beneath the floor, dressed in black then white as Taylor drifted from my arms to hers.

That's what I need to think about, what I did to Rick and what I didn't do. I've always allowed someone else to decide the hunting ground. They controlled what I wore and what weapons were used. I never took control of the situation until Rick, and I still didn't control much. All that will change tonight.

With one knee on the ground and the other supporting the arm that holds Taylor, I reach for the floor with my free hand. I look up into Jesse's face before closing my eyes, still humming.

"Touching lullaby, now give me the child," he quips and leans over to reach for her.

Before his hands make contact with Taylor, the room changes. The floors are no longer solid concrete. The walls aren't thick cinderblock. In their place, the ground beneath me is transparent blue and the walls are plain and seemingly endless. We're in the corridor of my dream.

My gown has changed to the black leather jacket and pants. The image of me in white waits below. I set Taylor on the floor, letting her slip through to the arms of my reflection and I look up to see Jesse's face turn red with anger.

"No! You can't change the dream I set. It's impossible," he shouts and swings his fist at me. I jolt backward, then scramble to my feet with my back to the wall.

In desperation, he falls to his knees and tries to put his hands through the solid tile, scratching and pounding in frustration just as I had in my dream.

"I didn't change the scene, *Mikey*. I only added to it. The jail still exists outside these walls. A barrier you can't penetrate."

At my revelation, he turns toward me, growling with fury, wanting to kill me, now.

Backed against the wall, I look Jesse up and down with amusement as he rises to his feet, moving toward me. He stops, seeing his reflection in the wall. He no longer wears jeans and a t-shirt. Instead, he has white pants, a gray shirt with black and white stripes near the top, black and white face paint and a top hat.

Jesse turns back to me with a cynical look on his face, his teeth grinding together. "Marcel Marceau? This is the best you can do?" Ripping the hat from his head, he throws it to the floor.

Hiding a smirk, I glare back at him. "I hate mimes."

As he throws a punch at me, I roll out of his way and he slams his fist against the wall. After shaking it off for a second, he comes for me again.

"Do you think I can't get to her anyway? I'll kill you here, Jaime Connor, then I'll kill her in her sleep. I'll tear her apart, just as I did your *father!*"

My cheeks turn hot as I realize it wasn't Rick and Sarah who killed Father. It was *him*.

Jesse sees my anger rise and a smile crosses his face.

"Yes, that's right. You didn't realize it was me, did you? Who do you think instructed Rick and Sarah on how to kill your husband? Ah, now the puzzle falls into place. You know, there was always the concern you'd allow him to die to save your own soul, especially after his devastating confession. I even considered stepping in and finishing you myself, but, unlike Sarah, I really wanted *you* more than I wanted you dead. An innocent baby is a different story now, isn't it? Having a child changes *everything*." He leans forward and his lips curve to a smirk, the one he had when he stabbed me in the abdomen in Thailand.

"You and Collin had a fortuitous night together. Fortuitous for *me*. Before you left the States, I smelled Taylor on you, letting you go, knowing it would only be a matter of time before I caught your scent again. You didn't even notice me on your plane. You never looked at me in Starbucks. All I wanted was small talk. A little chitchat. Oh, and to turn your soul over to Lucifer. Minor details."

He circles me and I keep him and Nancy in my line of

sight. They won't get the advantage on me, now that Taylor is safe.

"The true brilliance was when I learned you and Durudee had an old relationship. And when I led you to kill her, I knew it would be a stain on your soul that would prime you to turn rogue. But…" He turns away, giving a shrug. "If I have to use Taylor to achieve that end, I will. I will kill her slowly, horribly, until it drives you over the edge of sanity and right into being a rogue."

He grits his teeth as I do mine, remembering that night.

"Another inch to the left with my sword and you'd be a bigger mess than you already are. Right now, baby Taylor would be of no consequence and your allegiance to a selfish God would be lost."

I swallow the urge to tell him to fuck off, but I need him to reveal more of who he is, what he's done. "How did you find me?"

"Collin's whispers ultimately led me to Dublin. And although I wasn't sure if you'd let *him* die, I knew for a fact you wouldn't allow the same ending for *her*," he says and points to the floor.

Now I change the narrative. He loves to talk. I'll let him finish exposing his deception. I want his mind off Taylor.

"So, you *were* there, in Colorado. You watched while Sarah tortured Collin. And Rick, you waited in the shadows, watching while he cut and stabbed me, didn't you? Did you enjoy watching him running his hands over my body? Or are you more for the violence, delighting when he threw me against the rocks, cutting open my flesh? Maybe it was the part where he stabbed me with a pair of scissors, cut my face with the scalpel." I run my finger along the scar on my jaw line. "Did that make your blood race?"

He sighs. "Jaime. I don't get off on watching men hurt

women. I'm not like Dr. Stanton. And I'm not like Sarah, either. She enjoyed the kill. I guess that's what kept her going for so long, more than fifty years killing demons, until the day she turned."

He hesitates in reflection as I move to the far wall, still facing him.

"I found it rather disappointing when you eliminated the five guards I sent to assassinate you and Durudee in your sleep. They truly were my favorites. A shame, really. Oh well. What were we discussing before…? Ah, yes, business. You see, Jaime, what you fail to recognize is that I'm more of a *businessman*. I have a job to do and that's what I'm here for. That's why I don't make mistakes."

"But you made a mistake with me. In fact, you've made several mistakes. Underestimating my potential was your first."

His lips pucker in contemplation. "You're right about underestimating you, but you're wrong about making a mistake. Your daughter's not out of my reach, and I'm not finished thinking about her so don't change the topic. Granted, for now she's safe, but tomorrow she won't be. You know, I don't think Collin told you what happened to her at the hospital."

My mind suddenly spins. He didn't tell me. Whatever it was, he must have thought it'd be too much for me to handle.

"While you slept and Collin fought your demons, Nancy went into the nursery and held little Taylor's nose and mouth until she stopped breathing. When your husband rushed in, he found her nearly blue. Lucky she was in a hospital or he wouldn't have known how to resuscitate her and she would've died. Without you there to protect her, your husband will fight in his sleep and she'll be left alone and vulnerable. Anyone could come into your apartment and kill her while he sleeps and he could do nothing about it." He feigns sadness.

My gaze moves to Nancy. The smell of her fear is stronger than the look of terror in her eyes. She had better be afraid.

"Kill her now, Jesse," Nancy says.

"Calm down, she can't get to you as long as I'm here."

Nancy doesn't look convinced as I continue to glare at her. She tried to kill my daughter. "You *will* die tonight, you know that, don't you?"

"Jaime, she's getting pretty good at this, little Nancy here. As valuable as she's become, I'd hate to lose her. Yet, if I have to lose one of you, I prefer to make it a business arrangement we can both live with, if you know what I mean. Her life for your soul. I think it's a good trade, don't you? You don't realize the value of my girl here." He puts his arm around Nancy's shoulders. "She did help give me the alibi to poison the town against you. She's the one who killed Scotty in his sleep last night. I was surprised she was strong enough to run him through, but she did it."

I'm aghast at what he's admitting without a hint of regret in his eyes. "You monster. So proud of what you've done. And Curtis? And Joseph, did she kill them, too?"

"Curtis and Joseph? No. *No*, the druids killed *them*. I was busy, still in Colorado. Well, between there and here, trying to find *you* and trying to kill your husband, of course. My mind was on higher conquests than two mortals. And while I was preoccupied with *you*, you were giving me so many ways to turn the town against you. I mean, just look at you, all those scars on your body, they already didn't trust you. And then there's the matter of Curtis and Joseph. You allowed them to die. And now Scotty?" He laughs. "And when you hit your own husband in public? Well, I couldn't have molded a more perfect nail to drive into your coffin. A woman who could harm the man she loves is most definitely capable of killing a stranger."

"Wait a minute, back up a bit. The Druids. They were looking for a rogue, not a dark angel. How did you keep them from coming after *you*?"

"I made a trade on one of my visits to the Emerald Isles." A smile crosses his face, as if he's proud of his deal with the devil. "Offered up a baby. The unborn child of the dark angel who killed six people in one night."

"You're the one. You're responsible for Curtis and Joseph's deaths. If you hadn't sent the Druids after me, they wouldn't have killed those who associated with me. They could've killed everyone in this town just to reach me and you would've been okay with that?"

Michael yawns, then stretches his arms above his head. "This whole topic is really getting boring. Don't you agree?" His gaze narrows at me as if he's irritated that I'm not impressed. "Sometimes there's collateral damage."

"You have no conscience."

"The lives of those who populate this town are inconsequential to me. And a conscience only gets in the way of some of the most important matters in life. In this circumstance, the important matter would be the disposition of your soul. You owe me at least that much after destroying my Dark Angel's Trumpet fields. Oh, you have angered some powerful people in high places. You're lucky I reached you first."

"You find it so easy to justify your sociopathic tendencies. And that leaves a question burning in my heart. When the Druids didn't get what they traded for, what did you offer them?" By the look on his face I can tell he hasn't squared up with the spirits yet.

"Jerrica…"

I roll my eyes as my angel name crawls from his lips. *Patronizing asshole.*

Flashing a prideful smile, he continues as if we're discussing an exciting business venture. "You don't realize what a big deal this is. I've been on this earth for more than a hundred years. I've been killing demons since the Great War. You'd remember it as World War One."

Patronizing *and* pretentious.

He glares at me, clearly reading my mind again. "You don't understand. There was so much evil across the globe. And the handful of dark angels they sent weren't nearly enough to take care of the innocent. It was a miracle I didn't turn at that time. But then, just a few short decades later, the holocaust happened and I left the States for Europe once more."

It surprises me when he shakes his head, closing his eyes in disgust. There was once a conscience there. Maybe he still has one.

"When I saw what they were allowed to do to those people… *Any* angel would absorb the evil that emanated from those death camps. You wouldn't be any different."

My lip curls up in disgust. "Not possible. I couldn't watch that kind of slaughter and take any joy from it. Only an angel as *insane* as you could turn under those circumstances."

His teeth grind together as he rushes me, hand reaching for my throat. He moves so fast I'm slammed back against the wall before I know it. His face draws so close it nearly touches mine. "You weren't there!" He takes a deep breath, releases me, and steps back. "You weren't there." He takes yet another breath, clearly trying to get himself under control. But I'm unaffected by his confession.

"Maybe not, but I still don't see how anyone who swore allegiance to our God would let evil invade their soul the way you have, turning them so black, too stained with angel blood to ever return home again."

"Really, Jaime? You don't understand? I've seen you fight, remember? It was entertaining to watch you stand there while demons slipped their hands over you, pressed their bodies into you. Shall we discuss being too unclean to return home?" He puts his hands on my wrists and slides them up to my shoulders, then pulls me closer to him. "You could've killed them with the snap of your wrist, but you waited until they were through, enjoying every second, playing your cat and mouse game until the right moment. You use your past to take revenge on the wrong demon before you finish them off. Is that clean, Jaime? By the way, I'm beginning to *love* this black on you."

"I've never killed an innocent person," I tell him and knock his hands away. He draws his hand back to slap me across the face, but I block his blow. When I swing back, he catches my wrist then grabs my hair to pull me closer to him.

"Depends on what you consider innocent, *kitten*." His lips press into mine, then he shoves me away. "I've always wanted to do that. Now, where was I? That's right. You've never killed an innocent person. Ahh, yes. And with that, a name comes to mind. Challenging to pronounce. What was that name?"

"Shut. Up. You arrogant prick," I finally break in out of sheer anger.

"That's it! Durudee. Wasn't she your friend? Innocuous little Durudee? Innocently believing an assassin would behead her upon waking. Poor, desperate soul. So easy to manipulate. But I hadn't expected her to beg you to take her life before I did."

He reaches for the wall with the tips of his fingers, then nods appreciatively.

"I *really* like what you've done with the place. Very…clean.

So unlike your soul. We all knew how powerful you'd be if you reached full strength. Nearly as dangerous as Michael. The other Michael, of course. Rogue angels quaked at the idea of confronting you, but I didn't. I knew someday I'd turn you or kill you. I was patient. Seventy years I've waited for this moment."

"So, you've been in the United States, searching for me all this time?" He doesn't say a word, but I can see in his eyes the answer is affirmative. "How did you develop such a close relationship with the people of Dublin so quickly if you've been there all along? You haven't been here for more than, what, a week?"

"That's right, exactly seven days. There's a trick to it, you see. I planted memories of me in their minds while they slept. Aha, didn't know you could do that, did you? They think I've been here all their lives. They grew up with me, we went to school together. They knew me like their own brother with only a night's work from me."

"They don't know you at all." My voice is practically a whisper.

"They don't know *me*. They know Jesse, the *garda*. Hell, I even planted the idea of the extradition order in the heads of my counterparts. You know there's no such order, don't you? The Thai authorities think it was one of the gangs roaming the streets of Thailand who killed Durudee. Oh, so close. Unlike Colorado. They have *no* idea what happened to those people in that town. Bumbling fools. By the way, that was *brilliant* what you did to Rick, making him believe he ingested rat poison."

"The scene downtown today was only for the town's sake then." I shake my head.

"Totally. In fact, you two could've denied it out on that street and no one would have known the difference because I have no way to prove it. But you're too honest. That's what I like about you. And that's what I counted on."

"You sure had me fooled. *Clever.*" Now *I* sound sarcastic.

"You see! You're starting to get me. Now!" He claps his hands and rubs them together. "Getting down to business. You do realize why you can't win? These poor, gullible saps will string you up if anything happens to me, so you can't kill me. And if you lose, which inevitably you shall, I'll be the one to string you up." The look on his face is one of accomplishment.

His confession is sealed. Now is the time to make my move and end this. He hasn't beaten me yet. I close my eyes and let my mind listen to the walls. The wind whispers across the distant moors, blowing the scent of wet grass into my soul. I'm not alone, haven't been the entire time.

"You think your husband on the other side of the prison door is close enough to save you?"

"No. What I think is you're a petulant child who needs a good *spanking*. You can try and kill me, but you won't win. No matter what happens tonight… *You. Won't. Win.*"

Fury rages in his eyes as he brings his arm back to hit me. He swings at my face and I let him. It'll be his last. He has no idea what I've done and how fully I've changed the playing field once I changed this room. The more brutal he appears, the better. As my body flies to the floor I see Nancy moving toward me. Grabbing her by the ankle, I yank, throwing her to the ground.

When I push up to my knees, I glare at her. "Stay out of this. I'll deal with you in a minute." I turn on Jesse. "Did you think I'd be unprepared for you? Do you really think I'm incapable of stopping you?"

Jesse grabs my throat again and slams my back against the wall. I reach for his hands, but can't loosen them from encircling my neck. His voice is controlled, but angry. "Yes. You're completely unprepared and you're totally incapable of stopping me. You're weak and a fool, and I'll kill you right here, right now."

"You do, and the town will come after you and string you up." I look him directly in the eyes so he can see I'm telling the truth.

He bursts into laughter. "Jaime Connor, I'm gonna miss your sense of humor. And I'm gonna miss this little game we're playing, but we need to move it along."

I know his laughter isn't out of entertainment. He's worried I know something he doesn't. And he's right. "You must have me confused with someone else, Michael. Jaime Connor doesn't exist. My name's Jaime Leary."

He puts his hand over my mouth and nose and I struggle to pull his fingers free. "Well, Jaime *Leary*, I've grown bored with you." Clawing at his hand, I fight to breathe. "When I'm finished with you, they'll think you died in your sleep, Mrs. Leary. Suffocated by the pillow in your cell."

Forcing his hand from my mouth, I gasp in air. Slippery as a snake, he transitions back to my throat before I can get away. "No. They won't. They'll know *exactly* what happened." My eyes staring into his, I press my palms against the surface behind me.

As I do, the walls up and down both sides of the corridor light up and the faces of every resident in Dublin are illuminated, standing behind the façade, watching. Some hold their hands over their mouths in shock. Sean is standing in front, his forehead creased with anger, hands pressed against the wall. Collin is beside him, watching me intently.

"They've been here since I changed the field, when it became *my* hunting ground. I've brought them in their sleep to watch you and listen to you confess. They've heard every word you've said. Every. Gloating. Moment."

"Well, since you brought Collin and the whole town here to watch, shall we put on an entertaining show?"

Michael covers my mouth with kisses, biting my lips. I fight to get away from him, but can't. He has me pinned against the wall with his free hand sliding up my ribs, stopping at my breast. Gathering my anger, I bring my knee up as hard as I can into his groin, causing him to growl in pain. Rage rolls up his throat as he tightens his grip on my trachea. If I want to live, I'll have to act fast. Sliding my hands between his arms, I force them away, then head-butt him in the nose, spraying blood everywhere. He stumbles backward, holding his nose. His eyes narrow on me and he brings his arm out to his side. A katana appears in his free hand, just like the one I used against the druids. Shit. I gave him time to gather his thoughts and he took control of the dreamscape. I'll have to distract him to take it back. But it has to be enough to give me time for a significant disruption in his ability to fight.

From the corner of my eye, I notice Nancy moving along the wall. She's within arm's reach. What's she up to?

Michael lunges forward and I skip back several steps. A smile grows across his lips, perhaps as he remembers our last sword fight in Thailand. Nancy charges me and I knock her backward with a solid swing of my arm. Michael lunges just as I turn back to him and tears a hole in my jacket before I can vault out of his reach.

"Oh, Jerrica. Are we really here again? Are you going to give me the pleasure of running my sword through you once more?" He leaps forward and I jump back. "Oh, I like this. So much. Although, I must say it isn't nearly as thrilling as the thought of having you at my side for an eternity, or…of slicing your handsome husband and your tiny little baby into shreds. But, as Doris Day would say, *que sera, sera.*"

He springs forward and slashes the sword. Without the ability to materialize weapons into his dreamscape now that he regained control, I search the walls and ceiling for an idea. Anything. I look down to see Taylor sleeping soundly in my doppelganger's arms. He hasn't regained complete control. *Protect her*, I tell my duplicate with my mind. My eyes shift back to the ceiling and back to him.

As he's about to lunge again, I turn and sprint away from him.

Michael can't control the laughter forced up his throat. "Is that your game? Are we playing tag?" He laughs again. "Where will you go, Jaime? You can only run in circles. And I'm still much stronger than you. Just come back here and let's finish this, before you embarrass yourself."

When I stop at the other end of the corridor, I turn and glare into his eyes. No matter how hard I try, I can't keep the smile from creasing my face as his eyes narrow and curiosity fills them. He searches my thoughts, but I close my mind to him. In this moment of uncertainty, his weakness bleeds through as he forgets to control the dream. My opportunity. With my hands pushed out to my sides, palms to the wall, I force the energy in my arms to move the barriers. The deafening sound of shifting concrete startles those on the other side of the wall. Chunks of ceiling fall to the floor, compelling Michael to dodge them. Like on the bridge in Bangkok, he scrambles, unable to control the dream. This façade is mine to regulate. Another massive chunk of concrete falls as he leaps out of the way. The sword is knocked from his grasp. Now, it's my turn.

With a steady mind, I flip into the air and land on slabs the size of a car. I skip forward from one mangled chunk of cement to the next until I'm kneeling beside the katana. As I pull it into my hand, the unstable rubble shifts beneath my feet. I wobble then gain my balance to see the smile cross Michaels's face. Another sword appears in his hand. Without waiting for him to gain the advantage, I swipe at him, but he blocks my attack with his weapon. I swipe again, then once more until the katana is knocked from his grasp. I reach for the felled sword and continue toward him. A piece of rubble rolls my foot so that I catch myself, then turn back to Michael to see another weapon appear in each of his hands.

He steps backward, blocking my swipes and thrusts as he goes. "I'll kill you with all of them watching. Then, I'll wait for the next time your husband falls asleep." He glances to the walls, nodding toward Sean and the others who stand near him. "And I'll take down *anyone* in this town who tries to stop me."

My face still aches, and my body may be tired and weak, but I will be damned if I give up on these people of Dublin without a fight. I grit my teeth and tighten my fingers on the hilt of my sword. "We'll see about that," I answer, and begin another onslaught of slashes, swipes, and thrusts.

His balance thrown off, he falls, nearly dropping his weapons. His body slides backward on the slick floor, but he is on his feet before I reach him. For as strong as he may be, he's a surprisingly terrible swordsman. And it's this knowledge that feeds my spirit. I take a deep breath and head forward. For the sake of my mother country, I have to win this fight.

My new wave of attack is unmerciful as Michael blocks one assault after another. If I keep him on defense, there's a chance he won't gain control. I may be able to overcome him.

Michael backs down the corridor to avoid my wrath, but I continue forward until he's against the far wall. His blades go up between mine and he parries them away, then brings his full-circle to thrust inside. My blades stop his instead and knock them from his hands. I back him to the wall. He's defenseless. I have him where I want him.

Before he can make another weapon materialize, I drive my swords through the palms of his hands and nail them to the wall above his head. His screams echo through the room.

With my eyes trained on him, I step backward and bend down to reach his sword. The handle is warm in my grasp. I don't dare search for the other or he might seize the opportunity to slip his restraints. Besides, one sword is enough for what I have planned.

"You're finished, Michael," I say, crossing the piles of debris with careful footing. Once we're face-to-face again, I sweep my hand to force the blocks of cement several feet away from us.

I bring the tip of the katana in my hand to his throat, depressing the jugular vein until a small stream of blood appears.

Michael's eyes dilate then narrow to a pinpoint. A smirk grows across his face. The same he had the night he ran me through the abdomen. "Not quite." He answers.

My eyes turn up to his hands still pinned above his head. A sharp bite through my back and into my chest takes my breath away.

"*You're* finished, now, Jaime Leary."

I turn to see Nancy, backing away from me. She somehow found the courage to retrieve the sword. I drop to my knees and reach behind me, pulling the blade, cutting my fingers as I remove it from my back.

Nancy pulls the swords free that pin Michael to the wall. He cradles his hands to his abdomen. After drawing a deep breath, he takes a weapon from Nancy, grimacing as the hilt meets his torn palms, and limps over to me. The tip of the weapon lifts my chin, forcing my gaze to meet his. "Do you see your husband watching you die, Mrs. Leary? Do you think he'll cry over your corpse when he wakes and finally makes it to your cell? Or, instead, do you think he'll take Taylor and run from me like a coward? Will he take her to America, thinking he can hide from me there?"

What have I done? Rick was right when he said I make poor choices. Once again, my cockiness has caused a complication I hadn't anticipated. My husband and daughter are more at risk than ever before.

I turn my face to the wall to see Collin on the other side. His fists pound the barrier, but he can't make it through. He paces back and forth like a trapped animal in a cage, tearing his bloody hands through his hair and shouting something inaudible. Sean stands near him with panic in his eyes, shaking his head, looking hopeless. Suddenly, he also seems to be shouting my name. My head grows light, my body numb and cold.

In my final moments, I see all their faces, watching me die. Was it a mistake to bring them here, allowing them to see me breathe my final breath when there's nothing they can do? Tears steam down my cheeks, into the corners of my mouth. I have to stay strong, even knowing I'm near death.

"You have only seconds left, Jaime. I hate to gloat, but, who's the better angel, now? I suppose you wish you'd considered my proposal with a little more sincerity."

I drop to my hands and my elbows buckle beneath me. A puddle of red envelopes the floor as it drips over both sides of my back. My knees slip backward in the slick liquid. The cold floor meets my swollen cheek. Michael's hand lowers to my throat, pressing against my pulse as if to check it.

Darkness envelopes me and the pain leaves my body with my soul. I see myself from above as Michael's hands slowly lift away from me. Collin no longer paces. Tears stream down both sides of his face as he whispers my name. He stares at my body in shock, shaking his head in disbelief. Others around him are also silent, crying as they watch me die. Sean, Sandy, Annie, Mary, Matt, Amanda, Daniel, everyone. They don't move as Michael rises to his feet and stares down Collin.

He bends down again and lifts my body, like a cat presenting a dead mouse to his master to show them what he's done. He doesn't even have the decency to lower my eyelids.

Michael's expression is calm as he stares into Collin's furious face. "You'll go to sleep sometime, Leary. And when you do, you and your girl will join her in Hell." His smile turns to laughter as he allows my body to slip from his hands to the floor, splattering the blood in a pattern that resembles a pair of dark, red wings.

As I watch, a light appears near my silent corpse. No one else acts like they can see it. The sphere suddenly takes shape, wings at first then a human-like form. I hear my mother weeping, and my father, the same as I wept for them. I wonder how many times they've cried for what they've seen me experience, for what they've seen me do since their death. I wonder how many times they turned away in shame.

The light beside my still form smells familiar. He was one of those who watched in my dream, the one with the room of white walls and a transparent floor. Is this my father? It's so hard for me to tell since I haven't been near him in so long. When he lifts his eyes to see my soul, it startles me. I contemplate if I should hide, but I realize by the feel of his essence, his power, he doesn't mean me any harm. As my spirit grows calm in his presence, his gentle hands gather my soul to lift me away.

Thinking on Jesse's words about being unclean, I worry about my destination.

Where are you taking me? I wonder.

You're going home, Jerrica. His voice responds in my mind.

Whoever this is must not know what I've done in this mortal world. He doesn't realize it'd be impossible for me to return.

No. I can't go. I'm too stained.

Jerrica, your battles for righteousness washed away your sins. You've been purified by fire. And they're waiting to welcome you back. We've all been waiting for you.

I know the voice and it sends a thrill through my soul.

Michael? They sent you for me? I hadn't realized how badly I've missed him. The archangel Michael, my friend, who I fought beside in the time before my life on earth.

No. I came on my own.

Warmth rushes over my body and for once, I'm not in pain. All the stains of anger and hatred have finally washed clean from my soul. The joy and happiness I hadn't allowed in nearly a lifetime return to me, and I know peace once again.

While lifting my soul to the heavens, he heals the body still lying in a room of my nightmare. Scars disappear and broken bones mend. Blood stops dripping from the corner of my mortal mouth. Black leather clothing turns white. The blood-stained floor turns the color of snow.

Far away from me, I barely hear the rogue, Michael, ranting next to where my body turns cold, telling Collin exactly how he'll kill him and Taylor. He told me he'd tear my daughter apart like he did my father. He'll do the same to Collin. The thought is sickening. There's no question he'll do it if only to gain his revenge on me for refusing to follow him. And for destroying the crop of poisonous flowers.

Collin said he didn't think he could live if something happened to me. I realize I still didn't have a chance to tell him how I felt. He interrupted me the one time I tried. My husband still doesn't know what's in my heart.

With me gone, Taylor and Collin won't survive. I can't

leave them this way. There will be no more dark angels to defend the innocent once they're gone. Once we're all gone. The town still needs us for protection. The world still needs angels. I don't want to go back to earth, but I can't leave them, not yet.

Wait.

You've fulfilled your calling, Jerrica. Time to come home.

Archangel Michael smells like fresh air and love. I want to go with him, but know I can't. If I do, once Collin and Taylor are dead the world will fall into a deeper darkness than it has ever known. With us gone, Armageddon would begin. Michael understood this before he came for me. I feel his love surround me and how badly he would have liked to spare me the pain I've already known.

Please, Michael. Are you ready for earth to belong to Lucifer? Are you ready for the horrors that accompany that event? We cast him down there. This is our fault. We can end it. I…can at least hold it off.

Are you willing to live through Armageddon, Jerrica?

I don't understand and he senses my confusion.

Your body is a corpse. Your blood no longer feeds the heart or the brain. Without your soul, the life it once had no longer exists. The only possibility for your return would be to render you immortal. If you are immortal, you will never come home again. You'll walk the earth for an eternity. I feel the depth of sadness this admission causes him.

I have to save my daughter and husband. I can't stand by and watch them being tortured and I can't allow this country to be ravaged by this rogue, the world decimated by Lucifer.

Lucifer will decimate this world with or without you.

With me still on earth, we can buy time.

Jerrica, as an immortal you will be tied to the earthly plane. You'll never again see your family in heaven. When Taylor and Collin die, you'll also never see them again.

The thought strikes at my heart. I'll never see my parents again. Someday, I'll have to surrender Collin, and Taylor, also?

You will be on the earth and you will battle Lucifer until the end of time. If you deny your place in heaven now, you will be heaven's only personal witness to the horrors of the apocalypse. And, although you will never die, you will still know pain, physical and emotional agony. Are you prepared for that?

I didn't believe it possible for a soul to tremble, yet mine did.

I could save them all now, only to lose everything later. I'd never be able to return, never again stand beside my father in heaven, ever. And I'd battle evil for an eternity.

Rick Stanton once asked what I wanted from this life. I suppose, to decide if I was capable of being turned. The only answer I could consider was that I wanted to die so I could go home.

Now, I want to save my husband and child more. Am I willing to give up an eternity with them, to spare them the pain of dying at Jesse's unmerciful hand? The answer to this question doesn't only affect Collin and Taylor, though. My decision has a greater implication. My death is detrimental to all of Dublin. In fact, the entire world.

By choosing to stay on earth, becoming immortal, I'm only delaying the inevitable, I know. Can I delay Armageddon long enough to make it worth damning my soul to this forever? I wish Collin were here to help me decide.

Jerrica, come home. Your husband and child will soon join you.

I hesitate on the words I know I must say, finding the fortitude to utter them with conviction.

I can't.

Dublin is no longer disappearing far beneath me. We're suspended in place as Michael waits. He understands my heart. Still, my choice causes his heart to break. I feel it as surely as if it were my own.

You can't beat the angel killer.

Help me.

He hesitates.

Please.

After a moment of contemplation, he acquiesces. *I'll share my strength.* His expression changes to concern as he lowers his head. I believe I hear him say, *beloved angel*, but I'm not sure. His voice is soft, as if it was a thought I wasn't meant to hear.

Clouds drift away from me as we descend to earth and Dublin grows nearer. Michael returns me to the room where I lost the battle, kissing my cheek while presenting my soul to the lifeless body on the floor. An internal battle wages in his thoughts over his agreement to leave me with the angel killer. His essence still clings to mine, unwilling to set my soul free. His strong desire to protect me, encourage me to return with him, is evident. Yet, I'm unyielding.

Although I'm aware he knows more about the future of this world than I, my resolve is solid. This is a battle I'm determined to win and he must find a way to accept my decision. Still, Michael hesitates a moment longer, reluctant to release me. While he lingers, I sense the silent pain he's carried for decades, watching my battles destroy me.

The love of the most dangerous warrior in heaven surrounds me, averse to leaving my side again, but I promise him I'm ready. There's no way to relieve his mind, yet he respects my steadfastness. Grudgingly, he departs while my spirit longs for him to stay. I know that soon I'll meet my greatest challenge and fight an unrelenting foe who was once my brother in the preexistence. Lucifer waits for me. My destiny has been sealed. But first, I have a rat to fillet.

When my body has fully absorbed my soul, my eyes open to see Michael, standing in front of Collin at the partition, unaware I'm stirring. His singular focus is not on the life he'd ended moments before. Rather, he's more interested in the lives he intends to destroy. He could have stopped this dream long ago, but he draws it out to torment them all. Michael wants the world to fear him. *Arrogant prick.*

My lungs fill with air again, coughing and gasping for oxygen to help reanimate my limbs. Rolling to my side, I see that my leather jacket and pants, even my soul, are still white as snow. Only my hair remains dark.

At the sound of movement, Michael turns my way. "No. *No!* I *killed you!*"

The room appears different as I regard it now, brilliant and beautiful, as if I'm seeing it through heavenly eyes. I have no more fear. My body is strong and renewed. Archangel Michael's power surges through my veins. All mental and physical scars have permanently disappeared.

"Yes, you *did* kill me," I answer, my voice deep and hoarse. "But not again." I let out a slight chuckle. "Not even possible."

I still breathe heavily while rising to my knees. Being resurrected from death isn't an immediate return to full health. My body is growing stronger, but I'm not fully functional.

Michael returns to me and reaches for my throat, squeezing until I choke, but this time I don't feel fear, only determination. When I knock his hand away, he swings at me. This time I catch his fist in mine and tighten the muscles in my fingers while rising to my feet. Bones snap in my grasp while he screams in agony. Well, well.

"Bitch! I'll kill you!" he grinds through gritted teeth, cradling his hand.

Now it's my time to smirk back at him. "Really? Tell me how, *Jesse.*"

He releases his hand, teeth clenched, and rushes me, swinging with his opposing fist. I catch his blow with my forearm without a flinch and his eyes grow wild. He swings again and again. Each time, I block his blows with minimal effort. My God, I feel invincible. And I feel connected. Not only to the one who gave his power to me, but to those who left this earth before me. Those from as far back as the earliest recorded time and further.

Finally, I've had enough of this and glare back at him. Bringing my arm across my body, I swing and hear the crack as I connect with his cheek. His stumbles back, tumbles over ceiling rubble and into the wall.

My eyes close. I listen to the whispers of my ancestors blowing across the moors. The beautiful sound of my youth energizes me. Michael rises to his feet, once again cradling his broken hand. He can hear them as well. When I turn my eyes to him, I flash a knowing smile.

"You're finished, Michael. Or is it Jesse? This town will never fear you again."

The dread in his eyes doesn't bring me pleasure. The knowledge of his destiny causes me to pity him as I swing at his face, connecting with his jaw. Another crack and the swelling in both sides of his face grow prominent. His feet stumble over each other as he fights to catch his balance, hoping to escape my blows. He swings his arm through the air at me, attempting to defend himself, but missing each time. A final left hook to the chin makes a resounding snap and sends him to the floor.

While my back is still turned, Nancy rushes forward. Before she reaches me, however, I knock her backward with a fist to her face. Her screams blot out the sound of Jesse's cries. Blood pours through the fingers cupping her nose.

Backing away from Jesse, I close my eyes, hearing Collin in

my head, telling me to finish him off. "No," I whisper back. "This kill doesn't belong to me."

My concentration is clear again. My mind calls to the four winds, asking my ancestors to avenge the deaths of our people at the hands of a rogue angel. In an instant, I feel their presence. Their voices whisper, but not to me.

"Rogue angel…"

"I won't need angels to avenge my death, Michael. Unfortunately for you, you're not of druid descent."

A black cloud appears in a corner of the room, growing and slipping along the wall until it reaches the size of several men. As Michael realizes they've come for him, his eyes dilate in fear before his body is consumed by the cloud. Screams echo throughout the room and I turn away, unable to watch, no matter what he did to me, no matter what he's done to my family or this town.

As his shrieks subside, the cloud trails away into the corners of the room and we're left alone with Jesse's beaten and torn body. Only Nancy awaits, not far away. Still, I observe Jesse for a moment longer, watching for a sign of breathing. Soon, I'm positive his soul is in eternal darkness.

Once I know he's dead, I turn to Nancy. "You know I can't ignore you now, don't you?"

Moving in her direction, I don't take my eyes from her. "I'm a dark angel. I'm sent into dreams to dispose of killers like you. I can't leave," I sweep my arm toward the walls at the people watching intently. "*They* can't leave, and neither can you, until every killer in the dream dies."

Blood runs down to her chin and drips to the floor from her crooked nose. I feel her heart rate increase. Her eyes dart around the room, searching for an exit.

"Trust me, there's no way out for you. Jesse locked us in. We're all caught in this nightmare until it's over. And now it's just you and me. You know my strength. There's no way you can beat me, Better if you don't even try. I'll make it quick. And I promise, you'll feel only a slight amount of pain before you die. Far less than you afforded your victims."

Nancy pulls her hand from her pocket and I suddenly feel a searing pain in my arm. In her hand is a scalpel with a drop of my blood falling from the sharp edge to the floor. The leather of my white sleeve is sliced open to the skin of my bicep. She swings again and I catch her wrists and pull her into my arms. I tear the scalpel from her grasp and toss it to the floor before reaching for her chin. A quick flip of my wrist snaps her neck and I let her slip to the floor.

The moment her heart stops, I wake in my cell and reach for my arm. The scalpel was sharp, but didn't cut deep enough to tear any muscles. The blood clots, and the wound immediately heals, leaving my skin clear as if it had never been torn. Laying my head back on the pillow, I ponder my future and the idea of an eternity fighting Lucifer's followers, even Lucifer himself. Am I prepared for this?

Within minutes, Collin appears at my cell, holding Taylor and wiping tears from his eyes.

"Jaime. You're here. You're really alive."

He slips my daughter into my arms, then grabs me by the back of my head and around the waist. His lips find mine as he pulls me close. I don't remember him ever kissing me so hard.

Reaching for his cheek, I stare up into his eyes. "I love you, I love you so much. Don't you ever forget that, Collin Leary. I love you, I love you."

He smiles and shushes me while kissing my forehead. "I know."

The world around me distorts to a silvery haze as tears fill my eyes and I kiss him again.

Then he reaches for my arm. "Are you all right? Let me see." He lifts the sleeve of my t-shirt before I can pull away. A look of bewilderment crosses his face when he realizes there's no slice, no scar, not even one drop of dried blood on my back where I was impaled.

"It was nothing. She…only…scratched…um, the surface."

Confusion shows in his eyes. "I saw her drive a sword through your back," he replies. "Jaime?"

"Collin, let's just say, I took control of the dream."

He closes his eyes and shakes his head, then examines my back again.

There's no reason for me to tell him about the deal I'd struck with Michael. At least, not yet. He wouldn't understand. I'll have to find a way to break it to him, when the time is right.

As we turn to leave the prison block with a guard leading the way, I lean my head into Collin's chest and he wraps his arms tightly around me. Taking a deep breath, I smell the musky scent of the moorlands. His heart beats softly in my ear like the wind through wet grass. The worst battle of our lives is over. Starting today, I truly begin to live the way life was meant.

CHAPTER 29

MY eyes open to survey my surroundings. A darkened street with only a dim lamp near the distant corner stretches out before me. My gait is slow as I progress past empty brick buildings and shuttered businesses. I wonder how this street looked when it was alive with people and bustling with activity. These days, I wonder more about a previous life that has since been extinguished, rather than only seeing the results of its death. I find I'm taking that perspective more often in anything I do, even hunting. Especially while hunting.

Little time passes before I feel the presence of another. He knows I'm here, has been waiting for me to sleep. I'm ready.

When I reach the alley, before I can turn to see the one who waits in the shadows, hands reach out and pull me into the dark, pinning me against the wall. I'm not afraid as a scarred hand holds my shoulder in place while the other moves slowly up my thigh. He leers at my body as if I'm his prey.

Staring into his green eyes, I raise my brow. "I told you nothing short *or* tight. How do I fight in this?"

He smiles, green eyes gleaming as he examines the tight

black skirt and white cotton shirt unbuttoned below my bust. "Oh, but you look so damn good in this." He winks at me.

Sigh. "You did sexy librarian last night, Collin. Besides, sexy librarians don't wear such a short skirt. It barely covers my ass." I take off the glasses and drop them to the ground.

"I know." He smiles. "Tomorrow I'll switch it up. Leopard?"

What? "No."

"You'd look *hot.*"

I'd look *stupid.* "I don't do animal prints."

"There'll be cage dancing…"

"Uh, huh. Yeah…no."

"I'll wear a loin cloth…"

Hmm. Maybe.

He runs his fingers down my arm, locking them in mine and lifting my hand to his lips. The hairs on the back of my neck stand on end. My breathing is deep as my heart speeds its pace. His lips part again and he moves in as if he's going to kiss me on the mouth, but goes straight for my throat instead. My eyes close. Why do I love this so much? His touch still makes my skin tingle.

Suddenly, he stops kissing me, lifting his head for a second. "What?"

I'm not sure what he's asking, so I answer back. "What?" I take in a quick breath as he pulls my shirt to the side to kiss my shoulder.

He stops kissing again. "What?"

With my eyes still closed, I shake my head. "What, what? Don't stop now."

"Why are you tapping me?"

I open my eyes to see him staring back at me with a serious expression. "I'm not tapping you."

As the words leave my lips, my eyes fall on the demon

standing behind him, aiming a gun at his head.

When I point behind him, he turns. "Oh. Hey, what's up?"

"Hate to interrupt you two. You seem real cozy and all."

We both stare back at him in amusement.

Collin smiles. "Nah, it's no bother. We can do this later." He winks at me again. "Reconsider that leopard skin."

"Not a chance in hell." I smile and wink back.

He narrows his eyes at me, then turns to the demon. With a flick of his wrist he twists the gun out of the guy's hand, forcing it to discharge in the air and breaking the demons trigger finger in the act of doing so. I feel a piercing ache and reach for my hip. The wayward bullet has penetrated my skin and lodged in my bone.

"Shit!" I reach for the gaping wound and wait for it to heal as Collin calls over his shoulder.

"You okay, babe?"

"I'm good," I answer and bite back the pain until it subsides. The hole narrows and blood stops trickling down my skirt.

The demon shouts and cusses in the background as Collin saunters toward me and hands me the gun. Then he returns to the demon.

Glock? I roll my eyes and remove the clip, tossing it down my shirt then dropping the weapon to the ground. Even if the demon somehow gets the weapon back, he won't be firing it again.

The punk swings at Collin, but he doesn't try to dodge the punch. As his fist connects with Collin's chin the demon realizes what a bad idea it was and screams while holding his hand.

"What kind of criminal are you?" he scolds his opponent. "You should never swing at someone when your trigger finger is broken. Listen to you. Now you're screaming and holding your hand as if a shark bit it off."

Are you kidding me? "Collin…"

He follows the demon to the street and waits for him to recover. I shake my head. He's enjoying this way too much. Since the night at the jail, he hunts differently. He never used to play with the monster before he met me.

While I'm watching the killer's attempts to throw a punch with his left hand, I suddenly smell a strong odor. Caviar? *Yuck!* Then someone reaches for my shoulder and turns me toward them.

Good Lord! The man smiles, trying to look debonair in his navy-blue suit-jacket with some kind of crest on the pocket. He sports a white turtle neck beneath the jacket, white pants, and a white sea-captain's hat. "What are you?" I ask, my upper lip rising in distaste.

"I'm your captain of *love*."

I laugh. "Is that the best you can do?" Will I ever meet a demon with a good pick-up line?

"I have a yacht." He raises his eyebrows at me.

Really? I roll my eyes. "Well, that changes everything," I reply in the flattest voice possible.

Unfortunately, he doesn't recognize the sarcasm.

Collin, still engaged in his own mockery of a battle, leans back to avoid another weak left-hand punch. "You okay, hun?"

"Yep, just chatting with Thurston Howell the third, here. Says he's got a *yacht*. Wanna trade?"

"Really? No. No trades."

"My name's Jack, not Thurston," the demon replies.

Hilarious as his appearance is, the demon's intentions are dark as hell. I can feel them, see them in his mind. "Yeah? Hey, Collin, he secretly wants to take me for a ride, then drown me in his swimming pool. What do you think? Fun night?" I turn back to yacht boy. "Captain Jack, eh? Any relation to... Nah, never mind. It's too easy." There are so many places I could go with that.

Collin trips his demon to the ground. The man screams, having hit his broken finger again. Collin turns to me, barely breaking a sweat. "Well, it's up to you, hun. Sounds...*classy?* Except for that part about the swimming pool."

I turn back to Captain Jack and shrug. "That's my husband. He's a kill-joy sometimes."

Captain Jack turns back to me from watching Collin fighting the thug. He smiles again, imagining me in the same bikini his four previous victims had worn. As he leers at me, the skimpy apparel appears on my body. *Jerk.* I shake my head at him. Idiot thinks he has control.

I imagine myself in black leather from neck to ankle covering the tiny bikini. "That's where I draw the line, *Jack.* No bikinis."

"It'll be fun. I promise." He wiggles his eyebrows again. Ugh! The perverted grin on his face is more than I can stomach. That and the fish scent alone are enough to get him killed.

"I just remembered. I have plans." I'm not smiling anymore as I reach up and snap his neck.

When Captain Jack sinks to the pavement, I turn to watch Collin. He has a big smile across his face, still playing with his demon. Slipping to the ground beside the dead serial killer, my back to the brick wall, I watch Collin and the predator fight while dabbing the blood from my hands with Captain Jack's jacket. Collin glances my direction every now and then and I shake my head at him to show my disapproval. He takes far too long and I usually end up waiting at least ten more minutes before he finally finishes them off.

When he does and the dream ends, I open my eyes to

Collin staring back at me with a wry grin on his face.

I shake my head at him once more. "You're such a *slowpoke.*"

His grin grows wider and he rolls on top of me. "I'll show you slowpoke." He rips open the front of my pajama top and goes straight for my neck.

"Hey, that was my favorite…wait, stop that. And animal prints, tonight? Not only no, but hell—" He bites my neck, then moves down to my breasts, nudging my bra aside to reach the flesh beneath. I scream, then laugh as he nips at my skin. "No, *ah*, stop that, it tickles. Kissing only."

Soon he peers up at me and his eyes tell me he's serious. There will be some pain and oh, so much more ecstasy. I feel the flush of my skin as my mood turns to lust and my teeth grind together in eager anticipation. My nails dig into his shoulders as he lowers his mouth to kiss the tender skin of my tummy, trailing lower until he's between my legs. Dark green eyes catch mine once more, flashing that devilish look of the dark angel preparing for the hunt. His brows narrow as he licks his lips. My muscles contract in answer and I gasp as my fingers weave through his hair.

***

Collin made good on his promise. He had everything regarding our future handled once the nightmare with Michael was over. I figured he had money when he lived in Colorado but didn't know just how much. Turns out his crystal sculptures and hand-blown creations are popular around the world, have been for quite some time. A skill he perfected as a child. His pieces show intricate detail and beauty the buyers clamor for. Beauty, something I didn't have time to appreciate before. Now I'm surrounded by more than I could ever imagine.

The clothes, watches, and vehicles he owned in the past grossly understated the large sum he made and stored away. I'm humbled by his humility and amazing skill. He worked hard to develop his abilities as soon as he could hold a tool, intending to create a haven for us, a place where we would live together someday. He started planning for me from the time he was a young boy.

Before leaving for the States to find me, he purchased a large swath of farmland in central Ireland. There are no neighbors for miles around. All the land visible from our home is his. And now it belongs to us. Our home in Dublin is a restored, eighteenth-century, stone farmhouse with enough room for us to grow. It is a beautifully quaint home that's frigid in the winter and sweltering in the summer. And we love it.

When we finally settled into our new home and life became boring again, Collin finally told me more about his agreement in the preexistence. Seems he was warned he'd walk through hell if he chose this path. He decided long before that day he'd rather journey through fire than live without me. Until now, I never could've imagined loving anyone that much.

Understanding his heart, our God agreed to preordain with a contingency to protect my right of free will. What Collin didn't know, however, was that I'd walk the same fiery path with him. If he had known, he would have given up the opportunity to claim my heart. He would've put my best interest ahead of his instead, no matter how difficult it would've been. I'm glad neither of us knew of this life-altering detail. We might have made different choices.

We both realize, now, that Rick would've turned regardless of my status. He was too weak to withstand the torment an angel endures. No one ever said hunting demons was easy. Even with me at his side he'd have been too mentally feeble to resist. My life would've been in danger either way. The deciding powers must have known this, also. In the situation as it stands, I've found Collin instead and he's only strengthened my resolve, given me a reason to live.

The town of Dublin was resistant in allowing us to leave their midst, although most understood why it was necessary. In time, they realized their own safety was at risk with us amongst them. We're better equipped to fully protect them from a hidden distance. We need a place where no one knows us and their questions are that of normal neighbors. "Do ya think it'll rain today?" Not, "How many demons did ya kill last night?"

After learning from Michael, the rogue angel, that it was possible to plant suggestions into the minds of sleeping mortals by entering their dreams, I decided to try it for myself. Before we left, I reached into the dreams of our Dublin friends, just as Michael had done with them in the past, and changed their memories of us. As we walked the streets on our final evening there, people would smile respectfully, only seeing us as that nice couple who just had a baby, not as the angels that saved Dublin from a monster. They remember the angels as being taller, fairer and more muscular. Our names were Janice and Stewart. Some remember the silhouette of wings under our clothing. No one will notice Jaime and Collin Leary anymore as we stroll through any town across the country of Ireland. They're looking for angel wings, not dark souls. And the legend still lives on.

I don't think about those times in Colorado or my days in Dublin as much anymore. The pain of my worst memories was wiped away when Michael removed my physical scars and healed my broken bones. The thoughts I entertain now, mostly, are those that include me, Collin, and Taylor, smiling, laughing, and loving each other. I don't miss those dark days when I waited for my own death with welcoming arms. I know now I've missed out on so much of my life, so many opportunities having passed me by in a whirlwind. The simplest whispers of beauty that make our world wonderful — make it worth saving — are the ones I choose to focus on from this time forward.

Today marks the second year since we left the apartment in Dublin. The sun is out and Collin works in his shop on a special project. When I finish making sandwiches, I take Taylor by the hand and we walk out together to see her daddy. When we reach the door of the open barn that has become his workshop, Taylor catches sight of a gray goose and chases immediately after her. I laugh, watching her as Collin comes up behind me and I hand him his lunch. He drops his food on a nearby bench and brushes his fingers across my lips.

Smiling over my left shoulder at him, I say, "What do you think that goose'll do once Taylor catches her?"

"Probably what you did when I caught *you*. She'll fight for a while, but in due course, give in."

He kisses me on the shoulder and moves up the back of my neck.

Oh, Lord. If he doesn't stop soon… I might fight him off just a little, then let him catch me once again. *Mmm.* He knows I can't resist his lips on my neck. And he certainly knows how to capture me.

At the feel of his nip, I lean my head to the side and close my eyes. "Don't stop."

And he doesn't.

As my pulse quickens, muscles clench and breathing grows shallow. Our gray goose gives a high-pitched squawk in the distance. Taylor giggles loudly as she rushes back to me, carrying her protesting prize to the barn.

"Later, my love," I whisper quickly, much to Collin's

disappointment.

Taylor's green eyes have a mischievous glint as she runs with the goose held at arm's length in front of her, wings flapping in dissent.

"Look it that! Ya caught 'er! Good girl! Now what're ya gonna do with 'er?"

She tosses her catch to the ground then chases after her once again. I wink at Collin, who's watching in amusement. I doubt this goose will *ever* be complacent over Taylor's form of attention. That girl is an awful lot like her mother.

Collin smiles back at me, the electricity of his stare rushing down my belly to that very special place, making me gasp once again. I haven't told him yet about my agreement. That I've given up an eternity with him and Taylor in heaven to be here with them now. I don't know if I'll ever find the courage to explain my decision. Hope I'll never have to.

Collin retrieves his sandwich from the bench and reluctantly returns to working on the crystal statue. We'll be delivering it soon to the town of Dublin. This piece will rest behind the bar in Sean's tavern. A sculpture of Icarus, the boy who wanted to be like an angel and flew too close to the sun.

THE END

Thank you for reading! Find more from B. Hughes-Millman and the Dark Angel series at www.facebook.com/ShadowKiller.DarkAngel/

Please sign up for the City Owl Press newsletter for chances to win special subscriber-only contests and giveaways as well as receiving information on upcoming releases and special excerpts.

@ Bobbi_Bobbi

All reviews are welcome and appreciated. Please consider leaving one on your favorite social media and book buying sites.

For books in the world of romance and speculative fiction that embody Innovation, Creativity, and Affordability, check out City Owl Press at www.cityowlpress.com.

ACKNOWLEDGEMENTS

I want to thank the unsung heroes at City Owl, especially Heather McCorkle, Tina Moss and Yelena Casale, for believing in me and the Dark Angel Series. These hard-working women put their lives and souls into their work and their team of authors to make each novel that comes off the presses a polished gemstone.

Without them our hard work would go unnoticed and we would continue to toil in dark rooms, bent over our keyboards to produce prose for a limited audience. These women do all the challenging work for us, always adapting and evolving to enhance the publishing experience for us. No amount of thanks could ever compensate for the time and effort they put in for each of us. For that, I will be eternally grateful.

ABOUT THE AUTHOR

B. HUGHES-MILLMAN is an award-winning writer of short stories and author of young adult paranormal as well as adult urban fantasy and contemporary romance novels. She spends her time teaching English to professionals in France over the internet while participating as chief entertainer and chauffeur to her two sons along with her husband and partner in crime.

www.facebook.com/bhughesmillman

@bobbi_bobbi

ABOUT THE PUBLISHER

CITY OWL PRESS is a cutting edge indie publishing company, bringing the world of romance and speculative fiction to discerning readers.

www.cityowlpress.com

www.ingramcontent.com/pod-product-compliance
Lightning Source LLC
Chambersburg PA
CBHW032231010726
47494CB00002B/442